what

Alabama Summer Series, Book Five

i need

New York Times bestselling author

J. DANIELS

To all the Certified Bama Girls out there.

Thank you for wanting this story. And more importantly, for waiting for it.

what
Alabama Summer Series, Book Five
i need

"Never again, tequila. Never. Again. You're dead to me."
~Riley Tennyson

riley

"**A**RE YOU FUCKING serious? You're still going?"

I lift my eyes in the mirror and lower the tube of lipstick in my hand.

Richard is standing in the doorway of our bedroom, leaning against the frame with half hooded eyes and flushed cheeks, looking pissed and a beer or two away from being full blown drunk. He takes a swig from the bottle in his hand, squints, and points it at me.

"This is fucked up, Ri," he slurs. "Seriously. Way to back me."

I sigh as an ache pinches in the center of my chest. "He's my brother," I remind him. "Honestly, what do you expect me to do?" I stand from my vanity stool and walk over to the duffle bag opened on the bed, further explaining, "I can't miss Reed's wedding. And Beth is like, my closest friend. I'm in the wedding party. I have to go." I slip the tube of lipstick into my makeup bag, zip it closed and pack it inside the duffle. I grip the sides and look up at Richard when I'm finished. "I'm sorry," I tell him, hoping my words sink in this time. "I'm kind of stuck. You know I want you there with me. I don't want to go to this without you, it's just—"

"It's just your brother is a fucking dickhead and you're backing him instead of sticking up for me," he snaps, cutting me off. "Probably think he was right in firing me too."

My shoulders drop.

"Don't say that. You know that's not true."

"Yeah? Do I know?" His brows reach his dark hairline. Before I have the chance to respond, Richard straightens in the doorway and shakes his head, looking disappointed in me. "What-the-fuck-ever," he grates, swiping his free hand through the air in a brush-off motion. "Go. Do what you want. I don't really want you here right now anyway."

I blink. "What? Why?"

He doesn't really mean that, does he? Why wouldn't he want me here? What did I do? I didn't get him fired.

I move to offer some sort of comfort—my hand squeezing his or my arms wrapping around his back—needing to give it as much as I crave to feel it myself, but halt a foot away when Richard's head jerks up and I see his eyes. Eyes that are burning now, heated with anger and bitterness and blame.

And it's all for me.

"This is fucked up," he snarls. "You're *my girl*. We're together and I don't get invited to this shit?"

I bite the tremble in my lip. Tears threaten to build behind my lashes.

I can't really argue with Richard on this one. I feel the same way. But what can I do? I can't bring someone with me to the wedding who's specifically *not* invited. That'll just cause tension, and I don't want anything messing up this weekend. That wouldn't be right to Reed or Beth.

"I'm only staying tonight," I announce, hoping a shortened trip will help smooth things over. "I'm leaving after the wedding. Right after it's over. I'll probably be back before you even have time to miss me. And then I'll be home and we can look for jobs together. I'll help you." I take a step closer. "Okay?"

"No, it's not fucking *okay*." He narrows his eyes at me. "What the fuck? Are you seriously asking me that? You're still going, Ri. You're still taking his side over mine, so how the *fuck* can any of this be okay?"

"I'm not taking his side. I'm not taking anyone's side. I'm trying to do what's right, and I don't really know what that is. But I'm trying. I'm *trying*, Richard. Please understand. I-I . . ." I fall apart shaking my head. The pain in my chest seems to spread out and out and out until I can feel it everywhere. It's wrapped around me now. I take a deep, shuddering breath as tears roll past my cheeks. "I have to go," I whisper. "I'm sorry. Please don't hate me for this."

A hard smile tightens his mouth. Richard lifts his beer and takes a chug, keeping his unforgiving eyes locked with mine. When he's finished, he wipes at his mouth with the back of his hand.

"Trying to do what's right," he mocks, shaking his head. "Traitor."

I flinch. "I told you, I'm not choosing sides. I'm staying neutral," I remind him, wiping carefully underneath my eyes. "God, don't you see how difficult this is for me? I love you, but he's my brother."

"Bitch, you shouldn't be staying neutral. He fucked me over. Are you forgetting that? You should be choosing *me*. That's the problem right there, Riley."

I pull in a breath. I hear one word out of his mouth. One.

"What did you just call me?"

Richard shrugs and takes another swig of his beer. "You're acting like one. Just calling it like I see it."

My mouth drops open.

Richard's never spoken to me this way before. Never. Is it the alcohol?

How many has he had?

"Take it back," I whisper.

He stares at me. Eyes hard. "You still going?"

"I have to go."

"Then no. You're choosing him. You're a bitch."

I feel my jaw clench.

When people are angry, they say things they don't mean. And when alcohol is involved, that only loosens the tongue further.

But excuses aside, I break. A person can only take so much.

"Yeah, well, you know what? You're being a giant *dick*," I hiss, emotion causing my voice to shake. "I get that you're upset and mad at my brother, but you're taking it out on me. And I don't deserve it. I don't deserve *any* of it. I have done *nothing* but be supportive of you this past week after you got fired and this is what I get for it? No." I shake my head as more tears fall. "I change my mind. I don't want you coming with me this weekend. I'm glad Reed forbid you to be my plus one. And as of right now, I'm taking sides." I stick my hands on my hips and tip forward. "*His.*"

"Get the fuck out of my house," Richard growls. "Take your shit and go to that asshole's wedding. Do whatever the fuck you wanna do. Please. See if I give a fuck."

"Oh, I *will*! And just so you know, I'm going because I want to go, not because you're giving me permission. Trust me. There is nowhere else I would rather be this weekend."

"Yeah? Well I feel the same fucking way!" he roars, turning on his heel and disappearing into the hallway.

"Great!" I yell back, spinning around and marching toward the bed. Face a mess. Eyes still watering. Sniffling like crazy.

God . . . what just happened?

I pull myself together and make to leave. I begin frantically packing the rest of my things for the trip—my overnight clothes, my pillow, a few outfits—and even though Richard isn't standing in the doorway anymore, I still keep at him as if he hasn't moved.

"You're taking everything out on me, like I'm the one who fired you. All week you've been giving me shit about it. I don't deserve that. I deserve *better* than that! And you know what? I bet Reed would understand if I didn't show up this weekend, because he's an understanding person, but you're not! You're expecting me to choose between you and my family. That isn't fair. It's *not fair*. But you know what? I'll choose. You want me to choose? I'm choosing *right now*."

I step into my beige platform wedges, grab my clutch and keys off the night table, sling my duffle over my shoulder and march out of the room, fury in each step.

I pass Richard standing in the kitchen.

"Tell that fucker I said I hope she stands him up," he mumbles behind whichever number beer he's nursing.

Asshole.

"Tell him yourself next time you see him at work," I holler out. "Oh, that's right. You won't be seeing him, 'cause *you* don't have a job!"

I reach for the doorknob with my chin tipped up. I ignore the tremble in it.

"Fuck you!" Richard yells.

My back snaps straight. I swivel my head around. "Fuck *you!*" I yell back.

Then I slam the door shut behind me, getting myself into the driver's seat of my car before I break down again. With tears flowing freely, I back out of the driveway and head for Sparrow's Island.

Single.

riley

I'T'S STRANGE HOW quickly one emotion can morph into another. And how it can happen so seamlessly, you don't feel the change before it's too late.

One second you're upset. Sobbing. Hand to your mouth and heartbroken. And in the very next second . . .

You're angry.

I leave the house crying. I pull onto the freeway with tears streaming down my face and all of my pain, every shred of it directed at Richard, but as I drive farther and farther away from that house, something changes.

The blame shifts.

Reed.

My hands grow tighter around the wheel. I become furious and filled with aggravation.

And I have every right to feel this way.

Yes, Reed hates Richard, he has for a while, and yes, he had reason to fire him—you can only be late so many times before any employer grows tired of it—but did he really need to go as far as to *forbid* me to bring him as my date?

God, that hurt. That hurt a lot.

Maybe not Richard—he seemed more pissed about it than anything—but it hurt me. Reed hating the man I love hurt me. It always did. I didn't understand it, considering Reed never gave me a real reason for his strong dislike toward my boyfriend, but I ignored it. I got really good at ignoring unwanted opinions. I didn't let it affect my relationship. Not with Richard or my brother. But this? I can't take this.

Reed couldn't cut me a break this *one time*?

They could've stayed clear of each other. I'm sure the beach is big enough. And who's to say Richard would've even come with me? I don't know if I'd want to attend my ex-boss's wedding, but at least the invite would've been there. This wouldn't seem like a deliberately hurtful move on my brother's part. And Richard wouldn't feel as if I was choosing sides. The invitation should've been left open. I mean, come on, I think it's just common courtesy to invite your sister's long-term boyfriend to a family event, no matter if you like him or not.

But Reed couldn't be courteous. He couldn't be understanding of my feelings for one second. He couldn't stop and think about how banning Richard would affect me, and because of that, I'm angry.

But this is different than any other time I've been mad at Reed for something. Because right now, I'm angry on top of being hurt with him, a hurt I've been feeling for a while. This is a deep wound.

Probably the deepest I've ever had.

I arrive two hours late to the ocean front venue, and because I'm so wound up with frustration, I don't feel any guilt for missing the rehearsal dinner and not giving anyone a heads-up about it. I don't even feel the pain in my heart one would typically feel after a break-up.

It's as if I'm on auto pilot. I'm programmed to only feel that anger now.

After getting my room key from the nice woman at the front desk and tossing my things onto my bed, I take off in search of my brother.

I need to yell at him a little. Express my opinion. Then I'll feel better.

And shortly after that, I need to find some alcohol.

Then I'll *really* feel better.

I walk around the resort in search of the Tiki Bar.

During the drive, between the several missed calls from Reed I ignored, I received two texts from Beth. One asking if everything is okay since she knows what I've been dealing with at home, and one telling me they'd all be hanging out at the bar after the rehearsal and to come find them there.

So, that's where I go looking.

Walking around the resort, the cool breeze off the water tickles my bare neck as I follow the sandy path and the heavy bass from the music playing in the distance. As I get closer, I spot colored lanterns strung around palm trees and torches burning.

There are bodies everywhere on the dance floor. Packed like cattle, dancing and singing and celebrating.

Everyone appears to be in a great mood. Probably because they all have boyfriends who were invited to tag along on their vacations. I bet their brothers all approve of their relationships too.

Must be nice.

I scan the crowd first, then look over toward the bar, not seeing Reed or any of his friends. After cutting through the horde, I finally spot Ben Kelly sitting at a table.

He's hard to miss.

It's the muscles. And the tattoos. And the overall look of his face.

The man has a really nice face.

Ben's wife Mia is sitting beside him holding one of their kids. Next to her is Tessa, Reed's best friend and Ben's sister.

I've known her for years. A little on the crazy side, but she's always been nice to me. Luke Evans is sitting close to her, drinking his beer and smiling. He works with Ben on the police force and married Tessa last year.

He's also *very* hard to miss.

The bad cop to Ben's good cop. Luke Evans always looks a second away from beating the shit out of somebody.

And it's bizarrely hot.

Reed and Beth are sitting together at the end of the table, and once I see Reed I start moving with purpose.

I push my way through the crowd and march across the dance floor. I'm fuming by this point, mainly because I'm staring at the man who couldn't be reasonable for one second in his life and because of his actions, I am now a day away from being homeless.

Our eyes lock when I get a few feet away.

"Finally," Reed says through an exhausted breath after spotting me. He slides Beth off his lap and they both stand, her staying behind him, then he takes a step closer and regards me with irritation burning in his gaze. "Where have you been?" he questions harshly. "I've been calling you for hours. You know you missed the rehearsal?"

I narrow my eyes, ready to attack, then remember I'm not mad at anyone else here besides my brother and figure I need to cool it a little and address the group.

"Sorry I was late," I say. "But I don't really see what the big deal is. It doesn't take a genius to know how to carry a thing of flowers and walk twenty feet." I direct my attitude-heavy honesty at Reed before looking at the others.

I'm not close with anyone else here besides Beth, but I know everyone. We've been at the same get-togethers before. We've chatted a little. I'd consider us friendly.

I acknowledge the group with a weak smile. It's all I can seem to muster up right now.

Then before I direct my attention back at Reed, my eyes move past the table and freeze dead, locking onto a broad chest thick with big, bulging muscles.

I blink. Oh . . . *wow*. That's impressive looking. *Have I ever seen a chest like this before?*

The owner of this award-winning display of athletic physique is standing off to the side at the end of the table closest to Ben.

The crowd must've obstructed him when I first noticed everyone else. That's the only explanation I have for missing this guy, because I am certain I would've noticed whoever this is.

I'd have to be blind not to notice.

Curiosity finally tilts my head up, and I meet winter blue eyes. My breath catches the tiniest bit as I instantly recognize CJ Tully, another member of the Ruxton Police Department.

We've never met. Not officially, anyway. I've seen him with Ben and Luke around town. And we had a brief run-in once I'm betting he doesn't even remember. But before I ever saw CJ around Ruxton, Reed talked about him. Beth almost dated him too, which could've caused weirdness between the three of them, but it didn't. They're all good friends.

I know who CJ is, I've just never been in a situation where anyone would introduce us.

That's about to change though. We have to meet. He's in the wedding party.

My eyes widen as that thought blooms in my mind.

Oh, God . . . the wedding party.

I'm paired up with Mr. Fantastic Chest!

How did I forget that? I was told this information months

ago. *Shit.* All the arguing I've done with Richard the past couple of days must've distracted me and now I am *completely* unprepared for my duties involving close contact with a man who uses handcuffs on a daily basis, and who most likely looks phenomenal *using* those handcuffs.

CJ is hot.

Really hot.

From the neck down he's got it going on, and from the neck up?

God. It's almost unfair.

Short, light brown hair that has tints of auburn in it, styled but sort of messy in the front and sticking up a little. Straight nose. High cheek bones. Chiseled jaw. A thick five o'clock shadow reaching down his neck, making him look all rough and tough.

And . . . *huh*, he's staring at me. Why is he staring at me?

Maybe he's been arguing with someone too and forgot I was coming to this?

He jerks forward slightly, mumbling a "hey," that sounds as tense and unprepared for this as I feel, then clears his throat and offers out his hand. "Sorry. I don't think we've met yet. I'm CJ. I'll be your partner in crime at this shindig tomorrow." He furrows his brow, squints, and looks down with his hand still extended. "Did I really just use a cop reference?" he murmurs.

"Yep," Luke laughs, tilting his head up and smiling big. He throws his arm around Tessa. "Real smooth too."

I look back at CJ and take his hand, realizing he's likely to drop it soon if I don't take it.

And since it would be rude not to take it, I take it. That's the only reason. There is nothing else driving me. Not the urge to feel his hands or have him touch me the slightest bit.

Nope. That's not part of the reason at all.

"Hi," I reply softly, feeling the need to offer up an early explanation for what he should expect out of me during this weekend's festivities. "Sorry, but I'm probably going to be a raging bitch at this thing tomorrow. Don't take it personal," I tell him.

He smiles, half of his mouth lifting up in this adorably sexy way, gives my hand a gentle squeeze, then releases it and steps back, shoving his hands into his pockets.

"Sure thing, darlin'."

I feel my eyes flicker wider.

Darlin'? Did CJ Tully just *darlin'* me?

Is this really happening right now? Am I imagining things or did anyone else hear that?

"What?"

I turn my head at the sound of Reed's sharp, irritated voice, and watch him glare at CJ.

Oh yeah. He did. CJ darlin'd me. Reed heard it so that *totally* just happened.

Huh. I'm not sure what to make of this.

Reed's glare slides off CJ and hits me straight on. "Why are you going to be a raging bitch tomorrow? What's wrong with you?" he asks me.

My anger reawakens. I forget about just getting nicknamed and refocus my attention onto the one person on the entire planet I'm most frustrated with.

"You know exactly what's wrong with me," I snap, irritated I even have to explain myself to him.

Stupid.

"Don't play dumb, Reed," I add.

"He's not," Ben throws out on a chuckle.

I turn my head and watch Ben push to his feet, announcing as he looks toward the dance floor, "I'm going to take Nolan to the restroom. He's doing a different kind of dance now."

Luke follows. "I'll join you."

The two of them disappear through the crowd.

My gaze lands briefly on CJ. I'm expecting him to step away also and avoid the drama unfolding in front of him.

He doesn't.

He stands there, not smiling anymore, but he is watching me.

No one else. Not any of his friends or the other people in the crowd.

Me.

What's . . . happening right now?

"Is this because of Dick?" Reed asks, drawing my head back around. "Are you really going to be pissed at me because I fired him? Come on, Riley. I did you a solid."

My nostrils flare. *He did me a solid?*

Oh, my God. He did *not* just say that.

"His name is Richard," I hiss, hands clenching into fists and my bottom lip trembling as I turn my shoulders and square off with Reed. "And yes, I'm going to be pissed at you for firing him. *And* for not letting him come as my date. That was a really crappy move."

Reed sighs and tosses his hands into the air. "So sorry I didn't want to pay for some ex-employee of mine to eat salmon and drink tequila shots."

"He doesn't even *drink* tequila!" I yell. "But you know who does? Me! And guess what's going on your tab, big brother?"

I need to get out of here before I throw a punch. I'm angry, yes, but I'd hate to ruin Reed's wedding photos by giving him a black eye.

And I'm afraid it might come to that if I don't get away from him.

Spinning around, I make to storm off and knock straight into CJ, but I don't let his wall of a chest stop me. No. I steady myself and keep going, marching directly for the bar.

Tequila it is.

"I'll take some of that," I announce after claiming a stool at the high top counter. I point a finger at the bottle in the bartender's hands.

The older man, dressed in a Hawaiian shirt and wearing three different colored leis around his neck, looks over at me, then lifts his other hand holding a blender filled with a lime green concoction.

"A margarita?" he asks.

"No. The tequila," I specify. "Just set the bottle down when you're finished with it. I'll take it from there."

Laughing, he turns away and continues pouring into the blender.

He thinks I'm kidding.

I am definitely not kidding.

My brother is a jerk. My ex-boyfriend is an asshole. I've cried way too much over the past week.

I can totally handle a bottle of tequila right now.

"How about you start off with a shot and see how that goes?"

I turn my head at the sound of the deep voice next to me. CJ steps up to the bar, giving me his full attention.

My stomach clenches. I sit up taller on my stool.

Did he follow me over here?

What? Why in the world would he do that? And why would I think it?

Of course he didn't follow me over here. He's just thirsty. Look how big he is. He probably has to drink constantly to keep from passing out from dehydration.

I watch CJ continue to stare at me, his eyes bright and eager as he waits expectantly for a response because . . . *shit*. He asked me a question. What was it? Something about drinking and going somewhere with him?

Oh, my God . . . is that what he asked me? Does he want to take me somewhere?

I lick my lips, swallow whatever saliva I have left as I stare into his eyes, and respond with a confused, "Huh?"

Honestly, I just need clarification at this point. And I might be stalling.

Can I seriously leave with him right now? That's crazy. I don't even know him.

Holding his beer, CJ leans into the bar, bending his elbow on the counter and putting his weight on it. He looks down at me and smiles. "I don't know if you can handle that entire bottle, darlin'. You might want to go slow. That shit is harsh."

I blink.

Darlin'.

God. Is there anything hotter than the way he says that one word? All smooth, southern drawl and sweet to my ears.

CJ's chest rattles with a quiet laugh. "Are you hearing me?" he asks, tilting his head and grinning now. "You look a little lost, babe."

Babe.

Shit. He needs to stop. Stop talking and smiling and looking the way he does. I haven't even had a drink yet and I'm already considering things I should need a drink to consider.

He makes it easy though. Really easy.

Finding some sense, I ignore the rush of heat moving underneath my skin, tip my chin up defiantly and reply, "What makes you think I can't handle a bottle of tequila? You have no idea what my tolerance is for alcohol."

"I don't, but I'm betting you weigh a buck ten soaking wet," he counters. "I can't imagine a little thing like you slamming back a bottle and staying upright."

"I weigh a buck nineteen, actually," I correct him, giving him some sass with my tone and raising a finger. "And that's not even when I'm wet."

My eyes go round immediately after my giant sassy mouth quits moving.

Oh, God.

I did not just say that. Did I?

CJ smiles bigger, his eyes growing wider and brighter as they search my face.

"Now there's a sweet fucking visual," he says, looking me up and down. "You wanna explore that topic 'cause babe, I am down for that. Just say the words."

Annnd there's my confirmation. I said it.

Perfect.

I apparently need a set of rules when being in the general vicinity of CJ Tully.

Rule number one: Do not speak.

Jerking my head straight, I raise up higher on my stool, lean over the counter and snap my fingers at the bartender to get his attention.

"Hey! Tequila!" I shout.

If there is ever a time for alcohol, it's now. Just stick a bottle in my mouth and shut me up with it.

The man gives me an acknowledging lift of his chin as he finishes up with another customer. I take that and settle back on my stool, watching as he moves down the bar. He grabs the bottle of Patron and pours me a shot.

"Sorry about that. Here you go," he says, sliding a small plate of lime wedges next to the glass. He looks at CJ. "You want something?"

"I'm good for now, man. Thanks," CJ replies, lifting his bottle for the man to see.

I don't waste any time.

I grab the salt shaker, wet the back of my hand and sprinkle a thin layer there, then I lick it off and immediately shoot the tequila, following that up with a lime wedge I suck on until my cheeks pucker.

"Wow," I cough. *God, that's like breathing fire.* I rub at my throat, then I remember who is standing next to me and attentively watching, judging, thinking he knows me and what I can handle, so I lower my hand to the bar and slide the glass away from me, grabbing the bartender's attention again. "Another please?" I request. "That stuff's just . . . the best. So smooth, you know? I could drink it all night."

He tops me off, eyeing me warily as CJ chuckles under his breath.

"What? It is. I just love it," I announce, turning my head toward the lurking doubter and flashing him a smile. "It also makes you pretty. I read that in a Texas bathroom once."

CJ brings his beer to his mouth and takes a slow swig, observing me while he does it. Then he lowers the bottle and lick his lips. "Not sure you need help in that department," he says, his voice serious now. "I think you're set on looks, babe."

I watch his eyes wander lower . . . and lower.

My stomach clenches. I suddenly feel like I'm burning up.

I quickly look away and set myself up for shot number two.

Salt. Lime at the ready.

Then I watch my shot go sliding out of reach when CJ pulls it in front of himself after setting down his beer.

He keeps his fingers wrapped around the glass. Watching

me. Waiting . . .

"Are you . . . withholding my alcohol from me, Officer?" I ask, letting go of the shaker and lime wedge before swiveling a little on my stool.

CJ's brow lifts. "You know I'm a cop?"

"Yes."

"How do you know that?"

"Because I've seen you around."

"Really?" He tilts his head to the side, studying me. "And how the hell did I miss you?"

I feel my cheeks warm.

Mm. Must be the alcohol.

"We sort of ran into each other once. Like, literally ran into each other. I was walking into Sam's Deli and you were heading out. You knocked into me."

His brows pinch together in confusion. "Are you sure about that? 'Cause I'm thinking I'd remember running into you."

"I'm sure."

My one and only close encounter with CJ Tully. Not something I'd forget.

Imagine? Yes. Possibly. But I know that isn't the case here.

"When was this?" he asks.

"I don't know. A year ago, maybe? You were taking a call on your radio. You were in a hurry. I don't even think you looked at me. Just apologized and rushed out." I shrug. "Don't worry. I didn't take it personal."

CJ watches me cross one leg over the other, his brow lifting appreciatively.

"Good to know I didn't fuck up my chances," he murmurs.

I blink.

His chances? What chances? Wait. Is he talking about . . .

CJ chuckles, picks up his beer and takes a pull of it.

Good idea. I need more alcohol. I'm officially going nuts over here.

Clearing my throat, I sit forward and gesture at the glass he's still holding captive. "So, back to my drink. What's the deal? Are you monitoring how much alcohol I consume?"

CJ licks the beer off his lips and sets his bottle down. "Not yet. I think you can have a couple more before I need to keep my eye on you."

"And what are you doing right now exactly?"

He grins, admitting, "Trying *not* to keep my eye on you."

"Well, you suck at it," I tell him, smiling when he throws his head back with a laugh.

Oh, that's a really nice sound.

"Can I have my drink please?" I ask after his eyes reach mine again.

"Answer my question first?"

"Depends on what it is."

He narrows his stare and studies me for a moment while forcing a serious face, which is the exact opposite of what I'm doing.

I'm trying to contain a smile that's threatening to crack my cheeks wide open.

It's the tequila.

Honest. It has absolutely nothing to do with his easy charm.

CJ smirks, finally cracking. "Why were you pitching a shit fit with your brother? What was that about?"

I roll my eyes, losing most of my smile. "That's easy. He fired my boyfriend last week and forbid him to come with me to this. He was just being mean about it." I shrug, adding, "I thought it was rude, so I got rude back."

"You thought it was rude he fired him?"

"No, I thought it was rude he wouldn't let him come with me this weekend," I clarify. "I'm sure Reed had reason to fire him. He wouldn't have done it if he didn't. I know that. It's just . . . I think he could've still allowed me to bring him. Don't you think?"

CJ stares at me for a second, thinking on this, then shakes his head. "Yeah, sorry, darlin'. I'm siding with your brother on this one."

"What?" My brow furrows. "Why? I really don't think it would've been that awkward."

"Maybe not. Still. It's his wedding. If Reed doesn't want someone at it he has that right. Can't fault him for feeling that way." He leans closer to add, "Plus, it's better for me your guy's not here. I get a pretty girl to talk to all night and I get her without some asshole giving me shit about it."

I blink up at him, watching CJ slowly straighten up and resume leaning against the bar.

"You think I'm pretty?" I ask.

He stares at me, brow tightening. "Are you serious?"

I nod through a hard swallow. Memories of my evening before arriving here press like a heavy weight on my chest. "He called me a bitch tonight."

"Who did?"

"Richard. My now ex-boyfriend," I answer, looking down at my fingers twisting together in my lap. "He . . . we were fighting about the wedding. The past week, that's all we've been doing. He didn't think I should go and I didn't think he should put me in a position to make a choice like that. Then he called me a bitch." I shake my head, voice lowering when I continue. "I've never been called that before. Not by anyone. It felt like he slapped me, you know? It was like he hated me.

I could see it in his eyes." I look back up at CJ. "I was just try-ing to explain to him why I had to be here. I wanted him to understand. And if I'd been acting like a bitch *at all*, I might've let it slide, maybe, I don't know, but I wasn't. So I didn't let it slide. I got mad and I ended it. I won't be talked to like that."

"That's good, babe," CJ says. "You shouldn't let any man talk to you like that. And his ass was in the wrong anyway. He shouldn't be making shit hard on you and expecting you to choose between him or your family. That's fucked up."

Tension pulls from my shoulders.

Finally! Someone other than myself agrees with me.

"Thank you. That's exactly what I thought."

CJ shrugs, then releases the shot glass and slides it closer to me. "Straight up, though, that fucker doesn't really sound like much of a man if he couldn't let you handle your thing this weekend without crying about it. Don't let that shit get to you. Reed's your brother. You're right for being here."

I feel my mouth twitch.

CJ smiles at me, chuckles, then grips the back of his neck briefly before dropping his arm and shaking his head. "Shit. I really ran into you?"

I laugh, nodding. "Yep."

"*Fuck.*" He takes another pull of his beer.

As I watch his gaze move and fixate on a spot behind the bar, I remember CJ asking me if I was serious about wanting to know if he thought I was pretty, and further remember that I never finished pressing for confirmation on his earlier statement.

Confirmation would be super right now. I'd really like to know . . .

"So, yeah," I continue on a heavy sigh as I untangle my fingers only to tangle them together again.

I cannot believe I am doing this.

"After the night I had, or really, the last week, I'm serious. If it's true, it'd be nice to hear right about now. I couldn't tell you the last compliment I got."

He tips his chin at me. "What's that?"

I stare blankly at his face.

What's . . . that?

Crap. I'm going to have to trigger his memory.

"Uh, do you . . . you called me pretty, before, like, a minute ago, remember? And I was asking if you really thought that?"

My cheeks are burning by the time I finish speaking, then I watch a slow, satisfied smile drag across CJ's mouth while his brows lift in amusement and I realize he knows *exactly* what I'm talking about and he never stopped knowing *exactly* what I've been talking about.

Shit.

He starts chuckling.

Double shit!

I quickly lick the salt that is still on the back of my hand, grab the shooter he's no longer holding hostage, toss it back, swallow the fire quickly and then exchange the empty glass for a lime wedge, holding it with all of my fingers as I suck out the sour.

"Are you enjoying that?" he asks, watching me as if *he's* enjoying the display I'm putting on.

I nod behind my lime, then pull it away from my mouth, lick my lips and reply through a choked voice with eyes watering, "Yeah. Definitely."

God. I think I just broke all of my taste buds.

"Do you think I would've said something to you I don't mean?"

I turn my head and look at CJ after discarding my lime

wedge, noting the seriousness in his eyes after hearing it in his voice, and reply with honesty, "Maybe, if it was just the alcohol talking, which it could've been. I have no idea how much you've been drinking. Everyone could look like a pretty girl to you right now. Even the bartender."

"Well that sure as hell isn't the fucking case," he says, pointing at his beer. "It's not the alcohol, babe. That's my third."

My stomach clenches again.

"Okay," I reply with a quiet voice.

"I meant what I said. I do think that." CJ slides closer, his one hand flattening on the bar as he tips forward until he's practically hovering on top of me. Then he bends down and drops his head next to mine, tickling my cheek with his breath. "I probably shouldn't be thinking everything I'm thinking. You being Reed's sister and him being a good friend of mine. It's fucked up, darlin', but I'm having trouble concentrating on anything else right now. You want to know if I'm serious and I don't mind telling you, you look really fucking pretty sitting here next to me, Riley. On top of thinking that, I'm wondering how the *fuck* I've gone years without knowing about you."

I am no longer breathing. I have completely forgotten how to breathe.

CJ leans back but doesn't step away, so he's still hovering, his legs still pressing against mine and his large body shadowing me while he waits for my response.

And I want to give him one. It's just there's a lot to fo-cus on at the moment. CJ gives me plenty of information to respond to, like the thinking parts—him thinking things he shouldn't be thinking. What things? I want to ask about that but instead, I decide to explain his last inquiry.

Forcing air into my lungs, I look up into his summer

sky-blue eyes and say, "I don't usually spend time with Reed and his friends. Him and I are close, but we don't hang out like that. We never have. He's older than me, so—"

"How much older?"

The tone in CJ's voice grows more serious and dips lower. I know why he's asking this.

At least, I think I know.

"Five years."

"Which makes you . . ."

"Twenty-two."

I watch his eyes move over my face. He stares at my nose and my lips and my cheeks. I swear he can see every freckle I thought I hid with my makeup and is taking the time to count them.

Every. Single. One.

"How old are *you*?" I ask, sounding as nervous as I feel but hoping a question will distract me from it.

"Thirty."

"That's a good age. I like thirty."

God, what am I saying? I *like* thirty? I've never cared about a number before.

The corner of CJ's mouth lifts.

I half expect him to turn away now and find someone else to look at since I've clearly lost my mind, but he doesn't. He keeps looking at me.

And I suddenly realize how crushed I'd be if he did look somewhere else.

I like this. I like that it's *him* looking. There's something about CJ—something familiar and warm. I hardly know him, but I feel like I do.

Crazy. This is crazy. *I'm* crazy.

I'm probably imagining all of this. He's being friendly.

That's it. And I'm nervous and my heart is pounding. He isn't counting my freckles. God, what am I thinking? I need a distraction. I need to get the subject off me and my very legal age, and I need to do it before I go imagining anything else.

I decide on throwing out the first thought that pops into my head.

"Do all palm trees have coconuts?"

CJ blinks several times, jerking back. "Say what?" he asks, looking at me like I've suddenly grown two heads and he isn't interested in counting the freckles on either one of them.

Okay. There's more space between us. I can breathe a little now. This is good.

I feel my shoulders relax, then I lift both with a shrug and repeat, "Do all palm trees have coconuts? I've always wondered that."

"And you're wondering that *right now*?"

"Well, we are surrounded by them." I gesture at the tropical enclosure around the bar. "I honestly don't think they all have coconuts. Just the island ones, like where Tom Hanks got stranded. But I don't know for sure and thought maybe you knew the answer. I'm a naturally curious person."

CJ stares at me, then smiles through a shake of his head. "You're a naturally curious person," he repeats.

I nod, replying, "Yep."

"And you're curious about palm trees."

I feel my lips curve up. "Yep."

He steps back and looks around the bar while gripping the back of his neck. I watch his white tee ride up a little, exposing a hard, tanned stomach.

Would it be weird if I reached out and touched it?

Good Lord, what is wrong with me? Yes! Of course it would be weird. What am I thinking?

Rule number two when in the presence of CJ Tully: Do not *touch* anything. Don't even *think* about touching anything. And don't imagine he wants you to touch, because he doesn't.

After surveying our surroundings, he drops his arm and extends his hand to me.

"What?" I ask, looking between his hand and his face.

"You wanna know so bad, let's go find out."

I blink at him. "Really? You . . . you want me to go somewhere with you?"

I do a quick glance around the bar. *Did anyone else hear that? I'm not imagining full conversations now, am I?*

CJ laughs, drawing my head back around. "Absofuckinlutely," he says, wearing a smile full of mischief. "Come on, darlin'. Go somewhere with me."

I debate for a solid second about leaving the bar with CJ, and it might've been a longer debate if he wasn't smiling like he has some big secret he wants to share with me and dropping darlin's while offering his hand like a gentleman, but he is. I'm not dreaming this. I'm not crazy. And as much as I want to think maybe I shouldn't like the idea of holding this particular hand so much, I can't. I like CJ. And I want to know what this feels like.

Even if he only holds my hand for a second.

"The shots were on the Tennyson tab," I inform the bartender before taking the hand being held out for me and getting to my feet.

CJ moves us through the crowd, and he does this while keeping hold of me.

I can't stop smiling.

And *that* only quickens my steps and makes this decision that much easier.

CJ doesn't let go of my hand until we get to the other side of the resort and make it to a large grouping of palm trees separating the villas from the beach.

"I don't see any coconuts," he says, standing directly underneath one with his head tilted way back and his hands on his hips. "But I can't really see shit from down here. Hold up."

My eyes widen.

"Oh, my God," I giggle, slapping a hand over my mouth as CJ grabs one of the low hanging branches and uses it to hoist himself up the tree. I move closer and watch him climb up. "You're crazy! I don't think you're allowed to do that."

"What are they going to do? Call the cops? I *am* the motherfuckin' police."

My smile grows bigger. "And it would be a crime if we didn't crack this case, right?"

"Fucking A, babe," he calls out.

I press my hands to my cheeks as my heart races with excitement. The risk of getting caught quickens my breath.

When was the last time I had this much fun?

"Anything yet?" I ask after a couple of minutes pass.

CJ mumbles something I can't make out, then after a quick maneuver between branches he drops down, brushes his hands off on his shorts and moves to stand in front of me.

"They do not all have coconuts," he shares. "I think this is a date tree."

My mouth stretches into a grin. I tilt my head up and announce, "Then I guess I should've climbed it since *I* don't have a date."

His brows lift and his eyes brighten. "Wow," he laughs, looking down at me. "That was terrible."

"No. It was funny," I argue, knocking my fist against his chest. "Besides making me pretty, tequila also makes me a comedic genius. Admit it. You're finding me irresistible right now."

I move to lower my arm and step back, but CJ wraps his

hand around my wrist, keeping me there.

"That's got nothing to do with the tequila, babe," he shares.

I lick my lips. Breath moves slower in and out of my lungs. "Did you follow me to the bar?" I ask, growing bolder now.

CJ slides his free hand around my hip. "Yeah."

"And have you been looking at me like this, this whole time?"

"Yeah."

"I'm not imagining it?"

"No."

"Okay." I breathe a sigh of relief. "That's good to know."

CJ stares down at me, lips parted and eyes scorching hot.

I stare up at him.

"Tell me a secret," I request, thinking back to that look in his eyes before we left the bar.

He presses closer, lowering his gaze to my mouth. "I'm having a real hard time not kissing you right now," he reveals.

Thank. *God.*

A burst of air leaves me as my skin warms and tingles all over.

"You?" he asks, lifting his eyes to meet mine.

I swallow thickly.

Right. My turn. I can do this.

Feeling my heart rattling inside my ribcage, I fist the material of his shirt and step closer, pushing up against him. "I really want you to kiss me right now."

Nostrils flaring, his chest heaves against my knuckles. "Two shots. That's all you had tonight, right?" he questions.

I nod. "Why?"

His entire arm curves around my back, jerking me forward until we're pressing together, his solid against my soft, then he cups my face and brushes his thumb along my cheek. "'Cause I want to take you to my room and do all those things I've been thinking about doing since I first saw you storming across that dance floor, but I won't if you've had more than that, darlin'. I want you remembering this tomorrow."

I start breathing faster, so quick it's like I'm being chased. I wet my lips.

I'm not drunk, not at all, but I do feel a little mindless and wild and daring enough to roll up onto my toes, place my mouth a breath away from his and reply, "Then I suggest you make it good enough to remember."

I cannot believe I just said that. That wasn't me. It's the tequila talking. Honest.

Only . . .

It isn't. Not even a little bit.

His eyes flash with heat, then he's on me and we're kissing with hungry mouths and greedy tongues, and it's unlike I've ever kissed anyone before because I can't remember feeling a need like this burning through me. Not ever.

I've had passionate kisses. Ones that make my skin flush and my breath quick but nothing like this.

Nothing even close.

It's long and slow and unrestrained.

CJ keeps one arm curved around my back as his other hand slides along my face to my neck, breaking goosebumps out along my skin, then his fingers are delving into my hair, twisting in my messy practice wedding-day updo.

I want him to ruin it. I don't care that I've spent forty-five minutes getting it perfect. I want to look undone.

He tilts my head to deepen the kiss and does this thing with his tongue that has me gasping and groaning, then standing taller and pressing closer on shaking legs. I could stand here forever and kiss him, openly and witlessly.

But I don't.

My feet shift blindly beneath me as CJ moves us away, and I don't care where we end up, his room or mine, a remote spot or somewhere public where anyone could see, I don't care. I'm lost. So far gone to this kiss. I'm not thinking about anything besides his soft mouth and his rough hands and the scratch of his beard as it burns my skin and hopefully leaves evidence of tonight.

Whatever happens, I want to remember this.

His taste saturates my tongue. His frenzied touch squeezes my hips and presses low to my back as he heaves me closer and carries me when I'm doing nothing but dragging my feet and slowing us down.

And he never stops kissing me.

It's the hardest, deepest, most incredible kiss of my life, and I just want time to stop right now or the world to end so this is the last kiss I'll ever feel.

I'm shaking and moaning and making sounds I've never made before, and this is before we even make it to his room. And once that door shuts behind us and we separate long enough to look at each other, *really* look—his hair, wild from my fingers and my lips swollen and kiss-bitten—reality washes in to slow us down or stop us all together.

But it can't touch us.

Nothing can touch us. Nothing can stop this from happening. We both know it.

CJ moves first but only a second before I reach out to grab him, then we're stripping each other of clothes and kissing skin we've never seen, gripping and stroking while moving each other across the room until the bed catches us.

I cling to him as he moves on top of me, running my

hands up and down the hard planes of his back and wishing I could see what I look like beneath him.

Small and a little nervous and inexperienced. Are my eyes wild and are my hands shaking and do I look as fragile as I feel?

He sucks on my throat and the tops of my breasts. He teases my nipple with his tongue and lets me feel the sharp edge of his teeth.

I gasp and hold him tighter.

"Do you like that?" he asks, moving up to my neck and whispering there.

"Yeah."

My voice is breathless, quiet under the noise of my pounding heart.

I arch my back and spread my legs as he slides the palm of his hand down my body. Breasts, ribs, belly, hips. He touches and spends time on everything before he's moving over my clit and pressing lower.

"Oh, God," I pant, turning my face against the pillow as he pushes a finger inside me.

"You're fucking wet," he growls, kissing along my jaw. My cheek. I feel him smile. "I like that, darlin'."

Darlin'.

God . . .

I can't believe this is happening.

I can't . . . believe . . . this is happening.

And it happens again, and again . . . and again.

CJ spends his time on me and I spend my time on him, touching and learning what the other person likes. We're slow until we can't stand another second of waiting and wondering, and then we're desperate. It's unreal. He's everywhere, all over me, his mouth and his hands and the needy, broken words he presses into my skin as we explore every inch of each other.

I'm dizzy and delirious before he even fucks me.

And then he fucks me.

And if it's possible to look inside another person's soul, I swear CJ doesn't just peer at mine. He stares and studies it like I mean something to him. Like this is important.

Between the rough and the dirty he gives me sweet as if he really cares and this really matters, and my little naive heart believes it.

It believes all of it.

Five orgasms and two condoms later, CJ is sound asleep and snoring quietly, and I want to stay curled up against his side with my head on his chest and his arm curved around my back, liking the way it feels, but I can't.

If Reed catches us, I'll die.

CJ could die. Or Reed could die because CJ is a mountain and sports muscles unlike any I've ever seen.

So I quickly get dressed and tuck my wedges under my arm as I slip out the door, ready to make the dash to my villa.

Until I lift my head and see Mia standing there, holding her kid and staring at me.

Busted.

I gasp, pulling my wedges against my body as my eyes go round.

Shit!

Nonononono.

Mia is close with Reed. She could tell him she saw me.

Oh, God . . .

She could tell him whose villa she saw me leaving.

Double shit!

I look at her with pleading eyes and hope she reads my panic, shake my head and silently beg her to keep this between us, then before I risk running into anyone else, I turn on my heel and take off running down the path, getting to my room and bolting the door shut behind me.

And just in case she *does* tell Reed and he comes looking for me, I take my pillow and the soft, down feather comforter into the bathroom, lock that door too, and spend the night in the large soaking bathtub.

Dreaming about tequila kisses.

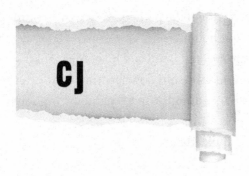

CJ

I WAKE TO the sound of my phone alarm blaring and blink against the pillow.

Why the fuck . . .

Then it hits me.

Right. Got shit to do today. That's why it's going off. Sure as fuck wouldn't have set it if I didn't.

Staying on my stomach, I reach out with a blind hand and smack along the top of the night table, searching for the phone so I can shut the damn thing off. My hand brushes against a condom wrapper. Then another.

My mouth twitches.

Fuck yeah. Riley Tennyson. What a sweet little surprise she turned out to be.

A sweet little surprise I should be feeling right now pressing close, only I don't.

Dozed off last night with her soft, warm body curling into mine, head on my chest, her leg thrown over my hip and her arm draped across my waist. I did not imagine that. So, what the fuck?

Brow furrowed, I silence my alarm, then I push up onto my elbow and turn my head.

The bed is empty beside me. Reaching out, I run my hand over the cold sheets.

Fuck.

She's been gone for a while. Why'd she leave? I didn't give her any reason to think she shouldn't stay here last night, did I?

I think back to our last conversation. My jaw tightens.

Fuck no. I damn sure did not give her any reason. In fact, I remember specifically telling Riley I wanted her ass in my bed, naked, and to not be surprised if I woke her up wanting another go.

"Baby," I mumble into her hair, moving my hand down her back to her ass and palming it.

Riley gasps, all fucking cute.

"Yeah?" she answers with a small voice. Her arm tightens across my waist.

"Look at me, darlin'."

Her head turns up and she looks at me, those big blue eyes blinking slow.

"I like this and what we just did," I tell her. "I like it enough I know I'm gonna want it again as soon as I get enough rest to give it to you, so heads up. We're not done. We're not even close to being done."

She blinks, sucking that fat bottom lip into her mouth. "Okay."

"You might wake up with me getting you ready if you aren't already there. I hope you're good with that."

Those bright blues flicker wider. A flush creeps across her one visible cheek. "I'll be good with that," she whispers.

I smile and tug her closer.

"Good. Now give me that sweet fucking mouth so I can go to sleep and recharge. You wore my ass out."

"I barely did anything," she argues while climbing higher until she's more on top of me than next to me, her heavy tits now pressing to my chest instead of the side of my ribs.

Her heart is pounding.

Keeping one hand on her ass, I cup her face and slide my mouth along hers, speaking inside our kiss. "Rode me. You forgetting that?"

Her breathing stops. "Oh," she whispers.

"Yeah. Oh."

Riley giggles, then deepens the kiss by tilting her head and working her tongue. She pulls away to ask me, "You get enough?"

My brow tightens.

"Enough of what?" I growl. "Didn't I just say—"

"I meant enough of my mouth so you can get to sleep and recharge," she explains.

I watch her drop down, flatten her hand on my chest and rest her chin there, doing this while smiling all cute for me.

"I'm gonna be honest with you, babe," I begin, tucking my one arm behind my head and raising up higher. "If I ever get to the point of getting enough of your mouth, I got a serious problem and most likely need medical attention."

The smile she's wearing softens, turning shy.

"So to answer your question, no, I didn't get enough of your mouth. But I am satisfied enough to shut my eyes knowing I'm gonna get it again the second I wake up. That work for you?"

"That works for me."

I smile. "Then, darlin', let's get some sleep. The sooner I recharge, the sooner I'm feeling you tighten around me again and hearing you scream my fucking name."

Now that flush is taking over both cheeks and burning out those freckles to the point they are no longer visible.

Riley slowly shifts down and settles against my side, swinging her leg over my hip and draping her arm over my waist as she lays her head on my chest. And I tuck her close, keeping one arm around her.

Yeah, I remember being pretty damn clear. And she seemed agreeable.

So, again, *what the fuck?*

My phone beeps with an incoming text. I grab it off the

nightstand and swing my legs over the side of the bed, sitting there as I swipe my thumb across the screen.

Reed: Breakfast is at Parrot's Bay in fifteen.

Right. This is why I'm awake. Everyone is meeting up for breakfast before all the wedding shit starts.

Everyone including Riley *fuck me* Tennyson.

I get out of bed and head for the shower, washing up quickly so I can get dressed and get going. I know I'm going to have to wait until after breakfast to get some answers out of Riley. Makes this breakfast something I'm not looking forward to. But maybe I can catch her before everyone else gets there. Once we all sit down and start eating, I'm screwed. No way will I be able to say shit to her about it.

Not unless I feel like making it awkward for everyone.

"Hey, Reed. I fucked the shit out of your sister last night and then she bailed on me while I was catching some shut eye. Can you believe that? Pass the juice, man."

Yeah . . .

It's the guy's wedding day. I should probably spare him the details of his sister's tight pussy and what all I did to it.

After toweling off, I get dressed in a pair of army green cargo shorts and a black tee. I grab my phone, my wallet, and my room key, tuck those into my pockets and head out, combing my wet hair with my fingers as I make my way toward the resort restaurant.

When I push through the glass doors and scan the room, I spot the guys sitting at a large round table near the back with their women, Nolan and Chase.

And no Riley.

Motherfucker.

Ben eyes me and motions for me to join, grabbing the

attention of Reed who then notices me along with everyone else, destroying my plans of backing out of the room and knocking on every goddamned door until I see freckles and blue flames.

She better be on her fucking way over here.

"Mornin'," I greet the group, pulling out the chair next to Tessa and sitting in it. I stare at the empty seat across from me, then lift my eyes when Ben starts talking.

"Where'd you end up last night? You stay at the bar?" he asks me.

Mia elbows him, careful of Chase who's sitting in her lap.

He gives her a look. "What?"

She subtly shakes her head, briefly looks at me, then grabs the purple stuffed octopus sitting on the table and bounces it in front of Chase, making him laugh.

My brow furrows.

I don't know what the fuck that's about so I grab my glass and shoot him a vague, "For a while," before taking a sip of my orange juice.

"You see my sister when you were over there?"

I cut my eyes to Reed.

Fuck.

Fuck.

"Yeah. She was taking shots," I tell him, figuring I'm in the clear admitting my knowledge of that. I did say I was at the bar. I would've seen her.

No fucking way would I have missed Riley. *Jesus.*

Can't believe I had the chance of meeting her a year ago at Sam's Deli. What the fuck? That must've been one helluva call for me to not notice a girl looking the way Riley does.

Damn.

"Great. She's probably too hungover to show up to this,"

Reed guesses, shaking his head and tossing a napkin on his empty plate.

I can clear that up real fast but I don't, because how the fuck would I know if Riley got drunk unless I was watching her *or* with her until she called it quits last night?

And considering how much watching I was doing and what all we did while I was with her, I keep my mouth shut.

"No. Look, there she is," Beth announces, raising her finger to point.

I set my glass down and turn my head, watching as love-me-and-leave-me makes her way across the room wearing a white midriff tee with the word Rebel scrolled in red across her tits, showing off her tanned and cute stomach, jean cutoffs and black badass-looking combat boots on her feet. Her hair is down, falling past her shoulders in a mess of waves, and her face is free of makeup. She looks like she just rolled out of bed.

Her own fucking bed. Not mine.

I feel my jaw clench.

But holy fucking shit, she looks good. A little rough and sharp edged. Far from the pretty thing pounding back shots of tequila and asking me for secrets, that's for damn sure.

Riley Tennyson looks ready to hop in my truck, not ask questions, and just let me take her.

And I will fucking take her.

She locks eyes with me, blue flames burning me up but only for a second before she cuts away, smiles shyly at the group and lifts her hand in a wave.

"Hey. Sorry I'm a little late. I forgot to set my alarm," she explains, rounding the table and moving across from me. She pulls out the vacant chair and sits in it, briefly catches my gaze, then leans over and nudges Beth's shoulder. "Happy wedding day," she says.

Beth's entire face lights up with a smile.

It's a smile that caught my attention last year and had me wanting to see more of it, but I'm over that now. Beth is Reed's. Has been since before I ever laid eyes on her.

I'm happy for them.

"Thanks. I'm so excited," Beth says, nudging Riley back.

Reed sits forward and plants his elbows on the table, linking his hands together. He sighs. "Look, Riley, I get why you're pissed at me and all, but—"

"It's fine, Reed. Really," she interrupts, leaning forward to see him. "I'm sorry for yelling at you the way I did. I get why you didn't want him here. I shouldn't have pressed. It's your wedding. Let's eat and just, enjoy the weekend, okay? I'd rather not talk about it anymore."

"It's *fine*?" Reed echoes. His brow lifts. "Are you sure? You were pissed last night. You looked ready to kill me. What happened?"

Riley slices her eyes to me, then looks down at her plate.

"Tequila happened," she answers, sitting back.

I feel my mouth twitch.

Fuck yeah. Looks like the Tully charm sticks with you even after you sneak out of my room. Good to fucking know.

"Really? You drink that stuff?" Mia asks with her nose scrunched in disgust. "I can't stand the taste."

"It's not so bad," I throw out, shrugging. "I like it mixed with something sweet."

Riley's eyes go round.

"Dude, really?" Luke asks me. "Somethin' sweet with *tequila*?"

I keep my eyes on Riley when I answer.

"Yep."

She pulls her lips between her teeth, blushes, and looks away.

"Well, whatever the reason, I'm glad you're here, Riley. It means a lot to me," Reed says, causing Riley's blush to turn a shade redder and her eyes to mist. He leans back and drapes his arm over the back of Beth's chair. "Plus, Christ, now we can order."

"Finally! I'm *starving!*" Nolan whines, dropping his head on his arm.

Ben laughs and rustles his hair.

Luke asks Reed something, and Ben joins in, stirring up conversation I'm not paying mind to while Mia, Tessa, and Beth start discussing wedding shit.

I stare at Riley, watching her pick up her glass and bring it to her lips. She looks at me over the rim.

"*What the fuck?*" I mouth.

She swallows some juice and licks the residue away. "*What?*" she mouths after lowering the glass.

What?

Is she serious?

I cock my head.

Then before I can get anything else out of her, the waitress steps up to the table and begins taking orders.

Riley gives hers. I rattle off mine without glancing at a menu, not really caring what I eat at this point. I'm more interested in wrapping this shit up fast and getting *someone* alone so I can get some answers.

I slide my gaze back to Riley when I'm finished speaking and watch as Beth ropes her into wedding conversation with the rest of the girls, completely screwing me out of keeping her attention, unless I feel like offering my opinion on false lashes and whatever-the-fuck breast tape is, which I don't. I don't even have an opinion on them. Don't wish to have an opinion, and sure as hell don't want to pretend that I do. And thanks to Reed and his hard-on for giant motherfucking tables,

I can't stretch out and nudge Riley's foot to get her out of that conversation and back into the silent one we were sharing.

Should've gone around banging on every door this morning until finding hers. Now I'm regretting it.

Fuck this breakfast.

Fuck these eggs. Fuck this juice.

I'm done eating in nine minutes, but I have to sit here for fifty-six more and watch Riley and every other person at this table take their time eating. It's torture. I swear these assholes are all in it together. They all know I want to get Riley alone and they're keeping that from happening.

Even Nolan.

Awesome kid. Always saying funny shit, except for today when he orders two more pancakes just when I think we're getting the check.

Swear to God. I almost lose it.

Ben gives me a look when he catches me glaring hard at his kid. I play it off, fake coughing and turning away, then I go back to watching Riley and the cock tease show she doesn't realize she's putting on.

Sucking egg yolk off her thumb. Licking jam off her lip. And don't even get me fucking started on the damn sausage she orders.

"You okay over there?" Beth asks me at one point when I let a groan slip out as I rub at my face.

Fuck no, I'm not okay. I'm getting hard in a family restaurant. But I can't tell her that.

"Just tired," I answer, letting my hands drop to my lap and rubbing them on my thighs.

Reed stands from his chair and reaches back for his wallet. "This was on us," he announces, tossing money onto the table. "Just a thanks for being here and sharing—"

"Great," I interrupt, getting to my feet and yanking out Tessa's chair for her. She yelps. "We're happy to be here. Thanks for the food. Let's get going."

I motion for everyone to stand and make their way toward the exit. When Nolan starts busting my balls again by requesting more color time, I step up behind him and lift his little cock blocking ass out of his seat.

"Here. Just take it with you," I say, grabbing the paper and the cup of crayons and pushing them into his hands.

"Cool!" he shouts, then holds them out to Ben who's standing close. "Daddy, look. I'm taking these. CJ says I can."

Ben picks him up.

"I don't know if we're allowed to do that," Mia observes, looking cautiously at Nolan while bouncing Chase.

"I'm sure it's fine, Angel," Ben argues, smiling down at her. "And if it isn't, what are they gonna do?"

"Nothing," Luke and I answer together, both of us sounding ready to jump any motherfucker that tries touching those crayons and stalling our exit. I look over, catch his smirk and the eye roll Tessa gives him, then gently gripping Mia's arm, I spin her around to face the door. "Come on. We're wasting time."

"Jesus, man," Luke chuckles, throwing his arm over Tessa's shoulders and looking back at me. "You in a rush to see Reed get married or somethin'?"

"Of course. Why wouldn't I be?" I lie, looking from Reed to Riley, then back to Reed when I feel his eyes still on me, eyes that are now looking suspicious until Beth grabs his chin and forces him to look down at her.

Whatever. This shit show has been going on long enough.

I stay behind Riley during the walk back to the villas, but only because she's walking beside Beth. Reed is holding tight to his girl while joining in on their conversation, so no way can I step up now and not have it seem motivated.

After Beth directs all the girls to meet in her villa and all the guys to meet in Ben's, the group splits up. When Reed steps away and I don't see anyone paying me any attention, I follow Riley, getting to her door a few seconds after she closes it.

I knock, and the minute it cracks open I'm pushing my way inside.

"Whoa, hey," Riley exclaims before I step out from behind the door and she sees it's me. "Oh, hi, uh . . . did anyone see you?" she asks in a quiet voice, glancing around me and then looking back into my face.

I shut the door and cross my arms over my chest. "Babe, what the fuck?" I ask, skipping over her question because I got a better one. "Why'd you leave last night?"

She blinks up at me.

"And what the hell was that shit at breakfast?"

"What do you mean?" she questions.

"*What do I mean?*" I echo back, a little firmer. "Ordering off the sex menu and putting on a show that made my balls ache. Thanks for that."

Those stormy blues go round.

"Then ignoring my ass like I'm not sitting there trying to get some answers out of you."

"But I didn't want to get caught," she argues. "And you were staring at me. If I would've stared back like I wanted to, someone would've seen us."

My brows lift when I probe, "You wanted to stare at me?"

She nods.

Nice. That feels good.

"And I wanted to explain why I left," she continues. "I didn't want you thinking it was because I didn't want to be there." Her hand comes up, crosses her body and grips her elbow. "I did. I wanted to be there."

"So, why'd you leave? `Cause I sure as fuck remember expressing wanting you in my bed, darlin'. We weren't done."

Riley lowers her eyes to my chest.

"You could've told me last night you were looking to bolt," I add, drawing her attention up again.

And I would've convinced her that plan was shit and mine was better.

"I could've," she begins. "But you were sleeping and I didn't decide on bolting until after you fell asleep. That was when I realized how it would look if someone came knocking on your door and I was in your room . . . without my clothes on." She swallows. "It would've been obvious you had taken part in removing my clothes."

"And?"

"And." She drags in a breath, then releases it tensely. "I just didn't think Reed finding out that way was in my best interest. Or yours. So I bolted and slept in my bathtub."

My brow pulls tight. "Say what?"

"My neck is a little stiff, actually." She rolls her head from shoulder to shoulder, wincing through her stretch.

"You slept in your bathtub?" I ask.

"Yes."

"You got a reason for doing that?"

"Mia saw me leaving your room and I was worried she'd tell Reed and he'd come looking for me."

I stare at her, trying to figure that one out and coming up short.

I focus on what I can understand.

"All right. So Mia knows," I offer, watching Riley nod her head. "And you took off `cause you don't want your brother knowing about us. That right?"

She does that wide-eyed blink again, not speaking.

"Babe," I prompt.

"There's an *us*?" she asks, leaning closer and looking shocked. "I . . . I wasn't, I mean, I just," she stammers, takes a deep breath, huffs it out, then attempts this again. "I had no idea you wanted to be an *anything*."

"You forgetting what all I said last night about not being done with you?"

"I wasn't expecting it," she answers quickly.

"You weren't expecting *what*, Riley?"

"You."

My brows reach my hairline. Something heavy presses on my chest.

Riley slides her hand down her arm and twists her fingers nervously together, looks away as if collecting her thoughts, does that, then meets my gaze again.

"I just got out of a really long relationship. Like, *just* got out of it. And I came here not thinking something like this would happen. I didn't think it would *ever* happen. Not with you. Then it did and you said you weren't done with me yet and I—"

"That's not what I said," I interrupt.

Riley tilts her head, asking, "Huh?"

I feel my mouth twitch.

Fuck, she's damn cute right now. I'd rather just kiss her than explain but I want her knowing this and I don't want there being any confusion about it.

Ever.

I step closer, keeping my arms tight across my chest. "I never said yet, darlin'," I begin, watching her lips part. "I said I wasn't done with you and that I wasn't anywhere near being done with you, but hear me, Riley, I never said *yet*. Fucked up thing to say and I wouldn't say it, especially not to a sweet girl like you. If some asshole gives you a deadline to make you aware shit'll be wrapping up for the two of you and he already knows it, drop him. No man deserves you if he's already thinking of an out. Do you understand?"

She wets her lips.

"Yes."

"Now, I'm hearing you say you weren't anticipating me and the shit that went down between us, and darlin', I feel that. 'Cause I sure as fuck was not anticipating you. That doesn't mean we should let go of something we're both wanting more of just 'cause it's tripping us up a little."

"I'm just not sure," Riley says quietly. Her eyes dance between mine.

"You're not sure or you're just nervous 'cause this is new and you haven't had new in a while, and possibly haven't had it this fucking good," I press, needing her to clarify.

After a breath, Riley responds. "I'm just nervous," she whispers.

I smirk, saying, "That's good, babe. Nervous is good. I can work with that."

"But what about Reed? I don't think this is the right time to lay this on him."

I can't argue with that. She has a point.

Not sure how that conversation is going to go down anyway, if it's a conversation I need to be having, and with the timing of things—Reed getting married in the next couple of hours—it doesn't feel right dropping the news now. He's got enough going on.

"Then we wait," I suggest after thinking it through. "Get back to Ruxton and if this is still something we're both feeling, we handle it then."

I watch Riley stare up at me. Then, when seconds pass and she hasn't agreed to my plan or said differently, I give her a little nudge.

I uncross my arms, drop my hands to her waist and bend down, sliding my lips over hers and speaking slowly.

"Tell me a secret, babe."

She smiles. I feel it twist across her mouth.

"I like you," she whispers.

"I like you too, darlin'."

Her smile stretches into a grin.

"Are you good on what I just said?" I ask.

"Yes."

"Good. Now hurry up and kiss me before your brother comes looking for my ass."

Heeding my warning and without hesitation, Riley throws her arms around my neck, stands taller on her toes, tilts her head and seals her lips against mine. I move my hands to her back where her shirt is revealing skin. She's smooth and warm and I hold tight, sliding to her hips as I dip my tongue inside her mouth, flicking and stroking it against hers.

She tastes like her juice, sweet with a bite, a little sour.

She tastes fucking *good*. Smells good too. And her skin . . . *fuck me*. Her skin is so damn soft. I want to stay here and touch her for hours.

I break the kiss instead.

"I gotta go," I share, knowing I'm pushing time.

She drops her arms and steps back.

Turning my head after opening the door, I give her a look that conveys I'm going to be getting more of that mouth later, and she reads it.

I watch heat burn across her freckles before I slip out and close the door behind me.

SUIT ON AND barefoot, standing next to Luke who's beside Ben, taking the spot as best man next to Reed, I watch as two good friends of mine come together and exchange vows.

The girls are all crying five minutes in, except Beth. She's holding strong and practically tackles Reed to the sand when she's told she can kiss him.

That's some funny shit to watch.

And knowing all eyes are on that scene happening and not glued to where I'm going to be looking, I do just that and *look*, taking in Riley as she stands across from me.

Blue dress showing shoulders and sun-kissed skin, stopping a few inches above her knees. Flowers in her hand and ones pinned in her hair, and bare feet toeing the sand. Her eyes are lined black and her lips are shiny, plump and peach colored, and when she feels my gaze she gives me hers back, lasting all of a second.

A second I'll take.

Then she looks away, doing this while fighting a smile.

Later that night, Riley sneaks into my room after dark. She's flushed and breathing heavy like she ran to get here, and she's still barefoot but her hair is down now, big, loose curls and windblown messy.

I dive my hands into it the second I get her pinned beneath me on the bed.

"You're lucky Reed was so preoccupied with Beth tonight. He could've seen you," Riley warns around her moan as I suck and kiss down the line of her throat.

"He could've seen me doing what?"

She must be referring to all the looking I did during the reception.

Big crowd. Lots of commotion.

I took my chances.

"Well, you were touching me a good bit."

"We were dancing."

"I know, but still."

"Babe, honest? I didn't care at that point if he saw me or not," I admit, burying my face in her neck and inhaling.

She smells like sun and beach and smoke from the lit tiki torches.

"You wanted to dance. We were dancing."

Riley giggles. "Thank you for that, by the way. I'm sure it got a little annoying."

Her fingers move out of my hair when I lean away to look at her. "Why would it get annoying?"

"I hit you up for every slow song."

"And?"

"There were a lot of slow songs."

"I gotta ask again, babe. And?"

She bites shyly at her lip. "Um, I don't know. Don't most guys get annoyed with that stuff?"

"With what stuff? Spending time with a gorgeous girl while doing an activity where it's encouraged I keep my hands on her? Nope. Sorry. That will never annoy me."

Riley blinks, all wide-eyed at me. "Oh. Well, okay." She smiles, running her hands up my arms, and seems to melt more into the mattress, as if hearing that relaxes her completely.

What the fuck? Is she speaking from experience? What idiot would ever complain about slow-dancing with her?

Before I can think any more on that, Riley grabs my face, yanks me down, and seals her lips against mine.

We both moan. My hand moves down her body, slipping under her dress and between her smooth thighs. I touch the wet spot on her panties.

"Jesus, babe. How long have you been like this?" I ask, pushing up and kneeling between her legs. I grip onto delicate satin and pull.

She presses her fingertips against her mouth, softly admitting, "A while," as she bends her knees and allows me to drag her panties off.

Fuck. A while?

Fuck.

I toss them on the floor and loosen my tie, shaking my head at Riley when she rubs her dirty feet against my dress shirt.

"You wanting to do my laundry?" I ask, cocking an eyebrow.

"Nope," she giggles, pressing her toes into my ribs. "I'm making it so you have to take that off. I like your chest. I want to see it."

"Yeah?"

She nods slowly while sucking on her bottom lip.

"I could say the same to you, darlin'," I tell her, wearing a smirk. When she blushes, I jerk my chin. "You first."

Without hesitation, Riley drops her feet, sits up, grabs the hem of her dress and yanks it over her head.

I watch as her fat tits bounce free, so full and heavy, her nipples hardening fast as the chilled air hits them.

My nostrils flare as I stare with hunger. Tie gone, I work at the buttons on my shirt and tip my head at the spot on the bed beside her. "Help me out, babe, will you?"

Her eyes find the condom I tossed there, then she's tearing the wrapper with her teeth and tugging at my slacks at the same time, undoing my belt so she can unbutton and unzip while I toss my dress shirt and tug off my white tee.

Riley's eyes jump to my chest and hold there, looking

from pec to pec.

I see the want in her gaze. The wonder. Maybe her ex isn't built like me and she isn't used to seeing bulk like this.

I touch her cheek. She blinks rapidly and tilts her head up. Our eyes catch.

"Waiting, babe," I prompt, the urge to fuck itching underneath my skin.

Riley nods her head. Then I watch as she goes about freeing my stiff cock. With trembling fingers, she rolls the condom down my length.

"I don't know what I'm doing," she admits in an anxious voice, keeping her focus.

I smile hearing that, liking how unpracticed she is.

"The amount of fucking I'm planning on doing tonight, you'll be an expert by morning," I promise.

She blushes pink, then pushes the rubber to my base, grips it there, and blinks up at me.

"This okay?" she asks, sounding unsure but looking eager, so fucking willing to please me and to get this right and do it better than anyone ever has.

It fucks with me, that look.

I take her face in my hands and kiss her hard and deep, pushing her to her back and not bothering with my pants or boxers. They stay shoved down to my thighs as I crawl closer and slide the tip of my cock inside her dripping wet pussy. I wait for that little gasp I know she's going to give me before I thrust home.

And she gives it.

"*CJ.*"

Riley squeezes my hips with her thighs and keeps one hand flat on my chest and one in my hair, fisting and tugging as I fuck her.

"Yeah, baby," I pant.

She whimpers and spreads her legs wider.

I feel her fingers move along my skin, tense and curl like she's trying to tear away pieces of me to keep as I pound into her. We're kissing and then I'm moving down, still fucking while I play and suck on her nipples.

"Fuck me, these tits," I growl, palming her left and moving my lips over her right. "So fucking full and heavy and tasting sweet as hell. *Fuck, babe.*"

Riley bites her lip and then releases it on a moan when I drag my tongue over her nipple.

I lift my head and raise up onto my knees, keeping one hand on her hip and using the other to stroke and touch. "I want you in my bed when we get back," I tell her, still thrusting slow but hitting deep and bottoming out each time. "I need this gorgeous fucking body in my bed, darlin'."

Her eyes flicker wider. She licks her lips.

"Okay," she pants.

I lean over her, brace my hand on the bed beside her halo of blonde, thrust in and slowly drag back out.

"Oh, God," she breathes, pleasure ripping through her.

"Not done with you," I growl.

Out, then back in.

"Not even close," I add.

Riley sucks in a breath. Her body starts tensing, thighs squeezing tighter and breaths coming quicker.

I keep thrusting.

Slower. Harder.

"God," she moans, closing her eyes. "CJ, oh, my *God.*"

Her hands move to my shoulders and grip. She tries to pull me down, to get me closer but I want to watch. I need to.

"Look at me, baby," I tell her. "I wanna see those blue

flames while you're coming."

I slide my hand between us and start working her clit with my thumb as I keep fucking, slow and hard.

Her eyes flash open, the center of a blaze burning there, flickering like wildfire.

"There it is," I murmur through a smirk.

Riley gasps, a shy smile lifting her lips.

I drop to my elbow, still working her with my fingers. My hips thrusting. My mouth a breath away. I build it in her fast, watching it in her eyes and feeling the way her body jumps and grows tighter. Then she goes off and she's grabbing my face and giving me that hot mouth, hard and desperate.

She's coming and moaning my name and *oh, God* while she clenches around my dick so goddamn tight I nearly stop breathing.

"Riley," I growl, pumping into her fast and getting there seconds after she does. "*Fuck . . . Riley.*"

I empty into the condom and bury my face in her neck.

We come down slow and we kiss even slower. Savoring this. She's trying to catch her breath and I'm trying to catch mine, both of us clutching at each other until I need to pull away to get cleaned up.

After disposing of the condom, I crawl back into bed, lay on my back and pull Riley close, half against my side and half sprawled across my chest, just like she was last night.

"You're staying," I tell her, in case she needs reminding of how I want this to be between us.

Riley's arm around me squeezes tight. She doesn't say anything. She doesn't need to.

I close my eyes. Content. Comfortable.

This feels good. Really fucking good.

The light touches of her fingers on my chest and the

curve of my ribs are the last things I remember before sleep pulls me under, and I let it.

Riley isn't going anywhere tonight.

riley

SHIFT THE gear into park and cut the engine of my car, staring at the house through the windshield.

I know what I'm about to do and I'm ready to do it, only I know it's most likely going to be awkward and difficult given the fact I'm pulled in the driveway behind Richard's Ford F150, meaning he'll be a witness to my pack-and-go, and I really don't want awkward and difficult.

I want this to be easy. I *need* this to be easy.

We were together for a year and a half, so unfortunately, I already know.

This isn't going to be easy.

Grabbing my keys, I get out of the car and head for the front door, squinting in the May sun. I test the knob when I step up onto the porch, and when it isn't locked, I enter.

The house is quiet until I close the door behind me. Then I hear a chair scooting across the tile floor, and when I look down the hallway, Richard is emerging from the kitchen.

"Jesus fuck," he murmurs, rubbing his hands down his face. He drops his arms and starts advancing toward me. "I've been calling you since Friday. Why haven't you answered me?"

I ignore the harshness of his tone when he stops a foot away, because now he's close enough I can see how bloodshot his eyes are and the shadows beneath them.

He hasn't been sleeping well.

Good.

"I switched my phone off," I admit.

No point in hiding that.

He nods as if accepting my excuse and the unspoken reason behind it.

"How was the wedding?" he asks with genuine interest in his voice.

I feel my brows pull together.

What in the actual fuck?

"What do you care? You didn't even want me to go," I remind him.

Richard looks down at the floor and grips the back of his neck with one hand. "Yeah, that was fucked up. I shouldn't have been like that to you. I'm sorry." He lifts his head and our eyes lock. I see his apology written all over his face. He really means it.

I feel a tinge of gratitude for his regret, but what's done is done.

"Fine." I go to pass him and head for the stairs when he sidesteps, blocking me. "Can you move? I need to get my stuff," I explain.

"Why are you getting your stuff?"

"Because I'm moving out."

He flinches, jerking his head back as if I had slapped him. "You're moving out?" he echoes. "Why? Because we had a fight?"

I blink up at him, starting to feel just as confused as he seems to be.

"We broke up, Richard. That was more than just a fight."

He crosses his arms over his chest and breathes a laugh. "We didn't break up," he mutters.

My brow furrows. "Excuse me?"

"I yelled and said shit I didn't mean. You yelled and said shit you didn't mean." He shrugs. "We had a fight, Riley. Had them before and I'm sure we'll have more of them. That's all it was."

I narrow my eyes and tip my chin up. "You called me a bitch," I snap. "More than once, if I'm remembering correctly."

"Yeah. That's part of the shit I didn't mean. Come on." He cocks his head as his eyes soften. "You know I don't think that about you. Have I ever called you anything like that before?"

I take a second to think, but I don't need it. I know the answer.

"No," I reply quietly.

"That's right, because I don't think like that." He reaches out and begins slowly running his hands up and down my arms in a soothing motion. "I was pissed and I took that shit out on you. That was my fuck up. I knew it wasn't your fault but I put it on you anyway because I needed someone to feel it, and all fucking weekend I've been regretting that. Did you listen to my messages?"

"I deleted them this morning." I step back, getting out of his reach when his hands start to irritate my skin.

His mouth twitches. "Guess I deserved that," he replies. "But if you had listened to them, you would've heard how sorry I was."

"It wouldn't have mattered," I counter.

His face hardens. "Why not?"

I sigh, pinch my lips together, and cock my head at the same angle his was cocked. "Because we *broke up*," I hiss, irritation spreading through me. "So you spending your weekend apologizing to me wouldn't have mattered. You were apologizing to someone who wasn't yours anymore."

I try and get past him again by squeezing between him

and the wall, but Richard steps over and blocks me.

He isn't a big guy. Not nearly as big as *some people* . . .

But I'm little, so unless I get a running start, I don't have a chance of pushing through.

"When the fuck did we break up?" he asks, eyes now full blown filled with confusion and searching my face. "Did you say it was over? Did *I?* Because I sure as fuck don't remember telling you we were done."

I open my mouth, ready to argue with conviction when memories flood me. My lips press together. Friday night plays back like a movie inside my head.

I'm packing my things and speaking as if Richard's still standing in the doorway.

"You're taking everything out on me, like I'm the one who fired you. All week you've been giving me shit about it. I don't deserve that. I deserve better than that! And you know what? I bet Reed would understand if I didn't show up this weekend, because he's an understanding person, but you're not! You're expecting me to choose between you and my family. That isn't fair. It's not fair. But you know what? I'll choose. You want me to choose? I'm choosing right now."

But he wasn't standing in the doorway anymore. I knew that. He was already downstairs, in the kitchen getting another beer.

Richard didn't say we were broken up. He said a lot of things, mean things, but he didn't say *it*. And I didn't say *it*. Not really. And what I did say, he didn't even hear.

Then I left. Hauled ass out of there wanting space and needing it to happen immediately. I left angry and upset and thinking we were broken up, but we weren't because neither one of us said *it*.

Oh, *God* . . .

I slept with CJ Tully when I had a boyfriend at home

waiting for me.

A boyfriend who was sorry.

A boyfriend who's been trying to contact me all weekend, but because I've kept my phone off, I didn't get his calls saying he's *still* my boyfriend.

Nonononono. This can't be happening. One of us said it. I *know* we did.

Except we didn't.

Shit.

Shit!

I thought we were over. I should've gotten confirmation before storming out, but I didn't. What's wrong with me?

"If anything, we were just on a break, which I'm not convinced of since neither one of us said we wanted that shit, but whatever," Richard says, pressing his forearm to the wall and leaning on it. "Now you're back so, break's over."

My mouth drops open. His does the thing that drew me in from the start; half of it lifting into a smile that looks both cute and inexplicably sexy. Then he pushes off from the wall, steps into me, and cups my face with both hands.

Hands that aren't as big or rough and feel so different now that I've felt another's.

"All of that shit I said and everything we've been fighting about, that's not me. You *know me*, Riley. How long have we been doing this?"

"A long time," I reply hoarsely.

"Year and a half," he clarifies, making my heart feel heavy. "We've got roots in this. You're the most important thing in my life. No way is a fight like that gonna tear us apart, baby. No fucking way."

My stomach drops.

"Baby," CJ moans when I lean over and suck him into my mouth.

"I love you, Riley."

My lip starts trembling as tears build behind my lashes.
What have I done?

"I thought we were broken up," I whisper with a shaky
voice.

He gives me a look like he understands, but he doesn't.
He can't.

"Come here." Richard pulls me against him and wraps
his arms around me, keeping one hand on the back of my
head and the other low on my back. He drops his face beside
mine. "I'm sorry. I'm so sorry, baby. I didn't mean that shit,
okay?" he whispers while stroking my hair.

Sobs vibrate in my throat and rattle inside my chest.
My tears soak into his shirt as arms that aren't as strong as
another's comfort me when they should be pushing me away.

I can't hold Richard back. I can't tell him what I've done.

And when he asks if I love him with his lips against my
ear, I can't lie and tell him I don't.

Like he said, we have roots in this.

I've only ever loved one man outside of my family. And
Richard is it. He's my first in a lot of ways. And you don't
easily let go of your first.

So I nod, not being able to say the words out loud, but instead, giving him my answer with my head buried in his chest.

He grips the back of my neck and brings his other hand
between us to lift my chin, then he lowers his mouth to mine
and kisses me the way he always kisses me, slow and full of
tongue and with lips that are familiar, and I force myself to
kiss him back because this is the mouth I should be kissing.
And when it feels off and not right, I grow determined and
slide my hands to his neck to pull him closer. I roll up onto
my toes, slant my mouth against his, and go for it.

"I'm having a real hard time not kissing you right now."

I break away choking on a sob.

"Jesus, Ri," Richard laughs as I wipe at my mouth with the back of my hand. "You trying to swallow my tongue or something?"

"Sorry," I mumble, looking up at him.

I feel sick and disgusting. I feel ashamed.

And I've made a terrible, *terrible* mistake.

A half smile hits me with eyes that are ignorant to my disgrace. Richard pulls a strand of my hair between his thumb and two fingers, studies it, then bends down and runs his nose along my temple.

I hear him inhale and I panic, quickly stepping back and getting out of his arms.

I know who I smell like.

"I need to shower. I probably still have sand on me," I lie, playing it up by brushing off my arms and the tops of my legs.

This time Richard lets me pass with a, "Cool, babe," because he knows I'm not going to get my stuff.

Because I'm not moving out.

Because we're still together.

Because we were never broken up.

We were never broken up.

I scramble into the bathroom and shut the door behind me. Then, after yanking open the shower curtain and turning on the water, I tug my phone out of my back pocket and scroll to the number that was programmed in it this morning.

While I was in bed, naked, with a big charming man sprawled over me, smelling like a mixture of sweat and sex.

The same mixture that is currently clinging to my skin.

"Tully."

I turn away from the door and wipe at my face.

"It's me," I reply, keeping my voice down just in case.

"*Jesus*," CJ murmurs. "Your voice on the phone is hot as shit, darlin'. Say something else to me."

"I can't do this."

There's a pause, then a breathy laugh breaks through the line. "Not exactly what I had in mind," he says before exhaling forcefully. "Right. Is this your nerves getting to you again? What'd I say about that?"

"No," I answer. "It's not my nerves."

"Then what the fuck happened?"

I begin pacing the small room, going back and forth between the toilet and the door as I explain.

"We weren't broken up. I thought we were but we weren't. We were on a break, I guess, but that isn't the same thing. We're *still together*. And I . . . *slept* with you. I slept with you when I had a boyfriend back at home."

"Did more than just sleep with me," CJ points out.

I close my eyes for a breath. "I know. But I wouldn't have done that if I thought Richard and I were still together. I'm not like that. I'm not that kinda girl. I swear."

My lip starts trembling again. I press my fingertips to it and bite back tears.

"I know that. I never thought you were, babe," he says. His voice is rougher now. "So what are you telling me? Are you staying with this guy?"

"I have to."

"What the fuck does that mean?" CJ growls. "Is he forcing you to stay? Give me your address. I'm thirty minutes out."

"No. That's not what I meant. He's not forcing me," I quickly reply.

Sheesh. He sounds ready to kill.

I stop in front of the mirror and stare at my reflection.

My eyes are red and puffy and glistening with tears. "It's just, we've been together for a long time and I don't know if I'm ready to let go of that yet," I confess.

I watch my lips form my next words.

"I love him."

CJ breathes tensely in my ear. "Hope it works out," he mutters.

"Really?" I ask, frowning.

"Don't ask me that shit. And what the fuck do you want me to say?"

God, he's right. What am I doing?

"Sorry," I rush out. "Sorry. That was stupid. I just, I can't believe this happened." I hold my hand to my cheek and shake my head, looking down at the sink.

"I'm gonna let you go," CJ says, talking about the phone call. I'm sure of it.

"Wait, um." I flatten my hand on the counter. My bottom lip trembles. "Please don't tell anyone what happened this weekend. Okay? *Please*. Especially not Reed. I don't want it getting back to Richard."

"You're not telling him?"

I shake my head as if he can see me. My silence gives me away.

"That's on you, babe," CJ points out. "Kinda fucked up if you ask me, but you're not asking."

"I'd rather just pretend it didn't happen," I return. "And I think it would be best if we forget about each other . . . in that way. You know?"

"Yeah. That's not happening."

I lift my eyes to my reflection again and watch my brows pull together. "Uh . . . sorry, what?"

CJ clears his throat, then goes on to elaborate. "You can

forget about me in *that way* all you want, or you can try and convince yourself that's what you're doing but I'm telling you now, Riley, I am not forgetting you. I got a taste of something I want more of and a taste like that, babe, there's no forgetting."

I pinch my eyes shut. I don't want my cheating heart to start warming right now but that's exactly what happens.

I try my best to ignore it.

Shaking my head, I return my gaze to the mirror. "I don't really know what to say to that," I admit, giving him my honesty.

"You don't need to say anything. I'm just letting you know how it is," CJ retorts. "Now, you making a choice means I need to back off, and even though I'm not feeling that choice, I'll respect it."

"Thank you." I smile a little, liking his attitude about this. "And I'd really like us to stay friends."

"Now you're pushing it."

My smile disappears and I'm back to frowning. "Huh?"

"I don't do that," he throws out.

"You don't do *what*?" I question with a little sass.

He better not tell me he doesn't have female acquaintances. Beth and him are tight. I know this for a fact.

"I don't keep friends with women who have had my dick in their mouth," CJ shares.

Oh . . .

Another fact, Beth has absolutely *not* done that. I would've been told about it.

This is different, but it's something I want, and it should be entirely possible. Why can't this work?

"Well, just pretend I didn't do that," I suggest.

"Do you need a reminder of the conversation we had not a *minute ago*?" he asks. "I'm not forgetting shit, Riley."

"Okay. Then . . . I guess we won't be friends." I feel my shoulders drop as I look to the door, then at the shower I'm supposed to be standing in. I sigh, telling him, "I should go."

"Fuck," he mumbles, voice tight. "Fine, goddamn it. We'll be friends."

Hope flutters in my stomach. "Really?" I ask.

"Yeah, really. But just remember, you wanted this. So when the Tully charm doesn't wash off, I don't want to hear shit about it."

I feel my forehead crease with a wrinkle. "All righty," I reply, not knowing how else to respond to that when I hardly understand it. "I really should go so, um, thanks for being so cool about this."

CJ chuckles. "Yeah. Sure thing."

I disconnect the call before he has the chance to throw out another 'darlin''. I'm not sure I can handle that right now. Then I quickly dial up Beth.

"Hello?"

"We were on a *break!*" I harshly whisper into the phone, pressing my free-hand against my stomach when it rolls with nausea. "Not broken up. *Oh, my God.* I feel like Ross."

Only my life is *not* a hilarious sitcom.

Reality sucks.

"What?" A shuffling noise comes through the line. "Wait, Reed, hold on a minute. Stop."

He grumbles, low and annoyed-sounding, then I hear his gruff voice ask an impatient, "Who is it?"

Most likely against some body-part of Beth's.

"Oh, crap. Am I interrupting honeymoon time?" I ask, wincing away from the shower. "I'm sorry."

"No, it's fine. You're fine," she assures me before whispering, "It's your sister."

"She can call back," Reed says.

"I can call back," I echo.

"What do you mean, you weren't really broken up?" Beth asks, ignoring us both. "So, you and Richard are still together? Is that what you want? You guys have been fighting a lot."

"Just because of the whole job thing," I reply quickly. "I want to be with him. I love him. I just . . . feel *really* terrible."

"Why?"

I bite my lip. "Uh . . ."

Beth doesn't know about my weekend with CJ. Nobody knows. Reed sure as hell doesn't. And if I discuss this with Beth right now, there's a chance he could overhear every single detail of my unfaithfulness.

And then go after CJ . . .

And get his ass beat.

I rush out a breath. "Nothing. I don't know. I just, wish I would've clarified our situation before I left." I try and peer at my reflection again, to see the guilt on my face, but condensation clouds the mirror. I rub at the dampness beading up on my neck.

"I don't think you have any reason to feel terrible, Riley."

I close my eyes. *You have no idea what I've done.*

"And you're not Ross," she laughs. "Ross messed up *big time.*"

I wince. My heart grows ten times heavier.

Beth giggles away from the phone, and says something I can't make out to my brother.

They're in love. Blissfully married and in honeymoon mode.

And I'm interrupting them.

"Okay. Go get back to whatever you were doing. I'll talk to you later."

We end the call with my new sister smiling through her farewell. I can't. Fresh tears well up in my eyes.

Then I finally strip and get my butt in the shower.

I have Tully charm to wash off.

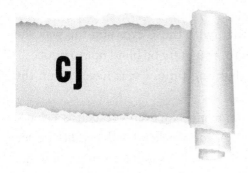

CJ

TOSS A few steaks into my cart, having finally decided on dinner, then head for the checkout so I can get out of here and get home to cook up some food.

The way Food Giant is laid out, if I'm coming from the meat department I gotta cut through produce to get to the front of the store. Normally that isn't a problem. What the fuck do I care? I like produce.

But today, when I turn the corner and catch sight of Riley standing near a crate that happens to be in the path I'm heading, it becomes a problem.

A major fucking problem.

Fuck. You gotta be shitting me.

Two years of living in Ruxton and not once do I remember ever seeing this girl around.

Yeah, I missed an opportunity a year ago. But shit, that doesn't even count, considering I don't remember it. And for some fucked in the head reason, I didn't even look at her during that run-in, but other than that? Not once have I ever seen Riley. Not on my lunch break when I was grabbing a sandwich. Not while I was shopping for food. *Nowhere.* Hell, I've spent most of my two years here not knowing she even existed. Even after I knew about her, I still never saw her around.

Ruxton isn't heavily populated. It's a small town. You remember faces. And anyone living and breathing sure as hell would remember hers.

Sweet face like that, with those eyes and the way she burns you up with them, you gotta be blind not to notice.

But aside from that one time, I was never given the opportunity.

Two years of not knowing. Not even so much as a glance in her direction. Then I spend a weekend with my dick buried inside Riley Tennyson and now I'm suddenly running into her at supermarkets? What the fuck is this shit?

Stopping a few feet away, I grip the cart with one hand and rake my other down my face, scrubbing over the stubble coating my jaw.

I'm supposed to be friends with this girl. That's what she wants. And when friends run into each other at supermarkets they say shit to one another. They don't contemplate ducking out and going unseen, which is exactly what I'm doing.

Only this is different. I've touched Riley. Tasted her. A taste I'm not expecting to forget any time soon. A taste I want more of, no matter if she's available to give it to me or not. Don't care. I can't turn it off.

And I sure as fuck don't want to be friends with her. Not after everything we've done.

So what do I do when she throws this option at me after taking away everything else? I agree to it. Not knowing what the hell I'm in for but figuring it can't be all that bad.

She wants to be friends? Sure. Why the fuck not?

Phone calls I can handle. Texts, probably. As long as she isn't trying to work me up with one. But face-to-face time?

Motherfucker.

Should've thought this through.

I can easily retreat. There's still time. She hasn't seen me yet, and chances are I can make it out of the store before she notices me at all.

But the kicker is, I *want* to talk to her. I enjoy it. Riley is a good fucking time.

And seeing her right now?

Yeah . . . I still want it.

I just need to decide if this is the right play for me, knowing damn well how bad I'll want to do more than just talk.

I stare at Riley's profile as I debate backing away and retreating to another aisle.

Her hair is up off her neck, tied up in a messy knot with a few blond pieces falling out and tucked behind her ear. She's wearing hospital scrubs. Dark blue ones. Stormy like her eyes after she comes.

Those blue flames.

Jesus.

Never seen eyes like hers.

What she's wearing isn't showing her shape but it doesn't need to. I know Riley's shape. I've felt it with my hands, gentle and with urgency. I've touched and grabbed and palmed. I know how it presses and curls into me when she's sleepy from sex.

And knowing everything I know, I shouldn't still be standing here, staring and allowing memories to trigger. I should be making my way to the checkout and getting the fuck gone.

She wants to be friends.

I want to throw her down right here, bury myself deep, and show her exactly why her idea is fucking terrible.

But I can't. And because I can't, I need to go. Pay for my food and get the hell out of here.

Fuck this. What am I doing?

Decision made, I start to retreat. But then I watch as Riley bends down to retrieve something out of the crate she's standing by, and I'm curious enough to pause and see what it is she's been staring at this whole time I've been staring at her.

What's held her attention for minutes?

She straightens up with the produce in her hand and holds it out. That's when I see it.

A coconut.

I smirk, because fuck me. There goes my decision. I'm going to have to go over there now. I can't ignore that.

That's ours.

You asked for this, Tully.

Ignoring all alarms in my head screaming that this is a bad idea, that doing a face-to-face with Riley is just going to make me want to fuck her even more, I push my cart over to where she's standing.

"Not all palm trees have those," I announce as I come up beside her, boxing Riley in with my cart so her only escape is to back away.

Her head snaps right and tilts up to see me. Then her eyes go round.

"You probably already know that though," I continue, keeping the smirk. "Considering how naturally curious you are."

"What are you doing here?" she asks with a quick voice, bringing the coconut against her chest and clutching it with both hands.

Her cheeks are now flushing pink. She's either embarrassed I caught her or nervous to see me.

I'll take either one.

"Robbing the joint," I reply, resting my forearms on the cart handle and angling my body forward.

Those burning blues grow rounder. "What?" she whispers.

I chuckle. "What do you think I'm doing here? I'm getting

food for dinner," I tell her, nodding at the coconut. "You got plans for that or were you just letting yourself remember?"

Riley smiles a little. Then she shakes her head and looks away to drop the coconut back into the crate. "I don't know what I was doing," she answers, turning back to look at me. "And before you say anything, the dates in my cart have absolutely no significance."

I cock an eyebrow.

"They are on sale this week," she adds quietly with a shrug. "That's why I'm buying them."

"Didn't say anything."

"I know, but just in case you were thinking something."

"I'm thinking a lot of things," I reply, watching her pink lips press tight together. Full and soft and tasting sweet as hell.

Jesus. What I wouldn't give to kiss that mouth right now. She's so damn pretty.

Fuck.

Fuck.

Why the hell did I think coming over here was a good idea?

Her eyes lower to my uniform. She clears her throat. "Did you just get off work?" she asks.

I nod, pushing thoughts away I can't make happen right now, then I jerk my chin. "You?" I question, brow furrowing. "Are you a nurse or something?"

I feel like a dickhead for asking this, considering how many times Riley and I have slept together, but truth be told, we didn't do much talking last weekend. If Riley wasn't offering information, I wasn't asking for it. Not because I didn't want it though.

My mouth was just busy doing other things.

"Hopefully in a year I will be," she replies, tugging on the bottom of her top and then smoothing it out. "I'm in nursing school. I had clinical today, hence the scrubs." Her nose wrinkles in distaste. "I hate wearing them," she shares. "They're so ugly."

I laugh under my breath, arguing, "I'm not hating them one damn bit," then flashing her a smile when her eyes widen.

"You *like* my scrubs?"

"What did I just say?"

"You said you didn't hate them."

"I think you can translate that to me feeling the opposite," I share. "Unless you need to hear me say it."

She drags her teeth across her lip, blinking slowly, then quickly looks away while shaking her head.

I know that look. I know what she's fighting against.

Riley wants to hear me say I like her scrubs. She wants to hear me say why I like them too. But she doesn't *want* to want it. That's the problem.

Hers, not mine. 'Cause I have zero fucking problems sharing my thoughts on Riley's uniform or anything else I like about her.

Another part of the look she's giving me? Shock. I've surprised her.

Riley's acting like the thought of me digging the outfit she's in right now is something she can't even fathom, which leads to me thinking that dickhead she's staying with has never said anything similar to her.

That pisses me off. He's touching all that every night and he's not appreciating it? What else doesn't this cocksucker do?

I don't waste any time finding out.

"What's he cooking for you?"

Riley cuts her eyes back to mine. Her brows pinch together. "What?" she asks, looking confused.

I tip my chin at her cart. "You're going home after this

for dinner, right? What's he cooking for you?"

She stares up at me. "Uh . . . nothing, I don't think. Why?"

"He doesn't cook for you?"

A laugh bubbles in her throat. "Not unless you want to count ordering takeout," she tells me, solidifying my opinion of this prick.

She wants to be friends with me? Ok. Part of this new arrangement should be me pointing out all the ways I'd be better for her.

Seems like the friendly thing to do.

"I'd cook for you," I share, letting some arrogance dance on my tongue, because fuck it. If she's going to know what all I'd do for her, I want her knowing how good I'd do it.

I watch for her reaction, expecting her smile to fade. Maybe her gaze to harden since I'm taking this conversation there. But neither happens.

With doe-like eyes blinking in wonder, she asks through the softest voice, "Why?"

I pull in a slow breath, staring into those flames and letting them burn me up.

Why? Simple.

"'Cause a girl like you should be having dinner made for her sometimes," I reply, giving her nothing but honesty. "You shouldn't be giving to a man who isn't man enough to give back."

"I don't mind cooking all the time," she's quick to inform me. "The way I was raised, it's normal for the woman in the relationship to take on that role. My mom cooks for my dad all the time."

"This has nothing to do with taking on roles," I argue back. "It's about showing your appreciation for someone and doing something for them they're always doing for you. Giving some of that good back."

She shrugs and keeps a soft smile. "I really don't mind cooking."

"You're not hearing me, darlin'," I inform her.

Her smile fades as she slowly draws in a breath.

Riley stands taller, suddenly looking uneasy. She grips the handles on her cart. "I should go," she says, backing away to make room so she can get around me.

I know why she's retreating. And I could let her go. I could let *this* go, but I don't.

I asked for this? No. She fucking asked for this.

I bridge the gap and box her in again, then I move to the side of my cart to get closer and take hold of the end of hers, preventing her from moving any further away.

"Is this how it's going to be?" I question, watching her eyes flicker wider.

"Is . . . this how *what's* going to be?" she asks.

"We see each other around and I say something that gets to you the way you don't want it to get to you, you freak, then you take off acting like you don't want what you just asked of me two days ago?"

"What are you talking about?"

"You wanted this," I remind her. "Wanted us to be friends, right?"

"Yes."

"This is what comes with being friends with me, Riley. I joke around. I flirt a little. And when a nickname sticks with a girl, it sticks hard. Now I get you not wanting me to call you that around people who might be suspicious, and honestly, I thought you got me when I didn't feel the need to assure you that'll never happen 'cause you know I'm not a dick. I guess I was wrong there. So here's your assurance—that'll never happen. You asked me not to say anything, and as long as I'm not being asked about it, I won't. And like I said to you before, I don't like the decision you made but you made it so I'm gonna respect it, meaning if I'm ever around you and you're with him, I'll stick with first names only. But babe, those two scenarios do not apply right now."

She stares up at me, breathing heavy through her nose and looking conflicted.

"I'm just giving it to you straight," I add, before she can give me her argument. "You want to be friends? We'll be friends, but I'm calling you darlin'. Name suits the girl and I like it."

"I just don't want this to be weird," she says, her hands pressing together on the cart handle so one's now on top of the other. "Or any weirder than it already is, considering . . ."

Her voice trails off.

I shrug, letting go of her cart and crossing my arms over my chest. "Won't be weird for me," I tell her.

I need to say this so she knows we can make this work.

Do I want to be friends with Riley? Fuck no.

Am I going to take what she gives me right now?

Yeah. I'll fucking take it.

No way am I letting her rip this shit away from me now. Hell. I'm invested.

Riley takes a few seconds to think it over, then apparently needing assurance and maybe that final push, she asks me, "Do you call any of your other friends darlin'?"

Jesus.

No. I don't. But I don't tell her that.

"Luke, but only when he's being sweet with me," I respond through a straight face, hoping to get the opposite reaction out of hers.

And I get it.

Her eyes go round a second before she bursts into laughter, hand to her chest and her head tilting up, showing me the line of her neck as she relaxes back into the girl who was sitting at the bar taking shots of tequila.

I smile watching her.

This is how I want Riley. Giggling underneath a palm tree and asking me for secrets. Open and acting her age. I don't want her guarded or worried I'm going to take this too far. Or worse, closing up on me all together and running away.

How the fuck is she going to see I'm the better man for her if she freezes me out?

"Okay, well, since I'm sharing the nickname with Luke, I guess it's fine," she says, her giggles fading out. "Just promise to keep it harmless, okay? The flirting stuff. I'd really like this to work out. I don't want to *not* be friends with you."

"Not sure I can promise something out of my control."

She cocks her head.

I cock mine, knowing the truth but only preparing to give her what she wants to hear, and what I need her to hear in order for this to play out.

"I'm harmless," I lie, the corner of my mouth lifting.

"How harmless?"

"Like a fucking kitten."

Riley presses her fingertips to her mouth, shielding me from her smile.

I don't shield mine. We're good to go.

"Do you have more shopping to do or are you done?" I ask her after glancing around the produce section.

She slides her hand to her cheek, picks up a lock of hair and tucks it behind her ear, answering, "I think I'm done."

I step back, grab my cart and give her room to pass,

waiting until she does this before I reach into the crate she was standing next to, grab a coconut, and keep it concealed behind my back as I follow behind her to a checkout lane.

Another lane opens beside the one Riley is standing in, and since she's already unloaded, I move to it.

After I hide the coconut under her reusable shopping bags.

I'm finished paying before her since I only have a few items. After collecting my change, I turn around to give Riley a smile and get one back paired with a wave before I head outside to my truck.

I'm expecting something. A call or a text.

And I almost make it out of the parking lot when my phone beeps. Then that smile I'm wearing in anticipation grows to a fucking grin.

Riley: VERY FUNNY.

LATER THAT NIGHT, after grilling the steaks, eating one and saving the other for tomorrow, then cleaning up the kitchen and putting everything away, I sprawl out on the couch, nursing my second beer and zoning out on SportsCenter. My phone rings, pulling my attention off the TV.

I sit forward, dropping my feet to the floor, and grab the device off the footlocker I use as a coffee table.

The name flashing on the screen brings the biggest smile to my face.

"Jesus Christ," I answer, settling back against the cushion and propping my feet up at the other end. "How the fuck are you? What's going on?"

"It's going," Jake says. His voice is rough. He sounds tired. "Just got back late last night. Fucking time difference is screwing me. I can't sleep."

"How was it this time?"

"How'd you think it was? It's Afghanistan." He pauses. I hear a can opening and wonder if he's missing it today. The drink. The drugs. "It's all a bunch of shit," he says. "Same as last time they sent my ass over there. Nothing's changing."

"How are *you* doing?" I press.

"I'm fine. Jesus. I'm not drinking. All right?" he's quick to reply, shooting down my worry. I listen as he takes a sip. "That's a Redbull that's got you freaking out. Relax."

"You're drinking a Redbull and you're tired?"

"Read somewhere it can have the opposite effect if you're really lacking. I thought I'd give it a shot."

I shake my head, smiling, then throw my arm behind me and use it as a pillow, propping myself up higher.

"Seriously though," he starts. "I'm fine. I know you worry about me and I appreciate it. I always have."

"You're my brother. And you're doing some pretty scary shit. You know I'm going to worry."

"Nothing scarier than what you're doing," he counters.

"Maybe, but I don't got shit in my past I gotta keep hold of."

"I'm not wanting to use," he bites out, shining a light on his demons. "All right? And if I start feeling those urges, I know to talk to someone. I got it handled."

"Just looking out for you, man. That's my job," I tell him. "And it's one I'm going to keep doing no matter how much you bitch about it, so get the fuck over it. You had a long deployment, Jake. I don't know what all kinds of shit you saw over there and I'm not asking, unless you want to share."

"Not really."

"Yeah, I figured."

"*Shit*," he mumbles. I hear shuffling through the line.

"What?"

"I just spilled my Redbull everywhere. God . . . *mother-fucker*. That was my last one."

I smirk. "Probably for the best. That shit makes you mean."

Jake breathes a laugh. "Whatever," he murmurs.

"Seriously though. I'm glad you're back and okay," I begin, hearing my phone beep with a message. "Hold up a sec."

I hold the phone out and read the text.

> *Riley: I just spent an HOUR trying to open that stupid coconut.*

Chuckling, I bring the phone back to my ear.

"What's up?" Jake asks.

"Nothing. This chick . . ."

"Uh oh," he murmurs.

"Nah, it isn't like that," I tell him, wincing. "Well, it is, but it's not." I shake my head. "I don't know. Shit's complicated."

"Sounds like a long fucking story I don't want to hear. Actually, tell it to me. It might put me out."

"Fuck you," I laugh. "How's Katie?"

"She's good, I think," he answers. "Didn't get to talk much while I was gone. I think that was hard on her."

"Sure it was."

"I'm planning on going to see her now that I'm back."

"You better be swinging by here if you're driving to Texas, shithead," I order.

Jake's stationed in South Carolina, so to get to his girl he has to drive through Alabama. And considering it's been over a year since I last saw him and he just survived another deployment, his third in six years, I'm going to be pretty firm on that request.

He chuckles. "I am. I'm gonna head up and see Mom and Dad too."

"When?"

"Shooting for a few weeks," he says. "I got some things I gotta do here, and I gotta wait for them to approve my leave. Bastards take their fucking time with that shit."

I know all about that. He's complained to me before. Jake doesn't hide shit that gets on his nerves. Ever.

He's better at hiding other stuff. Stuff he shouldn't be keeping locked in.

"Just give me a heads up when you're coming," I request. "I'll try and take off so we can hang out."

"Cool." His voice breaks with a yawn.

I smile.

Guess the Redbull does work.

"Fuck," he murmurs. "I better try and get some sleep. I'm gonna be dead tomorrow."

"All right, man. It was great talking to you," I tell him, feeling good about this phone call. "Keep me updated on shit."

"Yeah, I will."

"Later."

"Later."

The line disconnects.

Limbs heavy with relief, I relax further into the couch and pull up the text from Riley.

She's opening coconuts by herself? Using tools, no doubt? *That motherfucker . . .*

Me: He didn't help you with that?

Riley: I didn't ask for help.

Me: You shouldn't need to.

Riley: Stop it. It's not like he saw me struggling and refused to help.

Me: What did you open it with?

Riley: A hammer.

Me: And where'd you get the hammer?

Riley: His tool box.

Me: Did he see you get it?

Riley: Yeah.

Me: There you go.

Riley: ???

Me: I see my woman getting in my tools, I go find out why.

Riley: I know how to use a hammer.

Me: Not the point.

Riley: *rolls eyes*

Me: Roll them all you want. Just know if I were there, you wouldn't be handling your coconuts. That's my job.

Riley: Stop.

Me: Unless you wanna handle them while I supervise. I'm down for that.

Riley: STOP!

Me: ?

Riley: My COCONUTS?!? REALLY??

Me: I'm talking about the fruit. What the fuck are you talking about?

Riley: Nothing.

Me: Get your mind out of the gutter, pervert.

Riley: It just sounded like you were talking about something else . . .

Me: I was.

Riley: OMG BYE.

Laughing, I drop my phone to my chest and get back to zoning out on SportsCenter.

riley

Nine Days Later

PULL INTO the parking lot surrounding McGill's Pub and find a spot open next to Beth's silver monster truck, which isn't exactly what it is but I call it that considering how big the tires are and how much of a running start Beth needs to get herself up into that thing.

She loves it. I don't blame her. It really is fun to ride in.

Plus, you do feel kind of badass when you're sitting up that high. Especially when a guy pulls up next to you and you get to look down on him.

Seeing little Beth behind the wheel usually gets some curious looks.

Reed bought this truck for her last year when Beth left her car in Tennessee. Surprised her with it and had it modified to fit her, so he says.

Now they have matching trucks *and* matching last names, which I think is super cute.

I'm not sure how practical it'll be if they have any kids though. You can't exactly toss a baby up into that thing.

After turning my car off, I grab my keys and my phone, leaving my wallet in the backpack I carry around with me for class since I'm not staying long. Then I lock up and head inside.

McGill's is your typical small town bar. Warm atmosphere.

Great tasting food. Friendly service. And killer tunes always playing overhead. A sweet mix of rock-n-roll and country, which is exactly how I'd describe myself if someone was curious enough to ask.

I'll listen to Led Zeppelin and The Stones any day of the week, grew up on it and can belt out the tunes right along with my daddy, but I'm a southern girl down to my bones and true in my heart. I'll never let go of my roots.

It's nice to get a taste of both when I come around here.

I don't get to frequent much due to my school schedule and the hours I need to set aside for studying, but I imagine a lot of people do, making McGill's a second home to some.

I know Reed is one of those regulars. The rest of the guys? I'm not sure of, which is why I have my eyes on high alert as I make my way toward the bar after spotting Beth behind it.

I do not need to be running into CJ right now. Not with my main reason for being here.

I gotta share some things. Need to. There's just no holding it in any longer, and having CJ as an audience will make sharing this information that much harder.

I can't have him smiling at me and radiating that easy, downhome charm the way he does while *looking* the way he does, fully developed in all areas and more developed in some, with that wide chest and his thick muscles and those big, rough hands he'll use to fix every appliance in my house before suggesting he bang me all over it.

No way. He can't be here for this. I'll turn into a speechless freak and spend my entire time here staring.

"There's the sister I always wanted and finally have," Beth announces when she sees me claiming a stool, doing this after visually clearing the room of large, manly objects.

She smiles big, walking over to stand across from me in her worn Van Morrison tee and waitress apron tied around her tiny waist. Her long, dark hair is down and looking extra wavy, her skin is glowing, her finger is sparkling from the new rock decorating it, and she's got this cool double-winged thing going on with her eyeliner, which is a look I'm totally stealing.

"Your eyes look awesome like that," I share, never feeling the need to keep a compliment inside when it has potential to brighten someone's day.

Beth drops a coaster down on the bar, smiling at me. "Thanks," she says. "You want something? It's on the house. You know, since we're family and all."

"You love saying that, don't you?" I ask, wearing my own smile and not being able to help that one bit.

I love Beth Davis from McGill's. I love her even more now that she's Beth Tennyson and looking like the happiest girl in Ruxton, Alabama.

She shrugs, admitting, "Maybe a little." Then slides the coaster closer to me. "Drink?"

"No, thanks. I can't stay long."

I watch her slide the coaster away and add it to a small pile, noticing how dark the skin on her arm has gotten since I last saw her.

"So, how was the honeymoon?" I ask. I haven't spoken to Beth since I called right after breaking the news to CJ. I didn't want to bother her and Reed anymore. "I see my brother untied you long enough you were able to lay out a little."

Beth's eyes go wide before quickly cutting away. "I can't believe I told you he does that," she murmurs to a spot on the bar with the reddest cheeks I've ever seen. She looks at me again, quickly stressing, "*On occasion.*"

"Right. And by that you mean, every day that ends with a 'y'?"

She squints, lifts her eyes, and begins ticking off the days of the week in her head, by the looks of it, nodding through the process. After finishing up on Sunday, I guess, she focuses on me again.

"The honeymoon was everything I could've hoped for. Let's just leave it at that."

Laughing, I prop my elbow on the bar and rest my chin on my fist.

"Hey, Riley Girl," Ms. Hattie says, walking behind Beth and smiling at me. "You want anything? Something to eat?"

Hattie is Beth's aunt and owns McGill's with her husband, Danny. She's crazy sweet.

"No thanks," I reply. "I'm not staying."

"You sure?" She comes up to stand beside Beth. "Got Big Jon back there whipping up some of that tasty macaroni salad you liked so much last time you came 'round. Fresh batch." She smiles when I shake my head, then gives me a wink. "All right. You change your mind, you just holler out."

Hattie moves down the bar, grabbing a bottle on her way.

"I'll never look at all that rope in the bed of my brother's truck the same again," I tell Beth when her aunt gets out of earshot, just because I can't help myself and I'm dying to say it.

Beth makes a face.

I make one back.

"How's it going with Richard?" she asks after tossing a balled up napkin at my head. "Are you guys happy now that you're back together? Or," she tilts her head, "since you didn't really break up, I guess I should say, now that you're *still* together? Whatever. Are things better now?"

My phone begins vibrating from the front pocket of my scrubs. I reach for it while answering Beth. "Uh, yeah, sort of."

"Sort of?"

"Well, you know, it's just . . . taking some time. He's stressed out with the whole job hunting thing right now." I slide my thumb across the screen and pull up the text.

"He still hasn't found a job?"

> *CJ: Thought about your boobs earlier but I kept it on a friendly level. Just wanted you to know how committed I am to this arrangement.*

Laughter catches in my throat.

"How do you think about boobs on a friendly level?" I quietly ask myself while reading the text again.

"Riley."

"Mm?" I lift my eyes to Beth. "Oh, sorry. What did you ask me?"

She looks at the phone in my hand, then back into my face. "Did you just say something about *friendly boobs?*" She points at the device. "Is that Richard?"

Crap.

"Uh."

My hand buzzes with the next vibration. A new text.

I'm not going to read it. I'm going to keep looking at Beth, and I'm going to answer her original question.

If I can remember it.

> *CJ: Didn't even picture nipple. That takes dedication.*

I can't remember it so I read the text. And I totally laugh, again.

Why does he have to be so damn funny on top of being everything else?

"Riley."

"Yes. Right here." I put the phone down on the bar and look at her. "Repeat what you just asked me. I'm listening. I swear."

Beth's dark, perfectly sculpted brows pull together. "Well," she begins, eyes dancing between the phone and my face. "Let me think. I asked several things." She drums her blue painted nails on the bar and ponders for a few seconds.

"I'm just going to respond to this really quick while you think. I'm paying attention, I promise, I just don't want to be rude," I tell her, grabbing my phone again.

Me: Kinda weird that ur picturing my boobs without nipples.

I start to look up, but a new vibration drops my gaze back down.

CJ: You giving me the go ahead to picture nip? Fantastic. My day is looking up.

Me: Friends don't picture each other's boobs. No boobs or nip allowed.

CJ: You friend-zone me and it's a boob-free zone?

Oh, Lord.

Me: NO BOOBS OR NIP.

CJ: Should've been up front with that disclaimer. Can't be adding rules to this shit now. It's too late.

Me: These are unspoken rules that apply to every friendship. I don't picture Beth's boobs.

CJ: Totally imagining you picturing Beth's boobs right now.

Me: WHAT?!

CJ: Now she's thinking about yours.

"Oh, my God," I murmur, shaking my head through a laugh.

"Why are you and CJ discussing my boobs?"

Beth's voice jerks my head up and our eyes lock, hers so close to mine now I can count her lashes.

I guess I wasn't paying attention and held my phone out for curious eyes. Eyes that are apparently very capable of reading upside down.

Perfect.

This is so not how I wanted to broach this topic.

"Did you two always text?" she asks when I don't answer, leaning away but staying propped on her elbows. "You and CJ?"

"Uh." I put my phone down and saw my teeth over my bottom lip. "No, but—"

"I didn't think you two really even knew each other. How long has this been going on?" she interrupts.

"Didn't you ask me something about Richard?" I suggest, growing nervous from her line of questioning. "Right? Weren't you trying to remember what you asked me? Why don't we focus on those questions first and then we can move on? Did you remember them?"

"Riley."

"Okay. *Fine*," I groan, dropping my face into my hand. Pieces of hair that have fallen out of my ponytail tickle my cheek. "It's why I'm here anyway. I don't know why I'm avoiding this." I lift my head and look at her, lowering my hand to the bar. "The weekend of the wedding . . . I, uh, sort of slept with CJ a little," I confess with a soft voice.

Beth's eyes go round, taking up the majority of her face.

"And by *a little*, I mean a lot," I clarify.

"Oh, my God," she whispers.

"And when I say *slept with*, I mean there wasn't much

sleeping involved, except after we were finished *not sleeping."*

"Oh, my God," she whispers again.

"You sound like me that weekend," I say, shaking my head.

Beth blinks several times. She looks stunned.

"I think we would've continued what we were doing, maybe. He wanted to." I look down at the bar. "We both did," I admit quietly. "But I got home and Richard was there, and then I found out we weren't really broken up. And I couldn't do it. I couldn't . . ."

"You couldn't tell him or you couldn't leave?"

"Both." I look up at her. "I didn't want to hurt him. I love him. And CJ was just . . . a mistake. I couldn't throw away my relationship over something that was never meant to happen. And Richard and I, we're good together. *Great* together. We've just hit a bump. That's all."

A big bump. One that's taking us forever to clear, but we'll clear it.

I know we will.

"What about CJ?" Beth asks.

"We're friends. That's what I wanted." I tap my phone with the back of my hand, then wave her on. "Go ahead. Tell me I'm a horrible person. I deserve it."

"Why would I tell you you're a horrible person?" she questions.

"Because I cheated on Richard."

"But," her brow furrows. "You thought you were broken up, right? I mean, you *really* thought that."

I nod, grabbing the balled up napkin Beth used as a weapon and twisting it between my hands like I'm wringing out a towel. "I should've been absolutely sure though," I declare, swallowing down the sick creeping up the back of my throat. "I should've doubled checked. Triple checked. Why didn't I?"

Beth's face softens. She shakes her head. "You *were* sure, Riley," she tells me. "In your heart, you were sure. You didn't do anything wrong."

"Then why do I still feel so terrible every time I look at him?"

"Who?"

"Richard." I watch her lips press together, then lower my eyes to the napkin I'm now tearing into pieces. "He doesn't know anything. Not even about this new friendship I have," I confess. "I didn't tell anybody what happened that weekend until just now, and really, the only reason why I'm telling you is because I thought maybe if I told someone I'd stop thinking about it so much. I *need* to stop thinking about it."

I need to forget. Why can't I forget?

"You're thinking about it a lot?" she asks, drawing my gaze up again.

"Constantly."

"*Constantly*? Even," her eyes go round, "you know . . ."

I shake my head. "We haven't really done much of that lately," I admit. "Not since before Richard got fired. Things are just . . . off. I don't know. But other times? Yes. I'm thinking about it." My shoulders slouch. I sink lower onto my stool. "I try not to. I do, but they're just so different. *Everything* is different. Even their hands." I look down at my own, opening and closing them around the napkin. "I can't get over how different their hands are," I murmur.

Rough versus rougher. Richard has hands like he works outside but CJ has hands like he *lives* outside and has his entire life, built shelter for himself and kills what he eats. His fingers are longer and thicker and his palms are wider. But even if they weren't, he still touches differently.

I can't get over that most of all.

"Well," Beth begins. "I'm sure that's normal."

I snap my head up. "Fantasizing about a man who isn't your boyfriend is *normal*? For who?"

"I just mean having him on your mind still," she immediately clears up. "It just happened. I think as time goes on, you'll think about CJ less and less." She pauses, shrugging. "If that's what you want."

Our gazes lock, and I think she hears what I'm not saying and reads my worry.

I know I hear it—the words circling in my head and stabbing at my heart.

Is it what I want?

"Maybe you feel terrible because you made the wrong choice," she suggests delicately.

I shake my head and return to shredding the napkin.

No. I made the right choice. I know I did.

Didn't I?

Beth places her hand on top of one of mine. I blink up at her. "You're not a horrible person, Riley." Her voice is warm and sweet and full of honesty. Nothing else. "I think anyone would've done what you did knowing what you knew to be true. Really. I believe that."

"What about me wanting to be friends with CJ?" I ask. "Do you think I'm horrible for wanting that? For wanting *something* with him?"

She smiles softly. "No," she answers, giving my hand a squeeze. "I don't. CJ is a great guy. Really great. It's pretty impossible not to like him and want to be his friend."

"Unless you're Reed and find out your *friend* had sex with your sister."

Beth pulls in a sharp breath through her nose, blinking with wide eyes. "Yeah, I don't think he should find out about this," she suggests, pulling her hand away. "Maybe not ever. I don't know how Reed would take that."

"Right? No way. I'm not telling him. And I made CJ swear he won't say anything."

"What about Richard? Are you two—"

My eyes double in size. "I'm not telling him either! Are you nuts?"

"That's not what I was going to ask," she argues, scooping up the pieces of shredded napkin off the bar and disposing of them into the receptacle she's next to. "You already told me you weren't telling him, and I get that too."

"Oh." I bite my lip, handing over the remaining bits of napkin I'm clutching when she holds her hand out. "You do? Really?"

"Really."

I release a slow breath while Beth tosses out my mess.

"I just don't want to hurt Richard, you know?" I say. "I never meant for it to happen."

"I know. That's why I get it." Beth motions at a guy at the end of the bar who calls out for a refill, signaling for him to hold on. Then she looks at me. Her eyes are tender. "I just want to make sure you're happy with Richard. That this is really what you want."

"It is," I quickly answer, following her eyes to my phone and then meeting them when she lifts her gaze. "Really. I'm happy with him. Right now it's just hard with him struggling to find a job, but as soon as he finds one we'll be happy like we were. So happy. I just know it."

I know it.

"I'm sure you're right," she says, smiling a little. "And I'm sure he'll find a job soon."

"Yeah." I smile back, mine as weak as hers.

We stare at each other while silence lingers, that uncomfortable silence filled with unspoken words and unshared fears, and when I can't take it anymore I check the time on my phone.

"I gotta go. We have that concert tonight. The Killers. Richard bought us tickets a few months back." I stand from my stool and slip my phone away.

"Oh, that's right. Hey." Beth reaches into the front pocket of her apron and pulls out some cash. She holds it over the bar. "Can you get me a shirt? I don't have one of theirs."

I wave off her offer. "I got it. You know, since we're family now."

She grins, laughing lightly. "You just love saying that, don't you?" she says, bringing back my words from earlier as she tucks her money away.

"Maybe a little," I reply. "I'll give it to you on Sunday. Sound good?"

"Yep."

"And thanks for listening. Really. I'm so glad I have you to talk to about stuff like this. About everything."

"Anytime, little sis," she says, amusement in her voice as she makes her way to the man waiting on his refill. She lifts her hand and waves.

I wave back, doing this grinning because I have a sister now and she's awesome, and also because she gets what I'm doing. She understands.

Meaning I'm doing the right thing.

"I'M HOME!" I announce after stepping inside the house and shutting the door behind me.

I toss my book bag against the wall in the hallway and dart upstairs, knowing that's where Richard has been spending most of his time as of late, and find him in the office.

He's slouched back in the comfy desk chair we purchased months ago, still in the clothes he slept in last night, unshaved, looking exhausted and possibly irritated, I can't tell. The two seem to go hand in hand these days. Head tipped toward the ceiling, eyes unfocused, a bottle in his hand. Whiskey, by the looks of it. While two empty beer cans lay scattered on the desk amongst my school papers, laptop, and the bills I'm waiting to pay.

"Hey." I lean against the doorframe and wrap my hand around my forearm. "How'd it go today? Any luck?"

Richard doesn't turn his head or acknowledge me, meaning he's not possibly irritated. He's *absolutely* irritated.

He brings the bottle to his lips and takes a swig of the amber colored liquid.

"Well, you know, that's okay. Tomorrow's another day, right?" I step into the room. "I bet you'll find something tomorrow."

"You know how annoying you're being right now?" He slowly turns his head.

I stop a foot away from the desk when our eyes lock. I see the anger in his.

"Quit with the positivity bullshit, Ri," he snaps. "I'm sick of hearing it."

I shrug. "Sorry. I'm just—"

"You're just making it worse, all right?" he interrupts. "I don't need you telling me I'm gonna find a job and shoving down my fucking throat how qualified I am and then saying shit about how people are crazy if they don't hire me, and how *you* would hire me. What the fuck? You think that shit helps?" He takes another swig from the bottle, then jerks forward and slams the laptop closed. "There's no fucking jobs available right now," he spits. "There's *nothing*. How many times do I gotta tell you that? I can't get hired if I can't fucking apply to anything."

"Okay, okay, I'm sorry. Just . . ." I step closer until I'm standing beside the desk. "Please be careful with that," I request, pointing at the laptop. "I need it for school."

He sets the bottle on the desk and rakes his hands down his face. "Right," he murmurs before slamming back in the chair. He tilts his head up and glares at me. "Looks like you're the one who'll be providing for us so I guess I should be careful with the shit I bought you, back when I was working."

I feel my mouth grow tight.

Is Richard being rude and taking his frustrations out on me?

Absolutely.

Do I understand his frustration and know he really doesn't mean what he's saying?

Yes. This isn't him.

This is our bump.

Which is why I relax my mouth into a smile and let him see it before climbing onto his lap.

He doesn't reach out for me or draw me closer. He keeps his arms on the armrests.

"I think tonight will be good for you," I tell him, pulling my knees up, kissing his scratchy jaw and then resting my head on his shoulder while my fingers play in the frayed edges of his sleeve. "It'll get your mind off everything. Let you relax a little. You need it."

"What the fuck are you talking about?" he asks.

"The concert." I angle my head up and meet his eyes. "Remember? We've got tickets to see The Killers."

Richard stares at me.

"What?" I ask.

"You think I'm going to that shit after the day I've had?" He bumps my chest with his, signaling for me to climb off.

I twist in his lap, sitting tall so I can see him better. I do not climb off.

His arms stay on the armrests.

"Why wouldn't you go? You love them."

"No, I don't," he bites out. "*You* love them. When have you ever heard me listening to their music?"

"But, you got us tickets."

"Yeah, so you could take one of your friends. I never planned on going."

I look at him, my brow furrowing.

He never told me that. I would've said I wanted to go with him. I know I would've.

I relax my face and push my fingers through his dark hair until he yanks back, pulling out of reach, then I drop my hand to his shoulder. "I want to go with *you*," I tell him. "I don't want to go with a friend."

"Sorry," he mumbles coldly.

"Please?"

His face hardens.

"Jesus, Ri. *No*. What—"

"*Please*," I repeat, my voice shaking and stress filled as I resort to begging. "Please go with me. I want us to do something together. Something out of this house. We stay in all the time now. We don't do anything. You're job hunting and I'm watching you job hunt, and I feel like we need this. You're so stressed, Richard. It'll be good to get out. And look, we don't have to stay the whole time. We can leave whenever you're ready. I promise. And you can continue drinking. I don't mind. I'll drive. Just go with me." I hold his face with both of my hands and force him to look at me when his eyes start sliding away. "We used to do stuff together like this all the time. I miss it. Don't you?"

"Shit's different now. I can't afford stuff like this."

"Tickets are already paid for. There's free parking on the street. And you can sneak in your own booze. People do that, I think."

He inhales a slow, deep breath.

It's tense and tight and I think he's going to tell me no, and I don't know why, it's a stupid concert, it's *nothing*, but my lip starts trembling.

I duck my chin so he can't see it.

What's wrong with me? Why is this so important?

I'm worried. I'm stressed out and sick with worry.

"Fine," he grunts after several seconds, huffing out all the air in his lungs.

I lift my chin and look into his eyes.

"But I'm drinking. You're driving. And when I say it's time to go, it's fucking time to go. You give me shit about me wanting to leave and we're gonna have problems."

"I won't!" I throw my arms around his neck and squeeze him tight. Relief floods my veins and warms my skin all over. "I won't give you shit! I promise! And it'll be fun, you'll see. We'll have so much fun."

"All right. Get off me."

"Hold me back first," I request.

I need it, I whisper inside my mind. *We need it.*

A light touch grazes my hip.

I shake my head against his, then smile into the crook of his neck when he draws both arms around me and holds on, just like he used to.

I hold on too, closing my eyes.

Yes.
We are getting over this bump.

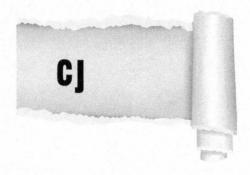

CJ

"YOU TULLY?"

I jerk my chin at the guy standing at the security booth after he speaks, then throw a look of appreciation at the bouncer who led me over here before he steps away.

"Name's Mark. I'm running things tonight. It's good to have you," the guy says.

We shake hands.

"Yeah. Don't mention it," I reply.

He looks around the venue and gestures. "Packed joint tonight. Shouldn't get too crazy with this band and the crowd it's bringing out, but we never wanna risk it. It's good having backup."

"How many of us you got?" I ask him over the music when the band starts playing, leaning closer to hear his response.

"You and another guy who's already here. He's hanging out up by the stage. Plus, a bunch of our guys." He hooks his thumb at the floor to ceiling windows along the front of the building, adding, "I got some uniforms on the street keeping that shit under control in case people get tossed out."

I nod, liking what I'm hearing.

The Red Door isn't the biggest venue I've worked security on, but it's big enough. Managing this shit alone can present a challenge. And by the looks of it, it's a sold out show.

The more eyes we got on the crowd, the better.

"You run into any problems yet?" I ask.

The guy shakes his head. "Nah. Just normal shit. People trying to sneak in their own booze," he replies, glancing at the door where everyone is filing in. "Confiscated it. No issues. Everything else seems to be running smooth."

"Good," I say when I meet his eyes. "I'll keep near the back since the other guy's covering the front."

"Sounds good, man."

We exchange another handshake, then I step away and move through the crowd.

I stop near the center of the room and stay to the back like I said so I can have full view of the floor that's packed with bodies, some keeping position and others moving away from me, pushing to get closer to the stage.

Bringing my arms across my chest, I stand tall and do a sweep of the place. I've been here before so I know the layout.

There's a bar to the right of where I'm standing, stretching the length of the wall. Restrooms are behind me. Other than the hallway leading to the rooms behind the stage where bands hang out, there isn't much that isn't visible. Plus, it's one level, standing room only, so I don't gotta worry about another floor I need to cover.

Should be an easy gig.

I do shit like this on the side for the extra cash. Venues hosting concerts are always looking for cops who are willing to come out and beef up security. We stay in civilian clothes so we blend in, and unless I'm having to act on something, I typically get out without anyone knowing I'm a cop.

Easy money. Nothing wrong with that.

I look back to the dance floor.

The lights are dimmed. Red and blue strobe lights

positioned on the ceiling illuminate the crowd, along with the bright, white lights shining from the stage. Visibility is good.

Another plus. I worked a few of these where it wasn't and that only presented problems.

But here, I can see faces. Can see other shit going on too if someone's dumb enough to try something.

I anticipate it. Events like this always bring out some of the stupidest motherfuckers. Which is exactly why they like having us work these things.

Security can only do so much.

I'm three songs into the set when the beat picks up. The bass vibrates along the floor. I feel it pulsing in my feet.

The faster rhythm stirs the crowd and shifts them around. More bodies gather and move closer to the stage, jumping up with their fists in the air and belting out lyrics, drawing people away from the bar. Others stay toward the back where there's room to dance.

That's where I'm looking, and that's where I see her.

Blonde.

I blink. My eyes refocus. Then I stare at waves the color of sand flowing down the back of a tiny thing swaying to the music.

Shirt tied off at the waist. Lower back showing. Hips shaking in some tight as shit black jeans. Ass looking fucking incredible.

Damn.

She reaches above her, bends her elbows and rakes her fingers through her hair, lifting it off her neck as her body keeps moving in ways I feel straight in my cock, then after letting her arms drop, she looks toward the bar with eyes searching, giving me full view of her profile.

My chest grows motherfucking *tight*.

I blink again, thinking I'm seeing things.

Riley Tennyson wets her lips.

Fuck.

I'm not seeing things.

Jesus Christ. This is just what I need.

Working this shit, needing to stay focused and eyes alert to all bodies in this room and now I know for damn sure that's not going to be happening, meaning this gig just went from easy to really fucking complicated.

There's only one body I'm interested in keeping eyes on, and it's the one making my dick hard.

Motherfucker.

Riley Tennyson is going to fucking kill me.

I pull in a deep breath, watching that sweet face get ripped out of view when Riley looks toward the stage again.

She keeps dancing. Keeps shaking that perfect ass and swaying those perfect hips, fingers curling in and lifting those long waves again, also perfect.

Every part of her. Every fucking inch.

Perfection.

And I'm not even considering what she's got going on in the front. Shouldn't even be considering it—we're friends, she's taken, and I'm not a fucking asshole—but that didn't stop me all day when I couldn't keep those spectacular tits off my mind, even going a step further into crazy when I shared that with her through a text.

I need to quit now. Stop this shit.

I can avoid it. I got options.

Switch with the guy hanging up by the stage, hoping Riley keeps her location. Or fuck it. Just pull out of this gig all together. Make up some excuse. I don't need the cash.

I don't need to be staring.

I sure as fuck don't need to be getting hard right now.

I got options. Just need to pick one.

Simple.

Yeah . . .

Real fucking simple.

I breathe in deep again, letting it out slowly. And I do this staring at her.

Only at her.

And the more staring I do the more I start to notice, like how she seems to be out there dancing alone, not with another person or a group of friends she came with. People around her are keeping to themselves or appearing to be together, throwing their arms around each other or sharing looks. Acting friendly. Just not with her.

Riley isn't meeting anyone's eyes. She's not trying to talk to anyone. She's in her own little world.

She's here alone.

He made her come to this shit *alone*.

Anger fills me. My jaw flexes while the muscles in my arms and shoulders start locking up.

My choice of options just grew by one.

Instead of charging through the crowd, which, no lie, is exactly what I want to be doing right now, I reach into the back pocket of my jeans and pull out my phone. I shoot out a quick text.

Me: *Tell me he's here.*

Lifting my eyes, I watch as Riley pauses mid ass-shake, slaps her back pocket, tugs out her phone and brings it in front of her. Her head tilts down, then a second later it's lifting and she's searching all around where she's standing, peering around people and standing taller. She finds me when she finally twists around, head first and then body following.

Her lips part. Her blue eyes go round, flames burning me up like they always do.

Riley starts moving my way and my eyes lower, first to her mouth, watching the slow smile twist across it and take shape.

She looks happy to see me. I shouldn't put stock into that, but I do. It's what I want.

Then my eyes keep dropping and I get full view of her tits. Her full, heavy, perfect fucking tits. Sitting high behind her tight white shirt and bouncing with her steps.

Jesus Christ.

My new friend has tits like that. And by the looks of it, she didn't bother putting on a bra either.

What the fuck did I do in a previous life to deserve this kind of torture?

"Hey. I didn't know you were coming to this," Riley says, all sweet sounding when she reaches me. Sweat gathers on her brow and in the hollow dip in her throat. She shoves her phone away and questions, "Why are you standing all the way back here? Don't you want to get closer so you can see the band?"

"Working," I tell her, lifting my eyes before I punch a hole through my jeans. I tuck my phone into my back pocket, adding, "Trust me. I can see plenty from where I'm standing."

Isn't that the fucking truth.

Riley blinks, then looks to my chest. "You're not wearing your uniform," she observes.

I squint at her mouth.

I got what she said, but I can barely hear her over the music. I don't like that.

I want to hear her.

"Come on." Grabbing her elbow, I pull Riley with me to the back corner of the room, stopping beside the hallway that leads to the restrooms and crowding the wall.

It's as far from the speakers as I can get her unless I take her outside, and I'm not sure I want to do that.

Only `cause I know I'll want to leave with her. Meaning I *absolutely* want to do that.

Shoulder pressing to the wall, I release her elbow after tugging Riley close. I pull my arms across my chest. "Not typically something I wanna advertise when I'm staying undercover," I say in response to her observation.

"Oh." She looks up at me, smiling and lifting her shoulders with a jerk. "Cool," she says.

I can see Riley better where we're standing now. The hallway light is shining on her, making her skin glow.

I look her over.

She wearing more makeup than I've ever seen her in. Black lines her eyes and her lashes are darker. Thicker too.

I like that.

Her cheeks are flushed from the dancing she was doing. That combined with whatever she's got on her face is hiding her freckles from me.

I don't like that. But I don't tell Riley. I keep looking.

Red lips, full and shiny. Cock sucking lips. I know that from experience.

Shit. Don't go there. I focus on her eyes again.

Blue and black, fading out to grey. Like a storm coming . . .

"You totally still look like a cop," Riley shares, jarring my focus. The corner of her mouth twitches. "You're not fooling anyone, CJ Tully."

My brows raise. "Yeah?"

She nods, laughing. "You look scary and pissed off. Smile a little."

I don't smile. Not even when she amps hers up and gives

it to me, pairing it with another soft giggle.

I get straight to the point with her, because getting off point with Riley is going to lead to this shit getting even more complicated, and fuck, I've looked enough tonight to run the risk of major fucking complications.

Plus, she's laughing. Smiling. Looking like she's thinking the same things I'm thinking.

Get to the fucking point, Tully.

"Are you going to answer my question?" I ask.

Her brow furrows. "What question?"

"I asked you if he was here."

"Oh." Nodding, Riley looks behind her in the direction of the bar, then meets my eyes again. "Yeah, he went to get a drink. He doesn't really want to be here. I kinda dragged him out."

"Why?"

"Why *what?*"

"Why'd you need to drag him out?"

Riley tilts her head. "Because . . . he doesn't really want to be here?" she repeats slowly, looking puzzled. "I just told you. He doesn't like The Killers."

"So?"

"*So?*"

"Yeah, babe. So."

She straightens her head, but her eyes narrow as if she's thinking hard. "You've lost me," she shares.

"Forget it," I mumble, looking away, knowing I got no business getting up in her shit the way I'm doing. I need to back off.

"No. What? Tell me." Riley reaches out and places her hand on my forearm.

I look down and watch her black painted fingers wrap

around and curl under. I feel them squeeze.

Our eyes lock.

"Tell me," she pleads, looking close to begging for this.

My blood starts running hot. Scorching. Hot.

Fuck it.

I'm getting up in her shit.

"I'm here because I'm working for extra cash, not because I'm digging the music," I share, staring into her eyes and seeing hers staring back, like what I'm revealing is something she needs to hear, not just something she's curious about. "Don't hate it. I listen to stuff like this on occasion but it's not something I'd pay money to see. That being said, my woman wants to come to a show like this, crowd this size, booze flowing, other shit possibly going on, she isn't coming alone. No discussion needed. I could hate this music to the point it makes my fucking ears bleed and I'm still going with her."

"Why?" Riley asks. "To protect her?"

"That." I jerk my chin. "And 'cause she's mine and a real man can deal with shitty music for a few hours if it means putting in time with his woman."

Riley drags her teeth along her bottom lip. Her chest starts working harder, moving stricter with her breaths.

I should stop now. The way she's looking at me . . .

I should stop.

I don't.

"Saw you dancing and thought you were here alone," I add, smirking. "Already hate that motherfucker for what he gets to touch every night. I thought I was going to have to kill him."

Riley stares up at me. She doesn't blink. Doesn't breathe.

"Babe," I probe.

"You shouldn't say that," she says, face serious.

Her hand squeezes tighter. She's anxious now, maybe. Or pissed. I don't know.

I decide to ease her mind if it's nerves getting to her.

"I wouldn't really kill him." My smirk grows into a smile. "Mess him up though."

"No. Not that." She shakes her head. "The other thing. *What he gets to touch.* You shouldn't say that."

"It's true."

"Even so. We're friends. You shouldn't say it."

I bend to get closer. "You might wanna take your hand off me if we're friends, darlin'," I warn.

Riley's eyes flicker wider. She yanks her hand back in a way it's like she forgot she even had it there, her movement driven by panic, but before she can lower her arm to her side, I'm grabbing onto her wrist and keeping it between us.

"What are you doing?" she asks.

I step closer, keeping my hold.

Her resistance is weak.

"You wouldn't be dragging me anywhere," I inform her, need vibrating in my throat so bad I can fucking taste it.

I run the risk of her hearing that need, but it's funny.

I just don't care.

Riley blinks. Her lips part.

And that resistance she's putting up goes from weak to non-existent.

"CJ," she murmurs under the sound of the music.

"Not anywhere, darlin'. Are you hearing me?"

I don't know why this is so important. I don't know why I need to make sure this sticks with her, but I do.

Hesitation keeps her still for a beat, or those damn nerves, I don't know, but she eventually nods.

"I'm hearing you," Riley mutters.

Good. It's sticking.

"We're just hitting a bump," she adds with a quick voice, suddenly looking uneasy. "It happens to everyone. We'll be better soon. I know we will."

My brow pulls tight.

They'll be better soon?

"What the fuck's that mean?" I ask her, not liking the way she's sounding or looking right now.

Riley opens her mouth to respond, but then her eyes dart away and focus over my shoulder. I watch them widen and fill with alarm.

"Hey. What the fuck is this?" a voice bellows at my back a second before a hand is shoving at my arm, trying to turn me.

My frame goes rigid. Unmovable and alive with awareness.

I turn when I want to turn, and it's right then to get a look at the dumb motherfucker trying to start something with me.

"Might wanna back off, friend," I warn, watching the guy step closer and recognizing his reaction. He's sizing me up.

I do the same.

He's tall, but I'm taller. Got some muscle to him but nothing I'm worried about. And his eyes are fixated on Riley in a way we can go ahead and skip the introductions.

My jaw clenches.

"Why are you touching my girl? Get your hands off her," the guy bites out.

Riley spins to face him, pulling her arm away that I was still holding, and wraps her hand around his bicep. "It's okay. He knows Reed," she says. Her other hand flattens on his chest. "Calm down, okay?"

"Listen to her," I suggest, glaring when he looks at me again.

He sniffs, then narrows his eyes, which are jumping between mine like he's chasing something.

"Fuck you. Why were you touching her?" he hisses through his teeth. "Huh? Why were you touching her, asshole?" He steps closer, bringing Riley with him since she's still holding on.

I don't move.

"Richard! Stop!" Riley yanks him back. "Calm down! What's wrong with you? I said he knows Reed. He's a friend."

"Yeah?" Richard turns his head, bends lower, and gets in her face. "He a piece of shit like Reed too? A worthless little *bitch*, like Reed?"

"Back off. I'm not gonna say it again," I warn, gaining his attention. He straightens up.

My voice draws some eyes from the crowd around us. I can feel them on me.

Richard bares his teeth. "Or what?" he asks, moving closer. "Huh? Or *what*? What are you gonna do?"

"He's a cop!" Riley yells, pulling his arm. "He's going to arrest you. Stop it!"

Richard stops, body going rigid and eyes swelling. The color drains from his face as he stares at me.

I figure he's just reacting to the threat of being arrested so I don't think much of his panic. Instead, I decide to fill him in on *one* of the issues I got with him right now.

"I know you got beef with Reed, but on top of him being her brother, something that should keep you from running your mouth the way you're doing out of respect for her, he's also a good friend of mine. You already stepped out of line with me once. Calm your shit."

Richard laughs. It sounds nervous. Then he sniffs a couple times and wipes at his nose with the back of his hand.

I narrow my eyes on him. That's when I start noticing more.

He can't stand still. He's shifting his weight around,

rocking his upper body, cracking his knuckles. Constantly sniffing and darting his eyes all over the place like he can't focus on one thing too long. He looks wired.

My jaw flexes again. The muscles in my back and shoulders tense up.

The other shit that sometimes goes on at these things has definitely been going on.

Richard is on something. Coke, by the looks of it. I recognize his behavior all too well.

Jesus fucking Christ.

Letting his woman out of his sight, looking the way she does in a crowd like this so he can score some blow.

Wasn't lying after all. I am going to kill him.

I move in so I'm standing in his space. "I'm going to ask you once and if you lie to me, this shit is going to end a helluva lot worse for you," I inform the prick, watching his eyes dart all over my face. "You got it on you or did you score it from someone?"

Richard leans back. "The fuck you talking about?"

"CJ . . ."

Riley's voice is at my shoulder. It's full of questions.

That I'm not surprised about.

I ignore her for now and stay on Richard. "The blow," I elaborate. "Did you bring it?"

He shakes his head, blinking fast. "What?"

I lean in. "Last time," I growl.

I've dealt with people on drugs a lot. I know their reactions can be unpredictable. You gotta be ready for anything.

I'm fucking ready.

Richard smiles like he knows something I don't, then he steps back, laughing and shaking his head. "Man, what the fuck? You're crazy. Come on, Ri."

He grabs her hand and tugs her away from me, wrapping

his arm around her waist, but it barely lands before I'm stepping up and separating them. I get Riley behind me and put myself between them.

"CJ!" she calls out, pushing up against my back.

I ignore her and get up in his face.

"Hey, man, what are you doing?" Richard tries to move around me to get to Riley. I side-step with him. His face turns red. "What the fuck, man? Move!"

The crowd around us starts stirring. Bodies knock into me and move past in a herd, fast, like they're all gathering for something. All three of us start getting pushed around the floor and separated.

I watch Richard. His eyes are all over the place, but I think he's looking for Riley.

"FIGHT!" someone yells from behind me.

"Fight! Fight! Fight! Fight!" others start chanting.

Chaos breaks out. People panic and rush in to see what's going on.

I turn my head to make sure Riley isn't anywhere near it, but I don't see her. I do see the fight that's broken out. It's coming from the hallway leading to the bathrooms. Three guys all throwing fists, some landing, some not, charging at each other and knocking into people who aren't sticking around to watch, but who are just trying to get away from it. Innocent people who don't want any part of it.

Shit like this can get out of control fast. People can get hurt.

Luckily, I don't need to intervene.

Security moves in, and I'm guessing the other guy working undercover, all of them swarming on the three jerkoffs and anyone else trying to get involved, locking that shit down quick.

Seeing that and knowing they got it handled, I turn back

around to keep with what I'm doing.

Richard isn't in front of me anymore. I look above heads and behind others. I search the crowd.

Nothing. I don't see him.

I don't see Riley either.

"Fuck," I growl.

I charge ahead, scanning faces as I push my way toward the floor where I first spotted Riley, thinking maybe she made for here when the fight broke out and knew I'd come looking for her.

The band is still playing. People are still dancing and oblivious.

I search, looking all over. Moving people when they don't clear for me and ignoring their bitching when I need to move them.

I don't see her.

Pushing toward the stage, I keep searching.

Nothing.

I check the bar, thinking maybe that asshole took her over there so he can get another fucking drink.

Nothing.

I head back to where we were standing and check near the restrooms, pushing through more people. Maybe I missed her and she's over here scared 'cause of the shit she's seeing.

I don't see her. Then a thought hits me as I look toward the entrance.

He's got her outside. He knows I'm onto him and he's trying to leave.

He's trying to leave with her.

Jaw clenching so hard my teeth fucking ache, I make for the door, heart pounding, nerves on edge, fists forming. I'm shoving people out of the way and knocking them to the ground. I don't care. I don't stop. I keep moving.

She's with him. And he's fucking high.

Getting outside, I scan the sidewalk, whipping my head left first and seeing the patrol cars parked along the curb. Two of them. The officers are standing on the sidewalk talking to some guy who looks pissed about something. He's yelling about his ticket.

I glance further down the sidewalk, thinking maybe Richard's moving with Riley and they're not near the door.

That's when I hear it.

"Stop! You're hurting me! Let go, Richard! What's wrong with you?"

My head whips right. I look past a crowd standing in front of the venue and see her.

Riley struggles in Richard's grasp. His hands are gripping onto her arms as he tries to move her further down the sidewalk. He's shoving her. He's making it so she has no choice but to go with him.

Fuck that. She has a choice.

"Hey!" I yell out, stalking in their direction.

"Move, Ri! We're fucking leaving! Go!"

He shoves at her again. Then he grabs her arm and forces her to walk.

"Get your hands off her!" I roar, gaining the attention of the other people on the sidewalk, just not the one person who needs to be hearing me. Richard doesn't even turn his head.

I shove at people to get through the crowd. They're slowing me down. They won't let me get to her.

"I don't want to go yet, Richard. Please!" Riley begs, stumbling as she tries to get away. "Let go of me! Why are you acting like this?"

He freezes. "Jesus, all you do is bitch, you know that?"

Richard grips both of her arms, yanks her against him and gets up in her face. "I'm gettin' the fuck outta here. You wanna stay? Fine. Fucking stay, you stupid cunt."

Richard throws Riley to the ground. Her body hits the concrete. Hard. I hear her cry out.

My heart drops to my fucking stomach.

I push the last asshole standing in my way so hard he stumbles and then falls over. I run at Riley.

I should be running at Richard. I should be remembering my job, my fucking duty, the fact that he put his hands on her. I should be reacting to that but I only see Riley.

On the ground. Possibly hurt.

I see the tears in her eyes when I get a foot away. I reach out to grab her, to hold her.

Riley. Only Riley.

In a crowd of people or just two, I'm only seeing her.

Richard charges at me when I'm nearly at her side and it's too late. I'm not expecting it. I'm watching *her*. All of my attention is on the girl I can't get out of my head, and because of that, I can't brace. I can't react to him.

His shoulder connects with my ribs, fast and with all of his weight behind it, sending a shooting pain up my side and knocking the wind out of me, then we're both sailing through the air until I hit something hard. It gives, shattering into pieces all around us.

The window at the front of the venue.

My back hits the floor inside The Red Door. Then my head, snapping back as a weight presses down on my chest.

People inside the club scream out.

I groan, eyes closed as I try and move my left leg. A fire spreads through it, burning me from below. I can feel the warmth flowing under my knee and up beneath my thigh. A thousand needles sting my back.

The weight on my chest is removed. Glass breaks around my head, then I hear my name being screamed, over and over.

"Oh, my God! Let me through! Move! Move out of the way!"

Riley.

Something presses on my knee, then a little lower where the fire is.

"Call 911! He needs to get to a hospital!"

I flinch, jerking my body. My shirt moves and fingers tug at my jeans.

"CJ, stay with me, okay?" Riley says through a shaky voice over the noise around us. Her warm hands hold my face and her breath tickles my lips. "Just hold on. I gotta use your belt as a tourniquet. I need to wrap it around your leg so we can stop the bleeding. An ambulance is coming, but you're bleeding a lot. I need to stop it."

I make a noise in my throat. I feel like I'm choking.

I want to look at Riley. I want to open my eyes and see those blue flames, let them burn me up instead of this fire I'm feeling now, but I can't.

I'm tired. My eyes are so fucking heavy. I can't open them.

Pain explodes in my leg as something tightens around it.

I groan, arching my back off the floor and gritting my teeth. I feel the flames everywhere now.

"Shh. It's okay," Riley cries over me. "Just hold on. They're coming. They'll be here soon."

My entire body starts shaking. Sweat breaks out all over as the fire continues to scald my skin. Continues to spread. It's burning fast now.

"CJ?"

I want to sleep.

Riley's hands are on my face again. I can taste her breath. Her tears are wetting my lips.

"Please," she whispers, voice breaking. "Please, hold on."

Darkness closes around me. The fire burns out.

I no longer feel it.

I no longer feel anything.

riley

CHEWING ON MY cuticle, I pace between the rows of chairs in the waiting room at St. Joseph's Hospital. Curious eyes follow my movement. I know why I'm being watched. I have blood all over me.

CJ's blood.

I can typically handle the sight of it, which is a good thing considering the profession I chose. It's never bothered me before. I'm not a squeamish girl. I never have been.

But seeing the puddle pooling around CJ, thick and bright red, and the way it was flowing like a river out of his leg . . .

I couldn't handle it.

I couldn't handle it because it was someone I knew and cared about. I couldn't handle it because it was CJ.

He lost consciousness. I watched him slipping away. I tried talking to him and keeping him with me, but the blood . . .

There was too much.

Thank God the paramedics arrived when they did.

I followed behind the ambulance while I made frantic phone calls and sent out texts. And now I'm waiting.

CJ is in surgery and I can't sit down or stand still. I can't stop looking up every time a hospital worker pushes through the doors leading to the back. They're carrying a clipboard and calling a name, but it's not CJ's name. It's never CJ's name.

What if they're having complications?

My stomach rolls as the Emergency Room doors slide open again. I glance up and watch Ben, Luke, and Tessa hurry through. This stops my pacing.

"What happened?" Ben asks me. He looks at the front of my shirt. "Jesus Christ. Are you all right?"

"Riley, are you bleeding?" Tessa wraps her hand around my arm. Her skin pales.

"No." I quickly shake my head. "No, it's not mine."

"*Fuck*," Luke mutters, pushing his hands through his hair and gripping the back of his head.

They all look concerned and as worried as I feel.

"He's in surgery," I inform them. "He cut his leg pretty bad. I don't know anything yet. I'm waiting."

"What the fuck happened?" Ben asks again, pulling his arms across his chest. He looks angry now.

With me? Do they all blame me for this?

Maybe they should.

I look between their faces, and then at the floor. "Um, he was pushed through a window . . . by my boyfriend. My ex-boyfriend."

For real this time. We're through. Over.

Officially over.

I made that clear after I watched Richard get arrested. I screamed our ending at the cop car window he sat behind. I made sure he knew we were finished before I followed the ambulance to the hospital. I didn't want any confusion or mishearing of words.

I sniffle when my nose begins to burn again. "He was trying to get me to leave with him and CJ saw. He knew Richard was on something."

"What was he on?" Ben asks.

"Coke."

"Oh, Jesus," Tessa says. She gives my arm a squeeze.

"Luke," Ben growls.

I lift my eyes.

"Yeah, I'm on it." Luke moves away while tugging his phone out of his pocket.

"Riley."

I turn back to Ben. "Mm?"

"You're not hurt? You're all right?"

"I'm not hurt," I reply with a quiet voice.

The pain in my chest calls me a liar.

The Emergency Room doors slide open again, and Reed and Beth walk through. Beth pulls her hand free and rushes over.

"Oh, my God," she whispers against my ear. Her warm arms wrap around me. She's in her pajamas. She doesn't mind that I have blood on my shirt. "Are you okay? Did he hurt you?"

I shake my head, locking eyes with Reed when he steps up behind his wife. He looks bothered and bone-breaking angry. I never thought Reed could hate Richard any more than he already did.

I was wrong.

Ben grabs his attention and fills him in on what I just shared, while Tessa and Beth fire a million questions at me.

"Did you know he was doing drugs?"

"Whose coke was it?"

"Was he doing it at home too?"

"Are you sure you're okay, Riley?"

I answer what I can, that I'm fine. I don't know the answers to anything else.

"He's being booked in Kent County," Luke announces, returning to the group. "Drug and assault charges. You trying to go down there?"

Ben lifts his chin. "Yeah. Let's get word on CJ first. I wanna make sure he's all right." Ben looks to Tessa. "Do me a favor and call Mia. She's up. Let her know what's going on."

Tessa nods and takes Luke's phone. They both move to grab a seat. Ben follows.

Beth keeps hold of my hand.

"Riley."

I look up at Reed after he speaks. My lip trembles. "I'm so sorry," I whisper with tears in my eyes.

He blinks, brow furrowing. "What? *Why*? Jesus, this wasn't your fault. It was that fucking dickhead's fault. Come here."

Reed grabs the back of my neck and pulls me against him, hugging me to his chest. He holds me tight.

I hold him tighter.

"You got nothing to be sorry for, okay?" he soothes against the top of my head.

I don't nod or say 'okay' back. I don't believe him.

"Thank fuck CJ was there. Shit. You could've left with that asshole."

Reed's words don't offer me the comfort he's trying to give. They can't.

My guilt is too heavy. It's the only thing I can feel.

"You're not hurt? You swear?" he asks.

"I swear."

"Tully? Do I have family here for CJ Tully?"

I turn out of Reed's hold and face the nurse who just spoke. She's wearing surgical scrubs and holding a patient file. The rest of the group crowds at my back.

"Yeah. How is he?" Luke asks.

She smiles gently. "He's doing fine. He's in recovery. You'll be able to see him in about an hour."

A collective sigh leaves the group. Beth gives my hand a

light squeeze, and I turn and look at her.

He's okay.

"Thank *fuck*," Ben says after the nurse moves away. He rakes his hands down his face, then turns to Luke. "All right. You ready?"

Luke nods. "Handle this, then we'll come back here." He looks to Tessa. "You stayin', babe?"

"Yep. I want to see him."

"We're hanging out too," Reed says, throwing his arm around Beth when she moves to stand beside him. "Why don't you head home, Riley? Get some rest."

My lips part. I look to Beth and watch her eyes soften and a frown tug at her mouth. She hears it too.

You don't belong here with us.

CJ is their friend. Not mine. Why would I hang around? I'm not a part of their group.

I don't belong here.

"Yeah, I probably should . . . get cleaned up," I say, tugging at the hem of my blood-stained shirt.

Ben and Luke utter their collective "Laters" and head out. Tessa gives me a smile before she reclaims her seat near the soda machine. I hug Beth one last time, then watch her and Reed join Tessa. They turn their chairs so they're facing each other, and wave at me as I walk past.

None of them ask me to stay. Nobody even suggests it.

I cry the entire way back to Richard's house.

IT'S BEEN TWO days since the night of the concert.

Two days of walking the same hospital halls and staring at the muted paint colors. Two days of smelling antiseptic in the air.

We've all been here—Reed and Beth and Tessa, Ben and Luke when they weren't working, and the boys, Nolan and Chase. Mia brought them. Everyone has been in and out of the hospital, visiting CJ.

Everyone but me.

I've been here, but I've gone unseen for the most part. I haven't been in his room to see him. Saturday, both times that I came by and Sunday when I showed up after I was finished at the soup kitchen I volunteer at, CJ had visitors. His friends and my family or other cops that were in uniform, they gathered in his room. People who should be visiting him. People he has history with. And once I saw his company, I left.

What did I have with him? Why would I have reason to visit? I didn't even belong in the waiting room with everyone else.

Besides not knowing if I have a reason to be in CJ's room, I'm scared to face him. So nervous my stomach is in knots as I walk in through the main hospital entrance on my third day in a row and head for the elevators.

It's my fault he's in here. It's my fault he had to have emergency surgery after lacerating his Achilles. I dragged Richard to that concert instead of letting him stay at home and because of that, CJ was hurt.

CJ was hurt and Richard is now in jail.

Not that I care about Richard anymore. I don't. Not after what he did. Not after I found out he was high that night. But I do care about CJ. He had gotten hurt trying to get to me. He wanted to protect me from the boy I gave my heart to. I know he did. I saw his face before he was pushed through that window. He tried to protect me and I got him hurt.

I did this. This is all my fault.

What if he doesn't want to see me now? What if he's

angry and he tells me I have no business visiting him?

What if he hates me for what I let happen?

Wiping my sweaty palms on my scrub pants, I step off the elevator and peer around the corner, looking for Reed or anyone else who might question my reason for being on this floor.

It's Monday, so everyone should be working, but I'm still cautious. I need to be.

The hallway is clear of anyone besides hospital workers filtering in and out of rooms. Feeling good about that, I round the corner and start moving.

I just want to tell CJ how sorry I am. And I really want to make sure he's going to be okay. I know his surgery went well, and Beth told me yesterday CJ seems to be making a steady recovery, but I want to see it for myself.

I need to see it for myself. I need to get the image of him lying in a pool of blood out of my head.

Deep voices stop me just before I reach CJ's room. I plaster myself against the wall and listen, head turned toward the door. I recognize one of the voices as Ben.

"You pulled this shit on purpose. Don't lie," he laughs. "I saw the nurses that are coming in here."

"For real. How many times has that one asked if you need your linens changed?" Luke's voice filters out into the hallway next.

I pinch my eyes shut.

Crap.

What if they see me? They could easily tell Reed I was lurking outside CJ's room. And that'll just stir up suspicions.

Although . . .

I look down at myself.

My uniform. *Yes.* I can just say I'm here for clinical, which

I am, just not entirely. I'll only be half-lying. I can pull off a half-lie. No problem.

Of course, they are cops. Human lie detectors. This could totally backfire on me.

Can I be thrown in jail for lying to the police?

Maybe I'll just try and see CJ on my lunch break . . .

"Later, man," Ben calls out, his voice louder as if he's closer to the door. Closer to *me*. "We'll drop by tomorrow."

"Or you can save us the hassle and quit fakin'. This visiting you shit is getting old," Luke throws out, his voice equally as loud as Ben's.

My head whips left and then right. I realize my best move here is to flee the scene so I don't risk jail time, but I unfortunately realize this a second too late.

Ben backs out of the room, turns his head and looks down at me. His eyes are assessing. He's dressed in his uniform.

So is Luke, who does the same, stepping out and following Ben's gaze.

Busted.

Body still plastered to the wall, I blink up at them. My panic filled eyes jump between their faces.

I watch Ben smile, that all knowing kind of smile that tells me he's connected the dots. He knows I've had sex with CJ. Why else would I be here? That or his wife has been blabbing and finally shared the news of my wedding weekend walk of shame. *Thanks a lot, Mia.* I swallow thickly, then I look to Luke.

Brow furrowed. Mouth tight. Eyes narrowing and dissecting.

Luke has no idea I've had sex with CJ. He's wondering what I'm doing here, since I obviously don't belong. I'm reading that loud and clear.

I push off from the wall and turn to face them both. "Hi,"

I greet them softly, looking to the doorway and then back into their faces. I clear my throat. "I was just, uh, getting my steps in before my rotation starts." I hold my wrist up and show them my FitBit. "And I heard your voices. I had no idea this was CJ's room. Some coincidence, huh?" Laughter catches in my throat.

Ben's eyebrows raise.

"This is my favorite floor to walk on. It smells the best," I quickly add, wincing when I hear how ridiculous that sounds.

It smells the best?

Shut up, Riley!

Keeping his smile and pairing it with the laughter he's holding in, Ben turns to Luke. "You ready?" he asks.

Smirking now, most likely due to my terrible lying I'm certain neither one of them are buying, Luke's eyes leave mine. He gives Ben a silent nod, then the two of them move past me and head down the hallway. I watch them disappear around the corner. They never look back.

Maybe they're going to pretend they didn't see me here? That would be seriously cool.

I should make a donation to the Ruxton Police Department. Of course, you need money to make a donation and I don't exactly have any . . .

"Are you coming in today, or what?" CJ calls out from inside the room, spinning me back around and startling me.

My eyes widen. I feel my cheeks warm.

He knows I've been here.

I slow my breaths as I step up to the doorway and fill it, peering inside CJ's room for the first time. I look over at him.

He's sitting up in bed, hospital gown on, sheets bunched up around his waist and tucked under his injured leg for easy examination. White bandages wrap around his ankle and halfway up his calf. It looks swollen. Parts of the bandage are stained brown.

My stomach clenches when I think about how much blood he lost. I know there were cuts on his back too. He was bleeding from those as well. He seemed to be bleeding from everywhere.

God, how many stitches did he need?

"Hey."

I lift my gaze after CJ speaks. He's staring at me, bright blue eyes looking alert but with shadows under them. Dark smudges revealing his exhaustion. Behind an overgrown beard that's a shade darker than his golden auburn hair, the corner of his mouth is lifted.

"Come here," he says. His voice is rough. He sounds tired.

I wonder how much pain he's in. Maybe he isn't sleeping well.

"Are you comfortable right now? Are they giving you anything?" I ask, hooking my thumb behind me as I keep my spot in the doorway. "You can ask them for something stronger. If what they have you on isn't working, they need to give you something else. I can ask them." I drop my hand and begin to pivot around. "Let me ask them . . ."

"Riley."

CJ's voice halts me. I stop mid-turn and look back at him, meeting his eyes.

"Come here," he repeats, a little firmer this time. His mouth is tight now.

I exhale a breath, then I step into the room and move around the bed so I'm on his non-injured side. I take a seat in the chair pulled up to the bedside and knot my fingers together in my lap.

The monitor CJ is hooked up to beeps when he shifts

back and sits up taller. I follow the tubing coming from his IV bag to the needle going into his arm.

"Are you in pain? Does your leg hurt?" I ask, lifting my gaze to his face.

"I'm all right," he says through an easy smile. It does nothing for my nerves or the guilt I feel eating away at me. That's deep in my bones. I fear it will never go away.

"And your back? Is your back okay? Did you need stitches there?"

CJ shakes his head.

"Anywhere else?"

"You're blaming yourself for this. You need to stop," he orders, reading my worry and ignoring my question. His face is serious now. "This wasn't you, babe. You didn't put me in here."

"He didn't want to go. I made him go," I reply. "I . . . I *begged* him. I don't know why it was so important to me. I should've just gone by myself. This never would've happened."

"You get him the coke he snorted?" CJ asks, even though I think he knows this answer already.

I bite my lip and shake my head.

"You push me into that window? Was that you?"

"No, but I—"

"Wasn't you, Riley," CJ interrupts. "What he did, the drugs he took, those consequences are on him. You're not taking the blame for this, babe. The only thing you did was ask your man to accompany you to shit he should've been going to in the first place. That's it. Me being here is not on you. That's on me and that's on your man."

"He's not my man," I rush out, watching CJ's eyebrows raise. "I, uh, ended it." I shrug. "When he got arrested, I ended it. It's over."

"You ended it `cause he got arrested?"

"We weren't doing good," I confess, and I see understanding flash in CJ's eyes. "Richard getting arrested and everything else that happened that night, that was just the final push. I think I would've broken up with him even if that wouldn't have happened. We just weren't working anymore." I sigh, shaking my head. "I was so stupid to think some concert he didn't even want to go to would fix that."

"You weren't stupid," CJ corrects me. "Wanting your man with you is not you being stupid, babe. So quit thinking that. Okay?"

I nod, letting CJ know I hear him. Then thinking back to his words from a minute ago, I tilt my head and ask, "What do you mean, *this was on you*? What did you do? It was all Richard."

How can CJ think he was responsible for any of this? He was trying to protect me.

CJ stares at me for a breath, then he rubs at his mouth and scratches his jaw. His eyes cast down to a spot on the bed. "I wasn't watching him like I should've been watching him," he begins to explain. "I'm trained to look out for stuff like that. To be ready for it. I wasn't. I was watching you." CJ lets his hand drop to the bed. Our eyes meet. "I couldn't brace when he hit me. I wasn't ready for it."

"He hit you really hard. I saw him." My stomach drops at the memory. "I don't think you could've braced for it. It was out of nowhere."

CJ's mouth twitches. He drops his head back, laughing a little. "Nice, babe. I'm already out for five months with the injuries I got. Are you trying to bruise my ego on top of it?"

I feel my eyes widen. Something sick twists in my gut.

Five months?

"Five months? You're going to be laid up for *five months*?"

I ask, leaning closer to the bed. "They said that?"

CJ lifts his head again and jerks his shoulder, answering, "Close to it, probably. Depending on how my PT goes. There's potential nerve damage."

I inhale sharply through my nose, feeling it tingle.

Nerve damage?

Oh, no. Nononono.

Oh, my God . . .

"*Potential*," CJ repeats, watching me. "They're not saying it's definite. I'm not worried about it."

"I'm so sorry," I whisper, emotion breaking in my voice.

CJ's mouth goes tight. "Babe," he starts, head tilting as he looks at me, wanting to shut me down again, I just know it, but I ignore him. I keep going.

"I hate that this happened. I know you were just trying to protect me. That's why you got me away from him before we were separated, right? You knew Richard was on something."

CJ nods.

"I should've stayed with you," I continue. "I never should've let him take me outside. This is my fault. I'm so sorry, CJ."

He pulls in a deep breath through his nose and exhales it noisily. His jaw is set. He looks ready to argue with me again, but a knock on the door turns his head and then mine.

I watch a nurse walk into the room. She's holding a folder in her hand and smiling at CJ. She doesn't even take notice of me.

"Hello. I just wanted to bring in the home nurse information I was telling you about. I went ahead and got it from your insurance company for you," she informs him, sounding proud of herself. She sets the folder on his food tray that's pulled up next to the bed.

"Thanks. Appreciate it," CJ replies.

The nurse smiles bigger. I think I see her batting her lashes, but maybe it's just the dry hospital air causing her to blink rapidly.

Or maybe she has a twitch she's not aware of . . .

"Shall I change your linens while I'm in here?" she asks, looking eager for that possibility. "It'll only take me a minute."

I look at the linens on the bed. They appear freshly changed to me. The top sheet still has creases in it.

My gaze returns to the nurse and narrows.

What's her deal?

Laughter rumbles in CJ's chest. "I'm good," he tells her, sounding polite. "Thanks. I'll let you know if I need that."

The nurse keeps her smile and fiddles with his IV, checking the line. Then after pressing a button on the monitor and messing with the leads on his chest, something I'm not sure needs to be done since his vitals seem to be registering just fine, she announces she'll be back in to check on him later and leaves the room.

I watch this happen, feeling CJ's eyes on my profile. And when I turn to look at him, at the bed he's in and the hospital gown his chest seems too big for, that same guilt hits me. But before I can open my mouth to apologize again, CJ grabs the folder off the tray and drops it in his lap.

"Do you live with him?" he asks, meeting my eyes again.

My brows pull tight. "Richard?"

CJ jerks his chin.

"Yeah. I mean, I *did*," I answer. "I need to move out. Even though he'll probably be in jail for a while, I don't want to live there."

"Are you getting an apartment?"

"I can't really afford one," I reply. "I don't work right now.

I can't with my school schedule. I have savings that pay for gas and groceries and stuff like that but I can't really afford rent. I'll probably just go live with my parents in Thomasville. It'll be a drive to school, but I don't have a lot of options."

"You could move in with me," CJ suggests.

My brows raise. "What?" I ask, voice quiet.

CJ taps the folder in his lap. "My insurance'll cover a nurse to stop by once a week. You're a nurse. Aside from making sure I'm healing properly, you could help me out around the house since I'm not going to be able to do much. They said I'll be on crutches for a while. I can't imagine keeping up with shit while I'm getting around on those. It's probably going to be a pain in the ass."

"But, I'm not a nurse," I tell him. "Not yet anyway. I'm not qualified for that."

"You're training to be one, aren't you?" he asks, the corner of his mouth lifting when I nod my head. His shoulder jerks. "Consider me practice. Hands on is the best way to learn, babe. And besides, Thomasville is over an hour away. That's really fucking far to be driving all the time."

"I can't afford rent though. I told you."

"Did I say anything about charging you rent?"

I think for a beat—*no, he didn't*—then I shake my head.

"You helping me out *is* your rent. You're doing me a solid," he explains.

I chew on my bottom lip, thinking on this.

Hmm. I'd be doing him a solid. He needs someone to help him. I can be that person. I *should* be that person. CJ wouldn't need anyone if it wasn't for me.

We can be roommates. We're friends so, why not? Yeah. Totally. This will work.

"Okay," I decide. "But what about sleeping arrangements?

We should probably work that out ahead of time."

A slow, satisfied smile twists from one corner of CJ's mouth to the other.

I sit up taller, blinking at him.

"I got two bedrooms. Relax," he says, voice wrapped around a chuckle. He lets his smile settle into a smirk. "Though, I'm all for sharing and will absolutely not fight you on it if that's something you're feeling strongly about."

"I think separate bedrooms is a good idea," I share, ignoring his charm. Or, at least, trying to ignore it. "I want to do this right. This is a job. I want to look at it as a job. If I'm going to be helping you get better, I don't want to be distracted."

CJ grins.

Oh, boy.

"I'm not saying *you're* distracting," I tell him, smiling a little because I can't help it.

And because he is a little distracting.

"That's exactly what you're saying," he counters, keeping the grin. "So, it's settled. You're shackin' up with me." He grabs the folder off his lap and chucks it back onto the tray.

"I'm moving in to help you heal," I correct him.

"Shackin' up," he reaffirms, giving me that grin again.

I shake my head, but let this argument go, mainly because I have something more important to discuss with CJ.

"I don't think we should tell Reed," I say, watching his grin slowly fade. "Not right away, anyway. He won't understand why I'm doing it. It'll just raise questions."

Questions that could lead to my brother hating CJ. They're friends. I would never want that.

"I'm not going to lie to him," CJ informs me, pulling his arms across his chest and leaning back. "If he asks if you're living with me, I'm giving him the truth."

I nod, telling him, "I get that. I'm not asking you to lie, I just don't think we should advertise it."

"You don't think he's going to ask where you're living now?"

"I'll just tell him I'm living with one of my friends from class. He won't question it."

CJ shakes his head, face still tense. "He finds out the truth, either from asking me or on his own, how he reacts is on you," he shares.

"I know," I say, thinking about how angry Reed could possibly get after catching me in my lie. But as long as he's angry at me and not CJ, I'm fine with that.

I push to my feet after checking the time on my FitBit.

"I should go. I need to check in with my supervisor before I'm marked as late," I say, pulling the bottom of my scrub top down and smoothing it out. "Do you know when you're getting released?"

"They're saying tomorrow. Wednesday at the latest," CJ says, looking at my scrubs and smiling. His eyes sparkle with mischief.

"What?" I ask slowly. Reluctantly. I'm not sure I want to know what CJ Tully has on his mind right now.

He lifts his gaze to my face. "Just thinking about how many times I would've had my linens changed if you were the one asking me," he shares, smile growing into a grin.

My eyes widen. I immediately turn and start moving around the bed, heading for the door. And because I'm moving in that direction, CJ has no idea how big I'm smiling right now.

He'll never know.

TWO DAYS LATER, I'm carrying two suitcases and straining

under the weight of the duffle bag slung around my neck as I step up onto CJ's porch.

His rancher style home is in the middle of nowhere, down a winding dirt road and set on a good amount of acreage, which I wasn't expecting. For some reason, I figured CJ lived in a neighborhood like Reed and Beth, or like my parents. But this seems to fit him more. Surrounded by woods and set back far from the road, CJ Tully can totally pull off the lumberjack look living here.

He can totally pull off the lumberjack look living in New York City too. He's got the build for it.

And the hands. I'm sure lumberjacks have big, rough hands.

I set one suitcase down in front of the door and knock, but only out of courtesy. I know CJ answering would require getting to his feet and using his crutches and I don't want that. I just want him knowing that I'm here. Even though I am moving in, I'm still a guest in his house. After making my arrival known, I twist the doorknob, push the door open, pick up my other suitcase, and step inside the house.

I look around the space and am instantly reminded of a log cabin.

Dark atmosphere. Natural wood floors. A big stone fireplace and animal heads on the wall; two deer with large antlers and what looks like a boar, I think. I've never actually seen one. There's also a gun rack and a crossbow mounted with arrows.

Sheesh. He really does eat what he kills.

Total lumberjack.

The foyer opens up to a large living room, decorated in oak and black furnishings, and this is where I find CJ.

Stretched out on the couch in a t-shirt and running shorts with a remote in his hand, his bandaged ankle is propped up on the arm rest.

"Hey," he greets me, muting the TV he's watching. He sets the remote down on the large trunk in front of the couch, which he uses as a coffee table, I'm assuming, then lifts his head from the cushion and begins to sit up.

"No, don't. I got it," I tell him, nudging the door shut with my hip. I step into the living room with my suitcases. "Just direct me where to go. I don't have that much to bring in."

CJ looks like he wants to argue with me after glancing at my suitcases, but drops his head back down instead and stays where he is. "Down the hallway, last bedroom on the right is yours," he says.

"Cool." I give him a smile. "Nice place. Very Daryl Dixon," I tell him as I pad around the couch and head down the hallway.

"Who?" he calls out.

My brow furrows.

Who?

"Walking Dead. The show. You don't watch it?" I yell, stepping inside the bedroom at the end of the hallway and setting my suitcases beside the bed. I lift my duffle bag off from around my neck and set that down as well, then I drop my head from side to side, stretching with my hands on my hips. I take a look around the room.

The bed is big, king-sized by the looks of it. And the room is fully furnished with a large dresser and two nightstands, both of which have framed pictures on them and a few books, along with some spare change, crumbled up dollar bills, and a pocket knife. As if someone emptied their pockets and placed the contents in this room, which would be strange . . .

Isn't this the spare bedroom? Why wouldn't CJ empty his pockets where he sleeps?

I exit the room and start to make my way back toward the living area, but curiosity gets the better of me, and I stop at the next bedroom door halfway down the hallway and push it open. I peer inside.

This bedroom is smaller, not just the room size but also the bed. It can't be bigger than a full. The paint job is unfinished—one and a half walls a grey-blue color, and the rest is still that builder's grade off-white. The only other furnishings in the room are a weight bench and a rack of dumbbells. That's it.

No nightstand. No dresser. The bed doesn't even have a comforter on it. There's just a sheet and one pillow.

What the hell?

"You said last bedroom on the right, *right?*" I ask CJ, coming to a stop behind the couch and looking down at him.

He turns his head, dragging his eyes off the TV, and peers up at me. "That's what I said."

"You sleep in the bedroom with the weights?"

"Yeah."

"That tiny bed. You sleep in that?"

"Wouldn't say it's tiny, but yeah," he says, bending his arm and propping his head on his hand.

I bring my hands to my hips. "CJ."

He smiles behind the scruff I'm used to seeing on him. He's shaved since he left the hospital. He looks good.

CJ scruff is really good scruff.

"Yeah, darlin'?"

His voice draws my eyes up. I connect with his.

Darlin'.

There he goes again.

My gaze narrows. "Am I sleeping in your bed? Did you give me the master bedroom?"

He stares up at me, doing nothing but smiling.

Oh, my God . . .

"You did, didn't you?"

Still, he doesn't answer. Holding that smile for another breath, CJ finally turns his head and resumes watching the TV, informing me, "Technically both beds are mine. The room I got you in is bigger, yeah, but it's not the master bedroom. I sleep in that."

"The master bedroom is the smaller one that looks more like a workout room than a *bedroom*?" I ask, doing this while leaning over the couch. I watch the corner of his mouth twitch.

I knew it. He's got me set up in the master.

That thoughtful jerk.

"Yep," he answers, lies hiding behind that charm.

Exhaling heavily, I rock back onto my heels and shake my head. "Just so you know, I don't believe you. But I don't have time to keep arguing. I have other stuff to bring inside."

"Anything heavy?" he asks.

"Not really," I answer before moving with purpose toward the door.

"OH, SHIT!" I cry out, slamming the box I'm carrying against the wall after barely making it inside. I ease it slowly to the floor, heart racing and breathing erratic. "Oh, my God," I pant. "That was so close. My laptop is in there."

I think I would've cried if I would've broken that.

"The fuck?"

"It's fine. I got it," I tell CJ, turning my head and watching over my shoulder as he gets up from the couch. "Don't! You shouldn't be on your feet."

He grabs his crutch and starts hobbling toward me. "Babe, hate to tell you, but I'm not about to sit on my ass and watch you struggle bringing stuff in," he says. "I wasn't raised like that."

God. He really is a . . .

My thoughts cut out as I watch CJ stumble after the foot of his crutch gets stuck on the throw rug. He puts weight on his injured leg.

I gasp.

"*Fuck!*" CJ roars, tossing the crutch, sending it sailing across the room toward the kitchen and then bending over to hold onto the armrest. He grits his teeth and hisses through them, dropping his blood-red face.

I leave the box on the floor and rush over. "It's okay. I got it. Really," I say, ducking under his arm and draping it over my shoulder. I help him straighten up, holding onto his wrist and wrapping my other hand around his waist. "Come on. Let's get you back on the couch."

He hesitates, but eventually lets me support him and hops a step.

"I could've managed myself. I just needed a minute," he grumbles.

"But I'm here. It's better if I help you." Stopping at the middle cushion, I lift my head and look up at CJ. He's smiling down at me.

I could say something snarky, or tease how he'll probably be stumbling more often to get this close to me again, but I don't.

"Thank you for wanting to help me though," I tell him, watching his grin soften. "That's really nice of you."

"Nothing nice about it. It's the right thing to do," he argues, stating that matter-of-factly.

I blink up at him, thinking about the day I moved into Richard's house and how he told me helping him carry things in would help *move this shit along*, and how when he saw me struggling with a box as heavy as the one I just carried inside, he laughed and said I needed to lift with my knees. That was the only help he offered that day.

My eyes fall to a spot on CJ's shirt.

"You all right?" he asks me.

No. Not at all, I think, but I don't tell him that.

I force a smile and give it to him. "Yep," I lie. "Come on. Back on the couch you go."

I get CJ re-situated on his back, boosting his ankle up with a pillow and handing him the remote, then I empty out the box a couple of items at a time and carry them to the master bedroom.

The bedroom I'll be sleeping in.

Later that night after a quick dinner of sandwiches and chips—CJ had lunchmeat that needed to be eaten and not much else in his refrigerator or cabinets, leaving us with little choice that didn't include takeout—I slip on a pair of sweats and a t-shirt, handle my bathroom routine, secure my hair up into messy bun, and climb into bed.

I draw the sheets around me as cold air blows out of the vent on the wall directly above my head.

CJ's smell is everywhere. On the pillow and the satin touching my skin. His summer meadow soap and that clean, masculine scent I took home with me after the weekend of the wedding.

I close my eyes.

More cold air blows out of the vent. My teeth chatter and a chill runs through me. I kick the covers off, swing my legs out of bed, and walk over to the suitcases I have yet to unpack.

I rifle through the one, looking for something with sleeves. When I flip open the lid of the second suitcase and stare at my collection of crop tops and frayed jean shorts, I give up and move to the dresser along the wall.

The bottom drawer holds what I'm looking for, and I slip on the light grey Ruxton Police Department hoodie with the word Tully in white screen-print on the back.

It's soft and well-worn and the sleeves are stretched out and fraying.

I never want to take it off.

I draw the hood over my head and climb back into bed. I close my eyes.

And I don't know if it's because I'm in CJ's house or in the bedroom I know is his, or if it's because he's all around me, in the sheets I'm tucking underneath my chin or the loved cotton against my cheek, but my mind goes back to that night at The Red Door. I can hear CJ calling out and I can feel Richard's harsh grip on my arms as he drags me down the sidewalk. And then I'm being thrown to the ground and he's there, CJ is right there, reaching out to me to make this better and to get me safe, and then he's gone, and there's shards of glass hitting me and people are screaming out.

I see him. He's lying there with his eyes closed and blood and broken glass beneath him. And Richard is getting pulled away by police and he's screaming at me, he's calling me a bitch and telling me to help him, but I need to help CJ. I need to, because this is all my fault.

It's my fault.

A sob catches in my throat as I press my cotton covered hand against my mouth. Again, I'm kicking the comforter off and swinging my legs out of bed, but instead of looking for more layers to keep warm with, I leave the bedroom I'm living in now and pad down the hallway to the other. I stand in the doorway.

CJ is lying on his side facing away from me. The moonlight is shining through the window. I can see him. He's shirtless and the sheet is gathered at his waist, and I don't make a sound but he hears me and turns his head, peering at me over his shoulder.

I don't know if I woke him or if he's having the same nightmares as me. I don't ask either.

He motions with his head for me to enter the room. I round the bed and crawl under the cool sheet, sliding closer until I can bury my face in his chest and get his arms around me.

"I'm so, so sorry," I cry, feeling my tears slide down my cheek and press into the skin above his heart.

CJ's arms tighten around me. He ducks his head close to mine and soothes me with his hand moving up and down my back. He doesn't say a word.

He holds me, and allows me to say mine.

And when I finally fall asleep a hundred apologies later, the nightmare doesn't follow.

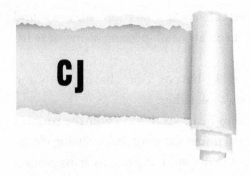

CJ

WAKE UP with Riley curled against my side, not wrapping herself around me like the last time we slept together but still pressing close.

Her head is on the pillow I gave her. Her hands are sleeve covered and shielding her mouth. She's breathing slowly and evenly. She looks peaceful.

Finally. Took hours of crying to get her here.

Riley came to my room needing to apologize. I got that. She was feeling that blame and had been feeling it. I saw it in her eyes at the hospital. Saw it again standing in my living room with her, and if she didn't give me her sorry and get that shit off her chest, it would eat away at her. She'd let that guilt tear her down. She'd keep it between us.

Fuck that. I didn't want that. I don't want anything between us.

That's the only reason I keep my mouth shut and let Riley do what she needed to do.

I sure as fuck don't want any apology from her. I don't blame her for what happened that night. Not for any part of it. And I don't want to see her crying—makes me want to go pay that cocksucker ex of hers a visit and pull his limbs off—but if it gets Riley past her guilt and allows us to move forward, fuck it. I'll lay here, hold her, and take it.

And that's exactly what I do.

Slept for shit 'cause I kept waking up needing to make sure she wasn't shedding tears again. My leg was killing me too. I could've used more of my pain meds, but I didn't want to move and risk waking Riley.

She didn't pass out until late. I have no idea what time, but she probably would've kept going if her body hadn't exhausted on her.

Thank fuck it did.

Riley needs sleep. I know she has a test in class today. She shared that with me last night when I asked why she was flipping through flashcards while we were eating dinner.

She looked nervous about it and said it was worth a huge chunk of her grade so yeah, she needs sleep.

And I need to quit looking at her and go get some fucking coffee.

After scrubbing at my face with both hands, I roll to my side and push up, swinging my legs over and sitting on the edge of the bed. I glance down at my wrapped ankle.

My left leg feels heavier than my right. It feels that way all the time. Not just when I move it. There's a constant dull ache running up my calf, worse now since I've gone all night without any pain meds. It hurts, but I can tolerate it. The Percocet they prescribed does its job, numbs it out for a while, but it also gives me that fucked up, foggy-head feeling. I don't like taking it during the day. I don't like feeling out of it. Maybe I'll save them up for when I start PT in a couple of weeks. I know that's going to suck. Not just 'cause I'll be working my injury for the first time, but also 'cause I know I'm going to be pushing myself.

No way am I staying laid up for five months.

I've always recovered quickly from injuries before. I broke my shoulder, ribs, and clavicle playing football growing up.

Healed up faster than the doctors were expecting with those. And I know this won't be any different.

I'm motivated. I can't stand this laying around shit. I need to get back to work.

After pulling on the white t-shirt I discarded at the foot of the bed last night, I reach for my crutches propped against the wall and use them to help me stand. Then keeping my foot up, I maneuver out of the bedroom and head down the hallway.

I can't put any weight on my left foot yet. Hurts like a motherfucker if I do—I found that out yesterday. But the second I'm able to, I'm ditching these crutches. They're a pain in the ass to use and I don't like needing something to help me get around.

I already got plans for them too. I figure they'll make good burning wood once I take off the rubber stoppers at the bottom and the padding around the handles.

I power on the Keurig and get my coffee made once I make it to the kitchen, then bracing against the counter for balance, I grab the box of Raisin Bran from on top of the fridge and go about pouring myself a bowl.

Back pressing to the hard edge of the granite, I stand in the kitchen and eat my breakfast, doing this while looking out into the living room.

My eyes cut to the notebooks Riley left out last night. They're sitting on the lip of the counter where the bar stools are pulled up. A few papers are scattered there too.

Ditching a crutch and keeping hold of my bowl, I hobble over to the sink and lean over it to look at the papers. One in particular grabs my attention: Riley's schedule. I glance it over while I shovel cereal into my mouth.

She has class on Tuesdays and Thursdays. Mostly in the morning and ending just after one, unless she has labs. Clinical eats up her time the rest of the week.

Good to know.

I'm scraping cereal off the bottom of my bowl when quiet footsteps cause me to turn my head.

Riley steps into the room and stops a few feet away, hood still up and one eye peering at me. She digs a sleeve covered knuckle into the other and offers me a sleepy, "Hey".

I lower my bowl and look at her, at the hoodie of mine she's swimming in and her black painted toes peeking out from underneath her pajamas. *Goddamn.* She looks good waking up in my house.

Really fucking good.

"Mornin'," I greet her, straightening up. I watch her brow pull tight after she lowers her hand. "What?"

"Why are you up? You should be off your feet," she says, raising a hand to point at my leg.

"Man's gotta eat, babe. I was hungry," I tell her. I lift my bowl to show her my evidence. "Besides, I'm pretty sure I'm allowed to stand around a little. Why the fuck else would they give me crutches?"

"I could've made you breakfast," she informs me. "You should've gotten me up."

"Make me breakfast now."

Riley looks from the bowl in my hand to my face again. She tilts her head. "But, you ate, didn't you?" she questions. "Isn't that bowl empty?"

I flash her a smile. "Yeah, it's empty. But I typically polish off half a box before I get going every morning. This was just my first bowl."

Her eyes go round. "You eat a half a box of cereal every morning? Really?" she asks, sounding and looking shocked.

"You see how big I am? Fuck yeah, I eat half a box of

cereal every morning. Sometimes more." I go to set my bowl in the sink, but hesitate, looking back to her and asking, "Are you going to make me something or should I pour myself another?"

Riley blinks, lets her eyes fall to my bicep and hold there for a breath, then looks back into my face. Reaching up, she pushes her hood back and starts walking toward me.

"Eggs okay?" she asks.

Hell yeah. She's making me something.

"Fuckin' A," I answer, freeing my hands up and then moving out of the kitchen to give her some space. I get around the counter and claim a stool, leaning my crutch against the seat beside me. Riley carries over the other I had propped against the stove and my coffee after she spots it. She hands them over. "Appreciate it, darlin'," I say before taking a sip.

Her cheeks pink up. She pulls in a breath through her nose and tucks her hair behind her ears. "Right. Eggs," she says, clapping her hands together. "You want sunny-side up or over easy?"

"Scrambled off the table?"

Her lips press together. "Mm, I've been told my scrambled needs work," she informs me, lifting her shoulder. "I always overcook them."

She looks a little uneasy sharing that, and I have a feeling it's not because of what she's sharing but rather who had that opinion and gave it to her.

I set my cup down and keep my hands around it, watching her gaze fall.

"Look at me," I tell her.

She lifts her eyes.

"Anything you feel like making me, I'm going to eat," I begin to share, keeping hold of her gaze. "I'm going to appreciate you for making it, no matter what it is, and I sure as fuck am not going to tell you *it needs work*. The fact that you're making it means I don't have to. That's not lost on me. So if you're feeling scrambled right now 'cause that's what you prefer making and fuck anyone who says you can't do it right, have at it, babe. If you set it in front of me, I'll eat it. I'll enjoy every fucking bite too."

Half of Riley's mouth is lifting by the time I finish speaking. She blinks at me, then drags her teeth across her bottom lip and nods her head, declaring, "I want to make scrambled. They're my favorite."

"Hell yeah. Do your thing, girl," I encourage, making her giggle. I smile at her, giving her that before she spins around to get started.

Riley Tennyson, smiling and laughing in my kitchen.

Fuck yeah. I like this.

I sip my coffee as she moves to the fridge and takes out the eggs. "I cooked them wrong for years until someone told me you gotta take them off the heat when they still look wet. I had no clue," I tell the back of her, wanting to offer up some advice without Riley knowing that's what I'm doing.

That dumbass she was with should've helped her out if he was bitching about what she was giving him. If you've got the balls to critique someone, you need to show them what they're doing wrong so they can learn. Otherwise, keep your fucking mouth shut.

I'm going to assume, since he is a dumbass, that Richard bitched and didn't offer up any advice.

Riley straightens up and looks at me over her shoulder after digging through a bottom cabinet and pulling out a pan. "Yeah. That's a . . . pretty important step. Otherwise you'll totally overcook them," she says, sounding sure of herself.

I smirk behind my coffee cup.

She starts getting everything ready—cracking eggs into a bowl and whisking them together with some milk while her pan is heating up.

I stare at the back of her, at my name written in white. The block lettering peeking out from underneath the hood.

"I'm going to go grocery shopping today, so let me know if you want anything specific," she says, lifting my gaze to her messy, bedhead blonde. I hear the sizzling of the pan as she pours in the egg mixture.

"Can't think of anything," I tell her. "Except maybe some more Raisin Bran. I'm running low."

"What?" she chuckles. "You have like, five boxes in your pantry. I saw them last night when I was getting out the bread."

"That's a two-day supply for me. We covered this."

Riley continues laughing quietly as she stirs. "Okay. I'll pick up some more while I'm out," she says through a smile I can't see. "I was thinking about making chili for dinner. Do you like chili?"

"I fucking love chili, but I wasn't lying. If you put it in front of me, I'll eat it. So if it's something you feel like making, make it, babe. Don't worry about what I like."

"But what if I make something, like chili, and you don't eat meat?" she asks, turning her head to peer back at me. "I need to know if you have any dietary restrictions. I can make it meatless."

I cock my head. "Aside from the fact that I got dead animals mounted on my wall, do I look like I don't eat meat to you?" I ask her.

Riley's eyes lower to my chest, hold there for a beat then quickly dart back up to my face. "No. You look like you eat meat," she says before turning back around. "A lot of it," she adds on a mumble.

I smirk as she continues stirring up the eggs.

"So, how are you getting to your appointment today? You can't drive, can you?"

"Nope. Truck's a stick," I answer, setting my cup down. "I'll probably just call a cab since I can't bum a ride. It's not a big deal."

"I'm sorry I can't take you," she says, turning sideways to look at me while keeping hold of the spatula. Her eyes are heavy with sadness. "I'd skip class if it wasn't for my test today, but they don't let us make those up. I really can't miss it. I'm sorry."

"I said it's not a big deal. Don't worry about it."

She presses her lips together, looking like she is worrying about it.

Fuck.

I don't want her worrying. And I don't want Riley thinking she needs to be apologizing either—I got enough of that shit last night.

"Riley, babe, I know you want to help me out as much as you can, I get that, I appreciate it too, but you gotta life and shit that's important. More important than giving me a ride," I tell her, needing this information to stick so we don't have this conversation again. "I got you here making me breakfast, darlin', and you're talking about making me dinner too. Honest, as much as I enjoy eating, I care about that more than you taking me to a doctor's appointment. So when I say don't worry about it, don't worry about it. Don't tell me you're sorry either. You don't need to be. Okay?"

She pulls in a breath through her nose, then nods her head. "Okay," she says quietly.

"Good. Shit's settled. No more apologizing."

Her mouth tips up in the corner.

I jerk my chin at the stove. "Now turn around so I can go back to watching your cute little ass making me eggs," I order.

Riley narrows her eyes while fighting an even bigger smile.

I don't fight shit. I give her my grin because I want her seeing it.

"Friends don't do that," she informs me with some sass before spinning back around.

"Friends don't do *what*?"

"Look at each other's asses. That's not a friendly thing to do."

"Fuck that," I grumble. "What'd I say about adding rules to this shit?" I watch Riley shake her head as she takes the eggs off the heat and separates them onto two plates. "Babe, don't even. The only way I'm not looking at your ass is if you quit having one. And I know you look at Beth's so don't play with me. Checking out asses *is* friendly."

"Oh, my God," Riley chuckles. She turns off the burner and carries over our plates, setting mine down in front of me. Our eyes lock over the top of the sink. "You probably think we make out all the time, don't you? Like at sleepovers? French kissing is friendly too, right? Is that what you're going to tell me next?"

I stare at her with a straight face as she takes a bite of her eggs.

"What?" she asks around her mouthful, shielding her lips with the back of her hand.

I smile.

Her hand lowers and her mouth grows tight. "Really?" she grumbles, rolling her eyes. "You're picturing that, aren't you? Me and her making out. You're totally thinking about that."

I take a bite of my eggs and give her a wink.

Yes, I am totally thinking about that.

Riley shakes her head and lowers her gaze to her plate. She takes another bite.

I do the same, chewing and swallowing before forking some more.

"These eggs are great. Cooked perfect," I tell her, wanting her to know she fucking nailed breakfast, because she did.

Riley blinks up at me, stops chewing, and smiles. And I can see in her shining eyes and the way her back goes straight and her chest heaves with a relieved breath how much hearing that means to her. And it makes me wonder something.

Aside from all the bitching about shit he didn't like, did that asshole ever compliment her when he *did* like something? Did he ever let her know she was appreciated?

My jaw clenches as I stare back, coming to my own conclusion.

He didn't.

Fuck. Jesus Christ, that pisses me off. And that's just shit I don't get. Who the fuck wouldn't want to see their woman looking like this? Smiling. Looking proud of herself. Who wouldn't want to see *her* looking like this?

"What?" Riley asks, jarring my focus.

I blink, relax my jaw, and give her a weak grin. "Nothing," I say, and Riley accepts that and grins back. I watch her go back to eating.

I do the same, and I do this thinking about all the ways I'm going to give her what she deserves.

I GET BACK home later that night, pay the cab driver and send him on his way, then I make it up the driveway, going between my truck and Riley's white Chevy Cruze. With the folded piece of paper held between my teeth, I hop up onto the porch, take the two steps to the front door, turn the knob and nudge it open using the foot of my crutch.

Riley turns at the sound of my entrance from where she's standing at the stove. She flashes me a smile, then immediately rounds the counter and starts moving toward me.

My eyes fall to her tanned legs shifting under the hem of my hoodie she's still wearing. Looks like she's claimed that as hers.

I smirk around the paper in my mouth.

"Here. Let me take that," Riley says, reaching up and taking the paper. She leans around me to push the door shut. "Hey, you got a boot."

I hear her observation and watch her eyes fall to my foot when she straightens back up, but I got a question of my own that needs answering, and I don't waste any time asking it.

"How was your test?"

Riley lifts her eyes to my face. She blinks, looking like the fact that I'm asking this means something big to her, which has me wondering about that shithead again, then gives me a proud smile and lifts her chin, stating, "I think I nailed it."

"Babe." I steady my crutch, then hold my hand up for her to high five.

She does, giggling.

"When do you find out?" I ask her.

"Couple weeks probably," she answers, rolling her eyes and sighing heavily. "It takes my teacher forever to grade anything. She likes to torture us."

"Make sure you share with me when you get the word. We'll celebrate."

Riley smiles big, letting me know she likes that plan. Then lifts the paper in the air she took from me. "Where do you want this?" she asks.

I gesture at the kitchen with my head. "Tack it up on the fridge for me, will you? It's my schedule for PT."

"Oh," she says with interest, unfolding it to read as she turns around and heads where I direct her.

I follow behind but cut a right and make for the couch.

"Hey, I can take you to all of these," she comments. "I don't have class Tuesday and Thursday afternoons. This is great."

"Huh," I mumble, keeping a straight face when Riley peers back at me with suspicion in her eyes. "What? That's what they had open. I had to take what they gave me."

She squints, trying to see through my bullshit. Her cheeks lift before she turns back around. "Dinner's ready. And don't worry. I didn't skimp out on the meat," she informs me. "There's basically an entire cow in there."

I'm chuckling, halfway to sitting down, but hearing she has dinner ready, I stand tall again.

"No, sit," Riley orders from the kitchen. "Relax. I'll bring you a bowl."

I give her a smile. "Appreciate it, darlin'." Then I lay my crutches on the floor beside the couch and fall back onto a cushion, propping my foot up on the trunk to keep it elevated. I drop my head back and look up at the ceiling. "Can you grab me a beer too? I'm fucking beat."

I should sleep good tonight, as long as Riley doesn't come crying to me again. And she shouldn't. I think I cleared her conscience.

"Do you want your pain meds?"

"Nah. I'm going to hold off," I reply. I scrub my hands down my face, ignoring the pain in my calf and ankle and the urge to rip this fucking boot off, then hearing Riley approaching, I lower my hands and drop my head to look over at her.

"Here you go," she says sweetly, stepping between the trunk and the couch and passing me my bowl. "I'll get your beer."

"And a bowl for you. You're eating with me," I tell her.

"I already ate."

"Oh." I crane my neck to watch her walk back to the kitchen.

Damn. I was wanting her to enjoy this with me.

"Yeah, sorry. I kinda ate while it was simmering. I was starving," she explains. "The only thing I had for lunch was a soft pretzel at Costco."

"You get your shopping done?"

"Yep. Got ten boxes of Raisin Bran. I think you're set through the weekend," she jokes, rounding the couch again with a beer for me and a glass of something for her.

"Cute," I tell her, taking the bottle she holds out.

She laughs quietly and takes a seat on the far cushion, left leg bent up off the floor and body angled toward me. "Hey, who's that guy in that picture with you on the fridge? The one in the uniform."

"My brother, Jake."

"Is he in the Army?"

"Marines," I answer, taking a sip of my beer and then setting it beside the couch. I scoop a heaping bite of chili into my mouth and chew it up, adding, "He's stationed in South Carolina. You might meet him. He's coming up in a few weeks."

"You two look alike," she shares, gathering her hair over one shoulder and then dropping the side of her head on the cushion. "Except," she looks at my arm, my chest, then lifts her gaze to my face, shyly adding, "I think you might be a little bit bigger."

"Yeah?" I smile. "Make sure you tell him that. The little punk thinks he can beat me."

Riley laughs. "Are you close in age?"

"Four years. He's twenty-six. We've always been tight though." I point my spoon at the bowl after swallowing the last of my bite. "This is good fucking chili, babe," I tell her, meaning that. "I hope you made a big batch 'cause I'm going to tear this up and will absolutely be going back for seconds." I take another bite, watching Riley's pink lips curl up before she takes a sip of her drink. "Here." I say, scooping out more. I hold the spoon out in front of her face. "Come on. You know you want this."

She shakes her head, laughing softly as she lowers her glass. "I already ate."

"Humor a broken man, will you?" I inch the spoon closer. "I want you enjoying this with me, Riley. This is probably the best damn chili I ever ate. Honest to God. Come on."

Riley looks from the spoon to my face, eyes big and bright and heat burning across her cheeks. And I know I've done it again—given her something she isn't used to getting.

I smile watching her. I hate that Riley hasn't had this before, but I can't deny it.

I like being the one giving her this.

Before I hit Riley with a more insistent request, she gives me a sweet look and leans forward, taking the bite I'm offering.

Two bowls (the second of which we end up sharing), two beers, and plenty of easy conversation later, I'm grabbing my crutches and standing from the couch as Riley cleans up dinner.

"I'm going to need your help with something when you get a minute," I call out, moving toward the hallway.

"Okay!" Riley shuts the fridge door and rushes out of the kitchen with a big grin on her face. She stops in front of me, rubbing her hands together. "That's why I'm here. What do you need?" she asks. Her voice jumps with excitement.

"I gotta take a bath."

Her grin fades, her mouth goes slack, and her hands slowly lower and separate, dropping to her sides. "Uh . . . you, gotta take a *what*?"

"A bath," I repeat, fighting a grin at her reaction. "It was hot as shit out today. I need a shower, but my doctor said I shouldn't be attempting that. I can't really get this wet yet." I look down at my foot, then back into her face. "I'm going to need you to help me out. They told me sponge baths are ideal."

Riley blinks. "They *did*?"

Now I'm fighting a grin hard, since I am completely lying here. Not about the showering thing—I was told that—but I'm sure I can manage washing up on my own.

"Oh yeah." I nod my head, face serious. "If my nurse was here, she'd be giving it, so . . ."

Another lie. Pretty sure that wouldn't be a requirement.

Riley straightens up and stands taller after hearing me. "Right. And that's me. I'm your nurse," she declares, owning that responsibility and looking prepared for the task. "Okay. Yeah. Let's get you a bath then. Are you ready? I'm ready." Her voice is quick. Anxious.

Fuck yeah. I'm ready.

riley

A SPONGE BATH.

I'm supposed to give CJ Tully, gorgeous police officer with a body like Thor, a sponge bath.

Sweet Jesus.

Okayokayokayokay. Don't panic, Riley. You can do this. Seeing penises is going to be part of your job after you graduate. Plenty of men come into the hospital, and those men might need to disrobe. You'll see penises. Tons of them. All of the dicks. It's bound to happen.

Of course, I doubt these will be penises I've had hours of fun with. But still. This is part of the job. CJ needs me. He needs *my* help. He wouldn't need *any* help if it wasn't for me, so, yeah, I can do this.

I can totally do this.

Be professional. And try not to stare.

Exhaling a deep breath, I walk past the hallway bathroom, knowing that one doesn't have a tub, and head for the master bath instead.

It's an impressive bathroom, with a large glass door shower that has one of those built in seats for . . . resting, I guess. A double vanity sink with all chrome fixtures, and a private room for the toilet.

And then there's the tub.

Tiled and big enough for two people, maybe more, unless one of those people is CJ.

He doesn't seem like the type of guy to takes baths though. He's big muscles and rough touches and doesn't shave for days. He's a shower after a hard day's work kind of guy. I bet this will be his first time using it.

"Do you take a lot of baths?" I ask when curiosity gets to me, turning to look back at him.

He stops just inside the bathroom and gives me a lopsided smile. "Wouldn't say a lot," he answers. "I've used it before. Two, three times, maybe."

"Really?" I laugh a little. "Did you light candles and set the mood for your alone time?"

I picture that in my mind—CJ with the lights dimmed and Enya playing from a nearby speaker.

He has to be the biggest guy I know. Manly to the extreme. He takes baths?

"I didn't say I was alone," he shares, his smile fading out.

I blink. A strange tightening forms in my stomach. "Oh . . . right. Of course," I mutter, gripping the strings of his hoodie and tugging them as my eyes fall to the tile floor.

God. Why did I even ask that question? Now I'm picturing CJ having an orgy in his bathtub, with the lights dimmed and candles lit and Enya playing in the background.

I was better off not knowing.

"Um, let me just," I spin around and move to the tub, "Get everything ready. Give me a minute." I push my sleeves up, turn the water on and test the temperature. "Do you like it hot? Warm?"

"On the hot side."

I twist the knob, getting the temperature warmer, and pull up the stopper to plug the tub. Then, hearing a knocking sound, I stay leaning over with my one hand flat on the tiled edge and peer over my shoulder.

I watch CJ prop his second crutch against the wall, brace his back against the sink and tug his shirt over his head. The faded grey cotton falls to the floor. My gaze lifts to his bare chest and moves lower, over the outline of his abs and the sharp, slanted indent of muscle narrowing underneath his waistband.

I've had my hands there. My lips there—tongue and breath when I kissed down his body to pull him into my—

"Babe."

Sucking in air through my nose, I blink up at CJ.

You're staring, Riley. And he totally caught you.

"Bubbles," I mumble.

His brows raise. "Say what?"

"Bubbles. We need bubbles."

Bubbles camouflage things hiding under the water. They inhibit staring. We need *lots* of bubbles.

"We need bubbles," CJ repeats, brows still raised, sounding like he doesn't understand this necessity.

I straighten up and spin around, hands on my hips as I look at him. "They promote relaxation," I explain, keeping my real reasoning to myself. "It'll loosen you up, and help with the healing process. You'll get better faster. Trust me."

CJ's stares at me, mouth ticking in the corner.

Please buy what I'm saying and just go with this, I think. I can't imagine playing this out with clear, unobstructed viewing water. I need muscles and large organs concealed.

"Whatever you say, darlin'," he finally gives me, and I feel my shoulders dip with relief.

Thank you, Jesus.

I look around the bathroom for what I need. Turning my head, my eyes fall to the collection of body washes on the seat in the shower.

I brought plenty. I like having a variety.

"Shower gel. That'll work," I say, mostly to myself as I move quickly to the glass door. I tug it open, grab the bottle of Mango Mandarin and carry it over to the tub, then I squeeze a copious amount into the running bath water—about half of the bottle—watching as the bubbles foam and spread across the surface.

They provide excellent coverage. I'm feeling good about this.

Sponge bath? No problem.

The tapping sound of CJ's crutches alerts me of his nearing proximity. I feel the heat of him at my back.

"I'm going to need to sit down to get these shorts off and get them over my boot," he shares. "Do you mind?"

I feel my eyes take up the majority of my face. Warmth blooms across my cheeks.

Okay . . . right. *Right.* He needs my help. CJ needs my help taking off his shorts.

Not a problem.

Straightening up and spinning around all in the same hurrying motion, as if I can't *wait* to get to this task, I knock into CJ with my elbow and jar his balance. He stumbles back with a grunt and I reach out, gasping, gripping his slim hips with my hands as he hops on his good leg and plants his crutches again to regain his posture.

"Sorry!" I exclaim with panic in my voice. *Shit! I am such an idiot!* "Oh, my God. I am *so sorry.* Are you okay?" I look up into his face and watch the corner of his mouth twitch.

"Yeah," he says with low laughter, brows lifting when he asks, "You? You seem a little . . ."

Flustered.

Horny.

Eager to disrobe.

"I'm great," I rush out before he has the chance to throw out any of those suggestions. "Just, you know, ready to help any way I can." I slide my hands to his warm abs and press my fingertips there, pausing for a pounding beat of my heart before finding the tied string on the front of his waistband. I watch his brows stay lifted as I tug and loosen. "What?" I ask, voice shaking with nerves.

Why is he looking at me like this?

He's staring, his eyes softening and the amusement on his lips pulling away before he glances down at my hands. "I just needed you to slide over a bit so I can grab a seat," CJ states, meeting my gaze again and offering me a kind smile. "I can get my shorts off, darlin'."

My fingers tense around worn fibers. As if they're scalding my skin, I hastily release the strings, pull my hands against my stomach and step back. "Cool," I blurt out. "Yeah, okay. Good for you. You do that. I'll . . . get you some towels." Spinning around, I wince as I move quickly to the linen closet because *oh, my God, he didn't need any help taking off his shorts . . .*

Seriously?

Good job, Riley. Strip a man against his will. Real professional.

The water sloshes behind me as I grab two white fluffy towels off the shelf.

"Jesus. You got enough bubbles in here?" CJ asks with laughter in his voice. "I'm going to smell like a goddamn fruit salad for the rest of my life."

"Promotes healing, remember?" I remind him. "The more bubbles, the better."

At least for me, anyway.

As I carry the towels over, set them down on the bath mat and snatch my loofah from the shower, CJ relaxes in the tub.

His head back, arms out of the water, bent and draped over the curved lip, and his left foot propped up on the opposite end, keeping his boot dry. I laugh when the bubbles reach his chin and stick to the stubble dotting his jaw.

Maybe I went a little overboard with the shower gel.

"Here." Smiling, I claim a seat on the tiled edge, push my sleeve up to my elbow again and cut off the water. Then I swipe the bubbles away from CJ's neck. Our eyes lock—his so close to mine . . ."Um," I quickly lean away. "Do you want to sit up?" I ask. "I can start with your back."

CJ smiles slowly, keeping my gaze as he leans forward. He slides his grip along the edge of the tub and bends his left knee so his boot turns on its side.

I dip the loofah into the water beside his hip, then I squeeze more of the shower gel onto it and work it into a lather.

"I appreciate you helping me out," he says. His voice sounding deeper, fuller now that it's not competing with the noise from the running water.

"Of course. That's why I'm here." I give him a smile, our eyes holding onto each other's, and I think maybe CJ wants to say something in response to that—his jaw ticks and his mouth hardens. He looks conflicted all of a sudden and ready to argue, but then he closes his eyes and with a heavy exhale, drops his head forward.

I take that as my cue, place my hand on his shoulder for balance, and begin working the loofah in small circles across his broad, muscled back.

Minutes pass with neither of us saying a word as I wash from shoulder to shoulder and down his spine. I cover the wide planes with suds and the sides of his ribs, leaning over to reach, then I move back up, dragging the loofah down his thick arm. I look at his profile as my hand moves idly over his bicep.

Eyes closed and lips parted, CJ pulls in a deep, relaxing breath and exhales it slowly.

I stare at his high cheekbone and the cut in his jawline. At his lips as they press together, twitch and curl up a second before he's turning his head to peer at me.

"I think my elbow is clean, babe," he shares, mouth twisting into a full smile.

I blink, looking down at my hand that's moving in lazy circles over his elbow and the lather spilling onto the tiled edge.

Oh, crap.

"So, what does the CJ stand for anyway?" I ask, playing off my distraction as I scoop the bubbles into the tub. I quickly wash his wrist and drag the loofah underneath his arm to his pec where I lather there, meeting his eyes when he doesn't answer. "What? Is it *that* bad?" I wrinkle my nose. "Is it a girl's name? Were you named after an aunt or something, Charlotte Jean Tully?"

Hmm. That's actually a really cute name.

A laugh shakes his chest. "I might actually prefer that," he says before leaning back to rest against the tub, pulling me with him in the process.

My hand stills against his sternum. "Tell me," I request, looking into his eyes. "Is it a secret? I won't tell anyone. I promise."

The muscle in his jaw jumps. I watch his nostrils flare with the breath he inhales, and I wonder if the same words are whispering inside his head, the ones we both pleaded to each other and pressed against skin.

Tell me a secret.

"You first."

I lift my eyes after he speaks. My brow furrows. *Me first?*

"What do you mean?" I question.

"The only people who know the name I was born with are my family," he shares. "I never went by it in school and got it legally changed to CJ when I was sixteen. Nobody calls me anything else anymore, except my mom, and she's in Tennessee. Nobody here knows it. I wasn't planning on anyone finding out either. I like going by CJ. I don't want people calling me anything different. So if I'm going to share that with you, you gotta give me something."

"Like what?" I ask.

"Why were you with him?"

CJ doesn't miss a beat, throwing his question out as if he can't wait to get it off his tongue and hear my explanation and the reasoning I did with myself.

I sit up tall and drop my arm to my knee, letting the loofah hang over the edge of the tub. "Because I loved him," I reply, nothing but truth in my voice.

"Yeah, babe, I know, and I'm going to be straight with you. I don't get that," he says, and CJ either hears his own harsh honesty or finds the need to explain himself after watching my face tighten. "Look, Riley," he begins, voice softer now. "I know I didn't see you two together aside from that one time, but from what I've been picking up on, I'm thinking he wasn't all that good to you."

"He was good to me."

"Yeah? He tell you that you can kick some serious fucking ass in the kitchen or show any interest in what you're working towards for a career? 'Cause I did, and darlin', you lit up for me like you'd never heard those words before."

I feel my shoulders sag.

He has a point. And CJ's right too—Richard didn't show much interest in my schooling or throw out compliments over every meal I made him. Not because he didn't think those things, I don't believe, it just wasn't him.

"He bought me that laptop when I first got accepted into the nursing program," I defend, feeling myself grow taller and my muscles stiffen. "He didn't need to do that, but he did. He cared about me. And I cared about him. I was with Richard because I *wanted* to be with him. It wasn't like he was forcing me or anything."

"I didn't say that," CJ replies.

"Well, it kinda feels like that's what you're saying, and it's not true. I loved him."

"Riley—"

"I didn't know there was different, okay?"

CJ blinks. His eyes soften and his lips press together. He looks regretful.

I sigh and look down at the bend in my knee. "I loved what I had and what he gave me. But it was all I knew," I explain. "I didn't know there was different, and when you don't have different to compare to, you don't question what you have. You don't know better until you're *with* better."

My truth tastes bitter on my tongue, but it is the truth. I didn't know men like CJ. And then I did, and still, I chose to stay with Richard.

Because we had history. Because CJ was mistake. We were never meant to happen.

Right?

I pinch my lips together, because I don't know which word will come out of my mouth, yes or no, and I'm a little scared of both answers.

"Cannon."

CJ's voice lifts my head and our eyes meet.

"Huh?"

Cannon? What?

He clears his throat, then cocks his head with a surrendering smile. "Cannon Jake Tully. That's what the CJ stands for," he reveals. "And before you ask, *yes*, my mom gave my brother my middle name. She liked it too much to not use it as a first, so she says."

I feel myself leaning closer as excitement quickens my breath. "Cannon. Really? Like . . . *cannonball?*" I ask.

"Yep."

"Your birth name is *Cannon Tully?*"

"Now you see why I changed it."

"What?" I sputter. "No way. I love it. That might be the coolest name I've ever heard."

CJ lifts his brows and stares at me for a beat. "You love it," he echoes back, looking and sounding unconvinced.

He doesn't believe a word I'm saying.

I nod quickly, smiling at him. "It's different," I explain. "I don't know anyone else with that name. And cannonballs are so fun. Your mom did good." I hold up my free hand between us.

Cannon Jake Tully.

Seriously cool.

CJ's eyes jump from my palm to my face. "You want to high five this?" he asks.

I shrug. "Why wouldn't I?"

"We high five things that are awesome, babe. Things worth celebrating. Not my shitty name."

"It's not shitty. It's totally badass."

"*Badass?*" CJ breathes a laugh, shaking his head. "Right."

"It is, *Officer Cannon Tully.* Kicking ass and taking names, one small town at a time." I stick my tongue out at him when he makes a face like he can't decide whether to be disagreeable or amused with me. Then I tilt forward, getting closer and leaning around my hand.

We lock eyes. His narrow. My smile stretches wider.

I get my high five.

"Thank you for telling me," I say after letting my hand drop. "I feel special knowing something most people don't know about you."

CJ's eyes shine with meaning. He gives me a warm smile, replying, "Same, darlin'," in that smooth, charming voice, the kind of charm that's hard to unhear and even harder to wash off.

My cheeks grow hot. I clear my throat and get through the rest of the bath at lightning speed, forcing CJ to do some of the washing because . . . well, *penis*, and asking him to towel himself off. Then I retire to my room, declining his offers of open door policies and free morning cuddles.

I find myself smiling until I fall asleep.

"MR. TULLY, HI, I'm Andrea. I'm one of the therapists here who will be working with you."

CJ gives the woman a friendly smile, gets to his feet with help from his crutches, and takes the hand she's offering, shaking it. "Nice to meet you," he says. He releases her hand and tips his head to where I'm sitting. "I brought my lady with me. Do you mind if she comes back and sees what all I'll be doing? She'll be making sure I keep up with it at home."

My eyes go round. I press my lips together and trap a giggle inside my mouth.

His *lady*? He did not just say that.

CJ looks over at me, mischievous smirk in place.

He totally said that.

I scrunch my nose up and make a face at him.

It's been two weeks of sponge baths, sharing meals I've prepared, and late night conversations that leave me with sore sides and cheeks from laughing so much. I know CJ pretty well at this point. I know he likes to joke around, it's part of his charm, and calling me his lady is just another example of that.

I think . . .

"Sure. She can come back. We have chairs back there," the therapist says, offering me her smile.

I stand and gently nudge CJ's ribs after the woman turns away to lead us. He feigns injury and I laugh.

"Are you coming?" he asks me, gesturing with his head toward the therapy room.

I nod and slip out my phone. "Yeah. I just want to make a call first," I tell him. "You go ahead. I'll be there in a minute."

CJ lifts his chin at me, accepting that. Then he follows behind the therapist and leaves me in the waiting room.

I sit back down and scroll through my contacts until I land on Beth.

I haven't seen or spoken to her since I moved in with CJ. She was out of town for some wedding in Chicago the one weekend and sick this past one, keeping her from making it to Holy Cross—the soup kitchen we both volunteer at. And lately, I've been slammed with school and busy doing other things. I just haven't found the time to return any of her calls.

And I need to speak to her. I need to tell someone what I'm doing—just one person so I don't feel like I'm lying to everyone—and she's a good someone to tell. A great person.

She's my sister. She'll understand. She always does.

"Hey you," Beth answers with a smile in her voice. "I was beginning to worry. I told Reed we might have to hunt you down on campus if we didn't hear from you soon."

"I'm living with CJ," I blurt out, skipping pleasantries for hand-to-heart honesty, and when Beth doesn't say anything for what feels like a solid minute, I look down at the fraying on my shorts and twist pieces of string around my finger. "So, how are you feeling?" I softly add.

Maybe my confession is enough. Maybe we don't even need to talk about this . . .

"You're living with CJ?" Her voice is a whisper now.

I flinch, hearing footsteps, then the creak of a door. I picture Beth hiding behind it.

"Um, yep. Mmhmm," I reply.

"Why?" she asks, sounding stunned. "And *how?* How did this even happen?"

"He needed someone to help him around the house since he's laid up, and I needed a place to live," I explain. "I couldn't stay at Richard's anymore. I needed to move out, and I didn't want to cramp your newlywed style. CJ offered, so I took it. I'm helping him out."

And I'm having the best time doing it, I think.

"You wouldn't have cramped our style, Riley. You're always welcome here," Beth informs me.

My mouth twitches.

Seriously the best sister ever. Reed did so good.

"Thank you," I tell her. "But, you know, this is better. I'm able to give CJ a hand."

"Is that *all* you're doing?"

My brow furrows. "What do you mean?"

"Riley . . ." Her voice trails off.

"What?" I ask. "I'm helping him."

"Are you sure nothing else is going on? You're *just* helping him? That's it?"

He makes me laugh. We can talk for hours. I'm smiling constantly.

I close my eyes and take in a deep breath, then I resume looking down at my shorts. "That's it," I answer, because nothing else *is* going on. We're talking and laughing. That's not stuff going on. That's just talking and laughing. And besides, nothing else *should* be going on. I'm CJ's nurse. He needs me—that's why he offered me a place to stay. The entire reason for us living together, and I want to do this right. I want to help him heal.

Speaking of which, I need to get in there and see what all exercises they have him doing. It's my job to make sure he continues with his PT at home.

"Riley," Beth speaks soothingly as I stand and take hold of the sketchpad I brought along to take notes in.

"Seriously. Nothing else is going on. I promise," I assure her. "But, still, can you do me a favor and not say anything to Reed? I'll deal with him when I'm ready."

Which might be never.

Beth exhales tensely in my ear, but gives me a promising, "I won't say anything."

"Thank you," I reply, feeling relieved and breathe-easy-good about this phone call. "Oh, and you never answered me. How are you feeling? Better, I hope." I hold the notepad against my chest and start moving toward the therapy room.

"Thanks. I will in eight months or so."

"Eight months?" I make a face. "What? Why eight months?"

"I'm pregnant."

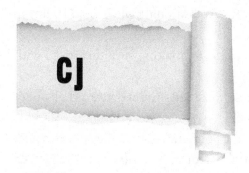

CJ

"**T**HIS IS AMAZING! I'm so excited for them. Oh, my God, I'm going to be an aunt!" Riley does a little dance in the driver's seat after starting up her car, wiggling her hips and smacking the steering wheel in celebration. Her tits bounce under the tight black sleeveless top she's wearing.

Jesus.

Never in my life have I hated an article of clothing as much as I do right fucking now. She couldn't have worn my hoodie today?

"Yeah, that's great," I mumble, wincing as I relax back against the seat. My ankle is throbbing from the PT. I'm regretting not taking any pain meds before we left the house. "I should give Reed a call and congratulate him."

"What? No, you can't!" Riley's head snaps in my direction and she looks at me with wide, panicked eyes. "You can't act like you know. Beth said she was only telling *me* right now. She's not telling anyone else until she gets a blood test done. You know, just to be sure." Riley frowns. Her brow furrows as her hands slide off the wheel. "I'm sorry," she adds, looking on the verge of giving me a couple hundred more apologies.

"It's cool. I hear you," I reply, understanding why Beth would feel that way. It would suck going back and telling everyone you weren't pregnant after sharing news like that.

"I just don't want Reed questioning why I would tell you, you know?" Riley adds.

"Babe." I give her a look, making sure this sticks with her. "I hear you," I repeat.

Her explanation isn't needed. And we sure as hell aren't doing any more sorrys.

Riley offers me a soft smile and drops her head with a nod, accepting this. "Are you in a lot of pain right now?" she asks.

"'Cause I can't call Reed? Crushed. But I think I'll get over it." I grin when she shoves at my arm. "Yeah, I'm a little sore. Those calf raises she had me doing sucked. I wasn't expecting to do all that on my first day. Figured I'd just get iced and rubbed down for an hour." I cock an eyebrow at her. "I'm still up for that, if you're offering."

Riley rolls her eyes but her smile grows. She likes when I joke with her.

Although, if I'm being honest, I'm not sure I'm ever really joking when it comes to Riley.

I want her. God . . . *fuck*, I want her. All the time. That hasn't changed.

"How about a special treat instead? You up for it?" She puts the car into reverse and backs us out of the space.

I watch her profile as we clear the lot and get out onto the main road. I stare at the curve in her mouth and the freckles dotting her lifted cheek. I want to tuck her hair behind her ear so I can see the delicate, tanned line of her neck, but I don't.

"My lady has prepared a special treat for me?" I tease, smiling with intrigue heavy on my tongue. "Fuck yeah, I'm up for it."

All kidding aside though, what the fuck could she have planned?

Riley doesn't react to the *lady* this time. Not with her

round eyes or her sweet restrained giggle. She just rolls with it, concentrating on the road ahead and only giving me a slight jerk of her shoulder in response.

"I just know you've been going a little crazy being stuck at home," she says, most likely referring to the fort I made yesterday on the couch using a blanket and my crutches. "You've only been out for doctor appointments and now this. And I knew today was going to be tough. So I thought maybe we could go do something fun. Maybe." Her profile tightens. "I don't know. I'm not one hundred percent sure if this *is* fun or not. I've never done it before, but I thought you might like it. I hope you like it." She clears her throat and slides her hands around the wheel. I watch her fingers tap restlessly against the leather. She's fidgeting.

"Relax, darlin'," I say, wanting to ease her nerves a little. "You took the time to plan this out. Put some thought into it. Rest assured, whatever it is, I'm going to like it. Trust me." She turns her head and gives me an easy smile. Getting that, I inquire further. "Seriously, what it is? What'd you plan?"

Riley shakes her head, then puts her eyes back on the road. "It's a surprise."

I rub at my mouth and jaw, a smile forming behind my hand. I turn to look out the windshield.

A surprise from Riley Tennyson. Well, fuck me.

This should be good.

"DUMB?" RILEY ASKS after shifting into park and looking over at me, wincing as though she knows I'm going to fucking hate this.

What is she, crazy?

"*Dumb?*" I echo. My eyes jump between her face and the

windshield where I look at the building we're parked in front of. "Your special treat is taking me to a pistol range?"

She winces. "Yes?"

"Are you for real?" I ask her, pointing at my chest. "Me, a guy who wanted to be a cop his entire fucking life, made guns out of everything laying around my house growing up and couldn't fucking *wait* 'til I was old enough to hold a real one. You're asking if bringing me here is *dumb*? Babe," I give her a look, "honest, if I wasn't worried I'd completely fuck up my leg permanently, I'd be running inside that building right now, carrying your sweet ass and hollering about how you're the shit for bringing me here. Straight up, this is awesome."

A smile starts in one corner of Riley's mouth and twists across to the other, stretching wide. "Well, I guess that means we won't be needing my back-up plan then," she says, cutting the engine and then leaning back in her seat. She lifts her hips to tuck her keys into her front shorts pocket.

"Which was . . ."

"A rubdown."

My brows raise. Riley starts giggling, pressing her fingertips to her mouth.

I bite back a grin, which is really fucking hard considering how sweet she looks right now teasing me, and feign disinterest. "Nah, this is better. I'm sure I'd hate every second of that. I can barely tolerate a sponge bath from you."

She lowers her hand and narrows her eyes.

Riley isn't buying the shit I'm saying, and she shouldn't. I'm lying out of my ass right now.

"Oh, really? You hate those?" she questions, disbelief in her voice.

"Twenty minutes of absolute torture," I reply, keeping up the charade. "You're so rough about it, and I'm a delicate man. Light, soothing touches only." I flatten my hand to my chest. "My heart isn't the only fragile thing about me, Riley. All of me needs to be nurtured."

"Oh, my God." She shakes her head through a laugh before turning away to open her door.

"I know you see all these muscles and think, *my, God, he can handle anything*, but really, babe, I'm sensitive. Don't let all this bulk fool you," I add as she climbs out of the car.

"Then maybe we need to quit with the sponge baths since I'm not doing it right," she suggests.

I lean over the console so she can see my face from where she's standing. "Hey, I didn't say that. Quitters never learn, babe. And I'm patient man. I'm willing to teach you how I like to be touched." I smirk, adding, "It'll probably take hours of instruction. And I'll, of course, need to touch you. This will be a hands-on process. *Very* hands on."

Riley's cheeks burn hot.

And really, I can't help myself at this point.

"We won't stop until we're both satisfied," I promise.

Her eyes flicker wider. Then she slams the car door, turns on her heel, and moves hastily toward the front of the building, leaving me laughing in the car.

"WELL SHIT, LOOK who it is."

I shake the hand Zeke is holding out for me, greeting him. "How's it going, man? How you been?"

Zeke is the owner of Heep Pistol Range. He's a retired Army Sergeant who is always doing stuff for the community and finding ways to support the local police and fire departments. He's a standup guy. I've known him for years.

"Good. Can't complain," he replies, running a hand over

his short gray hair before grabbing his hips. He lifts his chin at me. "How are you feeling? I heard about what happened. How long are you gonna be laid up for?"

"They're saying probably close to five months but I'm not hearing that, you know? I told my therapist today she has three months to fix me up. I can't stand lying around and not working."

Zeke nods, understanding me, then looks to Riley, who's standing at my left and keeping quiet. "You the little lady that called yesterday?"

I watch Riley smile. "That was me," she says, standing taller.

Zeke gives her a grin, then looks back to me. "I didn't know she was talking about bringing *you* in here," he tells me. "I would've told Leon you were coming in. He would've liked to see you."

Leon is Zeke's grandson. He runs the shop with Zeke and talks about becoming a cop someday. He's a good kid.

"Next time," I tell Zeke before turning to look at Riley. "You called here?"

She nods, explaining, "I wanted to make sure they'd let you sit while you did this. I figured you wouldn't want to stand."

I smile at her, liking how she prepared for this and thought of everything. Then, putting more weight on my crutches, I bend to get closer, staring into her eyes. "You're the shit. You know that, right?" I tell her, loud enough Zeke will hear me.

Riley blushes, lowering her gaze before shyness turns her head.

"Got you set up in lane one with a stool," Zeke offers. "If you don't like that, I got a chair I can bring back there."

"That should be fine," I tell him, meeting his eyes. "I

appreciate it, man."

"Anytime. You know that." Zeke spins around to grab some ear and eye protection for Riley and myself, setting the headphones and glasses on top of the display case between us. "Here you go," he says. "Let me grab you the paperwork to fill out."

"Oh, um . . . do I need these? I'm not shooting," Riley announces as she picks up the pink headphones and studies them.

"Doesn't matter. You need to wear those. It gets loud in there," I tell her. "Glasses too. Shells are going to be flying."

Riley slips the headphones over her ears and puts the glasses on. She pushes them up her nose, then adjusts the way the headphones are sitting before tilting her head up and smiling big at me. "How do I look?" she yells. "I feel like one of those air traffic controllers with the flashlights."

Laughter rumbles inside my chest as I lean on my crutches, steadying myself before reaching out to lift up one side of her headphones. "You look good," I say. "And I'm sure the people at the BP across the street share that same opinion. I think they heard you."

Riley's eyes widen as I set her headphone back on her ear. "Whoops," she giggles.

We share a laugh after she slips the headphones off.

Zeke returns with our paperwork, and I get Riley to fill out one too even though she says she isn't shooting—she could change her mind once we're in there. I'm hoping she does. I'd like her to try it out, but if she isn't comfortable, I won't push it. This needs to be something she *wants* to do. I tell her to go pick me out a target while I choose a firearm, sticking with a 9mm I've shot before when I've been here. It doesn't have a lot of kick-back and the handle is a little bigger and easier to grip. That'll help Riley if she wants to try it out. After getting a box of ammo from Zeke, I meet her at the door that leads to the range.

"So, you've always wanted to be a cop? Like forever?" Riley asks at my back as I spread everything out on the table in front of me and take a seat on the stool.

"Pretty much," I answer. "I think there was a week where I wanted to join the circus but other than that, yeah." I load the magazine, listening to Riley's muffled giggle through my headphones. "Don't laugh. I would've made a kickass lion tamer."

"Huh. I would've guessed clown."

"Funny." I hang up the target and move it out to the distance I want it at using the switch on the wall. Then I look back at Riley over my shoulder, watching as she drags her finger across her smiling bottom lip. "Ready?" I ask.

I want her comfortable with this, and I figure Riley hearing what this sounds like before I have her get any closer and possibly hold anything is the best way to do it. I know she's never shot a gun before and I'm going to assume she hasn't been around any either. She doesn't know what to expect.

Riley nods, wincing while reaching up to clamp her hands over her headphones.

I give her a smile before I turn around, staying angled on my stool with my left leg straight out in front of me and my right leg bent, foot bracing on the wood. I rack the gun, lift it to aim at the center of the target, and fire off ten rounds.

Adrenaline races through my blood.

"Wow!"

I set the gun down on the table and slide my headphones around my neck before turning my head to look back at her.

Eyes wide and blinking and lips parted, Riley smiles big

as she slowly lowers her hands and flattens one to her chest. "Holy crap, that scared me!" she says on a nervous sounding giggle. "It's still really loud, even with the headphones."

"You all right?"

She nods quickly. "Yeah. That was so cool." She looks past me briefly, then meets my eyes again. "Did you hit the target?"

I cock my head, face serious. Riley pulls her lips between her teeth and fights a grin.

"If I didn't, I'd have bigger problems than a bum leg. I'm going to need to choose a new career," I reply. She laughs, giving me her smile. As I'm bringing the target in to take a look at it, I gesture at her to move closer.

"Were you scared the first time you shot a gun?" she asks, reaching my side. Her headphones are around her neck now too.

"Nah. I've always been comfortable with it. But I started young. My dad taught me how to hunt when I was eight." I release the switch and grab onto the bottom of the target, pulling it over the table so it hangs without obstruction.

Riley steps closer, putting her one hand on my thigh. She reaches out with the other and traces her fingertip over the holes in the paper. "You hit the bullseye," she observes with wonder in her voice.

I look down at her hand on my leg. At her black painted nails and the way her fingers curl under and grip. "Good," I say. "I was aiming for it."

"Mm." She laughs a little. "Well, that settles that."

"*What* settles *what?*"

"I think you're the shit too, CJ Tully."

Her quiet confession lifts my head, and I briefly meet her eyes before she's looking down and away, hiding her blushing cheeks and pulling her hand from my leg.

Something swells inside my chest, pushing organs and bone out of the way. I want her eyes back on me and her touch and Jesus fucking Christ, I want her mouth.

"Riley . . ."

"It doesn't look real," she says, standing closer to the table now and pushing the target back to look down at the gun, hearing me but choosing to ignore because she knows what I'm about to say—*why the fuck are we just friends*—and she either doesn't want to have this talk with me or she's not ready to have it.

I've had moments with Riley like this since she moved in, where she gives me a look or her touch lingers, and the second I notice or open my mouth to question what the fuck we're doing, she does the same shit. She looks away or changes the subject. She acts unsure. And I don't want to rush her. I don't want Riley hesitating with me. I know what went down with her ex was a lot and she's still feeling that, but *fuck*, it kills me. All of this kills me. Her getting close and then pulling away. Knowing how she tastes and the way her body opens and moves, under and above me, her shaking limbs and quiet desires. I'm not forgetting shit.

I get off on the memory of Riley while she sleeps in the next room. I fantasize about touching her and fucking her.

I am the worst friend this girl could possibly have, because that's the last thing I want us to be.

"You know?"

Riley's question jars my focus and draws my attention to her face. She's looking at me over her shoulder. Her brows are lifted.

"I know *what*?" I ask, not following.

"The gun. It doesn't look real."

"Feels pretty damn real." I shift to the edge of the stool so

I can get closer to Riley and the table, then I pick up the gun and hold it out for her to see. "It's not loaded. Here. Look." I release the magazine, set that down, and rack the slide to show her the empty chamber. "You want to hold it?"

She reaches out. No hesitation. Not with this.

With me—when we get too close or look too long? Every damn time. But holding a firearm, Riley's all in.

Go fucking figure.

"Can I? Just for a second." She takes the gun from me and lets it rest in her hand, keeping her palm up. "Wow. It's heavy. I didn't think it would be this heavy," she comments, curling her fingers around it and flipping it over to study.

I could make a joke about that—something heavy in her hand—but I don't. Instead I slide my hand along the back of hers and move her grip. "Keep your finger off the trigger," I instruct. "Only time your finger should be there is if you're ready to shoot. Even if it's not loaded, it's a good habit to hold it like this. Okay?"

She nods, then lifts her arms and extends them out in front of her. "Like this? Am I doing it right?"

I grab her waist and twist her body so she's standing at an angle. "Right foot back, like you're ready to throw a punch. Don't lock your arms."

Riley follows instruction. She stands like a natural, and there's no need for me to be keeping hold of her right now, but I do it anyway. My knees on either side of her, my hands on her hips and my chest pressing up against her back.

I inhale her shampoo and the soft floral perfume she uses and *fuck me*, no woman has ever smelled this good.

"Look at you," I murmur beside her ear, watching the corner of her mouth twitch.

"Do I look good?"

"Dumb question, darlin'."

Riley smiles. She lowers her arms. "Can I," she looks back at me, teeth sawing across her bottom lip, "try and shoot it? Just once."

"You can shoot it as much as you like."

I load the gun with one round and run through how it fires and how she can aim for something, making sure she's comfortable with everything before handing it over. After sending the target back out and getting our headphones on, I resume how I was holding onto Riley before, keeping steady at her back so she feels me with her.

If she's nervous, I want her knowing I'm right here. That I've got her.

"Ready?" I ask.

"I think so."

"Don't worry about aiming. I just want you to shoot, okay? You do this and like it, we'll load it again."

Riley nods. I feel her body get into position before she extends her arms out in front of her. She holds there, breathing in, then out. Again. And once more. She knows to fire on an exhale.

And she does.

The gun goes off. I feel Riley's body tense with a startle. I grip her tighter while my eyes focus in on the target she just put a hole through.

Dead fucking centered.

"Holy shit," I murmur.

"Oh, my God!" she shrieks. "I did it! CJ, I did it!" Riley sets the gun down and spins around to face me. Her eyes are shining with pride and I've never seen a bigger smile on her face. "Did you see? I hit the target! I actually *hit* that son of a bitch." She pulls her headphones down.

I do the same, laughing. "No shit. You're a good fucking shot," I tell her, smiling as she clutches at her heaving chest. "You all right?"

She nods quickly. "My heart is beating so fast," she rushes out. "It's pounding. Here. Feel." Riley grabs hold of my wrist and brings my hand up to take the place of hers, pressing my palm flat against the space between her cleavage and her collarbones.

I quit breathing as her life races beneath my hand. Her skin is so goddamned soft and I'm touching her.

Fuck. I'm touching her.

"Do you feel that?" she asks me.

My lips part. A memory plays like a reel inside my head— *Riley's wide, stormy eyes holding me over her shoulder as I move inside her slowly. "Do you feel that? How fucking hard I am for you?"*

I blink her back into focus. *Do I feel that?*

Fuck.

Blood runs warmer in my veins and I'm hard beneath my shorts and I'm so close to losing my fucking mind on this girl. To pulling her into my arms and touching her more and kissing her kissing her kissing her and fuck being friends. It sucks.

Why would anyone want this when you can have everything else?

"CJ?" she presses when I don't answer her or the urges that itch beneath my skin. I can't.

This is what she wants. Friendship. Touches that don't mean more. And until Riley is showing me different, I won't take it further.

I can't. I care too much about her to fuck this up. Christ. I care so fucking much about her already. More than she knows.

Riley Tennyson got under my skin at that wedding and fucking stayed there.

So I pull my hand away instead of moving higher or lower or touching longer, bringing both to my face where I scrub up and then down. I grit my teeth. My groin throbs.

Fuck you. You should be used to this torture.

"Are you okay?" Riley's sweet voice fills my ears before she's getting handsy again with my thigh, and right now, with my dick threatening to punch through my zipper, I do not need her touching me.

"Fine," I grate out, letting my hands fall away. "I just want to shoot. Do you mind?" I don't mean to sound pissed off or angry with her, but I'm pretty sure that's how it comes out.

Because for the first time she since I met Riley Tennyson, I need her to back the fuck away from me.

She blinks before yanking her hand off my leg. "Sure. No problem," she rushes out, then Riley's moving out of my way and getting behind me again.

I pull in a deep breath and release it slowly, searching for calm, then I pick up the gun.

My next eighty-nine shots are aimed a little higher on the target, right where that motherfucker's heart would be.

I never miss.

I never touch Riley again either, not for the rest of the afternoon at the range or during the drive home. And she never reaches out for me. We're both stiff and quiet and this isn't how it ever is with her. Awkward glances and uncomfortable silence. It sucks. And it continues after we get back to the house.

Dinner is eaten with my eyes on the TV and Riley's attention on the textbook in her lap. When she stands, having finished with her meal, she picks up my empty plate off the trunk and then asks if it's okay for her to do that, to fucking *clean up* after me.

That's when I realize how much of an asshole I'm being.

I'm getting shitty with her when *I'm* the one getting fucking sponge baths every night. I send her texts about the cold side of my bed. I play with her and tease her and insinuate with Riley every chance I get. What the fuck right do I have getting on her case because I can't handle her dishing it back, if that's even what she's doing, and I'm honestly not sure if it is. This could just be Riley being comfortable with me. Friendly. Playful, the way I always am with her. She wants us to be friends. Feeling her heartbeat . . . sure. What the fuck? Friends do that.

Yeah . . .

Asshole. World's biggest, right here.

Huffing out a breath, I get to my feet and leave my crutches on the floor, choosing to walk on my boot instead since the therapist said I can start doing that now. My leg hurts a little but nothing compared to earlier, so I keep going. I round the couch, hobbling down the hallway in the direction Riley went after she cleaned up dinner.

The dinner she made, that I ate, enjoyed, and didn't say shit to her about.

Dick.

"Darlin', where you at?" I call out, reaching the bathroom and peering inside it. The light is still on and one of the cabinet doors is open. She was in here. But she's not anymore. I keep moving down the hallway, thumping my boot on the floor, and when I'm almost at the bedroom she's staying in, I hear Riley's lowered voice and it stops me.

"I'm glad you're sorry. You *should* be sorry. But that doesn't change what you did, Richard, and it doesn't make me forgive you either. I can't. I just . . . I *can't* forgive you."

Richard. My teeth clench.

Motherfucker.

I lean my shoulder against the wall just outside her room, crossing my arms over my chest and continuing to listen. That son of a bitch must've called her from jail, and now he's getting Riley upset. I can hear it in her voice.

"You didn't tell me things were getting so bad you were turning to drugs. You did *cocaine.* You should've talked to me. God, I was practically *begging* you to talk to me . . . no. No! Are you serious? That's *no excuse!*"

When Riley's voice cracks with a sob, I move, filling the doorway just as she's standing from the bed. She keeps her back to me, and I stare at my name, half hidden by her hair.

Jesus. I'm an asshole to her and she still puts on that fucking hoodie.

It's hers now. She's claimed it. And seeing Riley in something that used to be mine does weird shit to me. Having my name on her . . . I like it.

I like it way too fucking much.

"Don't call me again," she hisses into the phone. "If you do, I won't accept it. I promise you, I won't." Riley ends the call, lowers her hands to her sides and drops her head. Her breathing is loud and labored.

I want to break every bone in that motherfucker's body.

"Riley." I take a step into the room but halt when she turns around.

She looks surprised that I'm in here and that I'm speaking to her after the bullshit I put her through today, but she covers it quickly, closing her eyes and then wiping the tears from her face with her sleeve. When she looks at me again, there's nothing there. No shock. No hurt. Nothing. And knowing she's hiding how she feels from me is worse than actually seeing it. It makes my fucking chest ache.

"Babe, look I'm—"

"I'm really tired. I'm going to go to bed now," Riley interrupts, tucking her phone into her front pocket, pushing her hair behind her ears and then nervously pulling the sleeves over her hands to hide them. She lets her eyes fall to a spot on the floor between us.

She's waiting for me to leave.

I grip the back of my neck, squeezing hard.

I don't buy Riley being tired. That prick upset her after I made shit uncomfortable, and now she's wanting space.

Space from *me*.

I'll leave. Fuck. I'll do whatever she wants, but I'm not going anywhere until I know Riley's not going to be in here crying alone.

"You all right?" I ask her, dropping my hand.

She lifts her eyes to me. "I'm just tired," she says again, shoulder jerking and mouth trying to smile.

I still don't believe her. And that smile isn't hers. I know Riley's smile.

I pull in a deep breath, looking at her, watching her eyes cut away again.

Yeah. She's definitely wanting space. And I'll give it to her, whatever she wants, but I'm getting this out first.

"If you need to talk or if you just want someone to listen, you know where I am," I say, gaining her eyes again and watching them widen the slightest bit. "If you feel like crying, I don't want you staying in here alone, darlin'. I want you with me. Either come to my room or I'll come to you. I don't care what time it is. Okay?"

This isn't negotiable, and I think she hears that in my voice.

Riley hesitates for a breath, staring at me while she tugs

on her sleeves. "Okay," she says, voice quiet.

"Good." I drop my head with a nod. "And, babe?"

"Yes?"

"I fucked up today. Tomorrow won't be like that."

I watch Riley stop fidgeting, blink, and part her lips before I'm turning away from her and heading out of the room.

My legs feel heavy. I don't want to leave her.

"CJ?"

I stop just outside my bedroom door and look back over my shoulder. Riley is standing out in the hallway now too.

"Yeah?" I ask.

She gives me a soft smile, and the sweetest fucking "Goodnight," she's ever given me.

My chest gets tight. I stand there, watching her. Wanting her. *Jesus,* I want her. *But she wants space. If she needs you, she'll say it,* I remind myself. And she doesn't. Riley doesn't ask me to stay with her. So I don't linger when I want to. I give her what she needs.

"Goodnight, darlin'."

Getting that from me, Riley keeps her smile, steps back into her bedroom, and closes the door.

riley

RUSH HOME after clinical and park in the spot I've claimed as my own, beside CJ's old, white pick-up truck in the driveway.

I'm meeting up with Mia, Tessa, and Beth tonight for girl's night. Beth invited me. And I really want to shower and change before I head over to McGill's. I smell like a combination of hospital antiseptic and latex.

Not a good smell on any night of the week, but especially not a good one on a girl's night. I'd prefer to smell nice for this. I'm sure the rest of them will.

My left leg bounces against the seat after I shift the car out of drive. I've never hung around the group of them together before. Not in a setting like this. And on top of being excited that I'm being included—getting that text from Beth this morning while I was on my way to the hospital—I'm also slightly nervous. I'm comfortable around Beth. And Mia is really sweet. But Tessa? If I'm being honest, she frightens me a little.

Yes, I've known her the longest. She used to hang around my house all the time when she and Reed were in high school together. I'd consider us friendly. But what if Tessa doesn't want her best friend's little sister horning in on her girl's night? What if she asks me to leave?

I press my hand to my thigh and force my leg to quit

bouncing. I can't think about this right now. I'm short on time as it is. I need to focus on getting ready. So I push those worrying thoughts aside and turn the car off, grab my book bag off the passenger seat, hustle out, and hurry up the driveway.

I can hear music playing when I step up onto the porch. A steady beat with a heavy bass. Twisting the doorknob, I push the door open and step inside the house.

The living room and kitchen are empty, but the TV is on. CJ is typically lounging on the couch when I get home, either watching something or getting creative in his boredom. Just the other day, he set up glasses all along the living room floor and flipped quarters into them. And I also caught him building a castle out of a deck of cards on the trunk he uses as a coffee table. It even had a drawbridge and a moat. I was impressed.

This is CJ's go-to spot. But he's not here.

What could he be doing?

I pad across the room and down the hallway, heading toward the music and the shower I need to be taking. CJ's bedroom door is open, and curiosity has me stopping at it to take a look inside.

Just a peek, I think. *I'll say hi, then I'll hurry up and hop in the shower. A peek and a hi. That's it.*

I stop at the doorway. My eyes widen as the hand around my book bag strap tightens into a fist.

Holy . . .

No way is this going to be a peek.

CJ is shirtless and facing the far wall, his sculpted back bulging as he hangs from a bar mounted to the ceiling. Knees bent. Arms extended. Body shiny with sweat. Jay Z raps through the speakers *come and get me*, and the man with more muscles than anyone else on the planet—I'm sure of it—proceeds to knock out a never ending round of pull ups as if they are *nothing*.

My mouth falls open. I feel my pulse spike as I stand there, staring in awe at his power.

CJ's arms and shoulders and back flex and ripple and swell with tension, but he never slows. Rep after rep. *Boom. Boom. Boom.* One after the other. This is easy to him. It's nothing. And it's *killing me*. My God.

I may actually drool a little as I stand here. I can't help it though. This is better than porn.

Come and get me.

The song keeps playing. Goosebumps break out all over my body. I listen to the lyrics and to CJ's skin tingling grunts, which reminds me of the sounds he makes when he's having sex. And those memories paired with the visual I'm getting, plus Jay Z's goading permission, are a little too much to take right now. I know if CJ sees me or hears me getting ready in the next room, I'll have to face him, and honestly, I don't think I can handle that.

What if I touch him? What if I can't resist anymore and run my hands over his shiny skin? I'll curl my fingers around his muscles. I know I will, and CJ doesn't want me to do that. He said he fucked up yesterday—after touching me more than he has since we agreed to be friends. I can still feel his hands on my hips and his strong pressure above my heartbeat. But he got weird and quiet on me afterward. He got different. He didn't like it. Why else would he have acted the way he did?

I don't want that to happen again. But I won't be able to *not* touch him. Not today. Not anymore.

Boom. Boom. Boom.

CJ keeps going, rep after rep, and I can feel myself breathing heavier. I've never seen a man workout like this before. Honestly, I'm not sure I've ever seen a man before *period*. CJ

Tully might be my first.

You won't be able to fight this, desire whispers in my ear. I bite my lip.

Decision made—I need to sacrifice my appearance tonight.

After getting one last lingering look, I step back and move swiftly down the hallway, leaving the house as quickly as I arrived.

MCGILL'S IS CROWDED when I get there, which isn't surprising. It's Friday night. And as I scan the room for the faces I'm expecting to see, a sharp, whistling sound draws my attention through the crowd.

I spot the girls at a table near the bar. Beth and Mia are waving and smiling at me, all warm and welcoming, while Tessa side-eyes some girl twerking close by. I want to laugh because that's Tessa for you. She's not a girl's girl *at all*, but I'm also mildly terrified she might side-eye me next.

Please don't ask me to leave. I really want to be here.

"Hey. Sorry I'm late," I say, stopping behind the vacant chair between Beth and Mia.

Both of them are dressed in cute summer dresses, have their hair pulled up in messy buns and are wearing light make-up—bronzer, lip gloss, maybe some highlighter. They look like they're glowing. Tessa is wearing a white tank top with the word *No* written in bold, black letters across her chest. Her red hair is down and straightened, and her eyes are lined heavy. All three of them look girl's-night ready.

I'm wearing mascara. That's it.

I really need to start carrying makeup in my book bag.

"You're not late. We all just got here," Beth informs me,

head tilting in curiosity when she looks at my top. "I thought you were going home to change after clinical?"

I was, but CJ was shirtless and making sex noises.

I clear my throat. "Um, yeah, I got held up at the hospital, so I figured I would just come straight here," I lie, shrugging. "Sorry."

"If I looked that cute in scrubs, I'd wear them all the time," Mia shares, smiling up at me.

I feel my cheeks warm. *Gosh, Mia really is the sweetest.* "Thank y—"

"Yo, Riley Girl."

My head lifts and my eyes connect with Tessa's across the table.

Oh, God. Here it comes.

I brace myself and prepare to back away.

Tessa smirks after getting my attention. She leans forward in her chair and picks a chip from the nacho plate in the center of the table, snapping into it. "Have a seat. We have *loads* to talk about." Her voice floats with meaning.

My brow furrows. *We do?* "Are you not going to ask me to leave?" I question.

She blinks, looking at me like I suddenly sprouted two additional heads. "What?"

"Nothing," I rush out. I quickly claim my seat at the table and pick up the glass of water that's in front me, taking two gulps before setting it down.

"Ignore her, Riley," Mia says. "She's just teasing you."

"Um, hello." Tessa points her chip at me, but keeps her focus on Mia. "Her boyfriend is in the slammer and according to Luke, he'll be in there for a while. And I'd like to know how she feels about that." She looks at me then, asking, "So, what gives? You trying to bust him out?"

"What?" My back goes straight. "No! No way. Richard can rot there. I don't want him getting out. He hurt CJ."

Tessa's brows lift in interest. Beth clears her throat. I think I hear Mia mention something about really loving the cheese that's on the nachos, but my attention remains on Tessa.

She leans back in her chair, the corner of her mouth teasing with a smile as she continues biting into her chip.

I relax into my seat, feeling my stomach clench. Crap. *Crap!* I sound *way* too invested in CJ's wellbeing. And I shouldn't. Not in front of Tessa, anyway. She doesn't know about our weekend of sex or the fact that CJ and I are roommates now. And she's friends with him. Not me. I'm not supposed to be *anything* with him.

What am I doing? Keep a lid on it, Riley!

"Um, I just hate that Richard hurt one of your friends. That's all," I quickly add, trying to cover my slip-up. "And I told you. He's not my boyfriend anymore. I broke up with him."

"Mm." Tessa cocks her head to the side after hearing me. She's finished with her chip and full-on smiling now, meaning she knows something is up. And this is Tessa. She'll want to discuss details and positions and size and circumference. I just know she will. No question is off limits to her.

My palms begin to sweat. I rub them on my scrub pants and contemplate making a mad dash for my car.

Screw girl's night. Who needs it?

"You okay?" Tessa asks, following my nervousness.

"Yeah, I just . . . I'm super hungry." I lurch forward and grab a chip loaded with ground beef, cheese, black beans, sour cream, and salsa, and shove the entire thing into my mouth.

Tessa's brows lift. "You look ready to vomit because you're *super hungry?*" she asks.

I shrug and let my eyes fall away as I struggle to chew. *Do*

I look ready to vomit? I mean, I don't *feel* sick, but okay, if Tessa asks me how CJ's dick rides, I just might throw up a little.

She's Reed's best friend. She'll definitely tell him what I did.

"Riley, Riley, Riley."

The sound of my name being taunted lifts my gaze. I look at Tessa, watching the shake of her head and that all-knowing smile twist into something that makes me want to squirm in my seat, but she cuts me a break and shifts her attention to Beth. "So, what's up with you?" she asks, leaning forward and dropping her elbows on the table. "Your text to all of us made it seem like you had big news to share. Spill it, Tennyson. We're all here now."

Beth smiles big at Tessa, and I know it's in reaction to hearing her new last name. She's so happy being Reed's wife. "It did?" she questions, head cocked and lips pressing together.

"You used shouty caps, Bethie. And like, four exclamation points," Tessa explains. "I know you have news."

"I was just really wanting us all to hang out, that's all."

Straight-faced, Tessa looks from Beth, to myself, to Mia, and then back to Beth. Her eyes narrow. "Everyone at this table is a liar," she mumbles before reaching for another chip.

"I sort of have news," Mia throws out, then waves off Tessa when she shows an interest. "You already know about it. Nolan and his girlfriend?"

Tessa rolls her eyes through a smile. "Six-years-old and already pussy-whipped."

"Stop it," Mia scolds, giggling. "It's really sweet." She gives me her eyes then. "Nolan met this little girl at that wedding we went to a couple of weeks ago. He followed her around the whole time, and now he's like, completely obsessed. He calls her his princess. Princess Ryan."

"Aw." I smile. "That's so cute."

"Is he still sending her pictures he draws?" Tessa asks.

"Yep." Mia nods. "Everyday. I told him to space them out a little, but he won't. He's using up all of my stamps."

"They were adorable together at the wedding," Beth throws out. "Do you remember her dad? I thought he was going to have a heart attack. He kept giving Nolan looks."

"Smart man," Tessa says, a wicked gleam in her eye. "Those Kelly boys are trouble."

Mia gives Tessa a playful shove, then she turns back to me, keeping her smile. "Did Reed tell you about the party we're having? We planned it that weekend. Have you spoken to him?"

I shake my head. "No. Not recently."

"It's the last Saturday of July at our house," Mia shares. "Just a little get-together. All of us and our boys. I'd love for you to come."

"Really?" I ask.

Mia laughs at my shock. "Of course." She squeezes my hand that's on the table and leans closer to me, holding all kinds of meaning in her eyes. "You're one of us now," she says.

I'm one of them. A fourth to their girl's night. Part of their tight group of friends.

Finally.

I smile at her, loving how that sounds. "Okay. I'll definitely be there."

"Great." She gives my hand one last squeeze before releasing it.

"McGill's can provide the food, if you want," Beth announces. "I know you're not having a huge party or anything, but still. I can talk to my uncle about it."

"Really? That would be great. We could do like, a bunch of sides with burgers," Mia suggests. "Thanks, Beth."

"No problem." Beth takes a sip of her water, sets it down, and looks around the table, keeping her hand wrapped around her glass. "So, I sort of have something to share."

"I knew it." Tessa rolls her eyes. "Let me guess. Reed is allowing you to tie *him* up now. His kink goes both ways, doesn't it?" She rests her chin on her hand and wiggles her brows.

"Gross," I mumble, scrunching up my face.

Maybe hanging out with this group wasn't the best idea. I don't want to hear about my brother like that. When *I* joke about it, it's one thing. I don't talk specifics. And I sure as hell don't want any.

"Pipe down, missy," Tessa directs at me. "We'll get back to you in a minute."

My eyes widen. Hers twinkle with the promise of dick discussions.

I reach for another chip and stuff my mouth full.

"No. That's not it. Well, he's not *not* allowing me to tie him up." Beth tilts her head, thinking hard. "We haven't really gone there. And, I don't know. Honesty? I'm not really sure I want to. I like the way things are."

"Don't knock it 'til you try it," Tessa utters.

"*Luke* lets you do that?" Mia questions. "I find that hard to believe."

"He doesn't really have a say when he wakes up hand-cuffed to something." Tessa's smile is full of mischief.

The girls all share a laugh, while I picture hard-edged Luke Evans waking up cuffed to the bed.

He always looks so angry. I can't imagine him letting Tessa get away with that.

"Well, anyway, Reed's kink is not my news," Beth continues.

I breathe a sigh of relief. "Thank God."

Mia laughs. Tessa shoots me a challenging look, then puts her attention back on Beth. "Well, if that does happen, *please*, ignore Riley and let that be news," she says.

Beth smiles. Her shoulders rise and fall with the breath she takes in. "I'm pregnant," she reveals.

My eyes widen.

"WHAT? Oh, my God! *Really?*" Mia asks, leaning over the table. "You're pregnant?"

Beth quickly nods her head.

Mia squeals, jumping out of her seat and rushing around me to deliver hugs. "That is the *best* news you could ever share, Beth! Congratulations!"

"Thanks. We're really excited," Beth says through a grin, staying in her seat and propping her chin on Mia's shoulder as she reciprocates the hug.

"You should be! *Daddy Reed.* Oh, my God, I am *so* happy for you guys."

I smile at Beth when Mia moves back around me to reclaim her seat. "I thought you were going to wait until you had a blood test done before you told anybody," I remind her, thinking it's odd she's sharing this right now. I just found out yesterday.

She shrugs. "That was the plan, but I can't get in to see my doctor for another two weeks. And I took like, nine tests so . . ."

I lean forward and pull her into a hug, both of us giggling and holding tight. "I am so excited and happy for you," I tell her. "You're going to be such an amazing mom."

She is. Beth is so nurturing and gentle and kind. I can totally see her rocking parenthood.

"Thank you," she speaks against my ear.

"And I'm going to spoil that kid rotten. I'm buying them

everything they ask for. I don't even care."

Beth laughs as we separate. She sighs, looking almost as happy as she did the day she got married, but her smile fades when she turns her head and looks to Tessa. "What's the matter?" she asks.

I look across the table then too, catching the last bit of Tessa's head shake.

"Nothing. That's great," she says, breaking a chip in half and then dropping it back onto the stack of nachos, sounding and looking like Beth's news is anything *but* great. "I'm really happy for you guys."

"What's wrong?" Beth asks her again.

"Nothing," Tessa repeats, her mouth pulling into a frown. "It's just, can we like, get some alcohol or something? It's Friday night. We should be drinking." She gestures at her glass and then slams back in her chair, drawing her arms across her chest. "Well, you can't, but I can," she mumbles through a pout.

"What's wrong with you?" Mia probes. "Why are you acting like that? This is exciting news. It's Beth and Reed."

Tessa's lips press together and her face falls after hearing that. She pinches her eyes shut, then cuts them to Beth. "Shit. I'm sorry. Just ignore me, Beth. I'm being an asshole." She leans forward, grabs Beth's hand that's on the table and squeezes it between her own. "I'm really happy for you guys. I am. I promise. It's just . . ." Tessa's eyes fall away. "We've been trying, and I just got my stupid period again yesterday."

"You and Luke are trying to get pregnant?" Beth asks. "I didn't know that."

Tessa nods. She releases Beth's hand and slumps back into her seat again.

"Sweetie," Mia soothes, reaching out and rubbing Tessa's arm.

"I don't get it," Tessa begins. Her voice is soft against the music playing overhead, and I have to sit forward to hear her. "When I didn't even know if Luke and I were serious or not, I thought I was pregnant. We weren't trying then. Now I'm off my birth control, we're having sex every five minutes, and I can't get knocked up. What the hell?"

"How long have you been trying?" I ask.

"Not long, but still." Tessa gestures with her hand, as if to say any explanation for this isn't good enough. "I'm young. I'm fertile. Luke has a sex drive like he's just gone through puberty. I should be able to get pregnant like that." She snaps her fingers. "No problem."

"I think you're stressing out too much," Mia offers. "That can mess with things. Make it take longer than it should. I've read about that."

"Yeah, I've heard that. I think I saw it on Grey's Anatomy too," I share, trying to recall that episode.

"See!" Mia smiles at me, then looks back to Tessa, saying, "Grey's Anatomy. You love that show."

My reference doesn't seem to ease Tessa's mind any. Still pouting, she looks down at a spot on the table. "I want a family with him *so bad*," she shares, voice heartbreaking. "What if I can't give him one?"

Her question lingers heavy in the air. I don't know what to say, and neither does Mia. She's beginning to look just as sad, as if she's now unsure herself and worrying the same thing. The only comfort she can provide is her touch on Tessa's arm. That's it.

Someone has to say something. I look to Beth, hoping she has some comforting words to offer up, but she's too busy chewing on her cuticle and looking on the verge of gnawing her entire thumb off.

Damn it. What episode was that? Was it Izzy? I feel like it was Izzy . . .

"Well, Riley is living with CJ," Beth throws out like a grenade she wants to blow me apart with.

WHAT?

I cut my eyes to her as Tessa and Mia gasp in shock. "What the hell, Beth?" I snap. I can't believe she just blurted that out! "I told you that in *confidence*."

She shrugs and continues chewing on her thumb, still looking as uneasy as she did a minute ago.

"Wow. I had no idea," Mia softly proclaims.

"Hold the fuck up," Tessa bites out, drawing my attention to her. She's sitting up now and on the edge of her seat. "We're over here talking about how I can't get knocked up, killing the mood and making each and every one of us depressed on girl's night—a night that is *always* about a good time—and you're sitting on a secret *that* juicy? What gives, Tennyson?"

I open my mouth to explain, I think—really, I have nothing planned—when my big blabber-mouthed sister in law cuts me off.

"She slept with him at the wedding too."

"Beth!" I slap the table and glare at her. *What in the world?* "What is wrong with you? Do you need to go sit at another table?"

"Oh, yeah, I knew about that," Mia throws out, sounding confident.

"*What?*" Tessa's voice cuts through the air, demanding attention, but I keep my focus on Beth.

Eyes on me, soft and pleading for understanding, she mouths *"sorry"*, and I get it then. Her uneasiness. The harm to her poor thumbnail. She was wanting to get Tessa's mind off all the pregnancy talk. Beth felt bad about her announcement and the pain it was causing her friend. That's why she gave up my secret.

I sigh, shoulders sagging as I shake my head at her, but I lose my anger. This is Beth. She didn't do it to be mean.

But God . . . *damn it*. Now everyone knows.

"Um, *hello?*" Tessa's pressing voice turns my head, grabbing Mia and Beth's attention as well. "Why am I the only person at this table who didn't know you were riding the Tully train?" she asks me.

I frown.

The Tully train?

"Well, to be fair, I only had an idea that the two of them slept together," Mia reveals. "I didn't have confirmation on that."

"Yeah, and I'm the only person who knew they were roommates now," Beth adds. "I knew for sure they slept together though. Riley told me."

"How many times have I said there are no secrets within the squad? We share *everything*," Tessa proclaims, looking between Beth and Mia, then settling her disappointed gaze on me. "And how long have we known each other, Riley? My God. You couldn't tell me?"

"Sorry." I shrug. "I just . . . I didn't know I was even *in* the squad."

Really. I had no idea. This isn't just me making up excuses.

Tessa laughs a little, while Mia whispers, "I just love her," and Beth squeezes my wrist.

"Well, you are now," Tessa states, keeping her smile. "So, spill it. How's the big bull ride, anyway?"

I hesitate answering, looking from Mia to Beth—both of whom appear to be just as interested in what I have to say as Tessa. *Great.* Then I place my hands flat on the table, meet Tessa's eyes, and lean closer to ask, "You aren't going to mention this to Reed, are you?"

I need to make sure whatever I say stays here, at this table.

"*What?*" Tessa laughs, looking almost offended at the question. "Are you crazy? No, I'm not going to tell Reed. None of us are. What is said amongst the squad, stays within the squad. This is like Fight Club. You don't talk about it."

"She's right," Mia adds, looking at me with trust in her eyes. "Whatever you tell us, Riley, stays between us. Unless you say different."

I believe Mia, and I know the girls won't say anything now. I feel good about this.

"Okay." I nod before leaning back and settling in my seat. "Um, well, I'm not sleeping with him anymore," I announce, looking back to Tessa. "I'm just living with him. But I don't want Reed to know that either. Not yet."

Tessa shrugs. "Hey, to each their own. But you *were* sleeping with him." She gives me a knowing look.

"Just the weekend of the wedding," I clarify. *And I wish we were still doing it*, I don't share. "I, uh, thought I was single. And CJ and I hit it off at the bar and just, kept hitting it off. Then I got home and found out I was still with Richard, so, I asked CJ if we could be friends. We're just friends now."

"But you like him, right?" Mia asks.

I nod, looking between the three sets of gossip-absorbing eyes. "Yes. I do. I like him. I've always liked him, but . . ."

"But?"

I swear, they all say that in unison.

"But now I'm just helping him heal. That's it."

A strange tightness forms in my chest. I just told them the truth—I am only helping CJ heal. That's why he asked me to move in. That was all he wanted.

It's just not all I want. Not anymore.

"Oh, I bet you're healing him, all right," Tessa teases.

"Tessa," Mia scolds, mouth tight. She shakes her head.

"What?" Tessa gives her a look. "We are all curious here, Mia. Not just me. CJ is as big as Ben, and I'm wondering how well his stamina holds up." She drops her chin on her fist and looks at me expectantly. "So, spill it. What's it like?"

"*Nobody* is as big as Ben," Mia claims, saving me from having to give an answer. She makes a face at Tessa, and I get the feeling there is a hidden meaning behind her statement, one I'm not privy to.

"That is yet to be determined," Tessa argues, looking to me then. "Riley," she prompts.

"Yes?"

"Care to share? Is CJ bigger than nine?"

"Nine *what*?"

"Inches."

My eyes widen. I nearly swallow my tongue. "Ben is *nine inches*?" I ask, mouth agape at Mia. "Wow. That's . . . good for you. Congratulations."

She giggles, hand to her mouth and cheeks blushing pink. Beth joins in on the laughter as well, back to her happy, blissfully married self and no longer stressing about her big reveal. And seeing that, I smile.

Tessa looks across the table at me, and when she has my attention, holds her arms out in a welcoming gestures and grins.

"Welcome to the squad, Riley Girl."

HOURS OF CONVERSATION later, where I reveal little information about CJ's bedroom habits and instead share how well he's doing in his recovery, information Tessa pretends to care nothing about—but I know better—I arrive home, eyes sleep heavy and yawns on repeat. I'm desperate for a shower, my bed, and my new favorite hoodie.

I'm also anxious to see CJ. And to talk to him. And to just . . . be around him. Laugh and play the way we do. I feel like we haven't really spoken to each other since yesterday at the range. Hopefully he's done working out and fully clothed now. I don't hear any music when I reach the porch so I should be in the clear, but if not, I'll just sprint past his doorway with my eyes closed.

Using my house key, I unlock the front door and push it open. When I step inside the house and lift my head, turning it toward the living room, I smile.

CJ is asleep in his go-to spot, head at one end of the couch and feet at the other, wearing a shirt now—thank God—with one hand curling around the X-Box remote he has resting on his chest and the other tucked behind him. The football game he was playing is paused.

I drop my book bag onto a stool and empty out my pockets at the island, then I walk around the back of the couch and place my hand on top of his.

"CJ," I whisper.

He doesn't move. Doesn't pause in his breathing. His chest rises and falls slowly, evenly. I look at his messy auburn hair and his dark jaw. He skipped shaving today. But even with the rugged stubble and giant body, CJ still looks gentle when he sleeps. He always does. He's like a big, sexy, muscular teddy bear.

This isn't my first time catching him on the couch.

I decide to leave him there while I hop in the shower and wash off my day. Then after combing out my hair, brushing my teeth, and getting comfy in my rolled Victoria's Secret sweats and Tully hoodie, I walk back out into the living room.

I grab one of the pillows and slide it under CJ's injured ankle, boosting it up, then I take his remote, sit in front of the couch on the floor, bend my knees, and dig my toes into the side of the trunk.

It's late, and I *was* tired, but my shower woke me up. I want to play a little.

"Let's go boys," I say to the TV, keeping my voice quiet as I unpause the game.

My man, number twelve, runs around the field in circles while I get used to the controls. As the team huddles together, fingers move through my hair at the base of my neck, and I peer over my shoulder, meeting sleepy blue eyes.

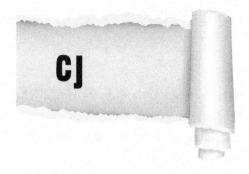

CJ

RILEY BLINKS AT me as my fingers weave through her damp hair and find the soft skin underneath.

"Hey," she says, voice quiet and mouth curving up.

"Darlin'."

Her smile grows. A flush burns across her cheek.

"You got in late. Did you have to stay at the hospital for something?" I ask, dropping my hand back on my chest.

Riley's mouth pulls down. She turns sideways to see me better. "No. I met up with Mia, Tessa, and Beth for girl's night," she answers. "I guess I should've called so you knew not to expect me for dinner. I'm sorry."

"You don't need to check in with me, babe. I was just asking." I give her a smile, easing her worry a little. "And I can handle my own meals occasionally. I am a man."

Her eyes widen with interest. "Oh yeah? What did you eat? A bear? A lion?"

"Half a box of Raisin Bran." My brow furrows. "Wait, did you say a *lion*?"

Riley pulls her lips between her teeth, fighting a grin, and shrugs.

I smile at her. *Fuck, she's so damn cute.* I missed this; playful Riley. The girl who's comfortable with me. Who's *herself* with me. "Did you have fun tonight?" I ask.

She nods quickly. "Yep. I'm part of their squad now. They

let me in," she states, sounding and looking really fucking happy about that development.

"Seems like a good squad to be a part of," I reply.

"It is. It's the *best*."

"I don't know." I drop my head to the side, wincing. "The one we got seems pretty fucking good too."

Riley sits up taller, smiling with pride and looking even happier about me calling this thing we got a squad. "You're right. Ours is better," she states. "Everyone else can suck it."

Laughing, I push up and slide back on the couch. "Do you want to watch something? You can turn that off," I tell her, tipping my chin at the TV.

"Nope. I want to play you."

My brows raise. I look from the paused game to her face. "Oh yeah?" I ask. "You sure about that, little girl? I'm pretty fucking good."

Riley rolls her eyes, hands over the remote and gets to her feet. "I'm a fast learner, *big boy*. Don't you remember how well I shot yesterday?"

"How could I forget?" I answer, swinging my legs off the couch to sit up as she grabs the other remote from the console. I roll my ankle to stretch it out.

It feels good. Even after all the exercising and walking on it I did today.

"You didn't even aim for the target and you hit it," I remind her.

"I aimed."

My face tightens. "Say what?" Riley giggles as she sits down beside me. "That's even more impressive," I tell her. "I thought you hitting it was just beginner's luck."

She aimed for bullseye and actually hit it? *Fuck.* She's not just a good shot. She's a *damn* good shot.

Riley shrugs, brushing her shoulder against mine as she smiles big at me. "Told you. Fast learner," she explains.

"Yeah, well this is Madden, baby. You need to play to get good at this," I say, holding up my remote. "Want me to run through the controls? Give you a few pointers?"

"I got it."

"You sure?"

Her eyes narrow. "Stalling? Afraid you're about to get your ass kicked, Tully?"

"*My* ass kicked? Do you have any idea how many years I've been playing video games? I'm about to school you."

Riley giggles and leans into me. "We'll see about that," she teases, turning toward the TV. She bends her knees and rests her feet on the trunk, curling her black painted toes over the edge.

I look away too and stretch my own legs out, propping my feet up and crossing them at the ankles so my injured one is being supported by the other. As I'm bringing up the menu to restart the game, Riley nudges her knee against my leg.

I smile and nudge her back. "Ready?"

"To win? Yep."

I slowly turn my head.

Riley's body is shaking with laughter as she giggles through pinched closed lips, eyes focused on the screen. She's really enjoying herself. Goofing off with me. Doing what we always do. Nothing is weird or uncomfortable like it was last night. We're back to this—us.

This is us.

"You know, for someone so fucking pretty, you sure talk a lot of smack," I share.

Her laughter stops and her mouth relaxes. Riley turns her head to look at me, blinks, and wets her lips. "Are you saying that because you mean it, or is this just part of your strategy?" she questions.

I stare at her, waiting for her to smile or to tell me she's joking by asking this. She doesn't do either.

"My *strategy*?"

"You want me off my game, so you're going to flirt with me. It's all just for show."

"I think I recall saying you were pretty before. Do you remember?"

Riley takes a second, one I'm not sure she really needs, then nods. "I remember."

"Have I ever said anything to you I didn't mean?"

"I don't think so."

"I haven't," I verify, needing her to know this as a fact. "Even if I needed a strategy, which I don't, I wouldn't be telling you something like that and having you feel it if it wasn't true. Everything I've ever said to you, I've meant, darlin'. The same goes for anything I'm ever going to say. You hear me?"

Riley pulls in a deep breath through her nose after I'm finished speaking, then looks away, exhaling forcefully. "I hear you," she says, voice rough and profile no longer relaxed. "Come on. Let's do this."

I watch her sit up and scoot to the edge of the couch so we're no longer touching. She looks ready to kick my ass. I figure Riley's just wanting to stay focused so she actually has a shot at beating me, and thinking about everything I've ever said to her is bound to jar that focus, same as us touching, so I don't question her sudden change in demeanor.

Smiling, I sit forward, drop my feet onto the floor and my elbows onto my knees. I choose *two player* and start the game.

"You're going down," I taunt under my breath.

"Don't think so," she says with some sass on her tongue.

"AW COME ON, defense! Wake up!" I slam back against the couch cushion and gesture at the TV as Riley springs to her feet. "Oh, that's nice. Taunting? Where's the flag?"

Riley giggles as her guy holds the ball out behind him, teasing my players with it, and then takes it into the end zone. "Booyah!" she cries, throwing her arms into air. "Oh yeah. Oh yeah oh yeah oh yeahhhh." She wiggles her hips, doing her celebratory dance next to the trunk.

I drop my head back and watch her, laughing when she breaks into the running man. "This is fucked up. You're like some secret gamer, aren't you?"

Seriously. She's kicking my ass.

"Nope! I'm just awesome at everything," she replies, smiling big as she turns to face me. Her cheeks are flushed and her eyes are shining bright. "Want to watch the replay again?" she asks, wiggling her brows and tucking her hair behind her ear.

"No thanks. I'm not sure my delicate man pride can handle it. I'm already depressed as fuck."

Riley presses her hand to her stomach, throws her head back, and laughs.

A sound comes from the kitchen, like an alert on a phone. Riley tosses her remote onto the couch and walks around it as I stretch out my legs. I check the time on the DVR. It's after midnight. We'll probably turn in soon.

I toss my remote beside hers and rub at my face, yawning. A quiet gasp turns my head.

"What's up?" I ask, watching Riley put her phone on the counter and start going through her book bag.

"Grades are posted," she says, voice anxious. "I can finally see what I got on that test." She grabs something out of the front zipper pouch, then pulls out her laptop and rushes over with it, sitting down beside me. She slips on a pair of glasses I've never seen her in.

"You wear glasses?" I ask.

Riley looks over at me after opening up her laptop. The glasses are black-rimmed and rectangular, and *fuck*, they make those big, blue eyes of hers pop even more. "I need them to read if I don't have my contacts in," she explains, sounding like she's apologizing for it, which tells me Riley isn't a fan of wearing them.

Or, that maybe some piece of shit never told her how pretty she looks wearing them.

I watch her long lashes blink behind the lenses. "You should skip the contacts more often," I suggest. "Trust me. They look really good on you."

Riley stares at my mouth as if she can't believe the words I just spoke, then lifts her gaze to my eyes again. She smiles, quick and shy, and ducks her chin to hide her blush, putting her attention back on the screen.

I figure even if I do point out that I saw what my compliment just did to her, she'll deny it. And right now, I know she's more concerned about finding out her grade. I am too. I'm curious.

"You thought you did good, right?" I ask.

Riley keeps her focus on the screen as she chews on the side of her thumb, pressing keys with her other hand and swirling her finger over the trackpad. She doesn't answer me. She's nervous.

"Hey." I place my hand on the small of her back and rub my thumb there. I get her eyes. "Remember how sure you were after you took it? You said you nailed it, babe. You wouldn't have felt that way if you didn't have this."

Riley stares at me, thinking back to the words she spoke,

then remembering them, she nods, but keeps chewing on her nail and holding onto that worry. She looks back to the screen, and I feel her body draw away from my hand as she pulls in a deep breath and clicks on the trackpad.

"Oh . . . my God," she whispers.

I drop my feet and sit forward, sliding my hand around to her side as I prepare to comfort her. "Hey . . ."

"Ninety-seven." Riley's head whips around. She beams at me. "I got a *ninety-seven*. A fucking *ninety-seven*! Holy crap! *CJ!*" She shifts her laptop to the couch, twists her body and throws her arms around my neck, pulling me into a crushing hug. "This was a unit test! It's worth so much of my grade. This is *awesome!*" Her excited breaths are sharp against my ear, and the quick pounding of her heart thumps beneath her hoodie.

"See? What'd I tell you?" I give her a squeeze, my other arm around her now too. "My girl's a fucking genius."

Riley giggles quietly, and for seconds we're just holding each other, neither one of us easing away or even relaxing the slightest bit. Her arms keep their pressure and mine hold her captive, circling her tiny waist. My face is half buried in her hair. I can smell her shampoo and the soap she uses on her skin. I can feel the blunt curve of her knee against my thigh, and I know if I were to lean back I'd pull her with me, forcing her to straddle my lap.

"You said we would celebrate when I got my grade," Riley reminds me.

"I did." I smile when she leans back enough to look at me. My grip slides to her hips. "Anything you want, darlin'. Name it."

She keeps one hand on my shoulder and brings her other up to stroke her chin. "Mm. Anything I want, huh?"

I chuckle.

She giggles at herself, then grips onto me again, sliding her fingers to the back of my neck and holding there. "You seem sure of yourself. I should say something you have no chance of following through with."

"Like?"

"Like," she looks over at the TV, then turns back to me, stating, "Fireworks."

"Fireworks?"

"Over a football field."

"Oh, you're getting specific . . ."

She drops her head into a firm nod. "I want to lay in the middle of the field on a pile of blankets and watch them together while we eat coconut inspired food and listen to music."

My chest rumbles with laughter.

Jesus. Riley was getting *very* specific. It's cute. I want her honest desires. All of them.

"Give me a week. I'll make it happen," I promise her, knowing this won't be a problem and feeling confident about it.

Riley tilts her head and stares into my eyes as if she's reading something hidden behind my irises. Her gaze narrows. Her mouth twitches. "And I want it to happen on July *fifth*," she states, voice victorious.

"Damn," I mumble through a grin, watching her smile stretch wider. "For a second, I thought you were going to make this easy on me."

"Not a chance," she chuckles. "And don't think you're getting off easy tonight either. *We* are still celebrating." Riley pulls back and leaps from the couch, hurrying into the kitchen. She heads straight for the refrigerator, yanks open the freezer door and takes out the bottle of tequila she bought and stuck in there, holding it above her head.

I groan and drop my head back against the cushion,

causing Riley to giggle before she starts hunting for glasses.

"You know what they say about that stuff—it makes you pretty. And I'm not sure you can handle me getting any more attractive, darlin'. Why don't we celebrate with you kicking my ass in Madden some more?"

I throw out this other suggestion hoping she'll take it, not because I hate tequila. Typically, I don't mind drinking it. I just don't think getting shit-faced off it right now is a good idea. Riley and I are touching again. We're both flirting. Me more than her, but she's giving it back. All in all though, we're keeping things friendly.

And there's nothing friendly about tequila.

"It only makes *girls* pretty. I doubt it said that in the men's bathroom," Riley argues. She rounds the couch and sets the bottle and shot glasses on the trunk, then she crouches behind it and pushes it closer to my knees. "There. And we don't have any limes, so we're drinking it straight."

"Awesome," I say, voice heavy with sarcasm as I sit forward more. I look at her with wide eyes as she claims the spot next to me.

Riley knocks against my shoulder. "It'll be fun," she says before pouring us both a shot.

"Famous last words," I mumble.

"A NINETY-SEVEN. THAT'S like, *so close* to a perfect score, CJ. They should really just give it to me, you know? I always have gum for everybody." Riley tosses a grape into the air, aiming to catch it in her mouth, but it hits her chin and bounces to the floor. "Ugh. I'm never going to get this."

"Hit me."

She smirks, leans forward, grabs another grape out of the bowl on the trunk, and tosses it at me. I bite into it.

"Show off," she mumbles before shooting back another shot.

Her sixth.

"I agree with you. Supplying gum to the class is worth three points, at least." I chew up my grape, laughing at Riley when she misses with another one. "Hey, you're a perfect score in my book, darlin'. Just remember that."

Cheesy? Yeah. But I'm one shot ahead of her so I can't be responsible for any of the shit I'm saying right now.

And I'm saying a lot. I just told her five minutes ago I thought she was my ideal woman.

Thanks to the tequila, Riley found that to be hilarious.

She slaps her hand over her mouth and giggles until her eyes water. "Oh, my God. I got a good one. Wait." She sets her shot glass down on the trunk, swaying a little as she rights herself, then once she's straight, she tucks her legs underneath her and gets up on her knees so she's hovering in front of me on the couch. One hand on the back cushion, she leans closer and points her finger at me, opens her mouth to speak, and then hesitates, closing it again. "Oh, wait. You need to sneeze first," she prompts.

I breathe a laugh. "What?"

"You do!" She shoves at my chest, laughing. "It won't work unless you sneeze. Come on."

"I can't sneeze on command."

"Just . . . pretend sneeze."

I stare at her, straight faced. "Ahchoo."

Her eyes widen and her cheeks lift. "I'd say God bless you, but it looks like he already did," she says, voice breaking with another giggle.

"Smooth." I hold my hand up, getting a high five from her. "I can top it though."

"Yeah? Try me."

I shoot back my seventh shot, wince as it goes down, and point at her with the hand holding the glass. "Did you sit in sugar? 'Cause you got a sweet ass, baby."

"Yes!" She pumps her fist into the air. "Oo! How about, are you a parking ticket? 'Cause you got *fine* written all over you."

"Do you have a name? Or can I call you mine?"

"You put the *stud* in bible study . . ."

I lean forward, set my glass on the trunk and slowly turn my head to look at her. "Christian pickup lines? Really?"

"What?" She shrugs, still laughing as she brushes hair out of her face using her sleeve covered hand. "I think it's a good one. Reed fell for it. Oo! Speaking of Reed . . ."

I lean back as Riley climbs off the couch, doing it like an animal would and planting her hands on the ground first, then pulling her feet down and crawling away.

"Goof," I chuckle. "What are you doing?"

She stands then, rushing into the kitchen, I think—I rub at my face instead of watching her. My head feels foggy. *Fucking tequila. I need to stop drinking.* When I lower my hands again, Riley is standing in the living room with her phone pressing to her ear.

I look at the time. It's after one.

"Who are you calling?" I ask.

Riley holds up her finger, listening to someone on the other end of the line as she looks at the floor. Then she smiles and meets my gaze. "Reed! My brotha from the same motha! I just wanted to let you know I'm living with CJ."

My eyes widen. *What the fuck? She's telling him?*

Riley waves at me, smiling even bigger now. "It's a business deal," she continues into the phone, twisting her body at the waist like she's excited about something and can't stand still. "So, yeah, we're roommates now . . . me and him. It's a squad thing. You wouldn't get it. But, anyway, I just wanted you to know that. Okay, so . . . have a good night. No! A good *morning!*" She giggles in delight as she lowers the phone and ends the call.

"Riley Tennyson, what the fuck has gotten into you?" I ask as she covers her mouth with her sleeve. A laugh rumbles inside my chest. "Come here, crazy girl."

She takes the three steps toward me and drops her knee on the couch. "I told him. Now he knows," she says, words slow and slurring. "It's not a secret anymore. I don't want it to be one." Riley crawls closer, puts her hand on my knee and drops her other to the center of my chest. She laughs quietly, bend downs, and whispers, "CJ," like she needs me to do something.

Do what? And *fuck*, she's drunk. I'm damn near it. If I do anything—touch her a little or look at her longer than I should—I'm not going to be able to stop.

"Babe," I say in warning when her eyes lower to my mouth.

She wets her lips. She doesn't say anything. She doesn't stop. Closer and closer, she moves in, until I can taste the tequila on her breath and just the slightest tilt of my head or slant of hers would put our mouths together.

"Tell me a secret," she whispers.

I close my eyes.

I want this so fucking bad, I don't say.

"Darlin'." I fight every desire I have screaming at me to just kiss her—*do it. It's all you want*—and instead, put my hand on her hip and sit up, easing her away. "I think we need to get you to bed," I suggest. "It's late."

Riley chuckles as she rocks back onto her heels, pulling

my hand off her. Her head flops sideways onto the cushion and she tilts it down, peering at me from behind her lashes. "Do you want to take me to bed, CJ Tully?" she asks in this low, raspy, sex-soaked voice I feel straight in my dick.

I inhale sharply through my nose before looking away. My jaw ticks.

Motherfucker. Why did I agree to tequila? Devil's nectar is what it is. It's completely fucking me over right now. Riley's dangling a hot as fuck carrot in front of me, I'm a starving rabbit, and I can't eat it. I shouldn't even be looking at the damn thing.

I grab my boot I discarded beside the couch and step into it, fastening the Velcro. I could go without it like I've been doing lately, but I won't. Not now. Then I stand from the couch and offer Riley my hand. "Come on. Can you walk?"

She smiles up at me with heavy-lidded eyes, and nods her head. "Nope," she says, voice breaking on a giggle, and I think Riley is going to make me carry her, which on any other night, I'd welcome the chance, just not tonight. I won't take advantage. I won't pretend Riley is meaning everything she's saying to me right now and every look she's giving. But then she tips over, kicks her legs out and gets to her feet, saving me the torment.

Thank fuck.

She rounds the couch, spinning around and walking backward down the hallway as I follow. "Do you need a bath? I could join you?"

Heat rushes to my groin. I slowly shake my head, nostrils flaring as I bridge the gap between us.

Either I'm walking faster to get to her or she's slowing down. I don't know.

Riley braces her hand on the doorframe, turns and backs

herself into the bedroom. She bites at her bottom lip.

"Quit, baby," I order.

"Do you really want me to?"

"Fuck no."

Riley's mouth tips up. "Well, then, maybe I shouldn't quit," she says, stopping when the back of her legs hit the mattress.

I get in front of her, toe-to-toe, and Riley has to tip her chin up to continue looking me in the eye.

"I mean, if you don't really want me to quit, then I shouldn't, right?"

"What I want and what I need you to do right now are two totally different things," I clarify for her. "You're drunk, babe. I've been drinking . . ."

"I'm not *that* drunk," Riley argues. Her fingers find their way beneath my shirt, brush against my abs and threaten to slip lower, teasing the band of my shorts.

My stomach clenches. "Darlin' . . ."

"Take me to bed, CJ. I want you to." She presses closer, slides her hands to my hips and rolls up onto her toes. "Please," she whispers, blinking slow. "I want it so bad. This isn't the tequila talking. I swear."

Groaning, I grab onto her wrists and pull her arms down. "You're killing me, babe. I'm not playing."

Finding my torture amusing, Riley chuckles under her breath before finally, thank fuck, falling back and plopping her ass on the bed. Then immediately after sitting down, she yawns, her first one of the night, as if hitting that soft surface triggered the sleep her body has been fighting against.

I bend down and grab her legs, swinging them up and twisting her so when she lays down, her head hits the dark blue pillow. "You want covers?"

"I want *you*."

Fuck.

"Riley," I groan, fists to the mattress as I lean over the bed. Chest heaving. Jaw clenching. And yes, my cock is rock fucking hard.

I need to just leave her. Forget about tucking her in. I got Riley to bed. She'll pass out soon. Any minute. She's yawning now.

Just leave, Tully. Get the fuck out of here.

"Cannon," she whispers.

My head snaps left and I meet her eyes, those big, stormy blues as a pressure builds inside my chest, making it grow tighter and tighter and tighter. Never in my life have I liked the sound of my name. Not once. Lived sixteen years with it before I got it changed and that day couldn't come fast enough for me. I couldn't wait to get rid of it.

Then Riley Tennyson says my name one time, one fucking time, and I don't just like it.

I fucking love it.

"Right. I'm going to say this, and then I'm leaving you to get some sleep," I begin, holding her gaze. I watch her sweet tongue peek out and wet those juicy, plump lips. "Jesus," I mumble, eyes pinching shut for a beat. I straighten up and rake my hand down my face, then I continue on, looking down at her. "I'm predicting you're going to be hungover as fuck tomorrow and I'm not going to be much better off. But come Sunday, we're both sober, I'm still feeling everything I've *been* feeling for you and you're offering me this, honest to God wanting me to take it, darlin', I'm taking it. Every fucking way I *can* take it. And once that happens, babe, we're not going back to being just friends. If I have you again, Riley, you're mine. My girl. My lady. My fucking woman. Yeah, we'll still be us, joking around and doing all the fun shit we always do, but we're gonna be fucking too. On the regular. Now, you got until Sunday to decide if that's something you want, or if this really *is* the tequila talking. Don't decide tonight. Get some sleep, think about it, and let me know Sunday."

I turn around then and cross the room. When I get to the door, I reach around to the back where the knob is and click the lock into place.

"Why are you doing that?" Riley asks me.

I peer over my shoulder and hold her eyes.

"'Cause locking it is the only way you're keeping me out of this room."

riley

KNOCK TWO Advil out of the bottle and drop them into my hand, then I pop the tablets in my mouth, exchange the bottle of pills for the cold water sitting in my cup holder, twist off the cap to that bottle, and start guzzling.

I'm dehydrated. I know I am, on account of all the vomiting I did yesterday. And even though I'd rather be drinking something with taste right now, I know water is the best thing for me.

There's a chance I'm also still hungover. That I'm not positive on, but my thoughts definitely feel half drunk.

You know when you have a dream and you go to tell someone about it, and the second you open your mouth, the details seem to scatter out through your ears and you're left with one or two things to share that don't seem to make much sense?

That's me today. It was me yesterday too.

Grasping for details. Trying to piece bits of conversation together. Getting glimpses that are doing nothing but confusing me. And I'm not even wanting to tell anyone about my Friday night/super early Saturday morning with CJ. I'd just like to know what happened for myself. Specifics. All of them.

I remember tequila—there's no forgetting that. Finding out my grade and celebrating together. I remember his low, rumbly laugh in my ear and his hold around my waist. Were we hugging? Dancing? I think I remember dancing. I *definitely* remember CJ in my bedroom—I can still see him standing over me, face tense, looking angry about something. What, I have no idea. All's I know is he didn't stay in my room. I didn't wake up next to him. In fact, I didn't even see him yesterday at all. The two times I pulled my head out of the toilet and went to the kitchen to get something to drink, CJ's door was closed. He never came out.

Why? Is he avoiding me? Did I do something or say something wrong?

I drop the bottle back into the cup holder and pinch the top of my nose, thinking back. Trying to remember.

Tequila. Dancing. CJ in my bedroom, not looking too thrilled to be there . . .

A sick feeling twists in my stomach.

Ohhh, no. Nonononono . . .

What if I *begged him*? What if *that's* why he was in my room? I know I wanted him in my bed—that's all I seem to want lately. What if I shared those desires and pleaded with CJ to carry them out? And now he feels embarrassed for me, and being the decent guy that he is, he's giving me space because he thinks I'll feel weird being around him after the way I acted.

Sloppy. Sex-starved.

He's *huge*. I didn't drag him into my room against his will, did I? Am I even capable of doing that?

Groaning, I drop my head forward until it hits the steering wheel. I squeeze my eyes shut.

Never again, tequila. Never. Again. You're dead to me.

After wallowing in my shame for a solid minute, I guzzle the rest of my water before dragging myself out of my car.

I can't just sit here forever. I have prep work to do. And I refuse to make people wait for their hot meal. It might be the only one they get all week.

I lock up and get halfway up the walkway to the front doors at Holy Cross when a loud horn startles me, halts my footwork, and whips my head around.

Reed's truck finishes pulling into a space two down from my car. I watch Beth lean over and kiss him through the windshield, then her door is opening and she's jumping down, those cute black flowered boots of hers smacking the asphalt.

I glance down at my own footwear, squint, and then shake my head when I realize I have on one black Chuck and one navy blue. *Awesome.*

Life- I've lost count. Me- somewhere in the negatives.

Beth leaves her door open and moves around it to step up onto the sidewalk. She walks toward me, smiling and lifting her hand in a wave. "Hey. He wants to talk to you," she says over the rumbling noise behind her. "I'll meet you inside."

I look from her face to the windshield, squinting. *Huh. I wonder what this is about?* "Uh, okay. Can you make sure Wendy puts out the fliers she made for the clothing drive? I want them on the tables before people start arriving."

Beth nods when I meet her eyes again. "Yep. I'll do that."

"Thanks. I'll be in in a sec."

"Okay."

We move past each other, and when I get close to Reed's truck, moving to the left of it to get to the open passenger side door, I wave at him through the windshield.

He doesn't wave back.

"Yo," I nearly shout just as Reed is cutting off the engine. I tilt my head up and peer across the seat. "What's up? I gotta get in there and delegate."

"What the *fuck*, Riley," he growls, his one arm bent, resting on the wheel, and his body angled, turned toward me and rigid against the leather.

I jerk back. "What? I'm not saying your wife can't delegate. I'm just saying, that's my job."

"You're *living with CJ*? How the fuck long has this been going on for?"

My mouth falls open. Panic floods me and causes my stomach to do a rollercoaster drop. "How do you know that?" I ask, voice so quiet I'm not sure Reed will be able to hear me.

His brows knit together. *He's hearing me.* "You told me you are. What do you mean, *how do I know that?* You left me a message saying you're living with him and in some sort of squad together, whatever the fuck that means."

You know when you forget parts of your dream, important, crucial parts, and then somebody reminds you of these forgotten moments and you just want to pretend you're not hearing them, these moments never happened, and you've suddenly gone deaf?

I blink and tilt my head to the side. "Huh?"

That's happening to me right now.

Reed scowls. "You know, we could've cleared this up yesterday if you would've answered your phone the thirty times I called it, but you didn't. So, before you go in and delegate, we're clearing it up. How long?" he asks.

"I kept my phone off all day."

"How long, Riley?" he presses.

I shrug. "I don't know what you're talking about."

"How." He leans over the seat. "Long."

I pinch my lips together, pull in a deep breath, hoping it'll relax me—it doesn't—and confess my truth. "Since he got out of the hospital. I moved in the next day."

"Are you serious? That was like, two months ago. What the fuck? Neither one of you thought I should know about it?"

"I asked CJ not to tell you. It isn't his fault. Really. Please don't be mad at him for it." I watch Reed sit back and shake his head, as if he doesn't believe me. "He thought you should know," I add. "He wanted to tell you."

"Why are you living with him?" Reed throws out. "If you needed a place to stay, you should've come to me. I'm your brother, Riley. You know I'll always help you out. Even if I didn't have room, I'd make room for you. Tell me you know that."

My shoulders sag. I pull my lips between my teeth and nod my head.

Sometimes I forget how good of a man Reed is, and just how much I love having him as a big brother.

It sucks when he has to remind me.

"I know you would've made room for me," I say, putting my hands on the edge of the passenger seat and stepping closer. "I know I could've come to you, but I didn't want to impose on you and Beth. You're newlyweds, Reed. You didn't need a third wheel."

He jerks his chin, accepting my explanation. "Fine. But that still doesn't explain why CJ. You don't even know him."

I flinch as if Reed's words literally slap me across the face. "*I know him*," I hiss. "I know him just as well as you do, or Beth, or anybody else. And he knows me. We're *tight*." I watch Reed's eyes narrow and the furrow in his brow deepen as he stares across the seat at me, and quickly realize I may want to reel this in a bit. I'm practically shouting. "I mean, you paired us up at the wedding," I clarify, voice calm and easy listening level. "We got to know each other pretty quickly that weekend between all the festivities. And don't forget, CJ wouldn't be out of work if it wasn't for me. *I* dragged Richard to that concert. So when CJ offered me a place to stay, rent free in exchange for being his live-in nurse, I took it. I'm helping him. I owe him, Reed. He saved me that night. Who knows what would've happened if I would've left with Richard."

Reed's nostrils flare as his lips press together, and I think maybe he's going to get on me about how aggressive I'm being in my defense, but he doesn't. He looks at the dash, rubs at his eyes with his hand relaxing off the wheel, thinks in silence for a breath, then turns his head back to me. And I recognize the look I'm getting now as the same look Reed gave me at the hospital.

It's a look of concern. That protective, brotherly look only Reed can give me.

"Every time I think about that night, I want to go find that asshole and kill him," he says, shaking his head and looking away briefly before meeting my eyes again. "You doing all right with everything that went down? Richard's going to be in jail awhile for assaulting a cop."

"Good," I bite out. "I hope he stays there and gets passed around between the big guys."

Reed's mouth twitches. He pushes his hand through his hair, saying, "I gotta be honest, I hate that you went through that, Riley, but I'm fucking ecstatic you're not with him anymore."

"I'm not surprised. You weren't shy about hating him."

"I won't be shy about the next worthless piece of shit either. I'm going to make that fucker jump through hoops."

My stomach knots up.

Reed smiles a little, but it does nothing to ease my lingering discomfort surrounding this topic. "So how come you couldn't tell me where you were living?" he asks. "What's the big secret?"

I swallow and feel my hands sliding off the seat. They

fall to my side where my fingers curl under the bottom of my shorts. "I just didn't think you would understand," I reply.

"What's there to understand? Is something *else* going on?"

I quickly shake my head. "No." My answer is firm and louder than my previous ones. It's also the truth. Nothing else *is* going on, but even if there was, I'm still worried how Reed would react. "I'm just helping him," I say. "That's it. We're friends."

I'm scared that's all we'll ever be.

Reed stares at me for a beat, eyes assessing, face expressionless while he considers my answer, then he tips his head toward the windshield. "All right. Go," he orders. "But next time, don't worry about me understanding or not. Just tell me what you're doing, Riley. And not in some drunken, middle-of-the-night phone call I can barely fucking understand."

I'm nodding, smiling, and so happy to hear the words *all right go*, that I don't even pay attention to anything else Reed is saying. Nothing else matters. *I'm off the hook! He doesn't seem to hate me. Thank God.* Taking a step back, I grip the edge of the door, ready to close it, but before I do, I remember one last thing that needs to be said.

"Congrats, by the way, Daddy Reed."

Seriously. This is amazing news.

Ear to ear, a smile stretches across my brother's mouth. And when men smile like this, beautifully, eyes shining and every muscle in their face reacting, it's something to look at, smile back at, and appreciate.

And I take the time to do just that before saying my farewells.

When I descend the stairs and step out into the basement of Holy Cross, I feel different. Better, in a way. I'm not keeping this giant secret from Reed anymore. He knows where I'm living now, and he seems okay with mine and CJ's arrangement, possibly even supportive of it. And having Reed's approval means a lot. So much more than anyone else's. It means *everything*. It always has.

"Looks like that conversation went well," Beth observes when I step into the kitchen wearing a relieved smile. She's standing at the long, metal counter in the middle of the room, several cans of green beans in front of her that she's opening up and dumping into a pot.

"Yep. I feel good about it," I reply, grabbing an apron off the wall and slipping the loop over my head. "I don't need to lie about where I'm living now, so that's a relief."

"And what about your other secrets involving CJ? Are you going to tell Reed about those?"

My smile disappears. That half-hungover feeling turns my stomach, but I know it has nothing to do with tequila.

Truth tastes bitter. No wonder people lie so much. I don't want to believe what I'm about to say any more than I want to say it.

I tie the string behind my back and cross the room. "I don't have multiple secrets," I clarify. "I have *one* secret—we slept together. We're not *sleeping together*. That's not happening, so it doesn't even matter. We can all move on." I meet her eyes—filled with questions and a pitying concern for me when I stop on the other side of the counter. My shoulders slouch. "I put CJ in the friend-zone and now I'm pretty sure he never wants to leave it," I add, frowning.

Her head tilts. "Why do you say that?" she asks. "Did he tell you he never wants to leave it?"

"Maybe," I answer. "CJ could've told me a lot of things the other night when I made that phone call to Reed. I can't remember."

Beth looks at me straight on as realization lifts her brows.

"Oh, right. Reed said you sounded drunk on that message. What's up with you Tennyson kids drinking too much and forgetting things?"

"It isn't *my* fault! I blame the tequila. And CJ was drinking it too. It wasn't just me."

I definitely remember clinking glasses.

Beth jerks her shoulders. "Well, then, if he got drunk too, maybe he forgets saying he wants to stay in the friend-zone."

My eyes narrow. Beth smiles unapologetically. *She's lucky I love her.*

"Sorry," she giggles, pursing her lips to fight her amusement. "What all *do you* remember? Anything?"

I firmly nod my head, then I lift my hand and start ticking off memories on my fingers. "Tequila. Some touching. Flirting done solely by *me*." I roll my eyes at that one. "CJ standing in my bedroom. And his resting bitch face."

Beth blinks. "What?" she sputters through a laugh. "*Resting bitch face*? He does not have one of those."

I shrug, dropping my hand to the counter. "Well, he didn't look happy being in my room," I tell her. "And he sure as hell didn't stay there after I *know* I flirted with him. I'm pretty sure I asked him to do, you know, *unfriendly things with me*, Beth, and he didn't do them. CJ didn't want to."

"And you wanted him to? You want to be more than friends now?"

"Yes." The word rushes out of my mouth like a breath of relief. I bend forward, drop my elbows on the counter and my face into my hands, groaning, "I do. I want it so badly."

He jokingly calls me his lady. I don't want it to be a joke.

"Oh, sweetie."

I lift my head and look at Beth again, staying hunched over and letting my arms fall between empty cans of beans. "He's just, he's *so fun* to be around," I tell her. "I laugh all the time when we're together. We play, you know? Like goofy, silly things I have the best time doing. And he's sweet and he's good. *God.* He's such a good man, Beth. And he says things to me and I think, *every girl needs to be with someone who talks to them like this.* He's *that guy.* There isn't better. I know in my heart there isn't."

By the time I finish speaking, Beth's mouth is doing this half-smiling/half-frowning thing. Her bottom lip is twitching, and her eyes are shining with emotion. And I don't know if she looks on the verge of tears because she's pregnant, or because she's sad for me and the giant mistake I've made, but I suddenly can't stomach the thought of staying on this subject a second longer. I know what she's going to say.

You chose Richard. You put CJ in the friend-zone. You brought this on yourself, Riley.

CJ never wanted this. He wanted *me*, and now he doesn't. He just sees me as his buddy. His roommate. His nurse. Drinking pals who occasionally flirt and share friendly touches, but that's where it ends. We're friend-zoned for life. It's too late for anything else.

"Riley," Beth begins.

I quickly straighten up and wave my hand at her, stopping any more of this discussion. Then I spin around, saying as I hustle away, "I don't want to talk about it. I need to get to work."

HOURS LATER, I'M halfway home, taking the long way and stalling for time when my phone beeps with an incoming text. I pull over to the side of the narrow dirt road I'm driving on—I know there isn't a red light for miles—lift my hips off the seat, and dig my phone out of my front pocket.

CJ: At Dellis' getting a bite. You want me to bring you back something?

I read the message, then read it again while gnawing on the side of my thumb.

Huh. I'm expecting all interactions with CJ to be hella awkward now—it's the whole reason I've been avoiding going home—but this isn't awkward at all. I wonder why he's being so . . . *CJ* with me?

Maybe his memory is as foggy as mine? I decide to inquire.

Me: So, Friday night was crazy, huh? Wow.

His response is immediate.

CJ: We'll talk about it when I get home. Food?

Crap. It looks like I'm going to be entering this conversation blind. This can't suck any more.

Figuring I've most likely reached my limit in begging this weekend, I don't try and persuade CJ to have this discussion now. Instead, I save what dignity I have left, if any, and picture the menu at Dellis'.

I am pretty hungry. I never eat when I volunteer at Holy Cross. The food isn't for me. It's for people who need it.

Me: Cream of crab soup would be awesome. Thanks. I'll pay you back.

CJ: No you won't.

I sigh and drop my phone onto the passenger seat.
See? He's *that* guy.

KNOWING CJ ISN'T at the house waiting for me gets me

off the back roads. I take the more direct route, saving myself roughly ten minutes of drive time, and once I'm home, it's all I can do *not* to go crazy.

I just want to get this conversation over with. And I have no idea how long CJ is going to be. It could be hours before he gets home, especially if he's sharing a meal with someone.

I need to find something to do . . .

I channel surf for five minutes. I play a little Madden, but it isn't as fun beating the machine. My mouth barely even twitches. Bored, I toss the remote onto the trunk, then I head to my room, grab the sketchpad I keep in in the nightstand drawer, and sit down on the bed with it.

I've always liked to draw. It's something I do for fun, and CJ knows this. He's seen me sketching while we sit on the couch together. It's how I occupy my time if he's watching something I'm not all that interested in. He's seen a few of the sketches I've completed.

He just hasn't seen what I've been drawing as of late.

I flip through the pages I've already filled, coming to my most recent pencil drawing of CJ, and give him more shadow on his jaw. I darken the outline of his t-shirt and sketch one of those coconut drinks in his hand. The ones with the umbrella straws sticking out of them. As I'm smudging in his jeans, I hear the front door open, lifting my head from my drawing and stilling my hand.

I close the sketchpad and push it aside to scramble off the bed, getting to my feet just as CJ takes the last remaining steps down the hallway to get to my room. He stops at the doorway, filling it, looking from my face to my bare feet curling against the hardwood, and back up again.

He's wearing a dark blue t-shirt and jeans that form to his strong thighs and I'm certain look amazing on his ass. I just don't think now is the best time to ask him for a view of it.

I open my mouth to say something, *hey* or *I'm sorry if I've made this weird*, but CJ beats me to it.

"How are you feeling?" he asks me.

"Better than yesterday." I give him a small smile. "Way better. I haven't thrown up any."

"Do you want to do this now, or do you want to eat first?"

His face is serious. And I know this man. I know if I say I want to eat first, no matter how badly he wants this talk to happen, CJ will sit beside me and let me eat every drop of the cream of crab soup he brought home before he utters a single word. He'll be fine.

But I won't be able to eat. I want this talk to happen just as bad as he does.

"Do this now, I guess." I lift my shoulder and gesture for him to come in. "Uh, here, or, do you want to go to the couch? I don't care."

"We might as well do it here," he says, but he keeps where he is, leaning his thick shoulder against the doorframe, crossing his booted foot over the other, and bringing his arms across his chest. "If this goes the way I'm hoping, this is where we're going to end up," he adds.

My brows raise. *This is where we're going to end up? What in the world?*

"Did you think about it?" CJ asks before I can get my own question out.

"Think about *what?*"

His mouth twitches. "If you meant what you were offering Friday night. Do you still want me to take it?"

I blink. *Take it?*

"What?" I whisper.

Take what? Good God. How hard did I flirt?

CJ holds my eyes for a breath, then he shakes his head and drops it. "Christ. You don't remember shit, do you?" He looks at me again. "You have no fucking clue what I'm talking about."

"I remember *some* shit," I tell him. "Just . . . not all the details."

"You asked me to take you to bed, darlin'."

My eyes widen. *Oh my God, I flirted so hard.*

"I didn't, considering how drunk you were and how close to being shit-faced I was," CJ continues. "Even though you told me it wasn't the tequila. Promised me it wasn't. Didn't matter. I needed to hear that sober, babe. You know? I couldn't risk you not meaning what you were saying to me."

I think back to that night—CJ standing in this room, hovering over my bed. Face tense.

Oh, my God . . .

He wasn't angry. He was struggling.

"You didn't want to leave me, did you?" I throw out, risking being wrong about this but suddenly not caring. I have to know. "You wanted what I wanted."

A slow moving smirk twists across his mouth, from one perfect corner to the other. "Fuck no, I didn't want to leave," he reveals. "I came back and tested that lock three times. I almost broke the goddamn door down."

My lungs seem to squeeze all of the air out of my body. "I thought you just wanted to stay friends," I say. "All day today, that's what I've thought. I didn't—"

"Fuck being friends. I want you."

Something must flash in my eyes, because CJ rights his head, his gaze hot and hungry all of a sudden as he stares across the distance between us, then immediately he's pushing off from the wall and stalking toward me.

"Do you want this?" he asks.

I swallow down a moan. *God, is this really happening?* "Yes," I answer, nodding my head.

"Do you want *me*, babe? The way I'm wanting to give you me?" CJ stops when we're toe-to-toe, curls his fingers under my chin and lifts it. "Do you wanna be my woman?" he murmurs.

My bones turn to jelly, and I whimper because being his woman sounds like the best thing in the entire world to me. Better than being any other man's *anything*. "Can I tell you a secret?" I request, running my hands up his body and stopping at his chest.

I can feel his heart pounding. I wonder if he can tell how fast he makes mine beat.

CJ gazes at my smiling lips, slides his hand along my jaw, and gives me that beautiful, charming grin of his. He bends closer, and closer, until he's asking, "Yeah. What's that, darlin'?" right against my mouth.

Eyes closed, I start to tell him that I've always wanted it, since that very first shot of tequila, but then his tongue touches my lower lip, and I don't know who groans first, him or me. But it's CJ jerking me against him and gripping my hair and growling, "God, I've missed this sweet fucking mouth," before he kisses me just like he did that first time—on the sand and underneath the stars.

Desperate. Hard, hot, deep, need this, *fuck*, need this now, kisses.

And I'm lost, caught up in the feel of his hands in places he hasn't touched in months and his mouth, expertly devouring, it makes me crazy. I want him. I want this man more than I've ever wanted anyone. It's beyond desire at this point. It's beyond anything I've ever felt.

If we don't do this, or if he stops or slows down, I think I might die.

I tear at his clothes, whipping his belt loose and unfastening his jeans. I shove them down with his boxers and wrap my hand around his dick and *God*, he's so hard and warm and big. He's big everywhere. I slowly stroke him, turning my wrist and rubbing the smooth, crowned head with my thumb. I do it just like CJ showed me that first night, squeezing harder at the base and being a little rough about it, a little sloppy, letting my nails touch his skin, and I know he likes what I'm doing, because he groans into my mouth and drags his teeth across my bottom lip. Then he's pulling back to tug off his shirt and toss it, and seeing his bare chest while feeling everything I'm feeling right now, holy crap, I lose my mind.

"I love your body," I tell him, rubbing my hands all over him while I kiss from pec to pec, lips and tongue teasing.

CJ has the sexiest chest I've ever seen. Broad, muscled, and dusted in a light amount of hair. The perfect amount. I can't kiss him enough. I can't touch him enough. I'm all over him. And when I move my mouth lower, over his ribs and the deep grooves of his abs, I realize I need more. I can't wait another second.

I don't pause to undress or give CJ time to remove anything I'm wearing. I can't. I'm still fully clothed when my knees hit the floor, and I love it. I love how desperate and frantic I feel. How hurried this is. How *real* this is. It's always been like this with him.

I take CJ into my mouth. I don't tease. I don't play. I suck him to the back of my throat and swallow around him.

Another thing he told me he likes.

"*Fuck*," he grunts. His hands fly to my hair and fist. "Riley . . . Jesus, ah, *fuck*, baby. Wait . . ."

My fingers dig into the back of his thighs and urge him to move.

I don't want CJ to think he needs to hold back. I'm not. I can't. I'm so turned on by this. As much as he is.

I moan and bob my head.

"God, you look so fucking hot," he rasps, thrusting his hips now and watching me take him. He stares down at me. Chest heaving. Lips parted. Face beautifully blissed out. I can feel my pulse race beneath my ear as he rubs his thumb along my mouth, feeling how I stretch for him. He groans, *"fuck yeah"* when I lick from his balls to the tip and swirl my tongue there. He grits his teeth and pumps his hips faster, pushing my hair out of my face so he can see me and I can see him.

I don't know why, but I feel like the most precious thing in the world when I'm on my knees in front of CJ. I shouldn't, I suppose. I'm letting him use me, taking everything he can give while I do nothing short of worship him. But I know what this means to CJ. I can see it in his eyes and feel it in the way he strokes my cheek. And when he rasps, "Darlin'," I know that's mine. Only mine.

I can't get enough of him. I'll never want less than this again. Never.

"Riley," he groans, strong thighs tensing. "Babe, I'm gonna come." He curls his hands around fistfuls of my hair and tugs.

I don't let him pull me off. I hold CJ's eyes, silently telling him I want it. *Please, please, please.* I want all of this man. Every part of him and everything he can offer me.

His nostrils flare with a savage desire for this, for what I'm giving him, but his eyes are all CJ, looking at me like he's the one worshipping as his hands tighten harder and harder in my hair. His hips start thrusting quicker, fucking my mouth deeper, and then he growls, exploding into my mouth and spilling down the back of my throat.

I swallow every drop. I take it all.

Nothing less than this. Never again.

"Jesus, fuck, babe," he pants, his body still jerking in pleasure as he watches me suck and lick him like he's the best meal I've ever had.

I hum around his length one last time, then I pull off and sit back on my heels. I blink up at him and watch his eyes follow my tongue as it sweeps across my bottom lip.

"Damn," he mutters. "I kinda want to ask you to marry me after that. Jesus Christ, Riley."

I smile from ear-to-ear, feeling triumphant. "Wanna high five?" I ask since, you know, we celebrate awesome things.

And that was *so totally awesome.*

Laughing rich and smooth inside his chest, CJ reaches down and takes my face between his hands, moving his thumb over my cheek. "Maybe later," he murmurs, looking at my mouth, then back into my eyes. "Are you gonna give me that pussy now?"

"I thought you were going to take it," I challenge.

CJ's eyes flash, then I'm being jerked up and tossed through the air, giggling and squealing as I land on my back in the middle of the mattress.

Yes. He's totally going to take it.

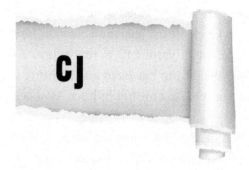

CJ

I WATCH RILEY lay back on the bed, pop the button on her shorts and shimmy out of them while I pull at the straps on my boot.

"Leave those on," I order when her fingers loop under the string of her panties. "I wanna feel how soaked you got them just from having my dick in your mouth."

Her eyes flicker wider, and the sweetest fucking blush creeps across her face. She sits up, leaving her panties, grabs the hem of her shirt and rips it off, then cups her breast through her bra and thumbs her nipple. "This too?" she asks, voice teasing and teeth dragging across her bottom lip.

I toss my boot and stand tall, pulling in a deep breath as I watch her nipple harden under the sheer material. "If I ever tell you to cover up your tits when we're about to fuck, honest to God, there's something wrong with me," I share, meeting her eyes and lifting my hand to point. "In fact, go ahead and burn that along with all your other bras. Tits that sweet, it's almost a crime keeping them imprisoned like that."

She giggles, dropping her hands to the mattress and rubbing her heels on the sheet. "Burning them all would be nice. Not buying them in the first place would be better. They're so expensive." She sighs and wrinkles her nose before gazing down at herself. "I wish my boobs were smaller so I didn't even need to spend the money."

She wishes her boobs were smaller? What in the . . . fuck?

My brow furrows as I kick off my jeans and boxers. "Bite your tongue, woman. We don't blaspheme in this house."

"I'm serious," she says, lifting her head and fighting a smile. "They aren't fun for me. And big boobs hurt. My back is always sore."

I step up to the side of the bed, smirking when Riley's gaze lingers on my half hard cock. "That's an easy solution, darlin'. Your back hurts? You come to me. I'm your man. I'll take care of every little ache you got." I drop my knee to the mattress and crawl closer. "As far as your tits go, I think God knows what he's doing. Let's not question his work."

Riley rolls her eyes. "You'll give me back rubs? Really?" she asks, reaching behind her to unclasp her bra.

"Yep."

"Back rubs that keep your hands on my *back*?" She slips her bra off and tosses it off the bed.

I stare at her nipples. "I make no promises of where my hands end up," I answer, gripping her ankle and pulling her down so she's spread out on her back beneath me. "After a long day held captive in that torture device, it would be wrong of me not to show them some attention. They've earned it." I drop my head and whisper against her cleavage, "Haven't you?"

Riley giggles. Her hands push through my hair. "Did you just ask my boobs that?"

"Shh. We're having a moment."

I feel her body quake against my lips as I kiss down to her nipple. "I know. *God*, I've missed you too. And she said some awful things, didn't she? She should be punished. What do you think? Should I spank her?"

Riley gasps. Her hands tighten in my hair when I close my mouth around her and suck. "Oh, God, please," she begs.

I tilt my head up, releasing her nipple, and smirk at that hot, hungry look in her eyes. "Goddamn. You want me rough, don't you?" I ask, watching her cheeks warm. "I was going to take my time," I kiss her skin, "savor you while I make you come every fucking way I can, but you don't want that. You want me wild."

"I want you how I feel."

"How's that?"

"Crazy," she rushes out, licking her lips. "I don't want you to be able to breathe. I can't. I'm . . ." Her legs shift beneath me. "I'd beg for this, CJ. For us to happen. I don't care how pathetic that sounds. I would. I know I would."

Pathetic? Yeah fucking right. If she had any idea some of the shit I've been thinking . . .

I press a kiss to her ribs and to the dip in her stomach, my hands curling around her tiny waist and roaming up her sides. "You think I didn't sit in that room every day for the past two months and go out of my fucking mind knowing you were in here?" I ask, gazing up at her. Her wide eyes blink. "Every time you looked at me, Riley, every time you touched me, even just putting your hand on my leg when you were wrapping it, do you think I didn't want that to mean more? 'Cause, babe, I did. I wanted that."

A sadness passes over her face. "I'm sorry I didn't do this sooner. With everything that happened, I just—"

"Don't do that," I cut her off, raising up a little to see her better. "We're here now. We're doing this. No sorrys, babe. We got here."

The corner of her mouth twitches. "No sorrys," she echoes, dropping her chin with a nod and no doubt thinking back to the no-apologizing rule I gave her when she first moved in. Her warm hands slide out of my hair to my face and cup my cheeks. "So, um, about the spanking . . ."

I raise my brows, knowing what she wants but already having an idea in mind how I plan on giving it to her. She's going to have to wait. I shuffle back, kneel between her legs, and wrap my hand around her thigh, pushing it back. "Spread your legs, baby. Let me see that pussy I can't stop thinking about."

Riley bites at her lip. She bends her knee and drops it to the side, keeping her other one straight until I'm guiding her to open up wider.

I stare at the wet spot on her panties as I stretch out, hanging halfway off the bed. My knees on the floor. My hard cock rubbing against the side of the mattress. "Look at you," I murmur, dipping my head so I'm hovering my mouth there. "Dirty girl. You made a mess. Do you think I can get you any wetter?"

Riley's response is a long, low groan when I bury my nose between her legs and inhale. She smells heady and rich, almost as good as she tastes, and it makes my fucking mouth water. I drag her panties down her legs and drop them off the bed, then I'm leaning over her again and swiping my tongue through her pussy.

"*CJ*," she gasps. She's breathless, back arching and hands wrapping around my forearms that are keeping her lower half pinned down. "Don't stop. *Please*, oh, my God, don't stop."

I smile against her and stifle a laugh. "Do you think I'd stop? Do you think I could?" Our gazes lock. I drag my tongue over her clit and we moan together. "*Fuck*. A girl like you, there's no stopping, babe. I tried. Trust me."

Riley was talking about me working her until she comes. I'm talking about us—admitting how hung up I've been since that fucking wedding. We weren't friends. Never have been.

I never saw her as that.

Never. It's not normal to want to taste your friend's mouth every fucking time they open it.

Riley bites at her lip again, looking shy—at what I just said or having my tongue on her, I don't know. Then she's sitting up, sticking her hands behind her and staring down between her legs with wide, curious eyes.

"You want to watch me?"

"Yes."

"What do you want to watch me do?"

A flush reddens her cheeks. "Eat me out," she whispers.

I lick my lips, holding her eyes as I lower my head back down, closer and closer until Riley is whining and lifting her pelvis to hurry me the fuck up already. I chuckle and push her back down. "Watch me."

She gasps, body trembling when I nuzzle my mouth against her pussy. "Oh, my God . . . *yes*."

I move my face roughly between her legs. I give her exactly what she wants—crazy. There's no control or restraint. I'm not gentle with her. I don't ask if Riley likes what I'm doing or build it in her slow. I can't. I realize quickly that I'm not doing this for her. Or at least, not *just* for her. I can't take my time—my mouth is on her. I can't savor and drag this out— she's in my fucking bed and I'm touching her and kissing her and touching her. The woman I've been obsessing over for months. The one I can't get out of my head. The pretty girl who shoots tequila and who's naturally curious about palm trees. This isn't sedate. It can't be. I get her worked up and wet so fast, she drips down my chin and onto the sheet before I'm even fucking her with my tongue, and then I'm fucking her with my tongue. She comes for me, sweet and soft limbs shaking. I swallow her desire and groan when I taste her in my throat. And then I'm building it again, pressing my finger against her tight little ass and telling her she misses me there while I suck on her clit. And by the time she's coming and flooding my mouth a second time, my cock is so hard I'm practically humping the mattress.

"I'm gonna fuck you so good," I tell her as I get to my knees between her legs, my next words getting stuck in my throat when Riley jerks up, grabs my face and crashes our mouths together.

She pulls me down on top of her and sucks the taste of her pussy off my tongue. My lips. "Hurry," she pleads between kisses. Pressing her mouth to my cheek. Biting my jaw. "CJ, *please*, my God." She tilts her pelvis up, rubbing her soaking wet cunt against my dick.

Lust crackles in my blood.

"*Fuck*," I growl, fists to the mattress beside her head and stomach tensing as I press up.

Jesus fucking Christ, the feel of her.

Riley freezes beneath me, her entire body going stiff and her eyes flashing open, and I know she's realizing how close we are to doing what we haven't done—to saying fuck it and going at this bare.

Maybe we do need to slow the fuck down a little. Shit.

"Sorry," she whispers.

I look down into her anxious eyes and shake my head, cutting off her thoughts and the way I know they're going. I don't want her worrying about this or anything else tonight.

"We'll get there. We got time, babe. Relax," I say, bending down to kiss her. "Let me go grab something."

"Wait," she rushes out, smiling a little. "Don't. I have some in here." Riley presses against my chest to ease me up, and then she's scooting back, getting to her knees and reaching around me to the nightstand. She digs a box out of the drawer and hands it to me.

I look from the box to her face as she settles back against the pillow. My brows lift. "A *hundred pack*? Where in the hell did you find this?" I ask her.

"Costco." She presses her lips together and shrugs before softly admitting, "I was hopeful."

I stare at her.

She bought these for us? She's been to Costco once. She got these right after she moved in.

My mouth twitches.

She was wanting me even then. *Goddamn it.*

"My little wholesale shopper. You're gonna get fucked so hard," I tease, ripping the box open as Riley covers her smile with her hand. Condom on (and keeping a wrapped one close by before I stow away the box, since I know I'm going to need it) I crawl over Riley, settling between her hips. I drop my forehead to hers and push in.

And sweet fucking God, I forgot . . .

"You feel fucking *good*, baby," I groan, pumping my hips slowly as I stare into those stormy blue eyes.

"CJ," she whimpers, her hands in my hair, tugging, her legs wrapping around my back and heels digging in. "I missed you," she says. "This . . . so much."

"Yeah." I bend and take her mouth, kissing her with that same frenzy we shared minutes ago and letting it feed us both. My grip on her body tightens—on her ass, her tit as I palm it roughly. "I missed this more than you know, darlin'," I say, watching that softness touch her eyes. Rearing back, I slide my hands to her hips, lift her off the bed, and slam into her, making her cry out, again and again.

Riley starts begging. Asking me for harder. Deeper. *Please.*

Her fingernails rake up and down my stomach and dig into the backs of my thighs.

I drop to my elbows and thrust faster, bottoming out and kissing her, swallowing her hot, desperate little cries. I push back on her leg and prop her ankle on my shoulder, fucking her deeper.

"Yes," she pants. "*God*, yes."

"All night, gorgeous girl," I promise. "All fucking night, I'm worshiping this body. Every inch."

I power into her. We're both panting. Sweating. I'm grunting and smacking the headboard against the wall, and Riley's eyes are rolling back in her head and she's making all of these hot as shit noises, looking blissed out of her fucking mind.

"I'm going to come," she moans, pushing her tits against my chest and arching her neck. Her limbs start squeezing around me. Her entire body tenses up. "Oh, God, Cannon," she whimpers. "*Cannon . . .*"

Fuck.

I freeze and suck in a breath. My chest tightens.

FUCK. Why do I like that? Why the *fuck* do I like that so much?

"Fuck me," Riley pleads, grinding her hips up. "Please, CJ! Please please . . ."

I snap out of it and pump my hips, meeting her body repeatedly and going harder each time. I fuck Riley through her orgasm. I don't let up.

"Oh, my God," she pants, coming down slowly when I start grinding deep, but staying there, right on the edge when my hand snakes between us and I move my thumb over her clit. She leans up and kisses me, shoving her tongue inside my mouth, tugging my hair and groaning, "CJ, I'm . . . *God.* Holy shit."

I smile against her mouth. "On your knees, baby," I say as I'm flipping her, not really giving her a choice but it doesn't matter. As soon as she hears the order, Riley is moving with me and positioning herself. Her body is still shivering with pleasure. Her legs shake beneath her. Then I'm kneeling, hands on her hips and eyes staring at all that tanned, toned flesh. Her long, sloped back. Her peach shaped ass I want to taste.

And smack.

And fuck.

"Ah!" she cries out when my hand connects with one cheek. She whips her head around and gapes at me, but then her mouth goes slack and her eyes get heavy when I position my cock and push back in.

"*Goddamn,*" I groan, hips pumping hard and fast. I'm so fucking close, ready to let go with the feel of her—still tight around me, and the way she looks bent over like this. And knowing that, I wrap my arm around her ribs and yank her up, crushing her back against my front. She groans and wiggles her ass against me when I suck her neck. Her jaw. I press my lips to her ear and whisper, "You ready to get spanked?"

Riley tenses. Her head turns and her hand reaches blindly behind her, curling around my hip. "Um, that wasn't it? What you just did?" she asks, meeting my eyes.

I smile and kiss her cheek, not answering. Hand moving between her legs, I buck into Riley, slapping our bodies together as I rub her clit with two fingers. I moan into her neck. She wraps her hand around my arm and drops her head back against my shoulder and when I'm right there and she's right there, body locking up and begging, I lift my hand from her pussy and swiftly bring it down again.

Riley jumps and jerks against me. "God, *fuck!*" she cries out. "CJ!"

I do it again, slapping her just as she's coming. Riley spasms in my arms and soaks my hand. I feel her desire dripping down my legs as she squeezes the fuck out of my cock.

"Godfuckingdamn," I snarl, thrusting faster. My pleasure coils around me and closes in until . . ."Fuck. *Fuck*! I'm coming." I grab Riley's face and turn it so I can kiss her as I empty inside the condom. She sucks on my lip. I moan into her mouth, and then I'm collapsing sideways onto the mattress and dragging Riley down with me.

We're a pile of pounding hearts and sweat soaked limbs, tangled up in each other.

Friends? Fuck that. This is so much better.

"Holy shit," she giggles, trying to catch her breath.

Panting, I turn my head and look over at her, holding onto her legs that are thrown over my hip. Our eyes lock. She bites her lip.

"You spanked my pussy," she says.

I grin.

Riley's gaze lowers to my mouth, then jumps back up. Her cheeks flush darker. "It was awesome," she whispers.

Laughing, I roll over, shift her legs onto the bed, and prop my weight on my elbow so I can lean over her and bend down, kissing her soft, swollen lips. She moans and curls her arms around my back. "I gotta take care of this condom," I tell her.

"Okay."

"Do you need anything? A towel?"

"A towel would be super cool of you."

I smirk, leaning away. "I just made you come a fuckuva lot, babe. I don't think I need help in the *super cool* department."

Her mouth twitches.

"But, my lady wants a towel, she's getting a towel," I add, kissing her once more before I start to roll over, but Riley's arms circle my neck and she tugs me back down, taking my mouth again.

"I'm your lady," she murmurs inside our kiss, voice quick and sounding really fucking happy about being that.

I stroke her cheek, smiling as I look into her heavy-lidded eyes. "Fuck yeah, you are. Always were."

Riley blinks and smiles back, big and bright. Her dimples showing.

I kiss her nose and the corner of her mouth. "Let me go get you that towel," I say.

Riley presses her lips to my jaw once more, then releases me, letting her hands fall weightless to the mattress and humming softly in contentment.

I roll over and push off the bed, grabbing my boxers out of my jeans on the way to the bathroom.

After I discard the condom and wash up, I get a towel, dampen it and carry it back out into the bedroom.

Riley's sitting up now, her back against the headboard and her knees bent beneath the sheet. She's running her finger over her bottom lip and looking down into her lap, but when I step out into the room, she lifts her head, drops her hand, and leans forward. "You're walking without your boot," she observes, glancing at my leg. "That's great. It doesn't hurt when you put pressure on it?"

I stop beside the bed. *Fuck. I can't be doing that in front of her.* "Nah. It hurts," I say, wincing when I press down hard on my heel. Harder than I typically would. "I just didn't think to put the boot on before I got up. It happens. Here." I climb on the bed and tug the sheet down her body, pulling it to her knees when she stretches out on her back. I clean her up with the towel.

"Can I see your leg?" she asks after I toss the rag onto

the floor.

Riley does this a lot. She likes looking at my incision and making sure everything seems to be healing up nicely. And I appreciate her doing it. I appreciate everything she does for me, but right now, I don't want this to be about my leg, my injury, or anything else besides us, what we just did, and what we're going to continue doing as much as fucking possible.

"Later," I tell her.

She cocks her head. "I'm your nurse, CJ. And I haven't looked at it today. I want to see it."

"*Later*," I repeat firmly, watching Riley's lips pinch together in surrender before she's giving me a quick nod. "Come here." I stretch out on my back beside her, then I roll up onto my hip and reach out, grabbing her knees and twisting her toward me so her shoulder's pressing against my chest and her legs are bent against my stomach. I pull the sheet over us both, giving Riley more of it, then prop myself up to look at her, elbow on the mattress and head in my hand. "I want to make a few things clear before I go heat up your soup," I say.

Her eyes flick wider.

I interpret that as her being worried about what I'm about to tell her and quickly shut that down. "I know we talked already, but considering how much you don't remember of Friday night, I'm going to assume certain shit needs to be said again. It's good shit though. Nothing bad."

She shakes her head immediately after I finish speaking. "No, I . . . sorry. I just got super hungry thinking about my soup." Her hands press to her stomach. "I'm excited. I forgot about it."

I stare at her. She's serious. *Fuck*. Laughing, I trail my fingers up and down her arm. "I guess I'll make this quick then."

"I'd appreciate you forever if you did."

I shake my head.

Jesus. If she keeps being this fucking cute about every-thing, I'm going to end up going through another condom, or three, and she's not going to be eating *anything* any time soon.

I cup her face, hold her eyes and get to the point. "Now that we're here, babe, where you're giving me this, we're not ever going back," I begin, gently moving my thumb over her cheek. Her lips part. "This is the beginning of us, darlin'. I get why you wanted to be friends and why you needed the time you took, and I'd be lying if I said I didn't enjoy being with you like that, 'cause being with you in any way, babe, is something I'm really going to fucking like, but it wasn't enough. It'll never be enough. Now, you said you wanted me and you sure as hell acted pleased as fuck to be labeled my lady, and I hope you know how much I like hearing that. But babe, honest to God, I've been seeing you as mine for a long fucking time now. We were never just friends, Riley. Not to me. And I apologize for making you think I was okay with that, 'cause I was *never* okay with that. I was just taking what you were giving me, babe. That's it. If you're mad, I'll understand, but I want us moving forward so I gotta ask, is that something you think you can forgive?"

Riley blinks, her eyes holding all kinds of emotion. A shuddering breath pushes past her lips. "Yes," she whispers. "I can forgive that. Consider it forgiven."

"Do you understand what I mean when I say we are never going back to that?"

She nods. "No more just friends," she offers up. "Not even if something happens."

She gets it.

I bend down and kiss her then, giving and getting tongue, but it's gentle. Soft and slow. Her hands stroke my back and

slide tenderly through my hair. I'm nipping at her lips and kissing down to her jaw, and when we're both breathing heavier,
I pull away, slide my grip to the back of her neck and roll us
so we're both on our sides, close and facing each other. Legs
tangled together. Her body curling into mine.

Riley Tennyson, claiming me in my fucking bed.

"CJ?"

"Mm?"

"Tell me a secret. I'm staying in your room, aren't I?" she
asks. Her warm breath on my neck.

I smile, lips curling against her forehead. "What do you
think, darlin'?"

She sighs. Her fingers dance across my chest. "I think I
am. All of your stuff is in here. And that other bed is too small
for you. Your feet hang off the edge."

"It's my old bed from when I was a kid. I just keep it
around for when Jake comes to visit."

"Isn't he too big for it too? In that picture, you guys
seemed the same height."

"Oh yeah. He hangs off just as bad as me. I just think it's
funny as shit when he bitches about it."

He's my baby brother. I'm allowed to torment him a
little. It's all out of love.

"Well, *I* could've fit in it. I wouldn't hang off the edge,"
Riley informs me, giving up information I already know.

"You fit better in this one," I tell her.

I feel her head move.

"*We* fit better in this one," she corrects me.

"Not gonna argue with that." I curl my hand around the
back of her head and press a kiss to her forehead, breathing
deep. My mind heavy.

"What?" Riley asks, reading me. She leans back and looks

up into my eyes, jumping between the two of them. "CJ . . ."

"I never waited for anything like I waited for you," I admit, watching her lips slowly part. "And I would've kept waiting, babe. Given you what you needed. I would've been the best fucking friend you ever had if it meant getting my shot with you, 'cause you're worth it, Riley. You're worth so fucking much, including falling out of small as shit beds for, which, I'm gonna be honest, that happened more than once."

The sweetest fucking smile spreads across her mouth. Slowly. It's fucking beautiful to watch. Then she drops her head and burrows closer. "Thank you," she whispers.

I wrap my arms tighter around her. "You don't need to thank me, darlin'. I'm just letting you know how it is."

"And I'm just letting *you* know," her arm curls around my body and squeezes me. "Thank you."

I kiss the top of her head. "I'll go get you that soup now."

"No thanks."

"You no longer super hungry?"

"I am, but I'd rather you not move."

I smirk, liking Riley's thoughts on keeping me close, but knowing she really wants that soup I brought her motivates me to say my next words. "I got the same thing you ordered. Best fucking soup I ever ate."

Riley clears her throat and shifts a little against me. "Yeah. They do a real good job with it," she says. Her voice nonchalant.

I know better.

"Loaded with crab meat," I tell her. "They don't skimp. That's for damn sure . . ."

"Mmhmmm." Her fingertips drum restlessly on my left pec.

I go in for the kill.

"I think they threw in a couple of legs for you. They were heavy too. It'd be a shame if someone didn't—"

"I'm good with you moving now," she interrupts me, pushing a little against my chest.

Laughing, I lean back, looking into her smiling face. I give her a wink. "Get my lady set up then."

Riley eats her soup in bed, her legs thrown over mine, her side against my chest, ass practically in my lap. She finishes up and relaxes against me again, both of us lying under the sheets. Eyes closed, I feel her touch move over my ribs, down my abs and lower.

Lower . . .

Wrapping around me.

"This is the beginning of us," she whispers, repeating my words when I settle over her again, condom on. Mouth finding hers in the dark, I push inside and feel her body open.

Hands gripping. Pulling closer. Urging. *"Cannon."* Her voice is like a plea in my ear.

The beginning of us.

The start. And already, I never want to find our end.

riley

Five Days Later

SPRAWLED ACROSS CJ'S body, eyes closed, head on his bare chest, leg slung over his hip and arm curling around his waist, I think about how happy I am right now, laying naked except for a pair of panties on the couch in the middle of the afternoon while CJ watches baseball highlights.

Do I typically lay around mostly naked? No.

Do I enjoy listening to baseball highlights? It's okay. I don't hate it.

Aside from the two days this week when I've had class, have CJ and I left the house at all? Nope.

Coming to my conclusion and deciding it's too important to keep to myself, I share it.

"I don't think I have ever been this happy."

CJ's arm around my back gives me a squeeze, then his warm breath is in my hair. "Me either, baby," he murmurs in that deep, smooth as honey voice that feels like a touch moving over my body. And he means that. I know he does.

Scratch that. Now, hearing his response, I am *officially* at my happiest.

My reunion with CJ couldn't have come at a better time. Due to my schedule change this week, I've been off three days out of the five, meaning we've had *tons* of time to spend together. And all of that time, whether we're kissing and touching or doing nothing but this, has been *amazing*.

We've talked. We've laughed and played. We've gone to bed together and woken up together.

And we've had sex all over this house.

I'm pretty sure the only place we haven't done it yet is on top of the TV. It's a flat screen so, otherwise, I think it would've been attempted.

Never have I smiled this much with a guy. Never have I laughed and joked around the way I do with CJ. I know he said we could never be friends again, but I still kind of feel like we are. Just more. We're lovers who became friends who became . . . everything.

I wasn't lying. I have *never* been this happy.

There's just one minor issue we may have that needs to be discussed, and I've honestly been avoiding it. Not that CJ has been bringing it up, I've just made it a point not to. But I can't do that anymore. No more stalling. We need to talk about this today. Now.

Reed cannot know about us.

Turning my head, I press my lips to CJ's pec and stare at his profile, relaxed and fixated on the TV. The side of my foot rubs against his shin. I've been doing that for minutes and he hasn't said anything or moved the slightest. I think he might like it—me touching his injured leg when I'm not being medical about it. When I'm not rewrapping it or rubbing vitamin E on his scar or helping him do his exercises when he's not at PT. I lift up and slide my hand under my chin, tapping my fingers rhythmically as I continue looking at him, and that draws his attention.

His eyes search my face, then his brows pull together.

"Riley."

"Mm?"

"You got something on your mind?"

"I don't want to talk about it."

Now his brows are lifting and nearly reaching his hairline. "Is it about tonight?" he asks.

I blink. *He knows?*

"It sucks that you can't be there," CJ continues, face tensing a little. "You don't have PTO or anything you can take so you don't have to miss out on it?"

CJ thinks I'm sad about my overnight clinical rotation landing on July Fourth. And while it does suck that I'm going to miss all of the festivities, especially considering how much I love fireworks, that isn't what we needed to talk about.

I let out a deep sigh. "No, I can't take off," I tell him. "I'd get marks against me if I did."

"That's fucking lame. They shouldn't schedule you to work a holiday."

"When I'm a nurse I'm going to have to work holidays." I shrug. "It's fine. Hopefully I'll be able to see the fireworks next year."

CJ's mouth twitches. He looks like he knows something I don't. And although I'd love to lay here for the next hour and pick his brain, I really need to get to my point before we get sidetracked.

My nudity tends to lead to us getting sidetracked.

"Everyone will be there tonight," I begin, holding his eyes. "And I didn't know if you were planning on saying anything, but I'm just worried that "

A knock sounds on the door, cutting me off.

"Go away!" CJ hollers, his muscles beneath me flexing as he looks toward the noise. He meets my eyes again. "You're just worried that *what?*"

"Um," I look curiously over my shoulder, then back at CJ. "Well, it's just that "

Three more knocks interrupt me, these being made with a heavier fist.

CJ curses under his breath and glares at the door, face tense and angry, but he doesn't make any attempt at getting up to answer it.

"Maybe you should check and see who that is," I suggest. "They could keep knocking."

"They can come back," he replies curtly, eyes cutting to mine. "You got something you want to talk about. That's more important than whoever's at the door. Don't worry about them."

My lips press together as something wonderfully warm flutters in my stomach.

Holy *crap*, that's sweet. Those Publisher's Clearing House people could be here, holding one of those giant checks for CJ, and he'd rather listen to me talk than collect his millions.

I press a kiss to his chest instead of attacking his face like I want to do, knowing that will just lead to more sex, and we *really* need to have this talk. "Well, I didn't know what you were planning, but I just think that—"

The sound of the front door swinging open and a man's voice entering the house halts me from saying anything more.

"Fuck you. *Go away.* What . . . oh, damn. My bad."

I squeal as CJ curses under his breath, grabs onto me and flips us with lightning speed, covering me up with his massive body and shielding my nakedness from whoever just rudely walked into his house.

Seriously. I mean, unless you're family or something, why would you do that?

"What the *fuck*, Jake?" CJ roars, head whipping around to peer over his shoulder in the direction of the entryway. "Goddamn it. You couldn't wait a minute?"

I suck in a breath. *Jake?*

Oh, my God . . .

"Oh, fuck you. Like you were going to let me in," he replies, his voice similar to CJ's in tone, but sounding rougher, as if he needs to clear it. "I would've been standing out there all night."

My arms are bent up between our bodies. I uncurl my fists from underneath my neck and press my fingertips to my mouth. "Your brother just saw me *mostly naked*," I whisper.

CJ looks down at me. "No, he didn't."

"Yeah, I did."

My eyes widen. *Worst family introduction ever!* I cover my face with my hands and groan.

CJ shifts above me. "Turn around and stay that way until I fucking tell you otherwise, you hear me?"

"Yeah, yeah," Jake mutters. "God. Some welcome party."

"You didn't tell me you were coming today, asshole."

"I said I was coming in a few weeks. It's been a few weeks."

"You couldn't give me a heads up? Let me know you were dropping in on the fourth?"

"I didn't know I was approved for leave until last minute. This *is* your heads up. Goddamn."

CJ lets out an exhausted breath above me. "Come on, darlin'," he says, dropping his knee to the couch space between my legs. "Let's get you to the bedroom."

"I don't want to move," I grumble from behind my hands. "Just stuff me underneath the cushions and leave me here to die. My butt was *totally* hanging out of my underwear."

I feel his body quake with a laugh. He kisses the back

of my hand. "He's not looking anymore. And if he does, I'll kick his ass."

"You can try, *gimp*," Jake counters. "Pretty sure I'll have an advantage."

"Bro, for real? It's good to see you. Always is, but don't make me embarrass you in front of my woman." CJ pushes off me as Jake mumbles something I can't make out over the sound of my nervous breathing. The couch dips and I hear Velcro being pulled, and I know CJ is putting on his boot. Then before I have time to protest moving from my burial spot, yet again, I'm being scooped up off the couch, cradled against CJ's chest in a way my naked upper half is squished against his, and carried around the sofa and down the hallway.

"Sorry about that," he mumbles into my hair. His arm underneath my knees lifts me closer. "I really don't think he saw much, babe. I had my arm around you and my hand on your ass, but even if he did see something? Jake wouldn't get on you about it. He's a good guy. He's not a dick."

I open my eyes, thinking on that.

Mm. CJ *did* have his hand on my ass. And he has big hands. Awesome hands. They cover a lot of surface. And it wasn't like I was laying on my back. My boobs were pretty hidden.

Okay. Maybe this isn't so terrible.

We enter the bedroom, and CJ kicks the door closed behind us and lowers me to my feet. He takes my face between his hands and looks at my eyes, my mouth. He runs his thumb over my cheek, assessing me.

I know CJ is close with his brother. And I'd hate for their reunion to start off on a sour note. Besides, maybe Jake just saw a lot of leg? I can be okay with that.

Smiling up into his serious face, wanting to ease him, I grip CJ's hips above the waistband of his shorts and step closer. "It's nice that he's here for a visit," I say. "How long has it been?"

A deep-set V forms between CJ's brows. He blinks, looking all kinds of confused. And all kinds of hot, too. "A little over a year," he answers. "He just got finished with his third tour over in Afghanistan."

Wow. His third? I can not imagine that.

"Then you better go out there and give him his welcome party. He deserves it." I pop up onto my toes and give CJ a quick kiss, spinning around and slipping out of his hold to get to the dresser. "You go ahead. I'll get dressed and be out in a minute. Oo!" I whip back around and clap my hands together. "Tell him about the fireworks celebration. Maybe he can go!"

CJ stares at me for a breath, face expressionless, as if he is trying to play catch-up with his thoughts, then he closes his eyes through a shake of his head. His chest rattling with a low chuckle. "Jesus. You got over that pretty damn quick. I thought you wanted me to leave you out there to die?"

"I'm just focusing on the positive," I tell him, arms crossing under my chest, which apparently does something stare-worthy to my boobs, because CJ drops his eyes immediately and blinks slowly at them. "And you seeing your baby brother after a year of not seeing him trumps my butt hanging out. This is important."

He lifts his eyes to my face. "So is that talk we were having that got interrupted," he points out, cocking his head.

Talk about starting off on a sour note. *Yikes.*

"It is," I agree, backing away slowly and maneuvering around the bed, while also maneuvering around this conversation. "And we'll get back to that after you go out there and welcome him."

I'd hate for CJ to not take our talk well and have it affect him and Jake's time together. I can wait another hour. Or two.

"All right," he says, jerking his chin at the dresser against the wall. "Toss me a shirt, will you?"

I grab a t-shirt out of the bottom drawer and toss it to him. He pulls it on as I'm grabbing some clothes for myself—jean shorts, a bra, and my Beach Don't Kill My Vibe tank top. I lay everything out on the bed.

"Don't take too long," CJ says, giving me a look before turning toward the door, like he'd come get me and drag me out of this bedroom if I do just that.

Tempting . . .

CJ steps out and pulls the door shut behind him. Seconds later, I hear the loud, boisterous welcome he gives his brother as I'm stepping into my shorts. Jake's voice is carrying down the hallway too. I can't make out what they're saying to each other as I finish getting dressed, but there is a lot of laughter. It's sweet to hear.

After taking a minute to brush out my hair, doing this so they have a little extra alone time, I step out of the bedroom and make my way back down the hallway.

Jake is sitting at the kitchen counter with a glass in front of him, digging Fritos out of a small chip bag and popping them into his mouth. And CJ is standing across from him at the sink, arms pulled across his chest, smiling, looking happy as anything to be watching his brother chow down like a starving man. They're not talking anymore so I don't feel like I'm interrupting anything when I walk into the room. But I do gain both of their attentions.

"Come here, darlin'," CJ says, motioning with his head for me to join him while giving me the smile he was just putting on Jake.

I hurry over and tuck under the arm he's holding out, getting that draped around my shoulders. My hand curls around his waist, and I give him a squeeze, smiling up at him.

"Riley, this is my brother, Jake." CJ lifts his head and looks across the counter, and I follow his eyes while his arm around me tightens and draws me closer to his body. "Jake, you rude motherfucker, meet my girl."

Jake snorts.

I do not snort. I inhale a sharp breath as bliss warms me all over.

His girl.

God, I love the way that sounds.

I uncurl my arm from around CJ and extend my hand to Jake over the sink. "It's nice to meet you, Jake. Now that I'm dressed . . ."

Jake smiles, looking from his brother back to me, then he wipes his hand off on his shirt and takes a hold of mine, shaking it.

Even though he's younger than CJ, Jake has this tired look about him, as if he's lived more years than his age. Shadows circle his dull blue eyes. He looks like he could sleep for months. He isn't smiling at me the way CJ does. He's being friendly, yes, but it almost feels forced, like he doesn't have the energy but he knows it's the polite thing to do.

I amp up my smile, appreciating the effort. I'm sure he *is* tired. He just got home after God knows how long.

"Complicated, huh?" Jake directs at CJ after releasing my hand. "The fuck happened to that?"

"What?" I ask. I turn to CJ, watching him glare at Jake and shake his head.

"Nothing," he mutters. "He's being a dumbass."

Jake laughs under his breath.

"Would you like me to make you something to eat?" I ask, watching Jake hit crumbs in his bag, tip his head back and knock the last remaining Fritos into his mouth. "I made taco lasagna last night. I could heat you up a plate. It's . . . well, it's exactly how it sounds. Tacos in the form of lasagna."

He crushes up the empty bag in his hand, shrugging. "Sure. Yeah, that sounds good. Thanks."

"No problem." I look up at CJ, meeting his eyes. *I wonder how long he's been looking at me?* "Are you hungry? Do you want some?"

"Yeah. Do you mind?"

"Not at all."

CJ kisses the top of my head, murmuring his appreciation, then releases me so I can go about fixing him and his brother a plate.

As I'm scooping out their servings and heating them up, I listen to their conversation.

They talk about Afghanistan, but only briefly, and I get the impression from Jake's short, to the point answers that this topic isn't something he wants to elaborate on. His voice is tight by the time he changes the subject, putting the focus on CJ's injury and getting the details of that night and his recovery so far. I carry the plates over to the counter and distribute them, along with forks and napkins. The guys are sitting beside each other, neither one of them looking up or breaking conversation when I walk over. I don't mind. I know they need this. I'm sure they missed each other a lot. You can tell CJ is the older brother out of the two. He slaps Jake on the back and roughs up his hair, and Jake lets him. He doesn't gripe at all. It's sweet.

I linger there, watching their reunion until CJ briefly glances at me before admitting to his leg still bothering him a good bit, and then I turn around and busy myself with dishes.

I scrub a pan with vigor, getting the hardened egg off the

bottom. My mouth set into a frown.

I can't help but feel a little sad. I know CJ isn't supposed to be healed up completely yet, but I hate hearing about how much pain he's still in. I want him healed.

I swear though, I think he's bringing some of it on himself. I've caught him several times forgetting about his boot.

"Babe!"

I jump and whip my head around, keeping my hands under the water. "Yeah?"

Shoot. Has he been calling me?

CJ laughs at me through closed lips, his fork hovering in the air with a bite. "Jake was just saying how good your food is," he shares, tipping his head at his brother and looking all kinds of proud of me.

I turn to Jake. My brows raise. "Do you like it? It's good, right?"

He nods, chewing up his bite.

I smile, wanting to do a little dance in celebration. I'm getting the family approval already. This is *awesome*!

I dry my hands on the towel that's hanging off the stove, then spin around to face the two of them. "Did CJ tell you about the fireworks tonight?" I ask. "There's a parade and everything in town. It's really fun."

"Yeah. I can't go, though," Jake replies. "People drink a lot at shit like that. I can't be around it."

My smile fades as Jake looks down at his plate and forks more of his food.

Crap. What is wrong with me? I know about Jake's history with drugs and the way alcohol brings that urge on for him. CJ told me he was a recovering addict. He said Jake struggled with it for years, and still does. And people drink a *ton* while watching the fireworks. It's like a big party in the middle of a field. I know this!

I look at CJ to give him my silent apology for having this stupid idea in the first place, but he doesn't seem the least bit mad at my suggestion. The eyes I meet are full of warmth, and his mouth is lifting in a gentle smile as he chews up his bite.

"How long are you staying for?" CJ asks, turning back to Jake. "Are you hanging out here for a while?"

Jake shakes his head. "Can't. I only got approved for four days, and I need to go up and see Mom before I head to Katie's. I just figured we could hang for a couple hours, if that's cool with you."

"Yeah, man. Whatever you want to do," CJ replies. "I don't have anything going on until later tonight. We can chill here or head into town. I don't care."

"Cool," Jake mutters before scraping up another bite and shoveling it into his mouth.

Nice. They are going to hang out today. Get some brotherly time in. This is great.

I smile, looking between the two of them.

"Babe?"

My eyes fall on CJ. "Mm?"

"Do you want to finish telling me what was on your mind?"

My mouth pulls down.

Do I *want* to finish telling him what was on your mind? No. Do I need to? Yes. Just not with an audience.

"Uh," I look to Jake, then back to CJ, shrugging. "That's okay. It's fine. I can wait."

"You want me to step out?" Jake asks, brows lifting, reading my apprehension and interpreting it wrong.

"No." I quickly shake my head. "No, please eat."

"Darlin', just say it," CJ returns, eyes serious when he

has mine. "You said you were worried about something. And there's no way I'm going to be able to get that worry out of your head unless you let me in there."

"It's fine. It can wait."

"Babe . . ."

"I don't think Reed should know about us," I blurt out.

His brows lift. "Say again?"

I knot my fingers together in front of my stomach. "Uh . . ."

Shit! I don't want to repeat it. CJ doesn't look like he's going to take this news well *at all*. This could ruin his entire day with Jake.

I pull my lips between my teeth and pretend I've gone mute.

CJ cocks his head just as Jake pushes his stool back, dragging the legs against the wood.

"I'm gonna step outside for a smoke. Give you two a minute," he announces, standing and moving with purpose toward the door, and I know he's really stepping out because I just made things crazy awkward.

God, I hope I didn't embarrass CJ. Why didn't I just get this out while I was half naked, standing in the bedroom with him?

When the door shuts behind Jake, I turn to assess my damage, but CJ doesn't look embarrassed. He doesn't look angry either. He looks unsettled. His brows pulling together and his mouth tense while he hunches over the counter, arms outstretched in front of him and hands steepled beside his plate.

My stomach rolls.

What the hell is wrong with me? He deserves an explanation. How could I say something like that and then pretend

I've gone mute?

"Reed hired Richard for the job he fired him from," I begin, stepping up to the sink. "Did I ever tell you that?"

CJ thinks for a beat, then shakes his head.

"He liked him at one point," I continue. "Richard said they got along, but then we started dating and for some reason, Reed would get on Richard about stuff at work, like single him out about things, and I don't know if he was doing it because of Richard messing up or because he was dating me. But eventually Reed just started to hate him. And it made things really uncomfortable. He talked bad about Richard in front of me all the time and called him Dick. It put a strain on us. And I know Richard is basically the absolute *worst*, I know that now, but in the beginning when this all started, he wasn't. Reed liked him, then we got together and he hated him. And the last thing I want is for Reed to start hating you. I won't let that happen."

CJ drags in a heavy breath, then slowly lets it out. "Riley, your brother and I go back a couple of years," he says, brow no longer furrowed, mouth no longer tight, but relaxed, and his eyes warm and full of understanding. "I get that you don't want him reacting badly to this and hating me, but that's something you need to let me worry about, darlin'. If he has a problem, I'll handle it."

"You handling it might make it worse and then he could hate you *even more*," I argue.

"Babe—"

"*Please*," I beg. "Just don't say anything. Not yet. I can't have Reed hate you, CJ. I can't ignore it like I did with Richard and pretend I don't care. Not when I like you this much."

CJ sits up taller, a look washing over his face like what I just said meant a whole lot to him. "Come here," he orders, twisting his torso on the stool.

I rush around the counter, step between his legs, and wrap my arms around his neck, getting gathered against his body.

"If he asks me, babe, I'm not lying to the man," CJ murmurs beside my ear. "That's fucked up and a guaranteed way for him to hate me."

I nod, replying, "I know. I'm not asking you to lie. I wouldn't want you to do that." I lean back just enough to look into his face, forcing my grip to his neck and his hands to slide to my hips. "I want everyone knowing about us," I say. "I promise. I love our secrets, CJ, but I don't want us to be one. I just want to wait a little while before we announce it. And it could be a good thing. Look how well Reed reacted when I left him that message about us living together months after I moved in."

CJ's mouth tips up in the corner.

He knows exactly how Reed reacted. I told him. And even though my brother was pissed off at first, he quickly cooled down and accepted it.

Hopefully, this won't be any different. We just need to wait.

CJ exhales a breath, pulling me firmer against him. "All right," he says. "I won't say shit about it tonight."

"Thank you." I tip my head up, inviting him in for a kiss he takes without hesitation. When it ends, I snuggle close, allowing CJ to wrap his arms around me once more. "Do you want me to leave you two alone so you can properly catch up?" I ask. "I don't mind."

"We can properly catch up with you in my arms, babe. That's where I want you."

I am so happy he says that.

I smile against his neck. And while I do that, I wonder

who holds the record for the time it took to fall in love with somebody, and further wonder if I'm on my way to breaking that record.

It's got to be close.

Leaning back, I slide my hands to CJ's face and go in for a deeper, hotter, heavier kiss he reciprocates with passion. Then I pull away, both of us panting, and press my lips lightly against his once more.

"Tell me a secret," he murmurs.

I smile against his mouth. "I'm falling so fast for you."

MY TWELVE-HOUR SHIFT is uneventful, which is a surprise. I'm expecting a few firework mishaps, but the worst I get is this adorable little boy who closed his hand around a sparkler. He was brave about it, big fat tears spilling down his face, but no cries escaping him as he held his mother's hand while the doctor and nurse I was shadowing did their thing. It's rare that I get an adult who takes pain like that. But kids? They can be some of the bravest people. It's inspiring.

It's almost nine in the morning by the time I get home, and I'm yawning like crazy. I don't know how people work overnight. I don't think I could do it. This whole sleeping with the sun up thing might mess with me, even though stepping inside the entryway of CJ's house, I feel like I could drop right here. Before that happens, I set my book bag on a stool and head straight for the bedroom.

CJ is still asleep, rolled up on his side and facing the window. I kick off my sneakers and move into the bathroom without disturbing him, strip out of my scrubs and sports bra, and wash up. I'm skipping a shower since I'm too exhausted for that, but I do run a wet washcloth over myself. After brushing my teeth and washing my face, I exit the bathroom, walk around the bed, and climb in under the covers, snuggling against CJ's warm chest when he lifts his arm as an invite.

"Hi," I whisper.

He presses a kiss to my forehead, and in a deep, sleep heavy voice, asks me, "Did you have a good night?"

"Yeah. I think I decided what I want to specialize in."

"What?"

"Pediatrics."

CJ's arm around me gives me a squeeze. "I'm sure you'll kick ass at it like everything else. You're fucking unstoppable."

He says that as if he *knows* I'd be good at this.

God . . .

I smile, leaning back to look at him and running my hand through his bedhead hair. "How was your night? Were the fireworks good?"

"They weren't bad," he answers, shoulder jerking. "I'm glad Jake didn't go though. There were a ton of people there getting fucked up."

"When will you see him again?"

"Not sure. He can't be taking leave all the time. And I don't think he's stopping here again before he heads back to South Carolina. He'll want to spend that time with his girl." CJ's hand comes up, and his heavy-lidded eyes follow his thumb as he brushes a strand of hair off my cheek. "I'm glad I got to see him though. I worry about him."

"You're a really good brother," I say, gathering that from the little time I spent with the two of them, and just from knowing the kind of man CJ is. Our eyes lock. I grin, but hold it for less than a second before I'm breaking it with a yawn I can't fight.

CJ draws me against him again, laughing softly inside his chest. "I'm going to get up," he murmurs, lips touching above my brow. "I got some stuff to do."

"Okay. I got some sleeping to do."

My eyes are closed before CJ's pulling away, the bed dipping with his weight. I feel the sheet slide up my shoulder and tuck against my neck, his touch on my hip, and his breath against my temple before he presses a kiss there.

"Night, darlin'."

"Morning," I tease.

He chuckles quietly and pulls away. And I never hear the door close. I'm asleep before then.

MY PHONE ALARM wakes me.

I stretch my limbs and snatch it off the pillow CJ uses, frowning at the screen.

I know I didn't put it there. I left my phone in the kitchen before coming to bed. And I *also* know I didn't set my alarm.

Yawning, I turn it off and check the time. It's nearly eight p.m.

Holy crap. I've been sleeping forever.

The house is quiet. I don't hear the TV on—or any noise for that matter—as I scoot out of bed and pull on my hoodie, going pantless for now. I'm just about to head out of the room and look for CJ when my phone beeps with a message.

> *CJ: Meet me at Calvert Stadium.*

Calvert Stadium? Huh? The high school?

> *Me: Hi ;) Did you mean to send that to me?*

> *CJ: Hi, beautiful. Yes I did.*

Beautiful.

I smile and rub at my sleepy eyes.

Me: Why am I meeting you there?

CJ: To celebrate.

To celebrate?
As soon as the question circles my mind, awareness shakes me. My pulse quickens as my thumbs hurry with a response.

Me: You didn't.

CJ: I did.

I gasp, hand flying up to my mouth. No way. *No. way.* He couldn't. It isn't possible. Fireworks on July *fifth?*

Me: Are you being serious right now? Am I really going to see fireworks? I don't believe you.

CJ: Believe it, babe.

I shriek into the silence of the room. My phone nearly slipping out of my hands.
This is why he set my alarm.

Me: OMGGGG I'm getting dressed and leaving RIGHT NOW!

I have to hurry. I cannot miss this.
Tossing my phone on the bed, I rip off my hoodie and tear into the dresser.

AFTER PARKING MY car at the open metal gate that wraps around the stadium seats, I take off running across the track and onto the field.

It's dark out so the lights are on. Bright white light beaming from above. It illuminates CJ's truck that's parked dead center and covering up the school logo.

When I'm nearly at mid-field, he stands up in the bed.

"Oh, my God! CJ!" I call out. "What are you doing? Are you even allowed to park out here?"

This has to be illegal. Or at least highly frowned upon.

His mouth is stretched into a big, beautiful grin as he steps to the back of truck, mindful of the blankets he's spread out.

A pile of them. Pillows too. And wait . . . yep. He has his stereo on. I recognize Sam Hunt.

This is *exactly* what I asked for.

God, is this seriously happening?

"A guy owes me a favor," he vaguely explains. "Don't worry about it. Come on. Let's get you up here." He reaches down with one hand, as if he's going to hoist me up like that.

Ha! Yeah, right.

I gape at him, laughing a little with my hands on my hips. "Uh . . . okay, but if I pull you out of that truck, it's your own fault." I take a hold of his hand and wrap my other around his forearm, and then I'm being lifted off the ground without so much as a grunt in exertion. I squeak when my feet hit the bed. "You're like Thor," I joke.

CJ chuckles. He grabs my waist and pulls me against him, kissing the top of my head.

"Hi," I murmur, pushing my hands through his hair and cupping his cheeks. "Is this real?"

I'm waiting to wake up from the best dream of my life.

He smiles down at me, his hands exploring my bottom and squeezing me roughly through my shorts. "It's what you wanted, right? I told you I'd make it happen."

He sure did.

"Yeah." I drag my thumb over his mouth and press, feeling the heat of CJ's tongue when he opens up and sucks me in. Pure need courses in my blood.

Holy crap, I'm horny.

"So." I drop my hands and wiggle out of his hold. Another second of ass-grabbing and I might beg CJ to take me home so we can fuck. And I don't want to miss his surprise. "Oo. What do we have here?" I kick off my Chucks before crawling over the mound of soft blankets to get to the cooler in the corner of the bed. I grip the handle and rattle it. Objects thump against the sides. "Did you bring us coconut treats?" I ask, voice teasing as I peer back at him over my shoulder.

I know I have to be beaming. This is too perfect.

"You were pretty damn specific in your request, remember?" he answers. "Right down to the exact date you wanted this to happen." He toes off his own sneakers and socks, and it's then I realize he isn't wearing his boot. My face must express my concern because CJ is quick to explain, "It's in the back. It's not like I'm walking around much up here."

"Oh." *That makes sense.* I smile at him, then look up into the dark, starless sky. "When does the show start? Did they tell you?"

"As soon are you're ready for it." CJ lifts his brows and digs his phone out of his pocket, waving it at me. "Just say the word, babe. We'll get this party started."

Excitement pinches in my stomach. *Seriously? He's controlling the fireworks too?* I feel like a kid waking up on Christmas day.

"Do it," I tell him, sitting tall on my knees. "I'm ready. I'm *so* ready."

CJ presses a button on his phone and brings it to his ear. "Yeah, hit it," he says. Three words. That's it, before he's disconnecting the call, stowing his phone away and crawling toward me.

I imagine some sniveling wimp on the other end of the line who cooperates with police in exchange for his freedom, and because of CJ's size and overall badassness, he does what he's told. No questions asked. Including rounding up leftover fireworks from the fourth and setting them off over the local high school football field.

This is all kinds of crazy.

"Is this legal?" I ask, scooting over to allow for room. I fluff a pillow behind me and press my back against it, then ready one for him.

"Sure." CJ gives me a wink. "Like I said, a guy owes me a favor." Our sides touch as the man who makes my heart pound sits down beside me, stretching his legs out. He reaches for the cooler.

"A criminal?" I ask.

His head slowly turns to look at me. "What? No, the coach. I helped him out with the team last year. They sucked. Thanks to me, they went All-state. Not that I'm trying to brag or anything."

"Oh. Well, where did he get the fireworks?"

"They shoot them off at homecoming. He gets them all the time." CJ's mouth twitches as his eyes narrow. He leans closer to me. "Did you think I had some fugitive back there I was keeping out of jail in exchange for making me look fucking awesome in front of you?"

"I don't know!" I giggle, knocking against his side so he straightens up. "This is crazy. We're in the middle of a football field and I'm about to see my first private firework show."

"And eat coconut inspired foods, don't forget." CJ pops the lid on the cooler, reaches inside, and drops two things into my lap.

A carton of coconut water and a Hostess Sno Ball.

I squeal and bounce my legs against the blanket. "Oh, my God! I *love* these!" I cry, tearing into the plastic package with my teeth and fishing out the spongy, flake covered cake. I bite into it and moan around my mouthful.

Coconut heaven.

"So good," I mumble with a sticky tongue.

CJ has his own unpackaged and is biting into it while I suck marshmallow cream off my fingertip.

I giggle when he turns to look at me. Pink coconut flakes cover his lips. He looks adorable. I swallow and lean over. "Here. Let me get that," I whisper, my clean hand bracing on CJ's thigh as I lick along his mouth. "Mm. Yummy."

He groans, tilting his head and pressing our lips together. We kiss, long and slow, and it tastes like candy. Sugar sweet and the richest chocolate. *I'm going to have the best high*, I think. Then the sky booms overhead, and I gasp and break away, looking up at the first burst of color that trickles down to the earth. Red and purple streams.

The smile I'm wearing can go down in the record books.

"Oh, my God! This is amazing!" The air whistles, and another burst of light blooms in the sky. It's white and spar-kles like diamonds. I lift my hand and point, yelling, "Look! Look at that one!"

Having inhaled his Sno Ball, CJ slides down so his head is on the pillow. He grabs my wrist and tugs me. I fall, giggling as I flop across his chest and nearly drop my cake on his face. We laugh together. Then I'm flipping over and resting my head in the crook of his shoulder, watching the sky and nibbling at the chocolate sponge.

The show goes on for at least twenty minutes. The bed of

the truck shaking beneath us with each boom. It's beautiful.
I swear, I've never seen an Alabama sky look like this before.

And I've gone and seen the Fourth of July celebrations
my entire life.

CJ moves his fingers in my hair as I drink my coconut
water and eat another Sno Ball, pointing out my favorite fireworks to him. The ones that glitter and fall down like willow
tree branches. We laugh together at the ones that look like
sperm darting across the sky, and at the duds that seem to poof
out before they're supposed to. CJ messages the coach, telling
him to save the pussy fireworks for homecoming (doing this
jokingly, of course), and I fall back against him and laugh until
my eyes water. We kiss and touch with tacky fingers. I nuzzle
against his side and he wraps his arms around me. And when
the finale starts, a rapid fire of the best of the best, I stand at
the foot of the truck with my arms raised in the air and cheer
at the top of my lungs.

"Wooooo! Yes! That was *awesome!*" I holler when the last
firework burns out and the sky fills with smoke. I close my
eyes and inhale the sulfur air.

Again, I can't remember ever being this happy.

I spin around with my eyes lowered, expecting CJ to still
be on his back, stretched out where I left him. But he's standing
now. I drag my gaze from his thighs and look up.

He tugs off his shirt and drops it on the blanket. Two
condoms he digs out of his pocket are next.

My feet shift beneath me. I fight the urge to run at this
man and hurl myself into his arms. I'm still buzzing from the
sugar and still horny from when he was clutching at my ass. I
can still hear his hot, helpless voice in my ear when I crawled
over him halfway through the show and rubbed my leg against
the bulge in his shorts.

"Here?" I ask, almost shyly, and clearly knowing the answer already. I just want to hear CJ say it, because I can't believe we're going to do this out in the open. I've never . . .

"I told my buddy to take a walk. It's just us," he says, eyes hungry and roaming over my body. They linger on the V in my top. "Show me."

Not needing another prompt, I lift the hem of my shirt over my head and drop it onto the blanket. CJ's nostrils flare. My breasts are smashed high and together behind the strict confines of my bra. I reach for the clasp in the front and slowly work it open, teasing us both. The summer air tickles my cleavage.

"Goddamn, your fucking body," CJ growls when I bare myself to him, hard nipples and heavy flesh that begins to ache. He shoves down his shorts and boxers, his stiff dick springing free and smacking against his stomach when he straightens up. "Lose the shorts, darlin'," he orders as he slowly strokes himself.

I watch his hand work, studying the way he pleasures himself. It feels good for him, I know, but I know CJ better. This is all for me.

My need goes into overdrive.

I step out of my shorts and panties, get halfway to CJ and stop to tug off my socks, cursing and causing him to laugh. Then I reach his outstretched arm. We pull each other down, both of us gripping and putting our mouths on as much skin as we can. My tongue on his chest and his lips warm and sucking on my neck.

"Oh, God," I moan, back arching off the blanket when CJ slips a finger inside me and nuzzles his mouth between my legs. I grasp at his hair and hook my legs over his thick shoulders, digging my heels into the large muscles in his back.

"More. *Please*, CJ please," I beg.

He pushes another finger inside me and pumps his hand, murmuring how sweet my pussy is. How tight. How perfect for him to fuck. I beg him to do it. I tell him to fuck me, but I know CJ well. I know he likes to make me come first before we do anything else. He says he needs it. Needs to watch and taste my sweet on his tongue. He acts like a starved animal finally being fed after days. And God, he looks so fucking good down there.

Messy hair and serious eyes. And mine.

My orgasm slams into me when he adds a third finger, and I cry out into the night. Then I'm the one starved and taking, taking, taking. I sit up and push CJ onto his back, grab a condom off the blanket and tear it open with my teeth. I stroke his cock, then slide the rubber down, fitting it like I know how to do now. CJ likes it when I put on a condom for him, and considering how much sex we've been having, I've had a lot of practice with it. And I like to do it, too. I like him watching me, like I'm the only woman who's ever done this for him before.

I like to imagine that's true.

I straddle his hips and reach behind me, wrapping my hand around him as he gropes at my breasts.

"Ride me, beautiful girl," CJ pants, his chest heaving as I position his thick shaft between my legs. I slowly lower down, his wet mouth opening and his head tilting back, eyes closing to moan, *"Fuck yes."* His hands fly to my hips and he squeezes when I'm stretched deliciously full.

I whimper and arch my neck, taking the second I need to get used to his size. Biting my lip and breathing heavy. And then I flatten my hands on his stomach, look down into his face and gently rock my hips back and forth.

Being above this strong, powerful man and giving him pleasure like this, there's nothing like it. The way CJ stares at me, nostrils flaring, the tightness in his jaw, how his fingers grip into my skin as I rock faster . . . and faster, it's so goddamn hot. I reach back and cup his balls, rolling them in my palm and squeezing a little. He growls, the sound tearing out of this throat, and I know my playtime is over.

CJ thrusts up into me, grabbing my thighs and slamming me down, making me bounce on his dick. His eyes stay on my breasts as they jerk and sway. He tells me he wants to fuck them, then gets them wet with his mouth and sucks hard on my nipple, making me moan and beg.

"God, you sound so fucking hot when you take me," he rasps, dropping his head back and staring up at my body. My mouth.

I give him a little smile, then I lean down and lick up his chest to his neck. I bite his jaw. "And you look so fucking good when you give it," I whisper in his ear.

He groans and slaps my ass.

I giggle, then I lean back and grind my hips down, hard, wanting to drive him wild. I grab his hand and suck sugar and the taste of my pussy off his fingers. CJ's eyes burn. He looks like he wants to eat me alive.

I tell him I love the way he looks at me. I almost tell him I think I love *him*.

We fuck and then we slow down and savor each other. I'm on my back and CJ is between my legs, hips swiveling and lips against my ear. I cling to his back and stare up at the night sky, listening to his whispered words and the sounds of his moans over the music playing.

"I'm crazy about you," he says, working his cock in and out while he stares down at me. His one hand between us, thumbing my nipple. "Fuck . . . you're all I think about anymore, Riley. Tell me you feel that."

Pleasure spirals through me. I don't know what does it, his words or how long CJ's been building this by moving inside me the way he's doing, but my legs tighten around his hips, all of my muscles locking up, and just like that I come, *so, freaking, hard.* "Oh, God," I groan. "Oh, God. *Oh, my God.*"

CJ's body jerks in my arms, and then he's crashing his mouth against mine while slamming into me, fucking me hard now.

"Fuck. *Fuck,*" he pants, at the edge. Right there . . . I feel him swell inside me. Then he buries his face in my neck, plants himself to the root and groans, deep and raw and beautiful.

All man. Nothing compares to the noises CJ makes. *Nothing.* And I've heard baby giggles.

I blink heavily and stare up at the endless night sky, moving my hands over the smooth planes of his back. "I feel it too," I whisper, biting my lip. "I'm crazy about you too. Insane. Like, mental institution crazy."

I want CJ to tell me he wouldn't do all of this for anyone else. To say I'm different. That's it's *me.* Only me.

To admit he's falling in love, so I can say it back.

But instead he holds me tighter, presses his lips to my neck, breathes deeply, and murmurs, "Darlin'," right below my ear.

Just *darlin'.* That's it. And I realize that is *all* I wanted and needed to hear him say.

With tears in my eyes and the biggest smile on my face, I am *officially* at my happiest.

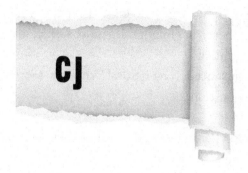

CJ

"**T**HIS IS GOING to be *so weird*."

I cut the engine of my truck and unlatch my seat belt, looking over at Riley after she speaks.

Her head is down, and her fingers are twisting nervously together in her lap. She started fidgeting more and more the closer we got to Ben and Mia's, bouncing her leg against the seat or chewing on the side of her thumb, but when she saw me noticing it, she'd stop and play it off with a smile.

She's not trying to hide it from me anymore. Or maybe she can't.

"What's that, darlin'?" I ask, throwing my arm behind her and gripping the back of the seat.

Riley sighs. "I'm not going to be able to kiss you in there, or sit real close or do anything that might give off the impression that we're totally banging all over your house." She looks over at me, pouting like this is going to kill her. "And you can't be putting your hands on me or stare at my chest the way you're always doing. We basically have to act repulsed by each other. And I honestly don't know if I'm going to be able to do that."

My mouth twitches. *Christ, she's damn cute when she's stressed out.* "I don't think we need to go *that* far with it," I counter. "Your brother knows you're living with me. If you start cussing me out in there, that might raise more suspicions than if we're sitting together."

"So, you think we just need to act natural," she says, more as a statement than a question.

"Sure. Why not?"

"Okay." Riley twists her upper body so she's facing me, sits up tall, and gives me an easy smile.

I give her one back. A second later, my eyes fall to her tits that are pushing out thanks to her change in posture.

Goddamn. I want to put my face all up in that.

"CJ!" she snaps.

I lift my gaze. Riley's doing this wide-eyed glare thing, tipping forward and pinching her lips together. "What?" I ask, looking out the windshield. I'm expecting to see Reed standing at the front of my truck, pointing Ben's gun at me. He isn't. "What's the problem?" I turn to look at Riley.

"You can't act *natural*. You were just staring at my boobs. If that's natural for you, we're going to have major problems at this shindig."

I cock my head. "We're alone, darlin'," I remind her. "Unless you go in there and tell your brother I was just checking out your killer fucking rack, he won't know I was doing it. I can be discreet when I need to be. Right now, sitting with you in my truck is not one of those times." I give her a smile, take my hand out from behind her shoulder and brush my knuckles along her cheek. "Riley, babe, I think you're worrying a little too much about this," I tell her. "It'll be fine. Trust me."

Seriously. What does she think I'm going to do? Bend her over the table and fuck her right there in front of everyone?

I mean, obviously, I'd wait for Reed to step out of the room.

Riley leans back, blinking. "You won't have a problem keeping things friendly in there?"

"I think I can handle it."

"Well, *I* might have a problem," she's quick to say, eyes widening in panic. "I'll want to kiss you. I know I will. You'll do that thing where you *look at me* . . ." Riley's voice trails off, then she drops her head and turns away, shyly tucking her hair behind her ear as her teeth rake across her lip.

"Where I *look at you?*" I chuckle. Riley jerks her shoulder. *Holy fuck, she's serious.*

Just me looking at her gets her going? Nice.

Grinning, I unlatch her seat belt, wrap my arm around her waist and yank her against me so she's pressed to my side. I drop my mouth beside her ear. "Maybe we should get it out of your system then. That way you're not fighting it too much," I murmur, pinching her chin between my thumb and finger and turning her head. My lips graze her cheek. I want Riley to take this opportunity. Take what she needs from me. "Nobody's out here," I remind her. "Nobody will see us." I press my lips to the corner of her mouth. Her jaw, when she tips her head back. I hear the quickness in her breath. "Kiss me," I say.

Riley leans forward on a gasp and seals our mouths together, moaning like she's desperate and dying for this. Her hand curls around my thigh while mine cups her cheek. I tilt my head, taking what I need from her too. I can't help it.

I told her I'll be able to handle this but the truth is, I don't want to have to. I want to kiss Riley whenever the fuck I want, in front of *whoever* I want. I want to put my arm around her and hold her hand and watch her from across the room. I want people assuming we're going to sit together because we *are* together. I've been keeping this shit to myself for what feels like a goddamn lifetime, and I really don't want to do that anymore. I don't want to go in there and pretend I'm not completely insane for this girl. I don't want to act like we're nothing. Fuck that. I think I can handle it? That's a damn lie. `Cause I have no fucking idea how I'm going to get through this.

Riley pushes up, pressing harder as her tongue flicks inside my mouth. She tastes like the peppermint she sucked on before we left the house.

She tastes like she's mine, and I gotta go in there and act like she isn't.

"*Fuck*," I rasp. "Let's just tell him. Let's just fucking say we're together."

Riley shakes her head, murmuring against my lips, "No. No, we can't. Not yet."

"Riley—"

"We *can't*," she insists, pulling back an inch to look at me. Her eyes jump between mine, and she grabs my face, begging with an anxious voice, "*Please*. We can't tell him, CJ. Not today. Not here."

I pull in a deep breath. My jaw clenches beneath her palms. *Fuck*. That's not what I want to hear.

Riley must see my bitter disappointment, because her eyes soften and her lips pull down. "This will be the first time Reed is seeing us together since I told him I'm living with you," she reminds me. "I want to see how he reacts to that first, you know? I want to make sure he's okay with it, `cause the first time he saw Richard and me together, he wasn't. Reed acted like he couldn't stand either one of us. And I just . . . I want to make sure he's good with seeing us together, okay?" She drops her hands to her lap and shakes her head. "I don't like this either," she says, sounding defeated. "I don't. But Reed . . . he said he's not going to be shy about hating the next person I date. He actually *said that* to me. And I just think easing him into this might be better. I'm sorry, CJ. I want to go in there and tell everybody. I do. Please don't be mad at me."

"I'm not mad at you," I tell her, understanding why she wants to feel him out. I watch Riley give me a weak smile in response, still looking just as sad and *fuck*, I feel like a dick. Could I bitch *any more*? Why am I pushing this with her? I don't want Riley apologizing to me.

Her hand smooths down the front of my shirt, and she opens her mouth to tell me something, probably another sorry I don't need to hear, so I grab the back of her neck and bend down, pressing my lips against hers again. I kiss her hard and quick, then jerking back, I end the kiss before I can't.

"Come on. Let's go," I say, pushing my door open. I hop out of the truck, turn back and watch Riley hesitate getting out, looking at the dash and smiling behind her fingertips.

A real smile. One I know well. She gives it to me a lot.

And when a man has a woman giving him a smile like that—daily, the way Riley does with me—he's one lucky motherfucker.

And he damn sure shouldn't be bitching, having what he's got.

Riley finally gets out of the truck and meets me around the driver's side. I'm still strapping on my boot after grabbing it out of the back seat.

"How's your leg after driving?" she asks.

I'm prepared for this question. I knew Riley was going to ask it. I haven't driven us anywhere together yet, and she was reluctant letting me do it today.

"Same," I answer. And that's the truth. I don't feel a difference after driving. I don't feel much of a difference after doing anything anymore. Not after PT. Not after walking on it. Not after doing shit she doesn't think I'm supposed to be doing. But I don't tell Riley that. Tipping my head up as I fasten the Velcro, I squint in the sun and watch her lips pull between her teeth. "What?"

"Maybe I should drive us home," she suggests.

"Did I just say my leg was killing me?"

"No, but it might start bothering you if you push it too much," she explains, her shoulders jerking. "I don't mind driving. Really."

She's adorable. I stand tall after finishing with the straps. "Don't take this the wrong way, darlin', but the only person driving this beauty is me," I tell her, lowering a heavy hand onto the lip of the bed and then stroking it lovingly. "I don't care how much you kick ass at everything you put your mind to. You're not driving my truck. *I'll* drive us home."

Riley cocks her head. "I know how to drive a stick," she shares.

"Oh, I know you do." I give her a wink, smiling at her.

Might as well get all of my innuendos out of the way now. I won't be able to say shit like that in front of Reed.

The sweetest look of confusion passes over Riley's face. "Uh, you've never seen me drive a stick," she says. "So how do you . . ." Her eyes widen, then she rolls them away, shaking her head and mumbling, "*Oh, my God.* I walked *right* into that one," before turning around and heading up the driveway.

Laughing, I follow behind, weaving in between the other cars. It looks like we're the last ones here. When we step up onto the porch, Riley knocks on the door and I stand beside her. I place my hand on her ass and give it a squeeze.

She gasps. Blush reddens her cheek. "CJ," she warns. Voice low and worry filled.

I drop my hand and fold my arm up behind me when the

door swings open. *See? I'm like a goddamn ninja.*

And she's stressing.

"Hey, you two," Mia greets us, smiling and stepping back to allow us room to enter. "Just in time. The burgers are almost ready."

"Were we supposed to bring anything?" Riley asks, stepping inside the house. "I couldn't remember if you said to."

"Nope. Beth brought the sides. We're good." Mia grabs Riley's hand, gives me a knowing look when I enter the house, then takes off down the hallway with my girl, whispering close and acting like she's in a hurry.

I close the door behind me and head in the same direction.

Everyone is outside gathered on the deck, the guys standing by the grill and Tessa standing at the opposite end by the table, looking out into the yard. Kids squeal below; Nolan and Chase. I'm guessing Beth is down there with them since she isn't up here.

When Riley gets close to Tessa, Tessa grabs her, gives me the same look Mia gave me over Riley's shoulder, and then smiles and turns away, engrossing Riley in conversation.

I don't know what the fuck I'm getting looks for.

Do the girls know about us? Has Riley been talking?

Christ. Whatever. If I keep looking over there this shit is going to seem obvious, and Reed's out here, so I don't. I cross the deck and step up next to Luke.

"What's up?" I say, looking around and getting acknowledged by Reed and Ben. My eyes land on some young guy I don't recognize. I couldn't see him when I walked up. He was being blocked by Luke.

"Beers are in the cooler," Luke shares, then he tips his bottle at the guy. "Meet your new partner. This is Grayson. He just got hired on."

My brows lift. I look from Luke back to Grayson. "No shit," I say, offering out my hand to him. "Did you just graduate?"

He grips my hand firmly. "Yeah. Damn, is it obvious?" he asks, sounding a little nervous. He releases me and pushes his hand through his short blonde hair.

I chuckle. "Rookies are pretty easy to spot. Plus, you're still sporting that Academy haircut. So's Luke though, so it's all good."

Luke side-eyes me while Ben laughs under his breath and continues flipping burgers.

"Christ. It's about time," I continue, pulling my arms across my chest. "I've been waiting for them to assign someone to me. My last partner was a fucking dickhead." I give Grayson a look. "You're not a fucking dickhead, are you?"

I'm just messing with him, but Grayson looks like he might shit his pants. The kid is actually sweating.

"I'm kidding, man," I tell him. "Relax. You seem cool."

"CJ likes to joke around," Reed announces, speaking up finally and wearing a smirk. "He thinks he's funny."

"I am funny. Ask your sister."

His brows pull together and his face hardens.

Fuck. Why'd I say that? I'm baiting him. Next he's going to ask me when Riley thinks I'm funny, and I'm of course going to answer *all the time, except for when we're making sweet, sweet love . . .*

"I heard about what happened to you," Grayson throws out, drawing Reed's attention and then my own, taking the heat off me. I like this kid already. He points at my boot. "Are you gonna be coming back soon?" he asks. "Do you know?"

I want to say yes. I want to say I don't even really need this fucking boot anymore, but I don't. Not with present company twenty-feet away.

"I'm not where I want to be yet, but I'm getting there," I tell him, risking a glance at Riley. I watch her press her hand to her chest and drop her head back with a laugh. *We're not where I want to be yet*, I think. Then I turn my head, knowing I can't be looking long, and when I catch his eye, Grayson tips his chin in understanding and takes a swig of his beer.

Good fucking idea.

Five minutes here and I've already made Reed suspicious. On top of that, I've noticed how fucking hot my woman looks when she's just hanging out with her girls. That's something I'd like to sit back and stare at. And since I can't, there's no way I'm getting through this without alcohol. I move to the cooler. "Anyone want another?" I ask, flipping back the lid.

"Grab me one, will you?" Ben requests. He takes the bottle I hold out, then looks over his shoulder across the deck. "Angel, you wanna bring out the rest of the food and get the table set? Burgers will be ready in two."

"Sure thing, babe," Mia replies.

I straighten up, twist the cap off my beer and take a swig, watching as Mia and Tessa head inside the house. Riley walks over to where the guys are all standing, meeting my eyes briefly before looking toward Reed. She steps up between Luke and Grayson and smiles. "Mia said I didn't need to help, but I want to. Is there anything I can do?" she asks, directing her question at Ben.

He finishes sliding a burger onto a plate and turns to look at her. "Yeah. You wanna help Beth get my boys up here? They're probably covered in dirt."

"Sure. Absolutely," Riley replies with enthusiasm. "I can do that."

"Appreciate it. Thanks." Ben turns back to the grill.

Grayson holds his hand out to Riley before she is able to move away. "Hey. I'm Grayson."

"Riley. Hi." She shakes his hand and smiles friendly. "Nice to meet you."

He gives her a lingering look, grinning after they separate. They got to be close in age. "Florida Georgia Line," he says, pointing at her top; the words *That's How We Do It Round Here* written in black and gold lettering. "Right?"

Riley nods, briefly looking down at herself. "Yeah. They're one of my favorite bands," she reveals.

"Me too," Grayson shares, looking really fucking happy about the two of them appreciating the same music. *Really fucking happy about it.*

Ah, Christ . . .

"Easy, man," Luke mumbles behind his bottle, speaking low enough I'm the only one hearing him.

I shoot him a look, then realize the expression I had watching my new partner hit on my girl is the exact same expression I'm hitting Luke with. Didn't even realize I was wearing one, but I am.

Arms across my chest. Mouth tight. Brow furrowed. Jaw clenching hard. And hand threatening to smash this beer bottle if I don't ease up with my grip.

Luke and Ben don't know shit about Riley and me except that we're living together. And that we had sex at the wedding—that information coming from their women, which they wasted no time busting my balls about when they both saw me on the Fourth. They don't know any more than that. I haven't said a word, and Riley hasn't either. But I'd be shocked if Luke wasn't at least suspicious now. And if *he's* suspicious . . .

I cut my eyes to Reed, meeting his narrowed ones.

Fuck.

Inhaling a deep breath, I try and relax, putting my attention back on Grayson as he keeps at it.

"I saw them live last year when I was living in Huntsville. They were awesome," he says. "They put on a real good show."

"Yeah, I heard that. I heard they were really good live."

"They might be coming to that South Will Rise festival in August," he shares. "I'm trying to get tickets. I could—"

I know exactly where this conversation is going. And over my dead body is it going there.

His too.

"Maybe you should hold up buying tickets to something like that," I interrupt, my suggestion sounding more like a fucking command he needs to follow.

Grayson quickly looks over at me, blinking like a deer in headlights.

I glance at Riley before I say any more and watch the blush warm her cheeks and her lips press together. "I'm just saying," I continue on a shrug, voice firm and eyes slicing back to Grayson. "We work a lot of weekends. I don't want you wasting your money."

Or your fucking time, which is exactly what you're doing here.

He nods slowly, thinking it over. "Yeah, that's true. Good idea. I'll probably wait," he agrees, seeming to genuinely appreciate the heads up I'm giving him. Grayson turns back to Riley.

I do the same.

Her eyes jump from him to me.

"Don't you gotta be helping with the boys?" I ask before Grayson opens his mouth first and suggests they go to fucking prom together. "Food's ready."

Riley's eyes widen and briefly land on the back of Ben, then she spins around and hurries to the stairs like she's worried he'll say something to her about not helping out yet.

Luke laughs under his breath, the all-knowing bastard. I'm sure his dumb ass is enjoying this.

I chug half of my beer and wonder what Jacobs—my old partner—is up to.

"Hats off to whoever built this deck," Reed says, grinning proudly. He leans his elbow against the rail and surveys his work, looking across the length of it. "Fine quality craftsmanship. I don't think I've seen better."

"Thanks," Ben smugly replies. "I remember doing most of the work myself."

Reed glares at him. "*You* did most of the work yourself? You *helped*, Ben. And I use that word lightly. The only real thing you did was bust my balls about Beth."

"`Cause you were fucked." Ben takes the last burger off the grill and slides it onto the plate. He laughs at Reed. "Don't try and deny it, man. We all remember how pathetic you were."

"Yep," Luke throws out, grinning.

Reed scowls, looking between the two of them. "Oh, like you two didn't act like a bunch of pussies when it came to your women. Fuck you," he says. His head turns just as Beth emerges from the stairs, then he straightens up, watching her smile at him. "Yeah, I'm pathetic. For her? I'll be pathetic all damn day," he mumbles, stepping away to get to his wife.

Luke and Ben laugh while walking over to the table. Grayson moves around me to get to the cooler, freeing up my line of sight.

I watch Riley step up onto the deck. She's carrying Chase, smiling at him and poking his stomach, making him giggle. My chest expands as I stare at her sweet dimples and the way the sun reflects off her hair.

"Hey, CJ."

I look down at Nolan after he speaks. He's got dirt smeared on his forehead and sand in his hair. "What's up, man? How you doing?"

"I'm okay." He stuffs his hands into his front pockets, keeping his head lowered. "Ms. Riley said she had to carry Chasey and couldn't carry me," he shares, looking disappointed.

"Well, he is a lot smaller than you."

"He can walk up the stairs. He does it all the time." Nolan sighs and kicks at the deck. "Did my dad tell you I got a girl now?" he asks, peering up at me.

My mouth twitches. "Oh yeah? What's her name?"

"Ryan. She's my age. I send her pictures I draw."

"Sounds serious."

Nolan nods, a heavy breath leaving him. "Yeah. I'm a wreck."

I chuckle, head turning. "I feel ya, man," I say, watching Riley take a wipe out of the pack on the table and clean off Chase's hands.

"Nolan, come get washed up," Mia calls from inside the house. The little guy walks around me. "Luke, CJ, can you grab some of this stuff so we can eat?"

I set my beer down on the corner of the table and step through the slider.

Mia hands me a bowl of potato salad and a plate of cut up tomatoes, gives Luke two things to carry, and then grabs some serving spoons. "Here." She sets them on top of the cellophane. "Tell everyone to start eating. I'll be out in a second," she informs us before ushering Nolan down the hallway and into the bathroom below the stairs.

Tessa moves around the counter carrying a serving tray of mac and cheese, grinning at me like she's in on some big secret.

My eyes narrow.

Yep. I fucking knew it. Riley has definitely been talking. And the fact that Tessa knows means I'm about to get all kinds of shit right now.

That's how she operates, especially if she's happy for you.

"How's it going?" Tessa asks me, stopping close.

"Fine," I grunt.

"Ha! Yeah, okay." She glances outside. "The new guy seems nice. *Very* friendly . . ."

My mouth hardens.

"Babe," Luke warns.

Tessa ignores him and gives me a wink. "Good luck out there, Tully," she says. "We're all rooting for you. Well, maybe not Reed." She smiles big before moving away and stepping through the slider.

"Unbelievable," I mumble. *The new guy seems nice? So much for friends.* I look to Luke.

"She ain't wrong," he offers. "He seems like a good kid. And you two should get along good, considering what all you got in common." A grin slowly spreads across his mouth.

I glare at him. Luke's grin keeps spreading.

"Shut the fuck up," I growl. "And move your ass already. I'm starving."

Throwing his head back with a laugh, Luke follows his wife outside.

The table is rectangular, with four chairs on each long side and one on each end. Ben is seated at the head of the table with Chase in his lap. Reed is next to him, then Beth and Riley, leaving one chair vacant on that side.

My chair. That's where I'm sitting, and I don't give a damn who's got something to say about it.

"Where's Mia?" Ben asks.

I step up to the table and set down what I'm carrying.

what i need 303

"She's getting Nolan cleaned up. She said to start," I tell him, head lifting when movement catches my eye.

Grayson slides out the seat next to Riley and claims it.

My nostrils flare.

What the fuck? Am I going to have to kill this kid?

"We'll wait," Ben announces, letting everyone know not to take a bite until his wife gets out here.

I kick out the chair next to Luke and slump down in it, planting myself directly across from Riley.

Ben and Reed start talking about baby proofing or some shit like that. Tessa chimes in. I don't pay attention. I'm watching Riley. She's smiling at Grayson, being polite and keeping their conversation going after he initiates it. I having no fucking clue what they're talking about though. Blood starts rushing in my ears when Grayson throws his arm on the back of Riley's chair. I hear my heart beat and the muffled voices of everyone around me, that's it. Then Grayson leans closer to Riley and laughs at something she says. Seeing that, I look over at Reed, thinking he should open his fucking mouth and say something to this kid for looking comfortable with his sister, but instead, he starts filling up his plate while keeping conversation with Ben.

My eyes narrow. *Really?* I so much as look at Riley and Reed's got a problem.

Asshole.

Luke and Ben go about filling up their plates too, and to keep myself from tossing Grayson off the deck, I do the same, scooping out helpings of sides and fixing up both of my burgers.

The slider opens and closes behind me. Nolan runs outside and climbs into the chair at my right. And when Mia finally claims her seat at the table, sitting directly across from Ben, everyone starts eating.

Conversation carries on between the group, minus me, while Grayson keeps hitting Riley up with questions. He's interested in her. That's for damn sure. Smiling. Keeping his arm on her chair instead of using two hands to eat.

Who the fuck eats a burger with one hand? There's something wrong with this kid.

"Hey." Luke nudges me with his elbow. He's talking low.

"What?" I grunt, not turning my head.

"You might wanna ease up on that fork. I think it belonged to Mia's mom or some shit."

I look down at the fork in my hand and notice my thumb pressing the handle into a bend.

Shit.

Dropping my hands to my lap, I straighten the silver so it's no longer curved.

"Relax," Luke mumbles.

"*You* relax," I mumble back. I toss the fork next to my plate.

Relax. *Right.* That's not happening. Now I know how Reed felt last year when I was making a play for Beth in front of him at game night. He sat there looking ready to rip my head off. And I am *right there* watching this kid with Riley. This fucking sucks.

Luke shakes his head before looking away and taking a pull of his beer.

Like he wouldn't shoot a motherfucker for even looking at Tessa. Fuck him.

Riley laughs at something Grayson says, getting my attention again. She's being friendly, that's all she's doing, I know that, but it still pisses me off.

I glare at the two of them while I sit forward and shovel

food into my mouth. Minutes pass. I don't talk much, except to Nolan when he shows me the Legos he has in his pocket, wanting my opinion on the figurine he built. Other than that, I don't engage. And when Riley eventually glances across the table at me, assessing my reaction to the shit I'm having to witness, the shit I've *been* having to witness, I don't hide it from her. I keep my eyes hard and narrowed. If she's expecting a smile and a thumbs up, she's not getting one. Riley can know how much this is bothering me. I don't care. What the fuck is she expecting me to do? Be *okay* with this?

Her face burns hot seeing my reaction. Then she looks away, turning back to Grayson when he speaks.

"Do you want to like, work in the OR? Have you decided what you want to do after you graduate?" he asks her.

"She's specializing in pediatrics," I answer, voice firm and loud enough it cuts into the conversations going on around me.

Riley's head snaps in my direction. Her eyes flicker wider in surprise.

Yeah, baby. I'm listening. And I fucking know you well enough to answer every goddamn question he's asking.

"Oh." Grayson's brows lift. "That's really cool," he tells her.

"I didn't know that," Reed throws out, leaning forward to look at Riley. "When did you decide?"

"Just recently," Riley answers. "I hadn't really told anyone yet."

"You told me," I say, smirking when I get her eyes.

Riley's blush creeps down to her neck. Beth quietly congratulates her while Riley drinks the rest of her water.

Grayson gets to his feet. "Do you want another?" he asks, pointing to her bottle. "I'll grab you one."

"Sit down," I growl.

Everyone goes fucking quiet. Even Nolan, who's been talking to himself while he walks his Lego knight around his plate, and Chase, who babbles constant nonsense. Nobody speaks. I feel ten sets of eyes on me but I'm only focusing on one. Riley looks like she might pass out—the color drains from her face. She knows I'm pissed.

As for everyone else, if it wasn't already obvious I got a problem watching someone hit on Riley, it's obvious now. I'm pretty sure Chase is even aware.

And you know what? Oh fucking well.

I shove my chair back and stand as Grayson slowly lowers himself into his seat, blinking at me. "I'll get it. I'm getting up anyway," I explain, snatching up my plate and empty beer bottle. I carry them with me inside, disposing of them in the trash and recycling bins underneath the kitchen counter.

Do I feel bad for exploding like that? Not one fucking bit. They're lucky it didn't happen sooner.

Lifting my head after closing the cabinet door, I look out the window above the sink.

Everyone is back to talking and eating, except Riley. She's picking at her burger bun and looking down at her plate.

Do I feel bad now? Yeah, okay. Maybe.

Grayson leans forward to look at her. He tucks her hair behind her ear to see her face.

"*Motherfucker*," I snarl, lips curling against my teeth.

I do that. I tuck Riley's hair behind her ear. I throw my arm behind her and talk real close and make her laugh. Not this guy. Not anyone else.

Me.

Fuck feeling bad and fuck this.

I spin around and prowl to the fridge, nearly ripping the door off the hinges I throw it open so hard.

I'm getting back out there and taking that seat. I don't give a fuck. Let Reed say something to me, I will straight up knock his ass out. He hasn't said shit to Grayson about being all over my girl and he's on the verge of fucking proposing.

I grab another bottled water for Riley and a beer I see hiding behind the milk for me. Might as well. I'm going to need it. When I turn to head back outside, the slider opens and Riley steps through it.

She closes the glass door and stares at me from where she's standing on the other side of the counter, telling me she's sorry with her eyes and her frowning lips, but she's saying something else too. I know that look. Goddamn, I know it. That heat in her eyes, blue flames burning 'cause she needs me and doesn't care where we're at right now or who could possibly catch us.

Her chest starts heaving.

Mine goes fucking *tight*.

Riley doesn't say a word before she starts moving. She takes off down the hallway, sneakers smacking against the wood, and as soon as I set the bottles down on the counter, I'm following close behind. I don't even look to see if anyone's coming in the house. I don't care.

We climb the stairs. I don't know where the fuck she's taking us. I've never been up here. I'm letting Riley lead.

She stops at the first door she comes to when she's finished climbing, puts her hand on the knob and glances back at me—for encouragement, for me to stop her, I don't know. If Riley's expecting me to be the one to have sense in this situation, she's shit out of luck. I want her. All the time and right now, so fucking bad. I'll take her right here if she doesn't get us somewhere private.

Reading that on my face or deciding for herself, Riley

twists the knob and steps inside.

"I'm sorry," she whispers when I grab her face and kiss her hard. I kick the door closed and slam her against it. She gasps and moans, purring deep in her throat. Her leg curls around the back of my thigh. "CJ . . ."

"I don't want him touching you," I growl. Riley starts whimpering *I know I know I know.* She's breathless. "I don't want him looking at you, thinking he has a chance. Thinking you're fucking his to take." I shove my tongue inside her mouth, slant her head with my hand and kiss her deeper. "I can't sit there anymore and act like I don't give a shit. I can't. You're mine, Riley. You're fucking *mine.* He needs to know that. I want him knowing, you hear me?"

"Yes . . . yes," she pants.

My other hand works frantically between us while Riley kisses the shit out of me—sucking on my tongue, my lips. Biting. Licking. Acting like she's never been this turned on before and just hearing me say she's mine is getting her there. I undo my shorts and free my cock. Her hand slides down my stomach and wraps around me, squeezing hard. We both groan.

"*Fuck.*"

"CJ . . ."

"Are we doing this?" I ask while I pop the button on her shorts, while I shove them down her legs and pull them past her Chucks. I don't give her time to answer and she doesn't ask for it. Riley jumps up, hitches her legs around my hips, grabs hold of my neck with one hand and pulls her panties to the side with the other, slanting her pelvis to take me.

"Yes," she whispers, nodding quickly. "Please, do it. Please now please . . ."

I stare at her begging lips and those big blue eyes and

fuck, I can smell her. How wet she is. How much she's wanting me. Wanting this to happen, right here and now, where anyone can find us.

I forget about consequences—getting caught. Reed finding out. This shit exploding in our faces. I forget about the condom I have inside my wallet or the fact that we haven't even bothered to lock the door. I only *feel*—Riley's nails digging into my neck and her legs tightening, drawing me closer. The precum beading up on my dick. I don't think. I don't fight this.

I grip her ass, hoist her up higher on the door and push in, groaning as her tight walls grip me.

"I'm bare," I tell her, kissing her hard. Growling. *Jesus fucking Christ.* "*Fuck*, Riley, if you don't want this . . ."

She moans when I bottom out, loud enough I have to cover her mouth with my hand to keep anyone else from hearing her.

"Baby." I lean back to get my answer. I need to know . . .

Eyes wide, she looks at me, nodding frantically while her breaths burst hot against my palm. "Please," she mumbles. "I want this with you. Fuck me, Cannon."

Pure adrenaline slams into me. My name, *goddamn*, when she says it . . . If there was anything stopping me from continuing on with this, one shred of sanity or clear thinking, that shit just went right out the window.

I cup her ass harder and drop my head beside hers, keeping my hand on her mouth. "I want to be all over you, darlin'," I say, sliding my cock through her pussy, in and out. Tiny thrusts that drive her wild. She gasps in tempo. "I want you fucking smelling like me when you go back outside. He wants to lean close to you, I want him knowing I've been here."

Riley whimpers against my hand.

I thrust up harder, steadily pounding into her. Her pussy

is so wet I can hear it and feel it dripping onto my balls. "I want everyone knowing what we were doing," I rasp, pressing my lips to her cheek. "What we have. What you're giving me. 'Cause you're giving it, baby, aren't you? You're giving me this sweet pussy to come in."

"Yes," she moans, eyes pinching shut. Nostrils flaring with her breaths.

Heat spreads underneath my ribcage. Hearing Riley tell me she wants me to fill her with my cum, *Jesus*, I've never . . . I can't hold back.

Muscles flexing, I buck into her like a wild animal, slamming her ass and the back of my hand against the door. *Thwap. Thwap. Thwap.* I'm grunting. Sweat beads up on my brow. My face is buried in her neck and I'm telling Riley how good she feels, how much I want her. Need her. "So much, baby. So fucking much." And she's crying out and whimpering and panting against my palm. Her heels digging into the back of my thighs and her nails cutting deeper, deeper, deeper. So deep.

"Fuck," I pant. My legs burning. "Riley, I need to come . . ."

She moans and starts tightening around me, as if she was waiting this whole time, waiting for me. Her eyes roll closed. Her pleasure moves through her. I feel her lips open against my palm and then . . .

The doorknob rattles and something pushes against it, but with our weight pressing in, it won't open.

"Hey," a little voice mutters.

Nolan.

I lift my head and turn it, gaging the room we're in for the first time since we stepped inside. Dragon posters cover the wall. There's toys on the nightstand. A twin-sized bed . . .

Jesus Christ. We're in his fucking bedroom.

Riley squeaks as her body tightens up. Her eyes flash open

and meet mine in panic but she's coming, she can't stop it. Nolan's calling out for Mia and rattling the knob and Riley's crying out against my hand, saying my name and soaking my dick.

I gasp and slam her body against the door. Pleasure grips onto me like a vise, and I thrust two, three times before I'm groaning into Riley's neck and coming deep inside her.

We're both panting, her against my palm and me into the soft skin of her shoulder. Chests heaving and hearts racing and mine, *fuck*, mine holding so much love for this girl. More than I've ever felt. More than it's held for anyone.

I am so goddamned fucked.

"Oh, my God," Riley whispers when I slide my hand off her mouth and onto her cheek. She doesn't say it out of worry. She doesn't say it out of panic, either. Her limbs are still wrapped softly around me. Her fingers are feathering through my hair, not pulling. She's not tense. She loves what we just did. "CJ . . ." her voice cuts with a gasp and her body jars against mine when the door tries to open.

"Mommy! My door is stuck!" Nolan yells. "I can't get to my *stuff!*"

"*Shit*," I growl under my breath. I blindly find the lock on the doorknob and secure it before setting Riley on her feet. "What do you want to do? What are we saying?" I ask her as I tug up my boxers and shorts.

The doorknob rattles again.

"What the *crap!*" Nolan whines. "Mommy!"

Riley bends down and steps into her shorts. "I don't know," she whispers. "Um . . . maybe one of us hides?"

My brow furrows. "*What?* I'm not hiding. What if Ben finds me? I don't want to be caught hiding out in his kid's room. That's fucking weird."

"Well, what if Reed comes up here to help Nolan?" Riley asks. She buttons her shorts, looks to the door and lets her hand fall heavy against her thigh while the other grips the back of her neck. "*Crap!* What are we going to do?" she whispers.

"Who's in there?" Nolan jolts the knob. "I can hear you . . ."

Riley whips her head around to look at me. Her eyes are filled with alarm.

"Jesus," I mumble. "Whatever. Easy solution—he's a kid." I take the three steps to get to the door, ignoring Riley's quiet protests and the tugging she does on my arm. The second I twist the lock, Nolan pushes the door open and stumbles inside the bedroom.

"Hey." He looks between Riley and me, blinking in confusion. "What are you guys doing in here?"

Riley squeaks.

Christ. Thank God I'm not leaving this plan up to her. She'd probably give us up immediately after forcing me under the bed.

I dig my wallet out of my pocket and pull out a bill. Then I bend down, getting eye level with Nolan. "Do you like money, kid?" I ask him.

His eyes brighten. He licks his lips. "Yes. I like money."

"Yeah? Have you ever seen a hundred dollar bill before?" I hold up the bill in front of his face.

"CJ," Riley whisper scolds behind me.

I ignore her. In my opinion, this is the only option that doesn't lead to me feeling like a giant fucking creep.

Nolan stares at the bill like he's just discovered buried treasure. Big, gray eyes going round. Lips parting in wonder. "Can I hold it?"

"Yeah, you can hold it. It's yours," I tell him, handing

over the bill.

He blinks at me. "It *is*?" He smiles big when I nod. "Aw, cool! I'm gonna put it in my piggy bank so I can save up for my sword!"

Nolan pivots around and hurries over to his nightstand. He grabs his piggy bank and sits on the bed with it, turning it over and dumping out the coins through the slot. Seeing that, I grab Riley's hand and tug her out of the room.

"I can't believe you just did that," she whispers. "You aren't worried he'll say something about seeing us?"

"No."

"Why not? *I'm* worried."

"I just gave a six-year-old more money than he's ever seen in his entire life. Did you see his face? He's probably already forgotten he caught us."

Riley blinks, realizing how fucking awesome this plan is. Then she giggles and leans into me as we walk down the stairs together. "That was so close," she says, voice racing again.

I kiss the top of her head, smelling her sweet shampoo. When we step off the stairs, I pull Riley into my arms and hold her in the entryway, prolonging this.

I don't want to go back outside. I don't want to pretend anymore. I want to talk about what we just did—what it means to her and what I know it means to me.

"Riley," I murmur into her hair, leaning away. She rubs my back. "I—"

"What the hell are you two doing?"

Riley's body stiffens in my arms. She tries to pull away. I don't let her.

Turning my head, I lock eyes with Reed.

riley

REED.

My stomach drops out. *Oh, God. I'm going to throw up all over CJ.*

I know how this looks—CJ's arms around me and my hands moving over his back. The sweet look on his face as he prepares to tell me something important, something *big*. Hearing the tone in Reed's voice, even before I turn my head and see his hard eyes staring back, I know *exactly* how this looks.

I also know from the way CJ is keeping hold of me as I try and wiggle away that he is *done* with our secret. He's ready. He's going to tell Reed.

But I'm not done with it. I'm not ready. The way Reed is looking at us and that sharp, assuming pitch in his voice, I know how he's going to react. Reed sounds big-brother angry. Disapproving. Nobody's good enough. *Fuck you, CJ. Get your hands off my sister.*

I can already hear his response in my ears and feel it saddening my heart, so I do what I have to do. For CJ. For *us*.

The words spill out of my mouth like water rushing through a broken dam. Once I start, I can't stop.

"I was sad about Richard," I say. My voice jumps with anxiousness. "You know, just thinking about what all had happened between us—him using drugs and not knowing he was using them, it just got to me. I was overwhelmed. CJ saw me and was just offering comfort."

My lie tastes sour and sounds so fucking ugly. I don't like it. I don't want to utter any name except CJ's while I'm standing in his arms, especially not *that* name, never again, but what can I do? I need to protect us. I need to give this more time. And even though I hate what I say and the way CJ's arms grow tighter around me and then fall away all too quickly, it works.

My lie works.

Reed should've made us, called me out and forced a confession, but instead he looks understanding after I speak and appreciative of CJ for what he's giving me. Relief floods me and sags my shoulders. I see this as a good sign.

CJ's arms had been around me and Reed wasn't telling him to fuck off while throwing a punch. We were making progress.

Reed doesn't say much besides what he always has to say about Richard.

"That guy was a prick. You're better off," he reminds me.

CJ doesn't say anything.

We all go back out onto the deck, and I feel relieved and a little sick to my stomach. Looking at CJ, watching him the rest of the night, I know he is frustrated with this and with me. I can see it. His gaze is cold and refuses to linger. And when he smiles at something Mia says, his jaw stays clenched.

I think hearing me turn down Grayson helps.

My response is polite and loud enough CJ's head swivels around and our eyes meet. I do that on purpose. I want CJ knowing that I'm his, that I belong to him, heart and body, and façade aside, I won't give out my number and pretend I don't. I would never take it that far.

He seems more relaxed after hearing me. And on the

drive home, in the privacy of his truck where we never have to pretend, CJ lets me know we're okay. He throws his arm around me when I burrow closer and presses his lips to my hair. I smile and rub his thigh.

I want us to talk. Not about my lie or why I needed to say it—I knew my reasoning was clear, and I honestly don't want to bring it up—but about what had happened in that bedroom. I want to know the big, important thing CJ wanted to tell me before we got interrupted.

"I'm on birth control," I reveal over the quiet tune playing on the radio. I figure this is a good lead in.

CJ reaches in front of me to shift gears, then he throws his arm over my shoulder again and kisses my temple. "I never had a girl I wanted to do that with before," he says, letting me know that was his first time going without a condom. "I'm glad it was you, babe. And that's something I want to keep doing with you, if you're wanting that with me."

Oh, my God. *Seriously?* I feel so happy hearing that, I think my heart is going to explode and kill me right here. And I would die with the biggest smile on my face. CJ Tully gave me that experience, and wants to *continue* giving me that experience. *Me.*

I hold his hand that is hanging off my shoulder and grin into his neck. As happy as I am, I have a feeling that wasn't the big, important thing he had wanted to share with me. Something in my gut has me wondering, but there is nothing else that needs to be said. Not now. This moment with CJ is already incredible. It couldn't get any better. So I let it go and kiss him long and lazy at the next red light. We don't even stop when the car behind us blows its horn.

"Fuck them," he growls against my mouth. I laugh inside our kiss. I feel giddy.

It's been two days since the dinner at Ben and Mia's. Two days of CJ being CJ with me—sweet, warm, funny. And so damn charming I'm certain he could teach a class on it. CJ isn't acting any different than he typically acts with me, but I'm still waiting . . .

I know he wanted to tell me something that had nothing to do with me tossing out our condom stash.

Closing my eyes under the shower spray, I let the warm water rush down my front. I left CJ in the other bedroom to finish his workout so I could get ready for class, but only after I lingered to watch him knock out a rapid round of pushups.

I can still hear those soft little grunts he makes. Sex grunts. *Yum.*

A shuffling sound turns my head. I swipe my hand across the condensation building on the glass and watch CJ step out of his shorts.

"No bath today?" I ask when the door opens and he moves inside the shower to join me.

His auburn hair is messy and his face is red from exertion. My eyes linger on his long body. His muscled torso and half hard cock.

God . . . Yum is right.

He chuckles darkly. CJ's told me before; he likes that awestruck look on my face when I stare at his body.

Makes me feel like a fucking king the way you look at me, darlin'.

I lick the water off my lips, staring at his thick shaft, veined and long. The crowned head.

He *should* feel like a king. He could totally rule empires with that.

"Hungry?" he asks, moving closer.

My eyes snap up to meet his as my back is pressed against

the cold tile, and I nod like one of those bobble head dolls that's just been flicked.

I'm *always* horny. It's like I've turned into some sort of nymphomaniac. I've never wanted sex this much before.

CJ palms my breast and squeezes it. I groan.

"I'm sweaty," he murmurs, bending low to kiss me.

"I like you sweaty." I smile when I feel his lips curl. "But, I don't know if showers are a good idea yet. Should you be standing in here? Isn't it a lot of pressure without your boot on?"

Since his incision is completely healed and doesn't need to be wrapped anymore, CJ can get his ankle wet. We do baths together now. It's fun. I think we get more water out of the tub than in it.

CJ drags his thumb across my nipple, making me shudder. "I wanna fuck. Can we not talk about my leg?" he asks.

He never wants to talk about his leg.

"I can't just shut off the nurse part of me. If I think there's a chance of you hurting yourself *more*, I'm going to say something." I gasp when he pinches my nipple. *Holy crap, that feels good.* Stay focused, Riley. "CJ . . ."

With a grunt, he pulls his hand away, pivots and steps back, sitting down on the tiled seat I keep my shampoos and soaps on.

"Better?" he asks.

I stare at his cock, sticking straight up like a rod between his legs. My chest rises with a breath. I lick my lips.

"You look fucking *good*," he says, leisurely stroking himself. "Come on, darlin'. Come sit down."

My stomach pinches with excitement.

He wants me to sit on his dick. And he's calling me *darlin'* in that honey smooth voice that makes my toes curl.

This is why I'm addicted to sex now—CJ Tully is the world's dirtiest charmer.

The water pelts the top of my head as I move under the stream. I grab hold of CJ's thick shoulders and straddle his lap. "So *this* is what this seat is for, huh?"

"Mm." He cocks his brow, smirking, grabs hold of my hips and eases me closer. He drops his head between my breasts. "I love this," he says.

"What?" I giggle. "Putting your face in my boobs?"

I know he loves that. He does it all the time. He has long, drawn out conversations with them.

How was your day?

I know I know. I told her to burn these stupid torture devices. Here. Let me rub it all better.

CJ doesn't answer me. He shifts my hips instead, forcing the head of his cock to slip between my legs.

I moan, neck arching and eyes closed. *I'll never get over how good he feels.*

"*This*," he finally says. He lowers my body, easing me onto him and stretching me wider and wider. His mouth is on my neck. "Not having to get a condom and just pushing inside you. Feeling how tight you grip me. How wet you are. So fucking wet, Riley. *Fuck*, I can feel you . . ."

I drop my head and thread my fingers through his hair. "I love it too," I tell him.

He lifts his head and we kiss. I taste the sweat on his skin when I move my mouth along his jaw, open and sucking. I press my lips to his ear.

"*Cannon*," I moan.

CJ groans hearing me say his name. He always does. Then he grips my ass with both hands and bounces me in his lap.

Our skin is slippery and warm. The sound of our thighs

slapping together resonates in the shower. CJ lifts and lowers me. He's doing all the work and I'm taking, taking, taking. Scraping my nails along his scalp and gasping in his ear.

"Yes," I pant. "CJ, please . . ."

"You always beg me to let you come. Do you think I won't?" He leans back to look at me, resting his head against the wall and rocking me in his lap. His wild eyes are electric. Dark blue and stormy. He parts his lips with a grunt.

Holy shit, he looks good.

I squeeze his neck, forcing my eyes to stay open when all I want to do is close them and lose my mind.

"I just . . . I feel like I need this," I reply. "When you touch me and . . ." I moan when his hand moves over my ass. "When you're inside me like this, it's so much more than just sex. It's bigger. That first night at the wedding, I felt it. Something . . . mm . . ." I shake my head, searching for the words while breathing heavier. His finger slips between my cheeks and rubs around and around and around. I gasp. "*God*, I don't know, it's just, it's always felt different. Awesome."

"Awesome?" he murmurs, mouth twitching.

"I can't think when you do that . . ."

CJ's finger presses against my ass and slips inside. "How about now, darlin'? Is this better?"

I groan and sink down, forcing his finger deeper. My head hits his shoulder. "I love that," I whimper.

"I know you do," he says against my ear, wiggling his digit inside me. "You come like crazy when I play with your ass."

"Stop."

My protest is halfhearted, and CJ knows as well as I do that I really don't mean it. My eyes are closed now and I'm hiding my blushing face in his neck, but holy crap, I'm wet. I can't deny how much I want this.

I start grinding in his lap, moving in slow, lazy circles. Fucking his finger as I ride his cock. "Oh, God," I breathe. I'm so full.

"I'd never deny you, Riley," CJ tells me, lips against my ear as he helps me move. "I couldn't. I need this too."

"Why? Because it means more?"

"Yeah," he rasps, meeting my eyes when I lift my head.

I grab his face. I want to ask what more means to him. If it's the same as what it means to me. If this feels different because it's love. But instead I relish the feel of CJ and that heavy look in his eyes. The look he's only ever given me, only me. I want to believe that so badly, because I know I've never looked at anyone else like this before.

We stare at each other, mouths close and open. We moan together. We move together. My pleasure doesn't feel like it's just my own anymore. It's ours.

One body. One heartbeat. One irresistible desire.

CJ squeezes my breast and sucks on my nipple. He whispers against my slippery flesh, *"Fuck, baby"* and *"I want to feel you come."*

I make a choking sound low in my throat as that sweet heat burns between my hips and up my spine. CJ is fucking my ass with his finger now and thrusting his hips. I can't move. I hold onto his neck, arch my back, and *yes, yes, yes.*

"CJ," I moan, shaking violently. My pussy growing tighter and tighter and . . ."Oh, God . . . Oh, my God."

He grunts, fucking me harder until he's pumping into me, cursing and spilling his release. I feel it wet and sticky on my thighs—our pleasure. It's exquisite.

CJ breathes heavily into my neck. His finger slips out of my ass, and I groan at the loss. He chuckles. "Miss me there already?"

Yes, I don't say. I grab his face and rub it between my breasts. When he growls like a wild animal and takes over, I squeal in delight.

We laugh and stand together under the water.

While I towel off and smear lotion on my body, CJ passes on my suggestion of a bath and finishes up in the shower. Still floating around on my post-sex high, I let it go, moving into the bedroom. I need to get ready.

Bra and panties on and shorts tossed on the bed (next to CJ's boot I set out for him), I pull on my shirt.

Without CJ's all-consuming stare and him moving inside me, I can think again. My mind immediately going to that big, important thing. *Why isn't he saying it?*

"What were you going to tell me the other day?" I ask when he exits the bathroom, white fluffy towel around his waist and chest dripping wet. I swallow and watch a bead of water trail between his pecs as he moves toward me.

Damn. He really should find a job that requires him to be in nothing but a bath towel.

"What was I going to tell you *when?*" CJ asks, running his hand over his hair. "You gotta give me more than *the other day,* babe. Narrow it down." He rummages through the drawers, shifting my clothes to get to his and making me smile. I've basically taken over his dresser. He grabs a pair of shorts, boxers, and a t-shirt and moves to the other side of the bed.

"At Ben and Mia's. After we . . . you know."

CJ tugs on his boxers and lifts his head. He smirks. "Oh. That."

"Yes. *That.* What were you going to say?"

"You're not ready for that," he states.

My head tilts. "Um, *sorry?* What do you mean?"

I'm not ready?

"Just what I said. You're not ready."

I glare at CJ as he pulls on a pair of running shorts. *What the . . .* "You were going to tell me the other day," I remind him.

"I know I was."

"Well . . . how come you won't tell me now?"

"'Cause you're not ready now."

"But I was ready *before . . .*"

CJ shrugs. He swipes his shirt off the bed and smiles at me as he pushes his arms through the sleeves. He smiles bigger when my eyes narrow.

"Stop smiling," I snap, hands flying to my hips and holding there.

"I can't."

"Yes, you can. You just . . . force your mouth not to do that."

"Are we having our first fight?" CJ's head pops through his shirt. He's grinning now, and it's so damn beautiful I feel my own lip curling up. "We are. *Fuck*, I'm excited," he says. "This is a milestone, babe. We did it. Come here."

A laugh catches in my throat as CJ holds out his hand for me to high five.

God, I love him.

"You're so weird," I murmur, reaching across the bed.

He slaps my hand and winks.

My cell phone rings from the dresser. I'm still giggling when I turn around to grab it. My parents' house number flashes on the screen.

"Hey, Mom," I answer, knowing it has to be her. My dad still works during the day at Tennyson Construction.

"Hi, sweetheart. How are you?"

"Fineeeow!" I spring up onto my toes as a sharp pain lashes across my bottom.

"Are you all right?" my mother asks with worry in her voice.

I whip my head around and watch CJ twirl up the towel I had my hair wrapped in. I suck in a breath. "You did not just do that," I scold.

"You liked it." He lifts his brow. "Turn around."

My eyes go wide and my cheeks burn hot. Both sets.

I did not like it.

Okay . . . I liked it. But only a little.

"Riley?"

"Sorry, Mom." I flip CJ off and he chuckles, tossing the towel and having a seat on the edge of the bed to put on his boot. "That was CJ. He's just super excited about us having our first fight."

"Oh," she says, sounding surprised. "This is the boy you're living with?"

My parents know I'm not still living at Richard's, which was what I had them assuming since I didn't say different. Once Reed found out about my new living arrangement, I didn't feel there was a point in keeping it from anyone.

"Yes. That's him." I dig my toes into the side of CJ's thigh.

The corner of his mouth twitches.

"Is there something going on with you two? Are you dating?"

"Uh." I drop my foot to the carpet and turn my head. *Crap.* Why does she have to ask me this? I can't say yes. My mom will totally mention it to Reed. She knows they know each other. "We're just friends, Mom," I tell her, wincing. "I'm helping him get better. Remember, I told you about his leg?" Before my mother has a chance to answer, I gaze back at CJ.

He's hunched over still, but he isn't working at strapping on his boot anymore. His head is turned. He's looking directly at me.

No smile. Not even the hint of one. CJ looks . . . pissed. Disappointed or both.

Shit.

My stomach tightens. Mom says something in my ear but I don't pay attention.

I watch CJ subtly shake his head before looking away, like a person would do when they're almost in disbelief of something they've seen or heard. Then he fastens the last remaining strap on his boot, stands from the bed and stalks toward the door.

I lower my phone and cover the mouthpiece with my hand. "CJ."

"This is why you're not ready," he says in a low, rough voice, turning back to look at me. His eyes are hard.

I blink and pull in a breath through my nose. My mouth opens, but he's out the door and down the hallway before I can utter a reply.

"*Shit,*" I whisper, eyes pinching shut.

"Riley?" My mom's voice is quiet, but I still hear her.

"Mom, I can't talk right now," I fume. I snatch my shorts off the bed and pinch the phone between my shoulder and ear. "I have class. I need to finish getting ready."

And I need to go apologize for that.

"Okay, sweetheart. Give me a ring later."

I say goodbye and disconnect the call. After pulling on my shorts and stepping into my Chucks, I head down the hallway, not even bothering to dry my hair or do anything with it. Finger combed waves soak the back of my shirt.

I stop just inside the living room. "Hey," I murmur to the back of CJ's head. He's sitting on the couch, leaning forward. I see the flash of his cell. "Um, look, I just worried she would say something to Reed, that's all. You know I don't think of you as a friend."

He has to know that.

CJ makes a noise deep in his throat, like a grunt, letting me know he hears me. He stands from the couch.

"I'm meeting up with Ben and Luke at McGill's," he shares, stuffing his phone into the pocket of his shorts and turning sideways to look over at me. "I'm heading over there now."

"Oh." I curl my fingers against my palms. My shoulders slouch. I suddenly feel smaller. Or maybe CJ just seems bigger to me. I swear he's grown inches in his anger. "Okay, um, well, I just wanted to make sure you knew why I said that to my mom. Why I had to . . ."

"Yeah, I get it," he bites out. He sounds impatient. "I get why *you* think you needed to do that, babe. It doesn't change how I feel about it."

"You're mad," I murmur.

"Getting there, yeah."

I press my lips together. That sick feeling twists in my stomach again and knots itself deep. I don't know what to do. I hate this. But CJ knows why I lied. What else can I say?

"You heading out now too?" he asks, tipping his chin in the direction of the door.

I want to stay here, convince CJ to skip McGill's and talk this out, but if I don't leave now, I'm going to be late to class. That shower sex took up all of the extra time I had.

Sighing, I nod and move to the stools pulled up to the counter, grabbing my book bag and slipping the strap over my arm. I fist my keys and turn toward the door, then shyly blink up at CJ when he takes my book bag from me.

"Thank you," I tell him.

His smile is halfhearted. An ache burns inside my chest.

I follow behind him outside and wrap my hands around his shoulders when he stops at my car. Standing on my toes, we kiss. It's brief and I'm more into it than he is. I tell him I'll see him after class and CJ squeezes my waist. He presses his lips to my forehead and opens my door.

No *okay, darlin'*. No last minute ass grab.

I'm pouting the entire drive to school.

This fucking sucks.

When I pull into the parking lot surrounding the health building, I see Allison walking back to her car. Jaylen is behind her. They're both classmates of mine.

"Hey. What's up?" I ask, slowing to a stop and rolling down my window.

"Class is canceled," Allison says. "There's a power outage or something. Free day." She flashes me a smile and continues walking.

Mm. Free day. We never have those.

And I know *exactly* what I want to do with it.

Spending time with CJ so we can talk this out is sure to stop him from becoming *completely* mad at me, since he's *getting there*, as he put it. And spending time with CJ in front of Ben and Luke, two people I don't necessarily need to pretend in front of, well shoot, that's even better.

I can finally be CJ's girlfriend in front of his friends. I feel like I've waited forever for that.

Foot on the gas, I pull a U-turn in the middle of the parking lot and head back in the direction I came.

WHEN I STEP inside McGill's, I spot the guys right away. They're playing pool at one of the vacant tables near the back.

Ben is lining up for a shot, while Luke stands at the opposite side to watch him. CJ is leaning his back against the wall, arms across his chest and cue in hand.

He grins and says something to Ben about his shot. I can't hear him over the music playing overhead and the lunch crowd commotion. It's one o'clock, so it's fairly busy in here.

I step out of the entryway so I don't block people coming and going and watch from the front of the room. I don't move any closer.

CJ pushes off from the wall. It's his turn. He bends over the table and lines up. I wish I had a different vantage point now. One from behind, preferably. When I shuffle a little to my right to improve my view, I notice CJ's well-worn sneakers on his feet. They aren't the ones he had at the house. I've seen this pair before. He keeps them in the back of his truck.

He took off his boot? Why? Why would he do that?

CJ takes his turn and pushes Luke sideways when he says something to him. The three of them share a laugh, then CJ leans his cue against the wall and carries the empty glass pitcher they're sharing over to the bar.

He's walking fine. He isn't limping like he does at the house—it's subtle and stops the second he puts on his boot, but I notice it. But CJ isn't doing that now. He's putting his full weight on his foot. He's pivoting on it. He's crossing his right ankle over his left and leaning against the bar while Hattie fills up the pitcher. He isn't supporting his injured leg *at all*.

I stand there and watch through the crowd, trying to make sense of what I'm seeing.

CJ would tell me if he was healed, wouldn't he? Why would he keep that from me? This must be . . . a mistake. My eyes playing tricks on me. He was just limping in the bedroom. I saw it. I don't understand.

Why would he keep this from me?

CJ walks back over to the table. Still no limp. No adjustment to his swagger. This is how he moves when he isn't injured, and although I should be happy to see him walk like this again, I'm not. I feel like someone just sucker punched me. I feel sick for a completely different reason now.

Before anyone notices I'm here, I slip back outside. I've seen enough.

I peel out of the parking lot and speed home, thinking about all of the times I caught CJ without his boot in the past weeks and the way he was always avoiding discussion about his leg. As if he didn't want to talk about it because he didn't *want* me to know.

Not now, he'd say. *Quit worrying, babe. It's fine.*

He even cut back on his PT. He said it wasn't doing him any good anymore and he could do the exercises at home. But now, I wonder if he just didn't need the therapy.

When I get to the house, I don't have a plan other than sitting around and waiting for CJ to get there. I want to hear him out. I want to believe he'd be honest with me and tell me over *anyone* if he was healed up enough to walk around like this. Not just because it's the right thing to do, but because we're together. I want to listen while CJ explains why he didn't have his boot on today, because today is *different*. He's not healed. He'll have an excuse, something that will make total sense, and then we'll laugh about the whole thing and spend the rest of my free day together in bed. We'll cuddle until our touches grow urgent.

That is the only plan I have for us, so I can't explain why I pack up my things.

It's over two hours later before CJ returns home.

I'm sitting on the couch reading over the discussion notes

my teacher posted for the class we missed when the door pushes open.

"Hey," he greets me.

I close my laptop and set it aside, dropping my feet to the carpet. Sitting forward, I notice CJ is back to wearing his boot. And the original, newer condition sneaker he left the house with.

He knew I would be home. My class would've gotten out by now. That's why he's wearing it.

With doubt whispering in my ear, I force a smile. "Hey. Did you have fun?"

"Yeah, it was all right." He tosses his keys on the counter. "How was class?"

"I didn't have it."

CJ frowns over his shoulder as he moves into the kitchen and opens the fridge. "You didn't?"

I shake my head. "There was a power outage. It was canceled. Now we have to do all of this stuff online, which sucks. I always have to email my teacher about things I don't understand. Hey. How's your leg feeling?" I throw my question at him in a rush. I can't say it fast enough.

CJ chuckles opening a bottle of Gatorade. He lifts it to his mouth.

"Any different? Better?" I continue to probe, my body hanging halfway off the couch as I twist to look at him. "Like, all of a sudden you're seeing a huge improvement and you don't think the boot is necessary anymore?"

"*All of a sudden?*" he echoes, wiping the back of his hand across his mouth. His brows are lifted.

"Yes. Like *today*. By the time you left here and got to McGill's. The boot was no longer necessary, so you took it off to play pool." I stand from the couch and spin around to face him.

CJ's mouth slowly goes tight and his brows pull together. He grips the back of his neck and looks to the floor.

"I was at McGill's," I explain.

"Yeah, I'm getting that."

"Are you . . . better? Is your leg healed?"

He sighs and lifts his head, dropping his arm to his side. "I don't know," he answers. "It's not like I've been cleared by the doctor or anything, but it doesn't bother me. I can walk on it. I've run on it a few times . . ."

"What?" My eyes widen. *He's run on it?*

"I wanted to see if I could do it and have that shit not bother me," he explains. "I gotta chase after people occasionally. It's part of the job."

"You aren't working right now, are you?" I ask. My voice shakes.

What else has he been lying about?

"What? No." CJ gives me a look like I'm crazy for asking that question. He walks over to the counter and sets his Gatorade down next to the paper towel holder. "I told you. I haven't been cleared."

"But you're better enough to walk around without your boot and *run*. You just throw your boot on in front of me, so *I* don't know you're better."

My chest is heaving now. I can feel myself getting worked up.

CJ cocks his head. He looks mildly remorseful. "Come on. Let's sit down and talk," he suggests, moving down the counter.

"I don't want to sit down."

He stops. "All right. We'll stand and talk."

"I just don't understand why you've been lying to me.

Why wouldn't you tell me your leg was healed up?"

"What would you have done?" he asks, bracing his hands on either side of the sink.

"What do you mean?"

"If I would've told you, what would you have done, Riley? Moved out? Gone to live with your brother? Your parents?"

I blink. I haven't even thought about that, but I suppose . . .

"Well, I guess I would've moved in with my parents," I answer, crossing my arms under my chest. "You wouldn't need a nurse here . . ."

CJ slowly shakes his head.

"What?" I ask.

"You're asking me why I didn't tell you? *That's* why," he says. His voice is sharper now. "Why the fuck wouldn't you stay here, Riley? Why would you leave? We're together."

My mouth opens, shuts, then opens again. "You would want me to live here, like, *officially?*"

"Why *wouldn't I?*"

We stare at each other across the room.

CJ's house is spacious. The living room and kitchen are fairly large. But I suddenly feel like the walls are closing in on me.

My shoulders slouch. "I just, I figured . . . well, you asked me to move in so I could be your nurse, CJ. That was our deal."

"Babe, that deal was up a long fucking time ago," he states. A hint of laughter touches his voice.

I feel my forehead wrinkle. He's laughing and I'm more confused than ever. I focus on the thing bothering me the most. "I don't understand," I tell him. "I just don't understand why you lied."

"The fact that you need a reason to stay here with me is why I didn't tell you," he shares. Quicker breaths begin to escape me. "I didn't want you leaving, Riley, and I knew you would. Just now, I was hoping you'd shock the shit outta me and tell me you wouldn't go if I was healed up, but you didn't. 'Cause you're not there with me yet. And that sucks for me, babe, 'cause I'm there. I've *been* there."

I blink, feeling my nose tingle. CJ only pauses to let what he just said sink in, I think, not because he's trying to find the words. I can tell—he already has them.

"I'm at the point where I want to live with you 'cause I don't see an end to this," he continues, voice sure and even. "Not next week. Not next month. Fifty fucking years from now, it's you, darlin'. In my bed. Walking around in that hoodie of mine you stole. Your clothes mixed up with mine. I want that and I know I'm never going to stop wanting that. You said this has always felt different, and you're right, it has. 'Cause we got it good, babe. The kinda good I know comes around once in a lifetime. The kinda good I'd suffer through months of 'just friends' bullshit for. I've watched my parents get it. Our friends. Your brother. They all got it. Not me. I've never had that until *you*, Riley. I want you here. But you're still keeping this shit a secret and needing a reason to stay. And I don't know what the fuck to say to that."

My mouth is hanging open by the time CJ finishes speaking.

I've wanted to hear so many things from him, things every girl wants to hear from their guy, and he just said them. All of them.

So why do I feel like my heart is breaking?

"You," I shake my head, trying to gather my thoughts, but it's no use. I dig the heel of my hands into my stinging eyes. "I think I should go," I whisper. I lower my hands to look at CJ. His brows are lifted. He heard me, but I repeat myself anyway, saying louder, "I should go," before scurrying along the front of the couch.

"You should go," he echoes in disbelief.

I don't respond to him. I drag my duffle bag out from underneath the legs of the stool and set it on the round seat. The rest of my things are already in my car. This is all I have left to take out. I tug the zipper open.

"Are you kidding me? You *packed*?"

My head snaps up and turns. I glare at CJ. "You *lied*," I hiss. I watch my accusation jar him. He blinks twice. "You've *been* lying to me. Do you have any idea how that feels? Richard lied. He kept stuff from me. Now *you're* lying. You don't tell me you're better and I just keep doing everything for you. Laundry. Helping you in and out of the bath. How long were you going to keep this up? Until I *get there* with you? I'm there! God . . . why do you think I've been keeping this from my brother?"

"He would've gotten over it." CJ's voice is murderously low. He stands tall and pulls his arms across his chest. "Whatever problem he would've had with us being together, I would've made sure he got over it."

Images of CJ pummeling Reed's face to a pulp enter my mind. I blink heavily and shove them out.

"You don't get it," I tell him.

"I don't get *what*?"

"You wouldn't need to make sure Reed got over it. If he had a problem, I wouldn't have a brother anymore. I'd choose *you*."

CJ's brows lift in surprise.

"I would," I say, standing taller. "That's how *there* I am with you." I bite down on the tremble in my lip and turn away, walking over to the couch to grab my laptop. "I ignored

Reed's problems with Richard," I continue. "I pretended they didn't exist. It bothered me but not like *this* would bother me. I wouldn't ignore it this time. I'd cut him out of my life. Out of *our* life." I meet CJ's eyes after I stuff my laptop inside my duffle. "It would make things awkward with Beth. She's my best friend. And the baby. I'd want to see her. I've decided it's a her." I sniffle and shrug, letting my eyes fall. "I don't know what I'd do about holidays. We always spend Christmases together with my parents. Thanksgivings. Easters. My mom likes massive get-togethers. All of the family in one place . . . she insists on it." I lift my eyes and meet his again. "But I'd insist on everyone accepting *you* or I wouldn't be a part of it. I love you. They need to love you too."

CJ's lips part. He looks ready to speak, and I'm almost too afraid to hear him say it.

It—*I love you too, darlin'.*

That would make leaving so much harder.

"I never lied to you, CJ. I always told you why I was keeping us a secret. I always talked to you, but *you*," I zip up the duffle and slide the long strap up to my shoulder, "you didn't talk to me. Even when I would ask you about your leg—you could've told me you were healed and you didn't. You kept a secret between us. And we don't keep secrets. We never have."

Tell me a secret.

The words are all around us. I hear them and I know he does too. How many times have we said them over the past couple of months? I've lost count.

He had every opportunity to tell me . . .

Bile burns my throat. I don't know what's worse, the taste of a lie or the sound it makes.

"You wouldn't need to choose me over your family, babe. I'd make sure of that," CJ shares when I'm halfway to the door.

I stop and turn back to look at him.

He blinks. I blink.

It's a standstill. He fucked up. Maybe we both did. I hated lying to my mom, and maybe I should've told Reed and dealt with the consequences or trusted CJ to take care of it. Maybe CJ should've asked me to move in after revealing his recovery, and not under the pretense of this being a business deal. I love him. I think he loves me too. We both did this. Or maybe we didn't.

It was just him . . .

This was all my fault . . .

I open the door and step outside, thinking about our last high five in the bedroom and CJ's adorable excitement.

I don't share it. Our first fight broke my heart.

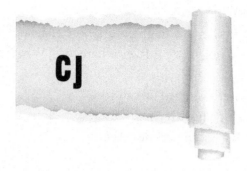

CJ

KNOCK THE side of my fist against the door and step back, stuffing my hands into my pockets.

I should've done this sooner. I should've done a lot of things sooner. I never regretted anything when it came to Riley before today. Not hooking up the way we did. Not being in her business and having that shit lead to getting put through a window. I could've had something worse happen and still, nope. No fucking way. I'd do it again. Even agreeing to be friends with her and suffering daily just so we could be *something*. I didn't have regrets. But now? Now I gotta live with the memory of Riley walking out my door with that pain in her eyes all because I didn't man the fuck up and handle this like I should've, and that's something I can regret all I fucking want but it doesn't change a thing.

I deserve to live with it. This is on me.

Yeah, coming to Reed when Riley didn't want me to tell him probably would've stirred up some shit, but like I told her before she walked out, she'd never have to choose between me and her family. I'd do anything. I'll *do* anything.

I'm not leaving here until he accepts this. I'm even prepared to camp out on this fucker's lawn. I tossed my tent in the truck before I left the house.

Whatever it takes.

My head lifts when the door swings open. Reed furrows

his brow. He isn't expecting me.

"What's up?" He lifts his chin in greeting before glancing behind me. Probably looking to see if Riley is here too. "What are you doing here?"

"You got some time? I want to talk to you."

Reed stares at me for a breath. His eyes are suspicious as he leans his shoulder against the frame. "About . . ."

"Your sister."

"What about her?"

"Can you just step outside so we can talk?"

His brows lift. "Is there a reason we aren't going to have this talk inside where I got my AC going? It's hot as shit out."

"There's a reason," I tell him. "One you'll understand in a minute. Come on."

I get out into the yard a few feet off the sidewalk. When I turn around, Reed is grumbling in annoyance and hopping down off the step. He stops in front of me.

"Well?" he probes. "You got me out here sweating my nuts off. What is it?" He crosses his arms over his chest.

I stuff my hands into my pockets again and think about what I want to say to Reed.

Riley and I are together. She's not just living with me. We've been together for a while. I love her.

I love her.

I've known. I've known it for a while, but I never said it. Not out loud. Not to anyone. But that's about to change. And the fact that it isn't Riley hearing these words from me the first time I say them fucking sucks. I should've told her.

Another mistake I'm going to have to live with. I'm really racking them up today.

"Christ," Reed mumbles, jarring my attention. He rubs at his mouth. "How long?"

I blink. "What?"

"How long have you been sleeping with my sister?"

My eyes narrow. His tone is cavalier. I feel a muscle in my jaw twitch. "We're together. It's not like that."

"Fine. *You're together*. How long?"

I breathe deep. I'm here to be honest with Reed. And that means not leaving anything out. If I do, that shit is just going to hang between him and Riley, and I don't want that.

"A few months, but this started back at your wedding," I share, watching disbelief widen his eyes. "Nothing else happened again until after Riley moved in with me. She was still with that asshole so we stayed friends. I didn't push anything with her. I wouldn't do that. We happened when she was ready."

"Dude." He gives me a hard look. "You hooked up with my sister at my *wedding*?"

"Hey, you're the one who paired us up," I remind him. "And don't fucking say it like that. I was never looking at getting with Riley as a one-time thing."

"Aren't you a little old for her?" he asks.

I stare at him for a breath.

"What?" he probes.

"Is that really a problem for you, or are you just fishing?"

"The fact that you both thought it would be better if you lied to me about it is a problem for me," he says, irritation flashing in his gaze. "I'm just pointing out the other thing."

"I wanted to tell you. Riley wanted to give it some time. She didn't want you hating on me like you did with her ex. She was worried. As for the other thing, there's eight years between us. We're both adults. It's been a few years since she became one so no, I don't think I'm a little old for her."

He grips the back of his neck, looking exasperated.

"I love her," I tell him, watching his brows tick. "I'm in love with her, man. I'm not playing around."

Reed drops his arm and blinks through a jerk of his head. He wasn't expecting me to say that. I watch his chest rise with a breath. "Well, shit," he mumbles. "It's like *that*? You're that deep?"

"I'm fucking buried."

"And she really thought I would hate you if I found out?"

"Yeah."

Reed thinks for a second. "If you hurt her, I will. I'll do worse than that," he informs me.

My mouth ticks. "Threatening a cop, Reed? Are you sure you wanna go there?"

"Fuck you. I'm threatening a good friend of mine," he counters, wearing a smirk and standing taller. "I don't give a damn that you're a cop, CJ. This is my sister. I *will* beat your ass if you make her cry." He looks me over, lingering on my biceps. "Or at least throw shit at you from a distance," he mumbles.

A laugh crackles inside my chest. I lift my chin in appreciation. "So, you're good with this then? With us being together? It doesn't bother you?"

"You really love her?"

I smile. Just thinking about Riley, thinking about how I'll answer this question makes my blood run warmer. I've never felt that shit. Not until her.

"Yeah, man. I do," I answer. "This is it. She's it for me."

It—I'm asking permission to date Reed's sister, but we both know, I'm talking about down the road and where I know this is headed.

The girl who can't handle tequila and who looks sexiest in hoodies three sizes too big for her. She's mine. There will never be anyone else.

Reed studies my seriousness, taking a second to do that. Then he nods his head, stepping forward and holding out his hand to me. "All right, Tully," he says.

All right. Simple as that.

Why . . . the . . . *fuck* didn't I do this sooner?

I shake his hand, laughing when he grips on tighter. I get it. I'd do the same thing.

"Right." We separate, and I roll my neck from side to side. "You get one punch. That's it."

His brow furrows in confusion. "Say what?"

"Look, I get it. If my friend was keeping shit like this from me, I'd want to hit him. Even if I accepted it, I'd still want to hit him. I'm sure you're feeling that."

"You're going to let me punch you?"

"Yep."

"And . . . you're *not* going to hit me back? I get a free shot?"

"As long as you don't go fucking nuts, yeah. But if you start wailing on me, Reed, I will *drop* your ass."

Reed thinks this over. He takes all of a second. "All right. Cool," he says, shrugging. He steps closer and rolls his right shoulder, loosening up his arm. "You ready? I have hit someone before, you know. I laid out that guy Beth used to live with."

"Good for you. Want a medal?"

Really, I don't mean that. I'm just moving this shit along. I got more important things to get to.

Reed narrows his eyes. My plan works.

He cocks his arm back and lands a punch that whips my head to the side. Pain spreads throughout my jaw. My skin tightens. I spit out blood in the grass.

"Nice one," I grumble, rubbing my aching chin.

"Fuck," Reed growls. He's shaking out his hand when

I turn back. "Is your face all muscle? Asshole. You and that fucking chiseled jaw." He flexes his fingers, glances at the blood in the grass and then at the cut in my lip. "Ah. I get why we're out here now. You didn't want to bleed all over my house." A grin twists his mouth. He looks smug.

I give this one to him. I did lie to the guy.

"So Riley sent you here to take the fall for this? Why isn't she with you?" Reed asks.

"I fucked up. I didn't tell her my leg was better. I didn't want her knowing."

His face hardens.

The next punch Reed throws is done with his other hand. I leave ten minutes later with a split lip and the beginnings of a black eye.

And his parents' address.

riley

LAYING ON MY back in the middle of my bed, I pick at the worn, fraying cuff of my sleeve as I look around my childhood bedroom.

I haven't lived here since before I moved in with Richard. Nothing has changed though. The walls are still painted hot pink and the ceiling is still decorated with those glow-in-the-dark stars. I stuck them up there without asking permission first. One is missing. It fell down sometime when I was in high school and took a patch of drywall with it.

My mom was thrilled. This is probably why she hasn't bothered to remove the rest. It'll ruin her ceiling.

I never expected to be back in this room. Once you move out of your parents' house, you think that's it. I used to love it here. The bright color. The walk-in closet where I'd sit and talk on the phone for hours with the door closed. And where I also hid my first minis I got at a party and anything else I didn't want my parents finding. But now, now the walls are too bright and the carpet irritates the bottoms of my feet. I miss CJ's room. The muted tones and the cold wood floors. The freezing air pumping out of the vents.

I tug at the collar of my hoodie as tears prick at my eyes. *It's so damn stuffy in here. I hate it.*

My phone rings. Rolling onto my hip, I stretch out and reach off the bed, swiping the device off one of the boxes I have yet to unpack. Beth's name flashes across the screen.

I tried calling her after I left CJ's house but it went straight to voicemail. I wanted to tell her what had happened. I wanted to tell someone aside from my mom, who couldn't really understand why I was so upset about moving out of a friend's house.

I didn't want to talk about it with her.

But Beth, she would understand. She'd tell me I did the right thing by leaving when I wasn't sure. She'd tell me everything was going to be okay when I didn't know.

"Hey," I answer, shifting onto my back again. I sigh into the phone. "You'll never guess where I am right now."

"Mom and Dad's."

Reed's voice startles me. I clench my stomach. "Uh . . . yeah." *How does he know?* "Good guess. Why are you calling me from Beth's phone? Is something wrong with yours?"

"I wanted you to answer," he says. "Figured you wouldn't if I called you from mine."

"I wouldn't?"

Reed breathes tensely in my ear. "Do you know why I hated that asshole, Riley?"

That asshole—Richard. I know that's who he means. There is no other person who fits that description on the planet. *Why is Reed bringing him up?* God, I'd rather talk about anything else.

"Can we not talk about him?" I ask. "Please? I'm not really in the mood."

"Yeah, he was a shit worker . . ." Reed starts, ignoring my request.

I roll my eyes.

"I was constantly having to stay on top of him. He fucked

up a lot. He was late a lot. He didn't take orders well, which is a major fucking problem if they're coming from me. And all of that added up. But the main reason I didn't like him was because I knew he wasn't good enough for you. And I'm allowed to do that, Riley. I'm allowed to hate some guy if I know my sister can do better. It'd be fucked up if that didn't bother me."

I blink and feel my hand grip tighter to my phone. "Uh . . . okay." I clear my throat. My eyes narrow. "So, you *did* hate him because he was with me."

"Not because he was *with* you. You're allowed to date, Riley. Jesus."

"I mean, because you liked him at first, remember? And then, I don't know, it just seemed like the second we got together, you switched, Reed. You stopped getting along."

"I liked him when I first hired him and didn't know any better," he explains. "The second that piece of shit tried telling me how to do *my* job, I realized I was going to have problems. That just happened to coincide with the two of you getting together. But it wasn't like I started hating on him because of that. It wasn't the fact that you were dating. I realized the kind of man he was, Riley, and it wasn't someone good enough for you."

My breaths start coming out quicker.

"How did you . . . realize it?" I ask, voice quiet.

"I don't know. Big brother instinct? I just knew. But you seemed happy, so I tried staying out of it."

My brow furrows. "You talked shit about him all the time in front of me, Reed," I argue, gaining volume. "How was that *staying out of it?*"

"Hey, I did my best. I could've talked shit about him *to* him in front of you. But I didn't."

"No, you rarely said *anything* to him. That made get-to-gethers fun." I sigh and shake my head, bending my knees up and digging my toes into the mattress.

God, why am I arguing in Richard's defense? I don't care about him. I *hate* him. What is wrong with me?

I miss CJ.

"Look," Reed begins. "I didn't like the guy. And I didn't like him for a bunch of reasons, but one of those reasons wasn't just because you were dating him, Riley. If he were a decent guy, I wouldn't have cared. He wasn't."

"*You wouldn't have cared?* You said you weren't going to be shy about hating the next person I date, Reed. So it wouldn't matter if he was a decent guy or not. You'd automatically hate him. The guy wouldn't stand a chance."

"I said I wouldn't be shy about hating the next *worthless piece of shit* you date," he corrects me. "He'd stand a chance, as long as he didn't fall into that category. Decent guy's typically don't."

"Oh," I breathe, wiping my sleeve across my wet lashes.

"CJ is a decent guy, Riley."

My hand falls heavy to the mattress. My eyes shift around my room as if Reed just spoke to me standing inside it. "Uh . . . okay. Why would you say that?"

"He's a decent guy," Reed repeats, saying it a little slower this time.

I feel my nose start tingling. *I know he is,* I think. *He's the best. Amazing. Better than you, even. Or at least equal.*

But why . . .

"Yeah, I might've gotten on him a little after finding out about you two 'cause he's a friend of mine, the same way Ben got on Luke about dating Tessa, but that shit is allowed. And it just means I got a higher expectation of him 'cause I know the guy personally. CJ would've understood that."

I hear the doorbell ring downstairs and the faint sound of
my mother greeting someone, but their voices are muffled.
Everything is muffled under the noise of my pounding heart
and heavy breathing and the words screaming inside my head.

Reed knows. He knows about me and CJ. He knows I lied.

"You should've told me," Reed continues on. His voice is
lower. Stern. "What if you and Beth were friends before I met
her and we kept that shit from you? How would you feel?"

I swallow thickly, sitting up and swinging my legs over
the side of the bed so I'm facing the window. "Shitty, I guess,"
I murmur. I tuck pieces of hair back into my hood and blink
at the carpet.

"Yeah. I felt pretty shitty an hour ago," Reed reveals.

"I'm really sorry." I pinch my eyes shut for a breath. "I
just . . . I liked him *so much* and I was scared you would hate
him just because he was with me. And I didn't want to lose
you, Reed. I was just trying to give it time. I think I was hoping
you would suggest we got together or something and I could
be like, 'We are! How awesome is that?'" My shoulders slouch.
"I was stupid," I whisper.

"Knowing what I know now, I probably would've sug-
gested it."

I blink. "Huh?"

"Is he there yet?" Reed asks, instead of elaborating. "I
gave that asshole plenty of time. Of course, he *was* injured.
That probably slowed him down a little." Reed chuckles quietly to himself.

I'm frowning at the window. *He was injured? Who was . . .*

A light tapping sound behind me precedes my mother's
gentle, "Hey, sweetheart."

I turn my head. She's smiling in the doorway. Beaming,
actually.

"I'm running out to the store to get some stuff for dinner.

I'll give you two some time."

You two—*me and Reed?* Privacy, maybe. But *time?* We're talking on the phone.

"Okay, Mom," I tell her.

"Tell Mom her favorite child says hi."

I ignore Reed and wave instead, watching my mother carry that beaming smile down the hallway.

"You are not her favorite. I am," I argue. "Dad's favorite, may . . ." the word dies on my tongue. CJ fills the doorway and leans his shoulder against the frame. I stare, mouth agape at his face.

His handsome, slightly mangled face.

"Oh, my God, you *hit him?*" I snap into the phone. I push to my feet and quickly round the bed.

"Ah, he's there. Good." Reed's smile touches his voice. "And he said I could do it. Relax. But even if he didn't, I was in my right. You both lied to me."

I stop in front of CJ and touch his cheek, running my fingers below the swelling around his eye. "Are you okay?" I whisper.

CJ's split lip twitches.

"My hand is a little sore . . ."

"Not *you*, you idiot," I hiss into the line, gripping the phone harder. "*God*, I cannot believe you hit him, Reed. I'm hanging up now."

"Hey, wait a second."

I drop my hand from CJ's face and glare at the carpet. "What?" I snap.

"He knows—if he hurts you, I'm coming after him," Reed warns.

My lungs fill with air. I blink. *Is this Reed's approval?*

"You . . . it's okay that we're, or that we were . . . um, I just, I need to know," my lip quivers. "Can I love him? Is that okay?" I whisper.

I feel CJ's hand push my hood down. He lifts my chin and holds my cheek as we look at each other.

"You fucking better love him," Reed says, laughing a little. "The man got his ass kicked for you."

My lips press together. "Am I not seeing a few bruises? It looks like you hit him, but I don't know about getting his ass kicked . . ."

CJ's mouth hardens. "Tell that motherfucker—"

I quickly disconnect the call before this escalates and Reed changes his mind. "Oops," I say, showing CJ my screen. "Sorry. I accidentally hung up."

He cocks his head, fighting a smile. His eyes slowly wander my face in that adoring way he does when we first wake up in the morning, as if it's been days, or weeks, since he last saw me. Not hours.

"Does it hurt?" I ask, looking at the puffy skin over his cheekbone.

"Yeah." He grabs my hand and forces it flat against his chest. "Right here. It's fucking *killing me.*"

My lips part with a breath. "You told Reed."

"Yeah, I did. I should've gone to him a long time ago. That's on me, darlin'."

"No." I shake my head, stepping closer. "*I* should've told him. I shouldn't have asked you to lie, CJ. That was wrong of me."

CJ releases my hand and grabs my face. "I'm your man, Riley," he says. "You were worried and I should've taken care of it. I didn't. That won't happen again. The same goes for me keeping stuff from you. It doesn't matter what reason I had, that was fucked up. I should've told you about my leg."

"It's okay."

"It isn't." His thumb moves over my cheek as he stares deep into my eyes. "I love you. Do you know that?"

My breaths come quicker. I hold onto his waist while I nod, needing the support. I swear, I feel like my legs are going to give out.

"God, I had no fucking idea it could feel this good," he murmurs, smiling. His chest moves with a laugh. "Reed, you motherfucker. Keeping my entire fucking world from me."

I giggle and roll up onto my toes, kissing him and then jerking back almost immediately. "Oh, sorry. Your lip . . ."

His hand snakes around my waist and yanks me against him. "My lip is fine. Kiss me."

I go back to kissing him, smiling so big through it, I'm not even sure he's getting any lips. "I'm right here," I say. "You know? You have me. Nobody is keeping me from you."

"Yeah," he breathes. He slides his mouth over mine. "Do you feel how good we got it?"

"I feel it."

"It'll never be less than this, darlin'. Never." CJ leans back to look into my eyes. His are brighter now. A soft smile tugs at his mouth. "I'm gonna make you so fucking happy," he says. He *promises,* holding so much meaning in his voice it sinks into my heart. His words never leaving. Never having to.

I'm his world. This beautiful, sweet man. I'm *his.*

And now we don't have to hide. Now I can tell everyone, strangers on the street and people who matter.

I cannot *wait.*

I wet my lips, my breaths leaving me in a rush. I've never been this excited. This happy. I want CJ to know how he makes me feel. "My mom left," I tell him instead, sliding my fingers underneath his shirt and touching his warm skin. "There's nobody here. It's just us."

I can tell him later . . .

His eyebrow lifts. "Mm." He bends to take my mouth, backing me into the room. The door slams behind him with the force of his foot. "Right here? Now?"

"Yes. Here. Now." I'm nodding frantically. I feel desperate. *"Please,* CJ."

"Call me Cannon," he rasps, pushing me back onto the bed and crawling over me. "I fucking *love* when you call me that."

I bite my lip as he sits back on his heels and drags my shorts and panties off. I moan when he palms my breast over my clothes. My back arches off the bed.

"Always wearing this," he murmurs appreciatively, talking about the hoodie of his I stole. "Always walking around wearing my name. Do you have any idea how good you look being mine? How good you've always looked?"

I whimper and reach for his shorts. *God, he's killing me. Why isn't he naked yet?* "Cannon," I beg. My legs shift around him. I'm squirming. I've never felt a need like this before.

Love—I've never felt it like this.

CJ's eyes grow hungry. Darker. He shoves his shorts down to his thighs and frees his cock, leaning over me.

He's still fully clothed and I'm still partially clothed and it's perfect.

I moan when he pushes inside me.

"I love you."

I say it, or maybe he does. I'm not sure. Those three words bounce between us as if they're the only ones we know. We moan them. We beg them. Inside savage kisses that taste like forever and against heated skin. CJ takes me soft and tender on my back, but on my knees from behind, he yanks my hair and tells me I'm his. I pant over my shoulder and watch his eyes. That wicked look he wears when we fuck. He's staring at his name on my back. He looks possessed. I tell him I want it—to wear his name. For it to be mine too. His nostrils flare as our eyes lock. My knees shift beneath me. The look on his face makes me tremble.

I've never seen a man so turned on before.

CJ pulls out, falls onto his hip and rolls, taking me with him. Our mouths devour again as I straddle his waist. He arches off the mattress when I sink down.

"*God*, ride me," he groans.

I bounce in CJ's lap and reach behind me to fondle his balls. I squeeze them when he rubs my clit.

"You moving back in with me?" he asks, his breathing ragged. Sweat beading up on his brow.

I nod, mouth open. I can't speak.

CJ sits up and crashes our mouths together. His hand in my hair. His other on my hip moving me on top of him, grinding me down, down, down. Faster.

"I'll never stop feeling this," he rasps. "What I've always felt for you. Never, Riley. This is us."

I close my eyes.

Us.

Lovers who fell in love being friends. Friends who always wanted more.

"I love you," I breathe against his mouth. I want to scream it. "I love you. I love you."

He growls and thrusts into me. The force of CJ's orgasm taking him like thunder moving underneath his skin. Face buried in my neck, he swears as my eyes water. My own pleasure swallows me up.

"Cannon," I moan, limbs shaking. "God. Oh, *God* . . ."

I'm already being held up by CJ but it feels like he catches me when I come down. His strong arms wrapping around me tighter. Protecting me like a shield. Always sheltering me. We lift our heads to look at each other.

He smiles.

I smile.

"No more secrets," I tell him, pushing his sweaty mess of hair off his forehead.

CJ's eyes warm. He tips his chin up, sliding my hands to his cheeks, and kisses me. Soft and slow.

"I got plans to marry you," he murmurs.

I gasp and lean back. "What?" I whisper. My eyes jump between his as I hold his face.

"You said no more secrets." CJ smiles cleverly. "I'm just saying, babe. But when I do ask, you're not knowing that in advance. You're going to have to deal with—"

He never finishes what he needs to say. I throw my arms around his neck with enough force it knocks CJ off balance. We tumble over together, laughing and kissing and I'm so happy—being us.

CJ and Riley. More than friends. Never less than this.

The *us* we were always meant to be.

The End

Read on for a sneak peek at

say i'm yours

jake

I'm sure you saw this coming. You know how miserable I've been. If you were stationed closer, things would be different. I can't keep doing this. We never see each other. Dale is here. He's here and you aren't. It just happened. I'm sorry. I'm really sorry, Jake. I love you. I only wish you the best.

Katie

THE TORN OUT notebook paper crumples inside my fist. I feel myself shaking. Jaw tight, I turn toward the wall, cock my free hand back and strike my knuckles against it, pounding until I see blood smear.

That bitch. That stupid fucking bitch.

"Fuck you! Fuck you! Fuck you!" I roar. I toss her bullshit onto the floor and tear through my room. I flip over the small table I keep shit on—shit of hers she gave me. Framed pictures and souvenirs from road trips and stupid fucking shit that means nothing. Two years of lies. Two years that were supposed to lead to more, but *it just happened*. Dale is there. I'm not. She's fucking him. She's giving him framed pictures and days that'll turn into two years. Fuck her. *Fuck. Her.* I send everything crashing to the floor. I crush it beneath my boot. The desk I share with my roommate—that piece of shit who said Katie didn't seem the type to handle deployments and distance well—is next. Fuck him for knowing. Cheap plywood splits apart when it hits the floor, and the laptop I'd use to Skype on crashes against the wall after I hurl it.

She told me she loved me on that. She got off watching me get off. She'd smile at me on the screen and tell me she couldn't wait to be done with school so she could move here.

She lied. She's done with me and wishing me the best and fucking her neighbor and "FUCK YOU!"

I pick up the end of my bed and toss it as far as I can. I rip the phone cord out of the wall and throw the receiver. I only got that shit because of her. Why the fuck would I need it now? The Walmart purchase crashes against the door. I punch the wall again. I keep moving. I keep pacing and kicking shit and breaking anything I can until I force myself to stop before I crush bone.

Chest heaving, I look around the room at my destruction.

My hands tremble. My skin burns and itches and I feel like I'm on fire. I grip my hair and squeeze my eyes shut as relief waters my mouth and rushes in my blood. The high I could chase to take all of this away is right there in my pocket. I just need to reach for it. It's simple. It's easy.

"*Do it,*" the best feeling in the world whispers in my ear. I just need to dial the number I know by heart. The one I can never forget. I need to go numb for a day or an hour or a minute. I need to stop feeling this.

I need to forget her.

I need to forget what she's done.

I need I need I need I need.

My phone is in my hand and the number I hate to love is on my screen and I can barely see it through the tears in my eyes. I want this. I hate this. My hand in my hair pulls. I can already feel better. My fingers shake.

I'm going to do it. I'm scared. I'm going to do it. I'll feel nothing in an hour. I'll hate myself tomorrow, but I'll feel good first.

The high is better than the fall down. It's worth it. It always is.

Dale—I can see that fucker in my head. He's touching her. Kissing her. Fucking the girl I bought a ring for. He's shaking my hand and telling me he'll keep an eye on what's mine. He's smiling. *They're* smiling. He's taking everything I have.

"Just one more time," my favorite memory beckons me. She loves me. Cocaine fueled and blackout drunk. She always will. There's no one else for her but me.

Katie doesn't feel that way. She won't love me ever again. She never did.

Never.

My back hits the wall and I slide to the floor. I almost hurl my phone across the room. Thank fuck I don't.

"What's up, man?" the rough voice in my ear sounds happy to hear from me. He's smiling.

I want to kill myself.

"I need your help," I croak. My throat feels like it's ripping apart.

"I'm leaving now." His tone changes to something that scares me. Something I've heard more times than I can count. "Give me two minutes and I'm out the door, Jake. Hold on. I'm coming."

My brother is coming.

Tears fall to my cheeks. I hang my head and begin to sob.

Say I'm Yours
Jake & Yvette's story
Add it to your TBR on Goodreads

acknowledgements

TO MY AMAZING husband, thank you for your support. To my family, blood and through friendship, thank you. Kellie, Lisa, Tiffany, Yvette, Sarah, my KGs Squad. Beth Cranford, we had fun with this one, didn't we? Thank you, boo.

Thank you to my readers, for loving this series as much as I do. My reader's group, J's Sweeties, you all are amazing. I'm so lucky to have you in my life.

To my agent, Kimberly Brower. Thank you! My sanity is in your hands.

To the amazing bloggers who I can never thank enough. Three years ago, I entered into this book world and you welcomed me with open arms. I am forever grateful.

And finally, to my Instagram girls. Your world is my favorite. Thank you for showing me so much love.

books by
J. DANIELS

SWEET ADDICTION SERIES
Sweet Addiction
Sweet Possession
Sweet Obsession

ALABAMA SUMMER SERIES
Where I Belong
All I Want
When I Fall
Where We Belong
What I Need
Say I'm Yours

DIRTY DEEDS SERIES
Four Letter Word
Hit the Spot

about the author

J DANIELS IS THE *New York Times* and *USA Today* bestselling author of the Sweet Addiction series, the Alabama Summer series, and the Dirty Deeds series.

She would rather bake than cook, she listens to music entirely too loud, and loves writing stories her children will never read. Her husband and children are her greatest loves, with cupcakes coming in at a close second.

J grew up in Baltimore and resides in Maryland with her family.

follow J at:

www.authorjdaniels.com

Facebook
www.facebook.com/jdanielsauthor

Twitter—@JDanielsbooks

Instagram—authorjdaniels

Goodreads
http://bit.ly/JDanielsGoodreads

Join her reader's group for the first look at upcoming projects, special giveaways, and loads of fun!

www.facebook.com/groups/JsSweeties

Sign up to receive her newsletter and get special offers and exclusive release info.

www.authorjdaniels.com/newsletter

playlist

Sippin' On Fire by Florida Georgia Line

Read My Mind by The Killers

So Good by B.O.B.

I See You by Luke Bryan

Come And Get Me by Jay Z

Mind Reader by Dustin Lynch

Sure Be Cool If You Did by Blake Shelton

Drunk On You by Luke Bryan

Put A Girl In It by Brooks & Dunn

It Goes Like This by Thomas Rhett

Make You Miss Me by Sam Hunt

Take A Little Ride by Jason Aldean

CPSIA information can be obtained
at www.ICGtesting.com
Printed in the USA
BVOW03s0039280217
477191BV00028B/29/P